For centuries, the Chevaliers de Rouen pledged to fight the monsters that inhabit France until their last breath. In the mid 1800s, Michel-Leon Parisee is the last of his line. The whispering memories of the chevaliers who passed before him offer help but have also driven other chevaliers mad with their constant advice, so Michel-Leon is forced to maintain a careful balance. When an ancient hunger threatens Paris, Michel-Leon must gather every tool he has to fight a terrifying threat that has eluded destruction before.

Constantin Severin is fey kissed, a man who walks the line between the fantastical and the mundane. He is determined to kill the magicman, the monster who destroyed his childhood, and rescue its young victims. In doing so, Constantin is in danger of becoming what he hates most. He needs a chevalier, but Michel-Leon is consumed with his own battle. Constantin must set aside old suspicions and his wandering ways if he is going to bargain for the help he needs.

Together, they can find the strength they need to battle their respective demons. They can learn they don't have to fight alone, but it will take trust. It will take letting down long erected barriers, and it will take love. If they fail, Paris will be destroyed by the creatures that threaten it when the swarm hatches and decimates the city.

THE MONSTER

WITHIN

MARGUERITE LABBE

A NineStar Press Publication
www.ninestarpress.com

The Monster Within

First Edition, October 2024

ISBN: 978-1-64890-811-8

Also available in eBook, ISBN: 978-1-64890-810-1

CONTENT WARNING:

This book contains sexually explicit content, which may only be suitable for mature readers. Depictions of graphic violence, the death of a secondary character, mutilation, fire, physical, mental, and magical abuse of adults and children, and suicidal thoughts.

In loving memory to my beloved husband, Keir, and wonderful mother, Carole. You both were always my biggest cheerleaders. I know you root for me still. I miss you every day.

Jusqu'à ce que je te revoie, je t'aime beaucoup.

Chapter One

DUSK SETTLED OVER the forested hills and rounded knobs of the mountainside as Michel-Leon Parisee crouched on an overlook and waited as patiently as any other predator waiting for its prey's nose to peek out of hiding. An early April snowstorm had blown through several days ago, and evidence remained by the snow lingering around gnarled roots and the bite that clung to the air.

"This could go bad before we know it," Régine Bardin commented as she hunkered down next to him, her gaze intent on the valley below. "The villagers are on edge and grumbling for payback."

"That's often the reaction when two worlds collide." Michel-Leon spared a glance for her. Rumors and whispers had abounded since she was a girl that she was his bastard half-sister. Their coloring was similar, though her hair was more of a true red and his gilded with gold and brown. She had a riot of curls she never could tame, and his tended more toward tousled waves. They both had the same long, lean body and warm smile, and though their temperaments were quite often opposite, they complemented each other.

He thought of her as a sister, and she wished for it for all the wrong reasons.

The stamping of horses and the creak of wagon wheels sounded behind him as the villagers unloaded his requested goods. It broke the silence among the birch and firs. Michel-Leon continued to wait as Régine shifted next to him.

"The tricksters are coming."

The voices whispered in his head, one warning coming out clear amongst the jumble of messages, as the first pinprick of yellow eyes appeared in the goblin holes that riddled the far hillside. The warning only he could hear—and Régine couldn't—proved, despite all the rumors and wishing, they didn't share blood.

"Here we go," Michel-Leon said as Régine stood and laid her hand on the hilt of her sheathed, long-bladed knife.

Another pair followed the first eyes and then a dozen until the mountain holes were lit like a swarm of fireflies. Michel-Leon straightened and glanced over his shoulder at the small group of men gathered outside the abandoned chapel doors. "Is the tribute ready?" he asked.

A low grumbling answered him as he turned his attention back to the waiting eyes. "*Oui.* But I don't see why we ought to give up the food we tilled and toiled for to a mob of troublesome creatures. You're a chevalier. Blow them out or bury them deep. Isn't that why we called you here?"

Régine rolled her eyes heavenward. The old ways were being forgotten, and Michel-Leon suppressed a sigh to echo Régine's sentiment. He pointed at the starry field of blinking eyes. "I could do it your way, but it would end up costing you a lot more than a few barrels of spirits, calves you were going to cull anyway, and some bushels of root vegetables you can afford to give up."

The other way would be bloody and long, and they'd never be

sure they got them all. If even one goblin survived, the stunts it would pull afterward would make the villagers long for the days of kicked over milk pails and holes bored in fences.

The grumbling returned. "What's to keep them from picking up their pranks and tricks again after you leave? The supplies won't last long. We don't figure to keep doing this each month."

"Don't worry, if they agree to the terms of the pact, they won't bother you for a long time." Michel-Leon patted his pocket to check if his surprise was still there. If this didn't cause a stir of interest among the creatures, nothing would. He started to walk away and then paused. "I'd wait in the chapel if I were you. Some of the more mischievous among them might see you as friendly targets to play with when they come to collect their booty. Staying out of sight is best. I'll let you know when it's over."

Michel-Leon took off in the gathering dark, one hand resting on his pistol as Régine strode beside him with the same posture. He wasn't worried they'd have to pull it, but he didn't want to chance the goblins would find the shiny metal fascinating and attempt to steal it. With his luck, one would blow its damn fool head off, and then negotiations would be over.

"I hope you have more tricks than they do," Régine muttered. "I've never seen an infestation this big."

"They have fewer places to parlay, and the machines with the iron and the steam, the gutting of the earth, make them uneasy."

Michel-Leon cocked his head to listen for any other nuggets of wisdom articulating itself in the endless whispers, but nothing stood out. "Times are changing, Régine. Too fast for the little ones to keep up. Science is outstripping magic."

"You sound regretful." Régine spared him a glance. "There will always be more monsters."

"Not everything different is monstrous." A fact Michel-Leon

believed fervently and one that had set him apart from other chevaliers when he was in training.

By the time they made it down to the narrow valley, they'd emerged from the trees and stars splashed across the night sky. Michel-Leon sensed all those eyes on them observing their progress, but if the creatures were planning an attack, the ancestral voices weren't warning him. He would take that as a positive sign even if it was unnerving to be the center of so much crafty scrutiny.

A figure scampered out of one of the holes and danced among the shadows toward him. As it drew closer, the gait changed to a slink until it came to a stop several feet away. The goblin was wizened and gnarled, its face pale in the faint light as it studied Michel-Leon and Régine with a crafty gleam in its eyes and a sly smile on its lips.

"You are not the local lord." It canted its head to the side and sidled a few steps away, pulling a fine woolen shawl around its bony shoulders. Michel-Leon recognized it from the list of many missing items. None of its clothing appeared dipped in blood and again the voices remained silent, so Michel-Leon relaxed. These goblins had not acquired a taste for death. "You are a chevalier."

It made a high-pitched whistling sound, and Michel-Leon stood still as many more amber eyes rushed toward him, cavorting around the disconcerting shadows. Régine's hand tightened on her gun, but she remained steady. He was grateful for her equilibrium and zeal for danger, even as he regretted the peril she put herself in for him and worried about her family's reaction.

"I am a chevalier. As you are the chief." He inclined his head with a nod of respect and kept his eyes on the chief. The hairs on the back of his neck stirred at the sensation of having so many behind him. "I've come on behalf of the village to parlay."

The other goblins gathering around them whispered "parlay" with increasing excitement until the chief gave them a fierce scowl and silence fell. It stroked the hanging fringe of its new shawl. "We won't give anything back. Finders keepers."

"It does look rather fetching on you," Michel-Leon agreed. "So, everything you've acquired already as well as the tribute on the hill, and in return, you'll leave them alone for another generation."

"No deal." The goblin chief drew itself up in outrage. "Do you think we'll sell our good behavior so cheaply?"

"No deal!" The other goblins chanted as they scampered and danced in wide circles around him. It was a good thing he'd left the villagers behind. All it would take would be one nervous fool and the situation would get out of hand.

"Michie," Régine warned, moving to guard his back as Michel-Leon kept his eyes on the chief. That was the one he needed to win over.

"No deal? No negotiation?" Michel-Leon asked, pulling a lighter from his pocket. He rubbed his thumb over the intricate brass work on the casing. He'd miss the little gadget, one of the many items his *grandpère* had loved to tinker with. "Not even for say…ten years of peace from your amusing pranks?"

The chief eyed the lighter with avid curiosity as Michel-Leon flipped the lid open and closed. The clinking sound caught the sea of gazes. "Ten years might be doable," the chief said, and its stare turned hard. "Then they won't forget us. They won't forget what we can do. A generation takes too long."

"I agree." Michel-Leon crouched so he could look the goblin in the eye. "The old ways are fading, *mon ami*. One day, beings like you and me will be an amusing memory for tales. So in honor of the old ways, let us come to an agreement. A half-dozen barrels of wine, double the number of calves, enough fodder to last you through the lean time, and of course the amusement you had in making the villagers dance to your tune again. That is more than enough for ten years of peace. Or…"

"What? What? What do you offer?" The goblin chief capered, its gaze still locked on the clicking lid of the lighter.

"This." Michel-Leon lifted the lighter, turning it so the creature could see it from all sides. "In exchange, you leave them alone until my firstborn is old enough to parlay with you."

The chief twitched, and its followers stirred as they murmured amongst themselves. The language was unearthly, coming out as a sigh among the trees, the babble of a brook, all with the undertone of distant music. It made Michel-Leon sad to think this might be the last time he heard it. There were creatures and monsters he didn't mind tussling with and felt no sorrow at their loss. The goblins were different. They were annoying. They could be dangerous, but usually they didn't mean harm. But with each generation the potential for actual violence grew, and it had taken all Michel-Leon's influence and fast-talking to prevent bloodshed here. He didn't want to witness that on either side.

The goblin chief hissed in disapproval and the others picked it up until the entire valley hummed with the sound of an army of angry tea-kettles. Régine started to draw her gun, but stopped when Michel-Leon laid his hand over hers.

"I hope you know what the hell you're doing. They are keyed for action," she said, trying to keep her eyes on all the scampering forms.

Michel-Leon had one gambit. If it didn't work, he'd have to think of something better in a decade.

"No deal!" the chief announced, tightening the shawl around it. "Ten years, then we'll play again and make the mayor's wife cry more tears. Collect the tribute," it snarled to its followers, and a group scampered away up the hill.

"Those fools had better stay in the chapel," Régine said, a frown marring her brow as they disappeared into the trees.

"We warned them." Michel-Leon straightened and slipped a cigarette out of his pocket. He gestured with it to the goblin. "If that is what you wish. Ten years then and the tribute. I'll see you again when that time is up." He brought it up to his lips and opened the lighter. The goblin chief paused, its hand lifted to swear. Michel-Leon flicked the striker and the flame flared.

"A spark! He's got a spark in a box!" The goblins hooted and hollered until the rolling hillsides up to the Vosges rang with the noise. Michel-Leon shut the lid and the flame disappeared.

"Do it again. Bring the spark back," the goblin chief demanded as it broke the line of the undrawn circle around Michel-Leon.

"This? I thought you didn't want it." Michel-Leon flipped it open again and worked the mechanism to make the flame reappear. "It's a bit of human craftsmanship. What you would call human magic."

The goblin reached out with greedy hands, its eyes fixed on the flame. "Does it always work?"

"I cannot promise it will work forever. Human magic doesn't work in the same way yours does, but my *grandpère* made this about thirty years ago, and I suspect it has at least that many years of sparks left in it. He was quite clever." Michel-Leon closed the lid on the flame once again and dropped the lighter in his pocket as the goblins moaned in disappointment. "So, do we have a deal on the ten years of peace along with the tribute?"

"No deal!" The chief tore its gaze away from Michel-Leon's pocket. "We want the spark in the box."

"I don't know," Régine cut in with a frown for the chief. "You keep changing your mind. How is the chevalier to know you mean it this time?"

"We swears. We swears." The chief held out its hands for the lighter, its eyes round with awe.

"I think the chief means it, Michie." Régine gave his shoulder an approving squeeze, but it didn't comfort him.

Michel-Leon squatted down again and watched the capering goblins with a sense of sadness. He would miss their wonder and tricky ways. Eventually, they'd figure out a loophole. They were goblins. But given the difference in time between his world and theirs, he doubted he'd ever see another one around these parts in his lifetime. He held up the lighter one more time. "The spark and in exchange you keep to your homes and the peace until my first born is old enough to parlay with you?"

"*Oui! Oui! Oui!* We have a deal." The goblin chief capered its hands outstretched to take the lighter.

Michel-Leon tossed it to the chief, and it grabbed it out of the air with a quicksilver motion. The goblins held their breath as the creature flicked it open and the flame flared to life. "We have the spark!" For a heartbeat, the goblins celebrated in the valley, and then they were gone.

Michel-Leon glanced at the now dark goblin holes and sighed. "Goodbye, little ones."

"Making a deal like that is chancy," Régine broke the silence and took his hand. "If they grasp your intent behind it, it'll anger them. Or you've given fate a reason to mess with you, challenging it like that. You might end up a father, after all."

"No children." Michel-Leon slung an arm around her shoulder. "I will buck the system as you do, only I have a thousand voices in my head screaming over my decisions. You merely must contend with your parents."

Régine grimaced. "*Maman* can equal at least half those voices." She took the cigarette from him and pulled in a deep breath. "When you asked for one of these, I thought you'd taken them up. Steadies the nerves, they say, though not something I think I'd want except on occasion."

"Your nerves needed no steadying. You did well." Michel-Leon had missed having someone he could trust at his back. Giving into her nagging had been a good decision.

"*She is not one of us.*"

Michel-Leon ignored the whispering voices that drowned out Régine's reply. The sky lit up with a bright white light streaking away from them toward the northwest. Michel-Leon squinted up at it as the voices went quiet in his mind. He watched it curiously, trying to identify it. Some type of comet. It was hard to make out any details as it undulated with a rainbow hue.

"What is it? It's beautiful," Régine said in awe. "Look at the colors in its tail."

Michel-Leon eyed the long body in the wake with a sense of foreboding. There was an impression of long, eel-like tails, but they were mere shadows in the glow. There was something familiar about the light and the overall shape mixed in with the importance of the time of year. It nagged at him. He fought off the rising tide of the voices roaring in his mind. It had to be bad for this many to be babbling at once. He sank to his knees, his legs weakening as he fought to remain present. The voices fed the fear, which only made the voices louder.

"Michel-Leon!" Régine cried, her fingers digging into his shoulders. "Stay with me. Remember the song."

He tried to concentrate on her voice, tried to focus his eyes on any point to ground him as the screaming began. Then Michel-Leon lost the battle and the voices swarmed over him. The surrounding landscape disappeared as Michel-Leon saw nothing but gray. The gray of nothingness. The gray of smoke and ash. The bitter, fearful remains of fire.

The screaming increased a hundredfold. Screams of pain and terror and with it the most horrid sounds Michel-Leon ever heard, the rending of flesh. He tried to close his eyes and cover his ears, rocking back and forth, but it never worked. He had no eyes and ears in this other realm.

"Metz. Metz. They overwhelmed us. The wings blotted out the sky. All the chevaliers perished."

"In Angers, hundreds disappeared even before the swarm hatched.

Hundreds. They all walked into the mists never to be seen again."

"One in ten died in Lyon."

More and more testimonies came as the splintered memories of past chevaliers came forward. Figures appeared out of the mists, and Michel-Leon concentrated on one. That was the trick. Try to listen to them all and it would overwhelm any soul. Pick one voice, one story to hear, and pray to the Almighty he picked the right one.

The figure solidified into a large man missing an arm with half his face ripped away. *"Don't repeat my mistakes. Evacuate the city. Get them all out before it's too late."*

"Sweet Saint Jeanne, what happened?" Michel-Leon asked, reaching out to grasp the man's shoulders. "What happened with the mists and the swarm? What does the light in the sky portend? What's coming?"

He made a mistake, asked too many questions as the ancestors rushed to answer and tell their tale. The voices rose to a crescendo again, threatening to tear away his control, and the figure in front of him dissolved back into the gray. Michel-Leon reached in vain for him. "Come back. I need to know."

More and more of the figures surrounded him, all trying to talk at once, and the screaming wouldn't stop. He caught glimpses of hideous injuries, a promise of his own eventual fate, as the figures before him flickered in and out of sight. Every time he tried to focus on one, the rest hounded him more.

Michel-Leon concentrated on a spot over their shoulders, an unseeing spot in the distance and sang under his breath, paying attention to each word as if it were a lifeline. *"Frère Jacques, Frère Jacques, dormez-vous…"* If he couldn't make sense out of them, he had to turn to the histories he was painstakingly compiling. The voices tried to drown him out, but Michel-Leon sang louder. *"Sonnez les matines…"*

Strong hands gripped his shoulders, shaking him, and a loved voice returned him to reality. "Come back, Michie. Don't make me tell my *grandpère* I failed you. I'd never leave the kitchen again until I have littles of my own."

Michel-Leon focused on the familiar heart-shaped face before him with its stricken expression. Sense and memory returned. Régine. He grasped her arms. "We need to get back home. Trouble is coming. Trouble on wings."

Chapter Two

PARIS CRAWLED WITH activity. Wagons loaded with building materials or carrying the remains of ruins rumbled by as pedestrians darted out of their way. Vagabonds and urchins dodged the guards trying to nab them to be brought to the beggar's depot in *Saint-Denis*. No part of the city had been spared the touch of Haussmann in his quest to give Napoleon III the city he dreamed of, the jewel of Europe.

Constantin Severin had been here for hours, yet his ears and nose had not gotten used to the cacophony of sound and scent after the quiet of the countryside. The babble of voices and strident cries, the clanging of church bells, the stamp of horses and creak of wagon wheels all played under the noise of construction and deconstruction. The acrid sting of smoke masked the worst of the odor of unwashed bodies, stale urine, and sour wine, but the reek lingered beneath.

He could get lost in a city such as this and evade his past. He could remake himself here. Again. He leaned against a tavern wall as weariness settled over him. He studied the denizens thronging the streets, moving from one errand to another. What was the point? He'd lost too many homes to count, been forced to run from the monsters who shaped him and the more insidious ones who wouldn't allow a man to get his feet under him so he could build a life.

His gaze fell on a trio of boys roughhousing in the entryway of an alley. Shouts and laughter rang from the impromptu wrestling match. Constantin's mouth lifted at the sight and the reminder. He needed a steady job. One that kept his hands and mind occupied and to earn enough coin that he could send some along to his brothers in Toulouse. One that kept him out of the debtor's prison where he might attract the wrong eyes.

Constantin wasn't in danger of that yet. He had enough coin to pay for his lodgings for a week and to eat; then he'd be out. He'd arrived this morning on foot with a long line of others who had heard Paris was in need of laborers. It was a city in flux, transforming into a new era. Not that Constantin cared. One city was the same as any other.

He rummaged in his bag and pulled out the last of his bread. As he gnawed on the heel, he considered his options. He'd spent the last few hours searching for the fine mechanical work he excelled in, but with no references and the vagabond nature to his papers, potential employers had turned him away one after another.

Foremen were hiring laborers to erect earthworks for the new boulevards cutting through the city. Others were looking for men to help burn and tear down buildings slated for demolishing and to haul away the debris. It was honest work with a steady wage. It would keep him too tired to think. Hopefully, too tired for nightmares.

His chances of finding little fiddly bits he could pocket for his tinker toys were high. That right there decided him, and Constantin set out again seeking the ever-present work crews. The foremen were easy to spot at each site. They were often in a position to watch the activity with busy frowns or fierce scowls and a rough tongue. The latter

Constantin avoided. Experience had taught him the reception he would receive there. He spied a likely group where several foremen had gotten together during the lunch break to look over likely prospects.

The queue quickly shrank as each potential worker hurried forward to talk to the foremen, which underscored the demand for work, and Constantin felt a spark of hope. They weren't turning many away. However, when it was his turn to step up to the foreman, all he received was a scowl. "Aren't you a pretty one? Look too pretty for honest work. Go on down by the docks, or the cathedral." He leered at Constantin with a guffaw. "Those men in skirts are always praying to God in the light and fucking like whores at night."

Constantin stared at him in stony silence. He'd have to be in more desperate straits than these to go back to selling himself. Not for the first time he cursed the fey appearance and slight build he inherited from his mother, along with her ill luck. "I'm stronger than I look. Let me prove it. Put me on the work team."

One of the other foremen standing at the front gave him a curious glance. He had a sturdy and dusty appearance to him, a man who led by doing as much as saying. His beard was neatly trimmed and graying, and his hands were as work worn as many of the men standing in line.

"You're wasting my time, *putain*." The foreman shoved him away and turned to the next man in line as Constantin fisted his hands in helpless anger. His fey nature had given him some gifts, but what was the point if it caused more trouble than it helped?

His temper smoldering as he turned away, Constantin eyed another site down the road with wariness. He didn't want to spend the entire day waiting in one line after another if all the results were going to be the same. There were other ways to make money, even if some of the methods were dubious. The ground rumbled and Constantin's anger fled as fast as it had struck. He stared around in wonder as everyone went about their errands with no more than uneasy laughs and startled looks.

"Had a big one a last week," a man commented from the front of the line. "These are more afterthoughts, and they are getting fainter and farther apart. Nothing to fret over."

"Not near a nuisance as the fog that rolled through a couple days after and then again the day before yesterday," another man growled, gesturing around them with work-worn hands. "Pissed the foremen off good."

"Was damn near impossible to get any work done while it lasted," a third commented with a worried glance toward the sky. "It was the strangest thing, rolled up out of nowhere and disappeared just as fast."

Constantin stiffened as one of the foremen moved up beside him, the curious man who had been standing by the one who had rejected him. He eyed the demolition zone next to them and then turned the same assessing gaze on Constantin. "Half wages for today," he offered. "If you're as strong as you say you are and can keep up, full wages tomorrow."

It wasn't fair. If he did the full work by the end of the day he should earn the full amount, but one of the first lessons Constantin learned in life was that nothing was fair. Not even close to fair, but this would get him started. "It's a deal."

"You're a fool." The first foreman shook his head as he turned back to his crew. "That boy will shirk and give you pitiful eyes when it gets down to doing actual work."

Constantin was older than he looked, and his youthful appearance had been both a boon when he wanted to appear harmless and a hindrance when he wanted to be taken seriously. The older he got though, the more he resented his appearance. Only one person had looked beyond the glamour and had loved him for himself. And he had been gone for so long there were times when Constantin had trouble remembering his features.

"You're the fool. You lost near a dozen workers this week and I lost some too. We need every hand we get if we're going to keep up with Haussmann's demands," the head of Constantin's crew retorted and gestured toward the crew knocking down a row of buildings and cutting through the maze of winding alleys and slums. "You can start there."

"*Merci.*"

The line of demolished buildings stretched out impossibly long. In the distance, more edifices were being torn down in a haze of smoke wreathing the rooftops. He nodded and joined the workers, who muttered to each other in dark undertones as they cleared away the debris of ruins.

"What happened to the missing workers?" Constantin asked as he fell in line beside another laborer. The midmorning air held a damp chill, though the cloudless skies promised warmer weather.

"You haven't been in Paris long, have you? More people are coming into the city every day. You sound like you're not from this region," the man said with a cynical glint in his gaze as he eyed Constantin.

He found when he worked a job like this, the crew either saw him as a youth to be exploited or one to be protected. Constantin didn't fall for the first and didn't need the second. He'd been on his own for a long time.

"I'm not. Got here this morning." He'd found quarters quick enough in a room that had recently lost its tenant. That had been a stroke of luck with so many displaced. It was small, and the shutters needed to be fixed, but for now, it was his. If this job lasted, he'd get himself a few comforts and find someone to help him haul it up. He usually didn't stay in any one city for more than a season, but if the work kept up, he might linger.

"Depends on what you believe. The superstitious say they got called into the mists." The man shrugged as a couple nearby workers cast nervous glances at each other and the muttering picked up again. He spat into the dirt. "I say they found a better offer elsewhere. There are plenty of things that can drag a body down. When summer hits, just you wait, cholera's going to be a problem, but mists?" The man snorted, picked a section and hauled up broken boards to carry to a waiting wagon. "I'm not that gullible."

"Savaugeau's wife said he walked right out into the fog talking about the song." Another worker straightened, his arms full. "Acted like he couldn't hear her when she called after him."

"If I had his wife and pack of kids, I'd be hard of hearing too," the first man said as he walked away, spawning complaints from others about their own lives at home.

Constantin tried to listen and get a better understanding of the danger, even as he searched for scraps he could use. Everything of value had already been carried off to be reused in other building projects. He'd watched the method used to reduce these buildings at another site. The foundation and supports had been undermined and then propped up by timbers. Gradually those supports were burned away until the structure collapsed. That was the most dangerous part. The other fore-man had been doing that type of work, and Constantin resolved to be grateful he was an ass. He didn't trust him to look out for his laborers.

This job site was already in ruins, and all that remained was clear-ing away debris. Maybe the workers had been lost when the walls crum-bled. Losing that many people was a cause for concern, but nobody here acted worried about that danger.

Constantin carried off his own pile as he pondered the situation. If the foremen were terrible, he could understand people leaving a job, but a dozen was still too many for his comfort's sake. Men needed to eat. They needed to bring money home to their families, and walking away from work didn't feed starving bellies or keep a shelter over their heads. Those who couldn't pay their bills were sentenced to the depots and once there, it was hard to leave alive.

He didn't like getting involved with local affairs. That spelled trouble every time, so he'd do what he always did, keep his ears open and his mouth shut. If there was something sinister going on, he'd move along. There was always more work in another town, and he could keep at it until his body ached and he was too tired to dream and remember. He was a master at that, and his brothers were well-situated, though Constantin didn't like to wait too long before sending more money. It didn't take much to go from getting by to scraping for survival.

He lost himself in the rhythm of the work, pausing to wrap his hands with rags to protect himself from scrapes and bloody knuckles. He'd gotten soft in Arles, spoiled by fine food and the illusion of security. Good thing he always listened to his instincts and got out while he still could.

When the call to end the shift came, Constantin looked up in surprise along with the rest of the crew. There was still a couple hours of daylight left and other work gangs continued at their labor. His companions eyed each other uneasily, but they all gathered around the foreman.

"The air is turning again. More mists are going to roll through. I can smell it," the foreman said as he doled out the day's wages. "I expect each and every one of you here at first crack in the morning. A bonus if you come back, you hear? I'm not losing any more men. Get yourselves and your loved ones under shelter."

"*Nom de dieu.* Do you think it'll be that bad?" one of the workers asked.

"I wouldn't take any chances. Get on with you. First thing in the morning, mind?" The foreman shooed the man off as Constantin shuffled forward and shrugged into his coat to collect his wages. "Half as I said, but you worked hard. Come back tomorrow early and you'll get the full pay as well as the bonus."

Constantin slipped his coin into the pouch he carried under his shirt. No worries about him not showing up. The man worked them hard and had no patience for shirking. Constantin saw the evidence of that a few hours into his first shift, but he kept his word. "I'll be here."

As tiring as it was, this paid better than the work he'd found in St. Malo before he'd been chased out of there as well. He'd be able to get a hot meal tonight and hide some away for his brothers. Louis was saving for his own butcher's shop, and Damien had married and had a little one on the way. They could use every bit Constantin sent and more. His needs were few. Always had been. When they'd found themselves without their parents, he'd promised he'd take care of them. Didn't matter if they were grown, the promise still held.

As he headed toward the section of town that held his quarters, he slipped his hand into his pocket and pulled out some of the materials he'd managed to glean. The building that had been torn down had once been a factory, and there were all manner of gears, bits of metal, and fine spun wire among the debris. He'd noticed some of the others pocketing pieces as well, no doubt to sell what they could. The foreman pretended not to notice most of the time unless the pickings were too obvious. Constantin could work on his little inventions. They weren't much, but the delicate work soothed, and the results comforted him.

Church bells clanged all over the city, but Constantin's thoughts raced with ideas about what he could make, so much so that he didn't notice the activity on the street at first until the change in the city's music alerted him. People scurried, looking over their shoulders with expressions of concern. Stalls were packed and shut down despite the fact a few hours of daylight remained to sell.

Constantin pulled up the collar of his coat and headed toward the bridge with a faster stride. It was spring. He understood bad weather, but the reactions from the denizens of the streets unnerved him. They acted as if they expected a deadly storm, and the foreman's insistence on finding shelter rang in his mind.

The air went still with a quiet hush, and Constantin realized the street was deserted except for a few desperate souls who were taking advantage of the quiet to go through rubbish. Constantin glanced behind him and saw a fog bank rolling out among the maze of streets in a fast-moving sprawl.

Constantin froze. It didn't move like any mist he'd ever seen before. Tendrils drifted over doors and windows with restless fingers as if seeking a way inside. Filaments of black laced through, forming a delicate web. He thought he heard the shuffle of feet, but the mist muffled all sound from where it blanketed. His heart pounded and his skin crawled as the mist swallowed up a lingerer at the end of the street. He'd witnessed many strange and wondrous things as he'd wandered all over France, but there was something different about this phenomenon.

A noise in the alley caught his attention, and he tore his gaze away. Even the urchins were fleeing, running away from the promise of free pickings as the fog flowed faster toward them. Constantin retreated several streets and ducked into a tavern as it was closing its doors. The barkeep sighed and barred the door behind him. "There will be more missing when this clears. You could've been one of them. Foolishness to be outside now."

"How long does it last?" Constantin asked as he followed him to the bar. He glanced at the barred door. A fat roll of rags lay across the floor to keep the fog from coming underneath, and similar rolls covered the bottom of the windows to stop up any gaps. He wasn't sure if that would be effective or if it was the cheery fire pushing out warmth that kept the mists from entering. He rubbed his arm, trying to scour away the sensation of being trapped.

"Several hours. Just on the safe side those doors don't open until I'm well and certain it's gone. And I'll break the arms of any man or woman who tries." He cast a threatening look at Constantin, then turned it toward the other people crowding the tables. Lines of strain and worry marred his face, and Constantin believed he'd follow through on his promise. "My sister and half her family are still missing."

"I'm staying put." Grateful to find that this was one of those establishments that served food along with their beer and wine, Constantin ordered a mug. He'd get his hot meal and savor it for once. He found an empty spot at a table in the corner and pulled out his small array of tools, along with the bits of metal he'd scrounged. The mood in the tavern was subdued, with most of the patrons huddled over their drinks as they eyed the door. Any conversation was conducted in uneasy whispers that sent chills through him.

It was ridiculous to be so apprehensive over some foul weather that sprang up. He'd lived through true terror, but the grumblings of his companions only underscored his reaction. He couldn't see the world outside the shutters and door. It reminded him of the more claustrophobic days at the orphanage, when the men in charge would lock up offenders in the dark and breathless attic or take off choice children for special punishments.

Constantin's fingers trembled and he focused instead on his tiny tools and the pieces he worked with as his construct took shape. This one would be a cat, he decided. A miniature, slinky feline. The tinkering provided endless fascination. The creatures he created almost came alive for him. Once he discovered he could animate them with a breath of magic, in many ways they did come alive. They had no personality, no ability to make decisions, but they were amusing and occasionally useful.

"That is some fine work you do." The familiar voice of the foreman jerked Constantin out of his concentration. "You can find better work than what you're doing with skill like that."

Constantin glanced up from the creature. The foreman studied him with a considering expression. He went back to fine tuning his work, checking the joints to make sure they moved smoothly. "I'd need to find someone willing to take a chance on me or apprentice to someone." And Constantin was too old for that. He'd found careers for his brothers, and it had served them well, but he'd never found a place where he fit in. "When did you come in?"

"Not long before you did. I gathered I wouldn't make it to my room." The foreman stuck out his hand. "Perrin Lyon."

"Constantin Severin." He took the offered hand, trying to get a read on the other man. He didn't like the coincidence of him being here at the same time, and he couldn't help but question it. But the only thing he sensed was friendly curiosity, not the predatory energy of a man hunting. Sometimes a coincidence was just that, and getting nervy wouldn't help him at all.

"May I?" Perrin asked, gesturing to the cat taking shape in Constantin's hands. "Most of my workers who scrounge are looking for bits to sell. I figured you among them. Some foremen make them hand it over so they can sell it on their own and pocket the money. I figure I'm holding steady. I won't take food out of the mouth of my men. Didn't expect to see you making anything."

Constantin stamped down on his instant distrust. It got him into trouble more often than it helped him. He relinquished the little figure and sorted through his remaining pieces to find what would work best for its whiskers.

"I know a man who's hiring people to build train engines. He could use specialists who can handle fiddly bits like you. You follow orders well and work hard. I'd be willing to put in a word for you," Perrin said as he handed the figure back.

"What's in it for you?" Nothing for nothing. That's how the world worked. Constantin could haggle and hustle, but he had hard lines. His hand drifted to the dagger hidden under his coat before he made himself let go. There was nowhere to hide in the crowded common room, even with his unique ability to disappear. And running outside meant he'd have to go into the mists. He wanted to know more about what made everyone so cagey about them before he risked it.

"A onetime cut from you when you're settled, a bonus from him." Perrin shrugged. "We all help each other. I'll expect a payout from your first wages if it works out. I hate to lose you, but I can get grunt work. The type of work you're doing now is more in demand, especially these days."

Constantin considered the offer as he laid two tiny gears for the eyes. A whisper of magic set them in place more surely than any glue and opened him up to the man across from him in sharper detail. The deal was genuine. He'd exert his influence to get Constantin in place and keep his other demands to a minimum.

"Agreed." He shot the foreman a grateful look. The extra money would be helpful, and if the demands got to be too much, he would roll on to a new city with every coin he'd saved. In the meantime, he'd use the handout the man offered.

"You don't talk much," Perrin observed as Constantin bent over his project again.

"Not much to say." Constantin studied the progress he'd made. He'd need more parts to balance the little toy right, but he was pleased with the results. He tied the remaining pieces in a kerchief and started to wrap a rag around the little cat when a shiver of dread whispered across his mind.

Constantin's head jerked up as he stared hard at the door, his heart racing.

"The mists got everybody in a state," the foreman grumbled. "People disappearing like that. It doesn't make any sense."

Constantin paid no attention to the man's words. There was something out in the mists…something familiar. His hands shook as he finished wrapping up his bundle. He was imagining things, letting everyone's fear grab ahold of him. He'd left himself open when he'd read the man's intentions. That's all.

The magicman was in Toulouse, not here. And it was the reason Constantin could never go home again. The familiar energy was a frisson across his senses again, and Constantin's stomach roiled, upsetting the food he'd consumed. It had been twenty years. Twenty years and hundreds of kilometers. It had to be his imagination. He buried his face in his hands as dark memories swarmed over him, stealing his breath.

Chapter Three

THE WELCOMING SIGHT of the Inn of the Mountain greeted Michel-Leon and Régine as they made their way up the climbing, twisting street toward the building that sat on a knoll above the town. To the east of the inn sat the crumbling, fire-wrecked ruins of his ancestral home. The setting sun splashed red and orange over the gutted stone, making it appear as if it still burned. As always, Michel-Leon made a point of turning his face away. The reminder would agitate the shades of his ancestors and give him memories he didn't have time or desire to contend with. He didn't want to remember that night.

He concentrated instead on the questions and tasks ahead of him. He'd sit down, put his feet up, and have a hot meal as he read over his correspondence and gathered what he knew. There had to be notes somewhere that would help them prepare for what was coming.

"Do you think the creature has found a nest yet?" Régine asked.

"So, you're speaking to me again?" Michel-Leon replied with a tease to his voice he hoped would evoke a smile. The flinty look she gave him in return showed her anger hadn't cooled. He should've let her keep the trousers on and had her deal with her parents and the consequences. "I'm not sure. The information I'm getting from the ancestors is garbled at best. From what I can make out, the lifecycle is relatively short."

"How much time do we have before the swarm hatches?"

Michel-Leon stopped his horse and twisted in his saddle to face Régine. "By September at the most. Régine, I'm sorry about the dress. *Je suis désolé.* I'm going to need you the next few months. I don't want to risk your mother forcing you to stay home."

"You're the baron." Régine shot him a fulminating glare. Many of her curls had escaped their braid during the long ride and hung riotous around her face. "You could insist on taking me with you."

"I could, but that would lead to bad feelings all around. Your family kindly provided me with shelter and a home. I don't want the inn to cease to be a haven. When you're out with me, you can wear whatever the hell you want." Michel-Leon laid his fist over his heart. "I swear."

"It's not fair," Régine grumbled, though she was softening. Michel-Leon hated to see the lines of unhappiness around her mouth.

"I know." Michel-Leon looked toward the inn with longing. The lime rendered stone walls clambered up two stories to the blue-gray slate roof. The tower section at the meeting point of the two wings rose another story and was the place Michel-Leon called home. Behind the inn, the farm that provided the food sprawled over lush fields. Michel-Leon would miss watching spring blossoming into summer here.

Régine sighed and nudged her mare forward. "That's why it's hard to stay mad at you. You do understand. And you don't tell me life isn't fair when you know better than me it isn't."

"The world is changing, Régine," Michel-Leon said as he followed her into the courtyard. "And I expect you will be at the vanguard of those changes."

"You arrived back in good time, my lord," Hadrien Belanger called from the stables. He hurried out, wiping his hands on a cloth, to help them with their horses. He was a stocky man with a long face and silvering red curls cropped close to his head. Régine's uncle was one of the many members of her family who worked at the inn and farm, and he was a welcome sight.

"It's good to be back." He swung down from his horse and handed the reins to Hadrien with a sigh of relief. He was tired of being in the saddle for hours at a time.

"Régine, my little hoyden, it is good to see you too," Hadrien said with a smile of affection as she slid from her saddle. He tugged on one of her wayward curls, and she kissed his cheek in greeting.

"Where is *Maman*?" Régine asked. "Do they need help tonight?"

"*Non*, we weren't expecting you for another day, at least. I suspect she's in the kitchen. She'll want you to eat before she hands out more chores." He caught her horse's reins and gave the mare's nose a gentle pat. "I'll take care of your mounts and have Pierre bring up your saddlebags."

A meal sounded like the promise of heaven. "*Merci*, I'll eat in the common room tonight after I've spoken with Janvier. Do you know where I can find him?"

"My sister has *potee* on the menu tonight. It's been cooking all day." His grin widened when Michel-Leon's stomach rumbled. "I thought that would get your attention. Janvier is meeting with Monsieur Simon. They've been holed up in the library for the last hour."

Michel-Leon thought of his comfortable seat by the fire with a sense of longing. He could count on Marie filling him near to bursting with stew and freshly baked bread. He'd enjoy the company of those who knew him personally, where he wasn't the representation of a savior from their folklore, a man he couldn't possibly live up to.

His valet, Janvier, always told Michel-Leon to let him listen to the requests first, to weed out the chaff or those who could fend for themselves. He would bring those requests with genuine need to Michel-Leon's attention. Michel-Leon was never good at listening, though, not even to Janvier. But before he could indulge in the cozy seat by the fire, he needed to check in with Janvier and see if any of his queries yielded results. It was indicative that the telegraph master was here, meeting with his valet.

The scent of smoked meat and aromatic vegetables greeted him as he came through the door. The common room was half full, mostly with villagers who had come up for a drink after a long day, though a few travelers sat in the corner as Marie and Jean's daughters bustled around serving and clearing.

Marie smiled in welcome as she set a glass of plum brandy down on the little table by his chair. The fire crackled, beckoning to him, but duty's call was louder. "*Merci*, madame. I need to speak with Janvier, but I'll return, and I look forward to relaxing."

"See that you do, my lord. You've been running hither and yon all winter. You'll never get your book finished if you don't take a moment to sit." She gave him a tart look that would scandalize her husband, but Marie took her cue from Janvier and mothered him almost as much as she did the rest of her brood. "And you, young mademoiselle." She pointed her finger at her wayward daughter as Régine schooled her expression. "You are as bad as he is. After you eat, I'll have baths drawn up. Tomorrow, you can get back to work, Régine."

"*Oui, Maman*." Régine settled at the little table with a sigh of relief and was soon in conversation with her sisters, who had gathered around her, forgotten trays on their hips.

Michel-Leon wanted to get back to his book. He needed to get his impressions down about the goblins before the delay from traveling warped his memories. Well, he'd have to make the time. He took the stairs at a trot up to the tower room. The second level held his bed and bath with a cozy study across the hall. The third floor held Janvier's room and Michel-Leon's library. It contained every tome and journal compiled by chevaliers before him. He was attempting to fill in the considerable gaps. Unfortunately, too many chevaliers before him relied on the voices to guide them, but the ancestral memories carried their own dangers, and Michel-Leon would rather trust a method that wouldn't deteriorate when he lost his mind.

Low voices murmured from behind the library doors. Michel-Leon braced himself and opened the doors. His whipcord-thin, aging valet glanced up with a grave expression that had Michel-Leon's stomach sinking. The man next to him ran the telegraph station in town.

"My lord, I regret to inform you that you were right. The mists have returned," Janvier said.

"Where?" Michel-Leon strode to the large map of France dominating one wall. Notes he hadn't properly moved to his journals yet covered the surface.

"The mists."

The voices hissed and Michel-Leon sensed them gathering. He ruthlessly blocked them before they could start clamoring. He would be damned if he'd give into his inherited weakness instead of going with solid facts.

"Paris, my lord," Monsieur Simon replied as he picked up the telegram on the table and handed it over. "We've received several messages over the week. They reported three occurrences of the mists."

"Paris?" A chill settled over Michel-Leon's heart. The swarm had never settled in a city so populous before. He didn't want to contemplate the number of victims it could claim before the swarm took to the stars again. "Do they have any idea of the number of people missing?"

Monsieur Simon shook his head, his mouth turned down in distress. "There are some missing, but to be honest, the palace doesn't appear to be concerned. They don't know, my lord. They don't understand the dangers the way we do around here. Our informants insist they will need a Chevalier de Rouen."

"*Bien sûr.*" Michel-Leon waved him off with an impatient nod and made his way to the table on leaden legs. "Go get some food and rest. Let me confer with Janvier, and we will make plans to leave as soon as it is possible to do so."

The voices clamored at him, demanding he listen. Michel-Leon cautiously inched down the barrier enough to recognize the agitated chaos, to hear the screaming. He erected the barrier again with a shudder. He'd keep it up until they calmed down, or he'd be a useless wreck. It was frustrating in the extreme to have possible answers at his hands and unable to risk diving for them. There were too many ancestors upset by this new threat to risk trying to converse with them at this stage.

Michel-Leon buried his face in his hands, and Janvier settled his hand on his shoulder. His earliest memories were of Janvier, who served his *grandpère*. The two of them had contrived to give him some sense of family and home. He'd been the odd one out in the family. More interested in science than combat, wanting to know why and how things worked. His brother had been their father's prize. Not Michel-Leon.

"Michel-Leon, you will find a way. Chin up, boy."

Michel-Leon blinked up at Janvier's lined and worried face. "I haven't been a boy in a long time, old man."

Janvier straightened with a relieved expression as Michel-Leon let his hands fall away. "You didn't have an episode, but I'm assuming those blighted shades of yours spoke with you at some point. Did you get anything useful out of your encounter?" he asked as he poured Michel-Leon a hefty glass of cognac.

"A lot of place names, nothing concrete." He took a long swallow of the cognac, and the burn steadied him. "Do any of them mean anything to you? Angers, Metz, Lyon, if I remember correctly. There may have been others, but I swear every chevalier ghost who ever existed converged on me at once." Michel-Leon shuddered and took another swallow.

"Metz…" Janvier pulled out a chair and made an impatient gesture for Michel-Leon to sit as if he were still a recalcitrant child of ten. "When I was a little older than you are, I began serving your *grandpère* as his valet when my father retired. I remember him speaking of the disaster at Metz. Thousands died."

"Ah, *oui, oui*. I would've remembered that one if I hadn't been in such a hurry to return. They blamed the chevaliers for not giving enough of a warning and that began the decline of our order." Michel-Leon rubbed his temples as he organized his thoughts. It was less of a decline and more of a plummet.

"Have Régine come up with our dinners. It's going to be a long night. Send a telegram to Liam Dill in London on the off chance they have a record of these occurrences over there as well. Régine and I will start going through my family's journals to pick out what would be useful to take with me. Find out when the next train is leaving for Paris. I'll be on it."

The old man straightened to the best of his ability, eliciting a symphony of wince-inducing cracks from his lean frame, and gave Michel-Leon a hard glare from under bushy white eyebrows. "You have your pronouns confused, my lord. *We* will be on the next train to Paris."

Michel-Leon attempted to stare Janvier down. He had been more of a father to him than Michel-Leon's own, and when Janvier passed, he'd be utterly alone. He'd be damned if he did anything to quicken that time.

"You need me," Janvier insisted. "I know more of the château's secrets than you, and you'll need to stay there even if you hate it. You'll need the safety of those walls."

"We have a map of the château and a list of all the traps." Michel-

Leon tried to remember which journal it was in and added that to the list of what they…*he* should bring with him.

"You cannot trust your father's notes, nor unfortunately, your *grandpère's* at the end of his life. I served at the château for decades. I know how the minds of those two worked, even better than you, and I was alive when the disaster at Metz occurred, even if I wasn't there personally. I can help. *S'il vous plaît*, Michel-Leon, I never involved myself in your father's affairs out of fear. Your *grandpère* told me more than I wished to know, even more so after he saw I took on the responsibility of tending to you. They sought dark things and those things ate your father's soul raw. I watched him die two deaths and could do nothing to stop either." He looked at Michel-Leon, his blue eyes clouded with age and worry. "I would not lose you the same way. Not on that same dark path. I know you fear it too."

Michel-Leon stood to face his valet and laid a hand on his bony shoulder. Janvier deserved to spend his last days at the Inn of the Mountain in front of a fire with the comfort of his books and great-grandkids. If Michel-Leon had his burdens, then Janvier had an even greater one and that was keeping an eye on him. Michel-Leon could not deny him anything.

"*Mon ami*, I will not follow my father's path. I promise you. You can come on the sole promise that when I say it is time to leave, with or without me, you go. Swear to that."

Janvier regarded him a moment longer. "As you wish, my lord. But you swear in return to keep Régine by your side. I know her mother desires a different life for her, but Régine is determined to make her own path. She will be another set of eyes."

"I agree. And Régine will insist on it. She's better with a blade and pistol than I am." Michel-Leon smiled at Janvier's pained expression. "As you said, she goes her own way."

"Both of you do, my lord," Janvier replied at his most dry and wintery. Michel-Leon winced as Janvier turned away. At least he agreed to leave when ordered, even if Michel-Leon would have to put up with his return to formality until the old man forgave him. He eyed the long shelves of books and journals and dove in to make some sense out of the scanty, crazed notes.

*

THE TRAIN JERKED and swayed as it moved west through the French countryside. Michel-Leon pulled another journal out of the neat stack Janvier had stowed and shoved the trunk back under the bed. The cramped cabin he shared with Janvier was a mess of discarded books, scraps of notes, and ink stains on the blankets where Michel-Leon had more than one mishap.

"Disorganization and sloth are the true enemies of the superior mind," his father's voice whispered.

That had been the old baron's mantra. Michel-Leon found it scribbled on the first line of every journal that held his father's research and investigations. Michel-Leon had tried to live by the same credo, but the cluttered cabin was a testament to yet another way in which he fell short of the ideal his father set. It was bad enough knowing it. He didn't need a shade reminding him of his shortcomings.

"You know what's the enemy of the superior mind?" Michel-Leon retorted testily. "Bad recordkeeping. Didn't one of you consider writing down important details? Like what avenues of investigation you've tried that didn't pan out, so I'm not duplicating efforts. All I've found are the numbers of the dead and the patterns of the mists." Too many of the accounts broke off ominously or degraded into rambling bits of insanity. Maybe his ancestors meant to go back to finish their notes but were never given the opportunity, which reminded Michel-Leon of the guilty fact that he was behind on his own book.

He turned back to the information he had gleaned, which was

useful since it appeared to be consistent. The mists rolled out every third day to start with and then began spacing further and further apart before stopping altogether. They'd have two weeks at the most after the cycle stopped. Once the swarm hatched, it was over. Michel-Leon scribbled another note and ignored the vague mutterings in his mind. If they weren't going to give him anything useful, he wasn't going to listen.

"I would watch the habit of talking to yourself, my lord. Our friends at the inn take it in stride. I doubt they will be so open-minded in Paris."

Michel-Leon spared a glance for Janvier, who had appeared in the cabin. He hadn't even heard him open the door. "He plagues me. They all plague me with dire warnings, but no real information. At least Saint Jeanne's voices were useful."

"Indeed, right up to the moment where they burned her at the stake." Janvier straightened a pile of books as Michel-Leon grimaced. "It's time to eat, my lord. You have not left your room since we boarded, and the buffet car is quite nice for an iron tomb hurtling about at ridiculous speeds."

Michel-Leon waved an impatient hand at him. "No time. I'll take tea and whatever you slap on a plate that won't make a mess."

"Michel-Leon," Janvier said in such a firm voice that he looked up at his valet in surprise. "You will get up and accompany me to the buffet car, and you will take a break and eat a full meal. If you won't do it for the sake of a healthy mind and body, perhaps you'll do it because there is a gentleman from Metz dining there with this grandson. He survived the attack that decimated the city fifty-two years ago."

Michel-Leon stared at him blankly a moment, and then all the words came together in a rush. "Why didn't you lead with that?" He got up, scrubbing ineffectually at the ink stains on his fingers with his handkerchief. "Bah." He tossed it on top of his abandoned books and grabbed his coat before Janvier could comment on him showing up in the dining car in his shirtsleeves. "Suddenly, I'm famished."

"I can't imagine why, my lord," Janvier replied in a bland tone that made Michel-Leon wince. He could deliver a scathing retort that to everyone around them would appear innocuous, but Michel-Leon knew better.

He followed Janvier's erect figure as they made their way to the buffet car, the scents making his stomach growl. He couldn't remember what he had for breakfast, but he hadn't complained, so it must have tasted fine. Tables lined the buffet car on either side of the windows. The occupants dined on glass plates and tables covered in linen. A serving cart trundled along between the tables, laden down with empty dishes placed there by the diners. Its body carried eight legs that allowed it to steady itself as it moved along. Quite a clever mechanical device.

He turned to watch its steady progress. His *grandpère* had been the tinkerer in the family. He would've loved all the new gadgets and inventions that abounded today. Jean had bought a new device for the creamery that churned out the most amazing cheese. Michel-Leon was hopeless when it came to the steam-powered gadgets.

"Utter frippery," Janvier said, eying the glass and crystal. "I have to wonder what they waste on breakage going for opulence over common sense. That creepy monstrosity had to have cost a fortune merely to collect plates. This push toward automation will ruin us all."

Michel-Leon had to agree with him on the former, which was one of the reasons why they got along so well. His mother would've been horrified with how he lived his life. Michel-Leon had no patience for niceties. Despite his distaste for them, Janvier could get quite stubborn about it if he felt the situation warranted it and if it impacted Michel-Leon's standing in the community. However, the serving cart charmed Michel-Leon. It should be clumsy, but the mechanics of it flowed.

"The gentleman three tables down with the boy at his side,"

Janvier said in an undertone, and Michel-Leon's gaze zeroed in on him. Recognition jolted through the ancestors and the clamor rose up.

"Lost! Lost! We thought you were lost!" one cried out above the rest in agony and grief.

"The swarm ravaged, tearing apart the young and carrying them off."

"The wings blotted out the sky. The noise blotted out my reason. It was a slaughter."

Michel-Leon swayed as the voices pounded him, and he had to steel himself to push them down to a mutter. He needed no more confirmation the man had survived Metz than the ancestors' response to him. He focused on Janvier's voice before he lost himself again.

"I made some inquiries. His name is Auguste Vautrin, and his grandson is Raul." The older man was unkempt in the way of scholars, his hair in disarray and his clothing rumpled as he wrote feverishly in a journal. He looked to be in his late sixties and the boy with him old enough to behave and be of some assistance, though he spent his time staring out the window as he ate.

"Find Régine and send her to me. I could use her observations," Michel-Leon ordered. There was an air about the pair that was vaguely familiar, a quality the ancestors approved of, and they weren't welcoming to many. Probably damned grateful there were survivors of that horror.

"I alerted her first. She should be here as soon as she's dressed appropriately."

Michel-Leon left that comment unanswered. Janvier may disdain waste, but he had a strong sense of social niceties, especially when it came to appearances. "Do you mind if I join you?" Michel-Leon paused beside the table as Janvier disappeared.

The man looked up at him with an expression of vague irritation. "I'm busy. Go find another place to sit." He nudged his plate over so it took up more of the space on the table.

His grandson glanced at him and leaned over to whisper; his voice carried loud enough for Michel-Leon to hear. "*Grandpère*, it's the Chevalier de Rouen. The one the old gentlemen was talking about. Remember, you promised to answer some questions."

"My sister and I won't take up too much of your time," Michel-Leon assured him as Régine approached. She had neatly pinned her hair up, and her expression was more intrigued than irritated.

He pulled out a chair for her. "I had a few questions for you about the tragedy at Metz. Rather urgent questions. This is my sister, the Widow Bardin. I am Michel-Leon Parisee."

"*Je suis désolé.* I get lost in my notes sometimes." Vautrin looked down at his papers with a sigh and gathered them together. They looked like drawings of a mechanical device of a strange long, vertical configuration. "I am Auguste Vautrin, and this is my grandson Raul."

Régine gave him a winsome smile as she pulled out a notebook. "My brother has a similar reaction when I interrupt his studies. We understand your hesitation."

Michel-Leon drew out the chair next to the boy and sat. "*S'il vous plaît*, call me Michel-Leon. I'm not very formal." He gestured toward the pictures and notes as Vautrin tucked them inside a worn leather notebook. "I couldn't help but notice what you were working on. My *grandpère* loved such things. He was always inventing something new, though he had a particular fondness for clocks."

Auguste's eyes brightened and for the first time, he looked at Michel-Leon with welcome in his eyes instead of gazing at him as if he were an intruder. "It's a new mode of transportation. One that could revolutionize our world. Make this train seem like a wagon in comparison. With it, we could go to the stars."

That was an intriguing thought, and he wouldn't be the first inventor that had such dreams. Before Michel-Leon could question him further, another automaton appeared, laden down with a tray and a pot of tea. Since it stopped right by Michel-Leon's chair, he had no doubt Janvier had it sent. "I'd like to talk with you further about your invention sometime," he said as he set the dishes before him and Régine. Not that he had time for such conversation. One day, his life would calm down enough for him to pursue his own intellectual studies.

"But you're here to talk about Metz." The old man's eyes went distant with a remembered pain. "Not the sort of conversation one has over a meal."

"I have developed an iron stomach. Hazard of the job." Michel-Leon paused before digging in.

"We would not distress you with our questions if it wasn't urgent," Régine said, capturing Michel-Leon's gaze and casting a significant glance at Raul, who had gone back to watching out the window.

"Though perhaps not a talk your grandson should overhear," Michel-Leon suggested at the reminder that innocence was too fleeting in this world.

Auguste looked at his grandson with worry. "I was his age when the swarm came to Metz. He knows why we are fleeing the country. We are on our way to Normandy. We'll catch a boat there for England, where he'll be safe. I know the signs as well as any chevalier. I saw the light in the sky. The mists will return, and in time, the swarm and another city will face its destruction."

"*Oui*, this time the target is Paris." It never failed to send a chill down Michel-Leon's spine. A failure anywhere was bad, but the potential death count in Paris was so much worse. The city had expanded, and from what he'd been able to tell from his research and what he'd gleaned from the ancestors, the swarm's size was predicated on the size of the city. This swarm would dwarf any of the other ones.

"You have a formidable task ahead of you," Auguste murmured, and Raul threw him a glance, his brow knitting.

"Which is why I could use your help. Quite frankly, I need to know more about what I'm dealing with. Chevalier journals are sketchy at best. One of the things I'd like to do is leave a more complete record. So people know how to deal with monsters and situations as they arise instead of relying on oral tradition." Michel-Leon stopped himself before he could launch into his usual rant. Time was too precious.

"The chevaliers failed in many respects." August's small eyes glittered with an old anger.

Régine tensed, her shoulders stiffening. "The chevaliers are the only ones who stand between the people of France and the monsters preying on them."

"Peace, Régine. He is right. We failed." In more ways than at Metz. Michel-Leon pushed back the familiar frustrated anger. They had been human, sometimes deeply flawed, and the cracks had grown bigger until it had consumed them. "I agree with you, Monsieur Vautrin, but I cannot fail. Too many people depend on it. A city the size of Paris will never evacuate. So I need your help."

"I don't know how I can help. I was a boy when it happened. All I remember is chaos and screaming," Auguste trailed off, his voice going hoarse. "There was a frightful roaring, like a thousand wings flapping in my mind and this constant high-pitched buzzing. Underneath it was the music. It got into your head and wouldn't go away. It's still a distant song in my brain, and it's getting stronger."

Michel-Leon sympathized. He didn't want to recall his demons either, and he didn't want to cause this man more pain by bringing up painful wounds. But he had no choice. "*S'il vous plaît,* monsieur, any information you give me, no matter how small, may help me put the pieces together so I can help."

Auguste turned his brooding gaze on Michel-Leon. "Perhaps, you should understand the price of the chevalier's failure. Then you can impress on the others the danger of underestimating the destruction the swarm will cause."

"Go on, monsieur," Michel-Leon said quietly. "The chevaliers have already paid the price for their failure. That I promise you."

"How?" August demanded, and Régine stiffened again.

Michel-Leon laid his hand over hers before she jumped to his defense. He had more to gain with the truth than vague assurances. "People lost their faith in us. Leaders turned their backs. Our failure became a disease that ate us inside out and left us vulnerable. As a consequence, there are no more chevaliers. I am the last."

"And you alone seek to do what they could not? To grab your glory back?" Auguste sneered, and Raul's eyes widened.

"You should not speak to him in such a way," Régine said in a low, tight voice. "You do not know what he has done for —"

"Peace, Régine," Michel-Leon said again before she could get started, even as Auguste continued to drill him with his half-mad gaze.

"*Grandpère*, you can help him. You always said you wished you'd been able to help. This is your chance to make a difference." Raul sounded so distressed that Auguste's eyes softened.

Michel-Leon shook his head. "I do not have that level of hubris. Quite simply, Vautrin, there's no one else, and I cannot turn my back on a threat like this merely because I am alone."

"You are not alone," Régine cut in with a narrow-eyed stare. "I will be with you every step."

"You'll get yourself killed." Auguste's gaze tracked between the two of them. "Both of you."

Death was preferable to madness. Either way, one of them was his fate. "I'd rather die trying than doom Paris through inaction and fear." Michel-Leon leaned forward to convey his seriousness. "*S'il vous plaît*, monsieur, tell us your story."

"Fool." Vautrin stared out the window and touched his fingertips to his temple with a frown. "I don't remember much before the last day. I have some recollection of the mists and the pall of worry, the lists of the missing. And I clearly recall the aftermath. I don't know what drove me, but I spent weeks scouring the countryside until I found what I believe had been their lair. Only most everything in there that had been organic was consumed. There were no answers to be had."

Michel-Leon glanced at Régine, relieved to see her scribbling notes. Then he turned his attention back to Auguste's mesmerizing tale. Even the ancestors were hushed and listening.

"But the day that stands out the most is the day the swarm came. The sky was black with them when the sun rose above the horizon. They blotted out the sun and descended on Metz." His voice was hushed, his eyes wide with remembered horror. "The song they made paralyzed and confused. They carried people into the sky and tore them apart. There was nothing left to bury. No way to match the missing to the dead."

Vautrin's descriptions agitated the chevaliers who had died there. A keening rose in Michel-Leon's mind, the voices babbling. The words that slipped through matched Vautrin's description and put images in Michel-Leon's mind that would linger there for weeks. Sweat popped out on his head as he tried to stem the tide, and then Régine took his hand the way Janvier had so many times. "*Frere Jacques*, Michie, remember?" She hummed the melody softly.

Michel-Leon met her gaze, and the determination he saw in her blue eyes matched his own. They would not let this happen again, and he could not let the ancestors sweep him away.

Vautrin pressed his fist against his mouth and rocked. "They tore through buildings. The screams…the screams… I still hear them and the sound of rending flesh. There's no sound like it. All day long, they fed. When the sun set and the whir of the wings faded, some of the survivors, me among them, crept out of where we hid. We watched them go up…up, a black mass that blocked the light from the night sky. Then one by one they became shooting stars. So beautiful…so beautiful."

Chapter Four

CONSTANTIN STARED AT the long, three-story building with a growing uneasiness. Paris was a large city. It made sense they had orphanages. He hadn't visited a city yet that didn't have several. Families that were neglectful, imprisoned, or killed left too many children with no home or shelter. Constantin had tried to harden his heart against them all those years he'd been on the street himself, but he'd never been successful. Adults he could ignore, but not the lost and forgotten little ones.

There was something about this orphanage that made Constantin's skin crawl. An air of misery hung over it, though that was no different from many other places like it. This was the only one that provoked such a visceral reaction. Constantin grew ill looking at it. He feared getting closer would worsen the feeling. He touched trembling fingertips to his brow and found it damp with sweat.

He should walk away. He had a job waiting for him. A job that would give him security and means. That is, if the foreman Lyon wanted to help him anymore after not appearing for work the morning after the mists trapped them in the tavern. As soon as the doors opened, he'd started searching for the presence he'd felt prowling around outside. Days of combing the streets, scrounging for food, until his growing frustration led him to believe it had only been paranoia that rendered him incapable of keeping a job or having the semblance of a normal life. It was his curse.

Then he caught the thread of what he'd sensed again. It was an energy like no other, full of all the pain and sorrow of innocence destroyed. It had led him here. To this bleak house. Even the sun refused to shine here, as if all joy had been sucked out of the air. His whole being recoiled from it, and he prowled around the walls restlessly, caught between his fear of what he'd find and his desperate need to know.

Constantin forced himself to stillness and studied the grim edifice with a growing dread. It couldn't be the nightmare from his past. None of this was getting him any closer to the building and the answers it contained. He was stalling. He was afraid, and it shamed him. There were too many innocents locked inside for him to turn his back.

But you turned your back on the ones in Toulouse.

The insidious thought twisted his stomach. He'd tried. He'd tried to save them, and they'd spurned him. But did he try hard enough? He'd been a youth then, barely a man. He'd had his brothers to protect. That didn't excuse his avoidance later though, and he had shunned the city. He'd never set foot back since he'd left, not even to visit his family. He'd let the fear of his past rule him.

Constantin gauged the height of the wall surrounding the building. There wasn't a sign of any child, not playing outside in the courtyard, or staring out at the blue skies from the window. He had to get in there to know for sure. He wouldn't be able to rest until he had answers.

Moving into the deep shadows of another building a couple of streets away, Constantin glanced around to make sure no one was near. He concentrated on the shadows around him and twisted them so they wrapped him in a shroud. It was a trick he discovered not long after he'd been shoved out onto the streets to fend for himself. It made people overlook him, their gazes sliding past, but it did nothing to hide the noises he made, and the glamour broke the moment someone bumped into him. He'd learned over the years to be cautious.

He moved toward the orphanage again, studying the layout. Going through the gate wouldn't work. He'd have to wait until someone came through, and there had been minimal traffic. If someone spied the gate moving on its own, the glamour would break. Constantin hadn't survived this long by being a fool. The wall was high, but not too high.

Constantin ran, jumped, and caught the top of the wall. Muscles straining, he pulled himself up and crouched on the edge, listening to be sure no one heard leather scraping on stone. The courtyard remained empty. Now that he'd taken the first step to breach this place, the next was a little easier.

He eased down and moved around to the back of the building. Here there was activity. Children dressed all in black worked at garden tasks. None of them spoke, or smiled, or did any of the things a child their age should do. An air of terror hung over them as they bent to their chores with an occasional furtive glance over their shoulders at the open kitchen door.

Constantin's jaw clenched and the surge of anger chased away his fear. This was a travesty. Though the garden was sizable, all the children were underfed, judging from their skeletal frames. Their ages ranged from the long, lanky lad hauling water from the well with the new muscles of an adolescent to a waif who gathered eggs from the coop with tear-streaked cheeks and a swollen lip.

His resolve hardened, pushing past the fear gnawing on the edges of the anger. Constantin had to know if it was the nightmare from his past. He had to do something about it, whether it was or not, though the task appeared monumental. Constantin was nothing. He was powerless. But he had to find a way to make a difference.

He made his way toward the open door as a matron appeared with a hard glare toward the working children. "You drop another egg, Luca, and you'll be in the basement tonight with a thrashing as well."

Constantin glared at her as he neared, and his hands tightened into fists. She was not one of the tormentors of his youth, but she was like them. The same unsmiling mouth. The same cruel glint in her eyes. This place held no warmth, no love. That was the first lesson everyone learned upon entering the doors.

He slipped in behind her as she entered the kitchen again and moved out of the way of the bustling servants and children. Staff took the jobs which required skill and were busy kneading dough and stirring pots. Children did all the heavy work, from scrubbing the stone floors to washing the pile of dirty dishes.

Constantin longed to ease their labor. To give them a bit of a laugh or a sense of hope. Though he couldn't imagine what he could do. It would have to be something that wouldn't bring retaliation down on spirits already bent and bruised. He edged around the kitchen, following the progress of the matron as she made her way to the heavy wooden door tucked in the back.

Keys jangled at her waist as the matron drew the heavy ring off her belt and unlocked the door. Behind it a lightless maw descended. "Gabrielle, you may come up. The Master wants to see you."

A whimper came from the darkness, and a few moments later, a little girl appeared. Her large dark eyes were wide with fright, her black curls mashed into knots, and her dusky skin covered in soot and dirt. Still, she was impossibly beautiful with an otherworldly air that caught Constantin's attention. She was fey kissed, like him.

"*S'il vous plaît, non*, madame, not the hungry man." The little girl twisted her hands in her soiled skirts, her voice a bare whisper. She couldn't have been more than five or six, but it was hard to tell with the fey kissed. They often appeared younger than they were. "I'd rather go back to the basement."

"Ungrateful *garce*." The woman seized the girl by her ear and marched her toward a corridor leading away from the kitchen. "He asked for you specifically. You don't say no to the Master. Ever. Not if you know what's good for you."

"What's wrong with her?" one child muttered in a barely audible voice. "I'd rather see the Master than this pile of dishes. He at least gives a peppermint with his lecture."

"Gabrielle's always been strange. Soft in the head," another one answered as a kitchen helper rounded on them with a hiss to be quiet.

His stomach sinking, Constantin hurried after the matron on light feet. He remembered all too well how no one at the orphanage believed him when he said a monster lived among them. He hadn't known what the creature was at the time, but Constantin felt it feeding off the children's pain and misery. When they got inured to the daily abuse, the monster orchestrated more horrors for them to endure until they died, husks of their former selves. On occasion, there were ones like him who had crossed an invisible line he never understood and were booted out onto the streets because they were no longer of value.

It wasn't until much later that he figured out what the monster was: a magicman, a soul eater, and children were their favorite prey.

Gabrielle continued to cry as the matron hurried her through the dormitories. The scale of the orphanage made Constantin ill. It was twice the size of the one in Toulouse. Twice the number of children being tormented. At the end of the hall was another heavy door and stairwell. The matron opened it and shoved Gabrielle forward. "Off with you. I've wasted enough time with you. Go."

Constantin shrank back. Evil flowed down those stairs, the sense of it so familiar and sickening that every instinct in him screamed to flee.

Gabrielle grasped the railing and continued, a forlorn little figure, as the matron smirked. Constantin promised he'd do something about her later on. What, he didn't know. He had about as much power here as he had at the old orphanage, but he'd find a way. Nothing too extreme. As bad as it was, here the children had food and shelter. He didn't have the means to provide for himself after he didn't show up at work, much less this many children with various needs.

The matron turned away, satisfied Gabrielle would obey. As soon as her footsteps faded, Gabrielle paused, crying silently and shaking with terror. It called to something inside of him, and he had to answer that fear. Constantin followed and crouched down next to her. With her round eyes and unblinking gaze, she reminded him of a little owl. "You're not alone, *ma petite chouette*. You don't have to face the hungry man all by yourself."

She stiffened with a squeak, and her hands tightened on the railing. "Are you a ghost?"

"*Non*, I'm human like you. You just can't see me." Constantin leaned closer. They didn't have much time. If this was what he feared, the monster had little patience. "Reach out your hand, Gabrielle."

After a moment, she did and touched Constantin's cheek. The illusion shattered and her breath caught. Constantin smiled at her. "See, I'm flesh and blood."

"What's your name?" Gabrielle asked.

"Constantin Severin." He gave her a courtly bow that teased a wisp of a smile from her. "I can take you away from here."

He had no idea how he'd take care of her, but he couldn't send her in there knowing she'd sense what he did. It was different with the other children, who couldn't sense the monster. To them, it was the *grandpère* who let them cry on its shoulder and gave them peppermints, not the nightmare who savored their pain.

Another wave of nausea rolled through him, and he longed to kill the monster as he had dreamed of since he was a young boy. Hatred was a living creature that wanted to burst free, and the only thing that kept it at bay was knowing the monster could kill him with laughable ease. Stealing from the monster was almost as satisfying as killing it would be.

Gabrielle gnawed on her lip and shrank back away from him. "You'd hurt me. Like all of them."

"*Jamais*," Constantin vowed, but it would take time to show her he could be trusted. He cast about, searching for a way, and the only one that came to him was a nightmare he didn't want to face.

"I have to go. Hungry man will be mad." Gabrielle started back up the stairs, her little jaw tight with determination.

"I'll go with you, so you won't be alone," Constantin offered. "You won't be able to see me, but I'll be there." Perhaps that would bolster her.

She turned back, her luminous eyes wide with wonder. "You would?" She patted his cheek and gave him a tremulous smile. She really was a beautiful child. "Promise?"

"I promise." Constantin rose and held out his hand. She clung to it with a soft cry. If she could face her monster, he could too. Side by side, they climbed the stairs and paused before the heavy wooden door.

Constantin crouched beside her again and laid his hands on her shoulders. "I'm going to disappear again. You won't be able to see me or feel me, but I'll be there. I swear."

Gabrielle searched his face for a long moment, then nodded, fisting her hands in her skirts again. Constantin smiled at her and let go, wrapping the shadows around himself as her eyes widened. "You still there?" she whispered.

"I'm here," Constantin assured her.

Gabrielle bit her lip and knocked softly on the door.

"Come in, Gabrielle."

Constantin went cold all over. He knew that voice. He heard it in his nightmares every night. The tone was smooth, mellifluous, and it froze Constantin where he stood. How strange a voice that sweet could awaken such dark memories. Constantin braced himself with an effort to face the creature who had done its best to destroy him from the inside out.

Gabrielle clung to the doorknob. "Promise?" she whispered again in the broken voice of someone who has had too many promises stolen from them.

"I'm right here. I can't speak again until you leave, but I am right here." Constantin braced himself for his first sight of the monster. He couldn't act on instinct. Nightingale would kill him in a heartbeat, and then he wouldn't be able to help her or any of the other children.

The door swung open, and Andre Nightingale looked up from its comfortable chair by the fire and smiled at Gabrielle. "Come in, Gabrielle. I've been waiting for you."

Non, non, non.

He had wanted to believe Nightingale was in Toulouse, preying on the children there. From what Constantin had been able to determine, it had been there for decades before Constantin and his brothers had been tormented under Nightingale's roof. There would be no reason for the monster to leave. It had all the power there, unless it had caught the attention of the wrong people. Even a magicman had something to fear against an entire city rallied against it. A Chevalier de Rouen might've driven it out, though he couldn't imagine one that would leave such a demon alive.

Here it was. In Paris.

Constantin had the crazy urge to snatch up Gabrielle and bolt, but he had no chance of getting away. He couldn't mask her in the shadows without revealing himself first, and Nightingale wasn't human. It could move with a preternatural speed and strength when it wished.

It would enjoy torturing Constantin if he interfered with its plans again. He could only do what he'd promised to do and not leave Gabrielle alone. But he'd come up with a plan and free these children from their nightmare, the way he'd prayed so often to be saved.

Nightingale didn't look like a monster. It appeared so normal. There was nothing about it that stood out. If Constantin hadn't known what it was, he would've passed it on the street a dozen times without noticing it. That had always disturbed Constantin even more. If the creature was as ugly as its deeds, he could understand that, or supremely beautiful, to lure in new victims would be another thing, but not this normalcy. It could be anyone's *grandpère* with that bland, kindly face until you noticed its smile never touched its eyes.

Which was probably how it convinced people to give it so many children.

Constantin followed Gabrielle in and prayed Nightingale wouldn't notice his presence. There was a time when he wouldn't have been able to mask himself from it, but he counted the years without contact and his age to counteract any old links they once shared.

Gabrielle left Constantin's side and went to stand before Nightingale, her chin lifted and shoulders squared. That was good. It took better care of those who showed spirit. Nightingale stroked Gabrielle's cheek and smiled when she let out a soft whimper. "Still afraid of me? Don't worry, Gabrielle, I won't hurt you. Your fear is so strong. It calls to me."

Constantin tightened his hand on the knife he'd hidden under his coat. He didn't know what he'd do if he sensed the magicman feeding or even if he could sense it anymore. But his soul would be damned even more than it already was if he sat back and allowed it to happen.

"You are the hungry man," Gabrielle whispered. "I can feel you. You eat us. When we cry ourselves to sleep at night. I can feel you in the room even if I can't see you."

Any hope Constantin had that Nightingale's little ritual of comfort was playacting died with the cruel glint in the magicman's eyes. It was merely a way to gloat and draw out the pain of innocents betrayed. "I knew there was something special about you, Gabrielle." The magicman sat back, its fingers drumming on the arms of the chair. "I knew another like you once. He is the sweetest memory I had until he betrayed me." Its gaze turned hard, pinning Gabrielle, and she shivered. "You wouldn't betray me, would you, little one?"

Gabrielle shook her head so hard her hair whipped her face.

"I didn't think so." Nightingale laid its head back on the chair and closed its eyes with a reminiscent smile. "Since you know me as I know you for what you are, there is no need to pretend. You are stronger than the others. You will feed me a long time." The smile turned lazy as it focused on her again. "I'm going to have to consider this development. Go now."

Gabrielle spun around so fast she almost collided with Constantin, but he stepped out of the way in time. He followed her as she raced down the stairs, his heart beating so fast he was surprised the monster couldn't hear it. Gabrielle fled to an alcove in one of the dormitories and hid behind the curtain, crying softly. "Are you there? Are you still there?" she called.

"I am, *ma petite chouette*." Constantin crouched down beside her. He thinned the shadows around him enough so she could get a glimpse of him, and her eyes rounded with wonder as her tears dried. "I'm going to find a way to get rid of the monster."

Gabrielle clutched at his coat with strong hands for such a young girl. "Promise?"

Constantin patted her on the back and gave her a ghost of a smile. He never knew how to interact with adults most of the time, but children were easy. "I promise," he said fervently, feeling the oath locked into his soul. One way or another, there had to be a way to bring Nightingale down.

Chapter Five

"THE TRAIN WILL arrive within the hour, my lord," Janvier announced as he came into the cabin where Michel-Leon was attempting to organize his notes. "Hadrien arranged for the rental of a carriage. He should be ready by the time we disembark. His family will join us in a few days."

Janvier's kith and kin were extensive, and his ability to call on them at need had helped Michel-Leon out of more than one sticky situation. It made him uncomfortable to have them in Paris though. He didn't want to put any others in danger. There was enough going on, but Janvier had overrun every one of Michel-Leon's arguments, and Régine had championed him. He had no chance of winning against their united front.

"That should give us a chance to go through the château and mark the safe areas," Michel-Leon said, and it would ease his concerns. "We should establish ourselves in one wing. Who did Hadrien send for?"

"His wife and daughter to help with the cooking and cleaning. I don't believe you've met them before, but they are close to Régine," Janvier said as he began to organize and pack the chaos of Michel-Leon's research.

"Be sure to stress the dangers. The château isn't safe for staff. We don't want anyone wandering off and getting caught in a trap." Michel-Leon snatched up the stack of notes he'd been searching for.

"We need to stop by the palace before heading to the château," he said absently as he scowled at the scrawled script in his hands. Even he couldn't read his own handwriting. He'd have to do something about that. What good were notes if they were indecipherable?

"They are intelligent enough to understand the dangers. We'll keep most of the place locked up and only disarm the areas we'll be using," Janvier assured him before his voice took on a disapproving tone. "We should stop by the château first. If you are going to present yourself to the emperor, then you need to get cleaned up and arrange for an audience. Details make a difference."

Michel-Leon flapped his hand at Janvier and stuffed the notes into his pocket. He'd figure them out on the carriage ride. "Bother that. It will delay us hours, and we don't have time."

"Michel-Leon, you would cover me with shame if you demand an audience appearing like a down-and-out scholar or the rootless vagabond you aspire to be. You need to look the part of a Chevalier de Rouen if you have any hope of the emperor listening to you." Michel-Leon met Janvier's adamant stare. "Since we have some time before the train pulls into the station, you will put down your notes, wash up, and wear what I pull out for you. Do we have an understanding, my lord?"

In Janvier's eyes, Michel-Leon would forever be an unruly child with skinned knees and a dirty face. No one but Janvier and Régine spoke to him as frankly, and Michel-Leon enjoyed the bluntness. He needed somebody to rein him in. He gave Janvier a mischievous smile and swept him a bow. "I am, as always, your obedient son."

"*Merci,*" Janvier said with an amused gleam in his eyes. "I appreciate your efforts to keep the dignity of this family alive."

"Well, let's have it then. What torturous getup did you manage to sneak on board?"

"Several, my lord. Today we will go with your green silk twill and wool morning coat and the white trousers."

Michel-Leon winced and steeled himself to be fussed over. By the time the train rolled into the station, Michel-Leon had reached the limits of his patience. His shoes and top hat gleamed. His precisely knotted wide tie and the jeweled stickpin Janvier managed to get on him added another layer of irritation. The only thing he pulled out that pleased Michel-Leon was the sword cane. He didn't expect to get set upon by monsters at the palace, though one never knew, but it would be comforting to have a hidden weapon.

Michel-Leon felt like a fool in all the frippery, and Régine was sure to laugh, but if it granted him an audience, he'd put up with it. He had his doubts though. The chevaliers were not looked upon with favor since his *grandpère's* time. The discontent had been building for generations. The disaster at Metz had been the catalyst that set the avalanche off and buried the chevaliers in its wake.

His hope lay in the changes in government in the last fifty-two years. They were now in the Second Empire, and Michel-Leon's family had been old and well connected before their destruction. Or had been once. Michel-Leon hadn't fostered those connections. There was never enough time.

"I do wish you'd let me cut your hair, my lord," Janvier said with a sigh as he directed the porters to gather their belongings. "You look like a ragabout."

Michel-Leon raked a hand through his burnished curls. It was getting rather long. He could almost tie it back. "You already came after me with the razor." He touched his clean-shaven jaw. "When this entire ordeal with the mists is over, you can have at me with the shears."

"I suppose that will have to do, my lord." Janvier fell into step behind him as they paused by Régine's door and knocked.

She opened it immediately, and a smile tugged at her lips as she took in his clothes. Her eyes danced, no doubt from memory of their quarrel. "You look a fright, Michie. My sympathies."

Janvier shot her a quelling look as Michel-Leon grimaced and held out his arm for her. "I have to speak with the emperor. I weighed the entertainment factor of your acid commentary about the court against the dangers of putting you in a dress again. In the meantime, I'd like for you, Janvier, and Hadrien to talk to as many people as you can. See if you can get a feel for the mood in Paris and around the palace. Let me know if the people feel like anything official has been done to help them."

"*Merci,* for not making me go along," Régine said as they made their way down the corridor to the bustling platform.

"Did you talk with Monsieur Vautrin and relay my offer?" Michel-Leon asked Janvier.

"I did. He is interested in your patronage. He will contact you once he's settled in London. If you have any further questions, you can telegraph him there." Janvier studied the line of carriages nearby and nodded toward one. "That one is ours, my lord."

"Speaking of telegraphs. We should check the local office and see if my colleague in London responded." Michel-Leon checked his pocket watch with a frown. "We should also contact a printer. The last incident of the mists occurred yesterday, so by my calculations, another one should not happen until the day after tomorrow. If we are correct, and we have been so far, we should distribute warnings."

"I have already taken care of the telegraph," Janvier replied. "I sent a messenger the moment we stopped. By the time we are settled and the luggage loaded, he should be back with news."

"I'll look into the printer, Michie," Régine said as they stepped out onto the crowded platform. "I should have a list of reputable places and prices by the end of the day."

"I am forever grateful I have both of you, else I'd be continually lost." Michel-Leon studied the platform with a frown. Broadsides covered with the names of the missing papered the walls. People walked with tense steps, their gaze more on the horizon than around them, and the pickpockets were having a heyday, but even they kept an eye on the skies. Paris was a city under siege, and it showed.

"We should take the time to engage in gossip while *grandpère* is seeing to the carriage," Régine suggested. She scanned the crowd and nodded toward a prosperous couple, members of the bourgeois, by their dress, who had arrived on the platform. They stood with dignified calm as their servants bustled around them, unloading several good-sized trunks from a laden-down carriage. The pile of luggage was impressive. "That looks as if they plan on spending a serious amount of time away from Paris."

"It does indeed. I'd like to know what's been happening in the city since I was last here. Let's see if the couple is in a chatting mood." Michel-Leon and Régine strolled over to them. "*Bonjour*, monsieur, madame," Michel-Leon said, tipping his hat to them as he noticed the man lay a proprietary hand on the arm of the woman next to him. "I am Parisee, the Baron de Dagonville, this is my sister the Widow Bardin, and you are?"

"Monsieur and Madame Roy." A hint of curiosity brightened the older man's eyes. "What brings you to Paris at this time?"

"We needed a change of scenery, and I hear Paris is going through a number of changes with Haussmann's renovations. I look forward to seeing them," Michel-Leon replied.

"I also understand they're planning on an opera house," Régine said in a confidential tone to Madame Roy, who smiled back.

"Not for years yet, I'm afraid. There are several other projects in the works first," Madame Roy replied.

"Another reason to leave this madness for a while," Monsieur Roy grumbled. "The construction has gotten out of hand. Haussmann is letting his power and greed go to his head."

"Oh, I don't know, the parks and all those wide boulevards will be lovely." Madame Roy was quite a bit younger than her husband and charmingly pretty. "I'm sure when it is all done it will be worth the fuss despite Monsieur Hugo and his contemporaries' disapproval."

"He's annexed half the neighborhoods around the city. It's a disaster." Monsieur Roy's face screwed up in an expression of disgust. "It is a terrible mess, and the city is crawling with indigents. I'll be glad when it is over with and normalcy returns. The dream of turning Paris into the jewel of Europe is vanity we cannot afford."

Madame Roy cast him a nervous glance, and that was the opening Michel-Leon needed to steer the conversation back to what he wanted to discuss. "I have heard the most disturbing rumors coming out of Paris, and I merely wanted to verify a few details before I reopened my home here," Michel-Leon confided.

"*Oui,*" Régine chimed in. "We hear there's been a plague of mists covering the city and that people have gone missing. *S'il vous plaît,* tell me there is no truth to such ugly rumors."

The smile in Madame Roy's eyes vanished as terror leapt into her eyes. Monsieur Roy's mouth thinned. "That is silly rumormongering. Another way for the laborers to protest the amount of work they've been asked to handle. The only people missing are the ones who gave up and returned to shiftlessness. Doesn't matter; there's always another body to take their place. Paris is crawling with them. It'll cause trouble. You mark my words."

Madame Roy smiled tremulously, and her gloved hand tightened on her husband's arm. "*Cherie,* I think it's time to board. If you'll excuse us. We don't want to miss the train."

Intrigued, Michel-Leon watched them stroll off. They had plenty of time before the train left but clearly did not want to discuss the mists. "That shut them down rather fast, didn't it?"

"Indeed," Régine said. "They are quick enough to flee but not warn anyone else about it. Maybe they're afraid of sounding crazy."

They attempted a few more conversations with similar results before they returned to the waiting carriage. Hadrien opened the door for them and helped Régine up. "Where to first, my lord?" he asked as Michel-Leon stepped in after her.

Michel-Leon grimaced at the formality, but they weren't back home anymore. No doubt Janvier had drilled into his head the need for appearances while they were in Paris. "The palace and then on to the château."

"*Bien sûr*, my lord," Hadrien said solemnly as he closed the carriage door with an impish wink to him and Régine. The carriage rocked as he clambered up, and soon they were inching out of the waiting line and into traffic.

"This came for you." Janvier handed him a message slip after they settled and Michel-Leon unfolded it impatiently.

We had problems with mists in England in the far past. STOP. Will research and get back to you. STOP.

"I thought it was a long shot." Michel-Leon tucked the message into his pocket and folded his hands over his knee. "Each region has its own issues unique to them. He's going to research more though. What did you learn on the platform? Régine and I didn't have luck getting many details, but some who can afford to are leaving."

"They are uneasy. Everyone I spoke to has at least heard of someone going missing in the mists. To the point where most abandon their tasks and retreat indoors when it appears. The few construction crews that insisted on remaining outside have been decimated." Janvier had a troubled look in his faded blue eyes. "It's hard to get a correct gauge, this early in, as to how many are truly missing, but I'm alarmed."

"The people I talked to didn't want to admit there is a problem, which doesn't bode well for my reception at the palace, but they are frightened." Michel-Leon steepled his fingers and studied the city as the carriage rattled across the cobblestones. The number of changes in the last several years were astonishing, and he wondered what made the creature who begat the swarm select the city it did. And how did something that size hide so well? Michel-Leon vividly remembered its shape against the night sky.

There were several commonalities he'd been able to discern. All the cities were on or near a river and had caves nearby. His meeting with Vautrin had confirmed the creature nested and laid its eggs in a cave outside the city. When they reached the château, Michel-Leon would study a map of the surrounding area. They would have to conduct their search systematically if they wanted to make any headway.

"You must be careful at the palace, Michie," Régine urged, her eyes concerned. "Napoleon has little patience for detractors. He's exiled people for disagreeing with him. We can't afford that."

Michel-Leon grimaced. "I will be my diplomatic best. We need his help. Paris is too big to search the surrounding areas by ourselves in the time we have remaining. If we discover where the creature landed, that would give us an area to start with."

"If the court refuses to listen, I know you'll carry on anyway." Janvier gave him a fond look. "You are nothing if not persistent. We might as well start around the château; perhaps we'll get lucky. I'll visit the village and see if we can find any who know the surrounding area well."

"That is a good place to start. Give them the date Régine and I saw the creature and ask if anyone saw anything unusual," Michel-Leon said. They rolled on in silence until they reached the sentinels at the gates of the Tuileries Palace. Janvier opened the window and presented their papers. "The Baron de Dagonville, Chevalier de Rouen, is here to address the court."

Michel-Leon found all the pomp and ceremony tedious, but Janvier thrived on it and soon had them moving down the long boulevard toward the palace proper with its distinctive roofline and squared central dome. The gardens were in full spring bloom, and there was no sign of the menace that haunted Paris. In interludes like this, Michel-Leon liked to pretend for a blessed moment there were no monsters about.

"Wait for me here," Michel-Leon said as they came to a halt at the entrance in the middle of the grand façade. A servant in imperial livery waited at a discrete distance. "If they are willing to see me, I'll send a message and join you at the village later. *S'il vous plaît,* do not go into the château without me, even if you know the traps better than I. If they refuse to see me, I'll return immediately."

"*Bonne chance,*" Janvier said softly, and Michel-Leon flashed him a smile.

"*Merci,* I suspect I'll need it." Michel-Leon left his pistols with Régine and descended from the carriage. He glanced at Hadrien, who nodded. He'd take Régine and Janvier away if any danger loomed. Reassured, Michel-Leon followed the servant to the main doors and glanced back over his shoulder at the extensive gardens and the *Arc d'Triomphe* in the distance. The signs of the massive renovations were visible from here, and he hoped Paris would have a chance to see it come to its fulfillment.

Tuileries Palace had been the home for several different kings, and it showed in the gilt and carved wood that decorated every surface and the enormous chandeliers that vied for dominance with the paintings hanging everywhere. Michel-Leon went through the process of identifying himself again with veiled impatience as messengers in imperial livery scurried and courtiers whispered. It was sweltering inside, and Michel-Leon longed to ditch his coat and tie.

A minor functionary escorted him through the maze of corridors and rooms. As they approached the *salle du Trône*, the doors opened and a familiar figure emerged, shutting the doors behind him, and Michel-Leon's heart constricted. Lord Lennox blocked the way, a sneer already on his lips, and Michel-Leon cursed under his breath. Of all the useless sycophants who had attached themselves to the emperor, it had to be this one whom he had to convince he needed an audience. His prospects didn't look good.

Lennox flicked his fingers at the functionary, who had halted, plucking at Michel-Leon's sleeve for him to do the same. "You may go. I'll deal with this intrusion."

"*Oui*, my lord baron." The man didn't even look Michel-Leon's way before making himself scarce. It wouldn't surprise Michel-Leon to find out Lennox had been using intimidation tactics to garner power. After all, his family had once excelled at that.

"Are you the emperor's secretary now?" Michel-Leon asked as he came closer. He weighed the benefits of shoving Lennox aside and barging in over trying diplomacy first. Other supplicants milled in the corridor, listening and awaiting their chance to be seen.

It had been years since Michel-Leon had seen him, and doing so now stirred unwanted memories and conflicted emotions. Thibuat Lennox hadn't changed much. Dark brows arched over expressive green eyes, brooding lines bridged over the straight slash of his nose. It was an arresting face, used to being obeyed without question. There had been a time when Michel-Leon found that face to be captivating until he'd uncovered the mask. Lennox had toyed with his affections as a distraction.

"He trusts me to ensure only important matters are brought to his attention." Lennox's gaze flicked over him, cool and dismissive. "What brought you crawling back to Paris, Michel-Leon? I thought you were done with this place and were licking your wounds in Lorraine?" Their long acquaintance gave Lennox a familiarity that Michel-Leon wished he could take back.

There were a thousand responses Michel-Leon longed to make, but if he had any hope of gaining access to the emperor in this decade, he'd have to bite his tongue. "I heard Paris is beset with strange mists that are plaguing your populace. It is my duty to investigate such matters and to keep the emperor informed.

"From what I understand, a significant number of people have already gone missing." Michel-Leon shot him a level look. "And those disappearances coincide with the mists."

"Immigrants, laborers, and the poor," Lennox said with a sniff and a wave of his hand. "They breed like mice, and there will always be more crawling out to replace them."

"Your people, who are the backbone rebuilding your city. If you don't have them, the whole structure falls apart. If they get spooked, if they believe their needs aren't being met, they'll riot." Michel-Leon paused to let that threat sink home. The violent scars from the past had barely scabbed over. "You know this as well as I. *S'il vous plaît,* let me speak with Napoleon."

Lennox gave Michel-Leon a condescending smile. "The city is changing. The people cannot barricade themselves like they used to. We're tearing down their hidey-holes and the army will be ready for them if they try. This is a rule of law now. If I hear you've been fear-mongering and driving them into a frenzy, I'll have you arrested myself." His nostrils flared as he leaned closer and lowered his voice. "I have not forgotten how your family devastated mine."

"At least you still have some left." Michel-Leon clenched his jaw. Damn diplomacy and tact. "You were keeping a lich as a pet to threaten your detractors. If my family hadn't destroyed it, another chevalier would've. We showed more mercy to your family than you had to others. What other secrets would I find about the Lennox family if I dig deep enough? What other monsters are in your closets?"

"What a lively imagination you have." Lennox's eyes narrowed in a glare as the courtiers whispered, and he straightened with a dismissive sniff. "The emperor has no time for you today. He is preparing to move with the court to *Château de Saint-Cloud* as he does every spring. He won't be back until the end of the year."

Michel-Leon struggled for a patience he did not feel. "Our families may have been on opposite sides once, and they ruined each other. But there was a time when we cared about each other. I beg you to listen to me. What is happening here in Paris is the same menace that wiped out Metz fifty-two years ago. They are just beginning to recover. We do not want a repeat of that in a city this size. We can stop it if we work together. If we don't, there won't be a Paris to come back to."

"Whatever friendship we once had is in ashes, along with your family home. I know about Metz. The chevaliers were so sure they could stop the swarm from hatching and look at how wrong they were. You, by yourself, think to stop something that defeated your entire order?" Lennox laughed. "Now I know you're making up tales. Run along, chevalier. I'll make sure the emperor gets your message. If he wants to see you, he'll send for you."

Lennox's barb hit the scars on his heart. Michel-Leon had long suspected the Lennox family had been behind that final strike on his home. He'd survived because Janvier had plunged into the nightmare of smoke and fire to pull him free. He had just returned from his tour in Europe, studying with other monster hunters and learning the techniques unique to each region. Still, he didn't want to believe it to be true. Even more, he didn't want Lennox to know his words had wounded. That the mention of the destruction slicked his back with sweat.

At least he said he'd pass along the message, which was more than Michel-Leon had expected when he saw the man. He suspected he was hedging his bets as usual. He wouldn't want to find out later Michel-Leon had been telling the truth and have the emperor realize he'd been sitting on a warning. That would destroy his family's waning influence for good.

"Be sure you do," Michel-Leon admonished. He made it a point to meet the eyes of everyone present who might have overheard the last bit of their exchange to convey his urgency, and then he turned and left, leaving hushed silence behind him.

Michel-Leon clenched the shaft of his cane in his fist as he descended toward the waiting carriage. Fools. The entire lot of them were blind fools. Terrors such as mists and monsters had no care for station or wealth. They wouldn't hesitate to attack because of someone's pedigree. And the common people of France would not sit still and allow themselves to be abused. They had shown that mettle more than once. It was easier to concentrate on that than on the other. The horror Lennox had hinted at.

"I take it the interview went as bad as you feared," Janvier said dryly as Michel-Leon wrenched the door open and pounded on the roof with his cane before he even settled himself.

"Bah, what interview? Lennox intercepted me before I cleared the door. Damn prideful fool," Michel-Leon grumbled as the carriage started with a lurch. "He's still enraged that my brother destroyed their lich."

Régine's eyes widened with interest. "I never heard that story before. When did this happen?"

Michel-Leon stared out the window. He didn't like remembering that disastrous time. "I was barely old enough to be considered a young man. Still training as a chevalier. My brother did most of the grunt work for Father then. A few families had gotten together for a round of parties, visits, the usual thing. I don't think the Lennox entourage had expected us to be there. They had brought along their pet to intimidate those they were trying to strong-arm. One family came to us for assistance."

"I don't believe that is the only reason Lennox bears you enmity," Janvier said with a searching look. "You were quite close with him that summer."

Michel-Leon flushed. That was a reminder he did not need. Lennox had a silver tongue. He'd taught Michel-Leon more than one lesson about love and passion and heartbreak. Another reason for his vow.

"That is neither here nor there." Michel-Leon brooded out at the changing cityscape. He wanted to confess Lennox's insinuation, but Janvier carried wounds on his heart as well. He wouldn't open them without proof. Not when Lennox could be lying just to get at him and distract him from his purpose. He'd share his suspicions with Régine instead.

"The fool wouldn't grant me an audience. I'll try penning a letter, but in the meantime, I will not wait for them to act. I might be able to get around Lennox through another avenue." Michel-Leon's long fingers drummed with impatience on the knob of his cane. "We need more people. We need more information."

The task was overwhelming, and for a moment, Michel-Leon did not even know where to start. There were so many directions to go in, and he was only one disreputable chevalier with two more than capable assistants whom no one would listen to because they were an old servant and a young woman. Stupidity upon foolishness.

"Rest assured, those in power will change their mind as more people go missing and it starts to affect them. Be at ease, Michel-Leon," Janvier soothed. "We can recruit others to chase down rumors for us while we concentrate on the important details."

Once again Janvier saved him with the calm voice of reason,

pulling Michel-Leon back from his brooding abyss. "I don't want to put anyone in danger."

"They are already in danger." Janvier snorted. "The least they can do is help themselves get out of the cookpot."

Régine touched his hand, stilling his fingers. "You're not alone."

Michel-Leon forced a smile. "Then I am indeed blessed."

Chapter Six

CONSTANTIN FILLED HIS pockets with bread and retreated against the wall. Wrapping the shadows more tightly around himself, he stilled as a servant came by, bearing another platter of remnants from the manor's table. He eyed the tray of thinly sliced roast beef and untouched game hens with crispy skin. He hadn't had meat in well over a week, and they wouldn't miss it if he snatched some of that. The children at the orphanage could do with extra nourishment besides the slop they ate, so it wouldn't go to waste.

As the servants busied themselves with other tasks, Constantin slipped some of the meat into his canvas bag and grabbed a silver bowl of candied nuts. He was pressing his luck, and he needed to get moving. He'd promised Gabrielle he would visit today.

He made his way through the manor on quiet feet. He hated scrounging for sustenance like this. It brought too many memories of his dark days on the streets, but he couldn't work, visit the children, and scheme to take down Nightingale at the same time. In the last week that he'd been at this, he'd come no closer to an answer for getting rid of the monster. There had to be a way to drive it out of Paris.

Which would lead to different victims elsewhere. No, he had to kill the magicman now. No more victims.

Constantin had witnessed enough incidents as a child to know that Nightingale was monstrously strong. It had the ability to feed off souls, and what Constantin learned about the creatures since his time on his own didn't give him much faith in his ability to handle the problem alone. He needed more people and a specialized weapon. Constantin didn't even know what Nightingale was doing in Paris after the creature had terrorized Toulouse for so long. But that could've been the problem. People may have caught on. So if it had been forced to move, that might mean it had a weakness. Constantin had to figure out what it was, or perhaps he was grasping at false hope.

As he neared the side door that he'd used to sneak into the manor, he slowed with a mental curse. Maids dusted and swept in the rooms beside it, talking amongst themselves. There was enough activity between them that Constantin didn't want to risk alerting them by opening the door. He gauged the amount of work left and determined he was better off waiting than searching for another place to slip outside.

The maids gossiped about the other servants as Constantin eavesdropped. Information could be quite profitable if he could find a buyer. He crept closer to listen.

"Many of Madeline's family disappeared, her cousins on her mom's side. The few left don't know what happened during the night. There was no noise to indicate they'd been taken against their will. Even stranger, her great uncle was bedridden, but he's gone stark raving mad. Keeps talking about how he wants to go to the song. If I was stuck in a bed all day and all night, I'd want to go meet my maker too." The maid surveyed the room with her hands on her hips. "He won't tell anyone what happened to his family, but they're sure he knows something."

"It's been happening everywhere, people leaving tasks undone, food half eaten," another responded. "I heard from Yannick, whose brother is a footman at the palace, that a Chevalier de Rouen appeared and tried to warn the court about the mists, but they booted him out."

"I didn't realize there were any chevaliers left," the maid's voice brightened. "If anyone will know what to do about the mystery, they will. Though, I suppose, if one showed up, it's not good news, is it? It means it's serious."

A subdued silence fell over the room. Then the maids gathered their cleaning items and marched down the hall to the next set of rooms. Constantin slipped out the door and closed it quietly behind him. The manor house was in the city, which made it convenient as loaded down as Constantin was. He should remain wrapped in the shadows, though the more he used it, the more like a shadow he felt. The more alone he became. Still, he didn't want to draw attention to his bag full of purloined food and silver.

The orphanage wasn't far away, and the mood on the street was uneasy. People kept half their attention on the horizon, their bodies tense as if they were constantly ready to flee. They reminded Constantin forcibly of rabbits with their quivering noses and ears. Prey. They were all prey to an unknown phenomenon. He tried to recall when the last mist had rolled through, but his attention hadn't been on that phenomenon. He should be more observant. The last thing he needed was to be caught out in it. He'd never be able to help the children if he disappeared.

The garden was deserted when he arrived, and all the doors to the orphanage shut. No matter, Constantin had studied every entrance and learned the best ways of getting in. He pressed his ear against the door nearest the coal shed. It was always unlocked and busy only a few times a day. It sounded quiet, so Constantin eased the door open a crack and listened again before slipping through and latching it behind him.

Down the short hall through another open door, the noise of busy clatter came from the kitchens.

The last time he'd visited, they had locked Gabrielle in the basement again for being defiant, and he'd had no way of getting to her. His frustration had been acute. But he had a solution of sorts. Something that would give her a sense of not being utterly alone. That is, if he couldn't convince her to run away this time. At the moment, Gabrielle's fear of the world outside was still bigger than her fear of Nightingale.

Constantin moved away from the kitchen, deeper into the bowels of the orphanage. He'd learned all the ways to get to the dormitories and the rooms where the children worked from sunup to sundown if they weren't toiling in the garden. He checked all the favorite punishment spots that he could get to. The room where they forced the children to kneel on wires for hours at a time until their knees bled. The cold storage for food that held barely clad shivering littles.

Constantin's fists clenched. More than one master and matron had met with an accident in the last week. He was not sorry in the least. It didn't take care of the monster who ruled over the entire place, but it made the children breathe easier to have a few of the worst out of their lives. He kept reminding himself he had to be careful and not attract attention, but that mattered little when he came upon a situation he could do something about.

He made his way up to the niche where he met Gabrielle and left presents when he could.

It was empty. Outside the window Constantin spied the mist slithering along the ground in a darting, fast moving dance with its familiar black filaments. He shivered with dread. There was nothing natural about that occurrence, and he'd be stuck inside the orphanage for several hours until it cleared out as quickly as it arrived.

His fingers curled into claws. Maybe he could arrange another accident while he was here. If a few more evil people disappeared into the mists, no one would comment on it, but before he hunted them, he needed to check on Gabrielle.

Constantin slipped a small object out of his pocket and held it up. It was a beetle, no bigger than his thumbnail, made of metal and wire, but so meticulously crafted that it had a life of its own. He concentrated on an image of Gabrielle, offering a tiny thread of his soul's energy, and felt wings whir against his palm. He lifted the beetle to his lips. "I'm here," he whispered, and the device took off in a blur of wings.

It shouldn't work. Constantin still didn't know how he did it, but ever since he found himself scrabbling on the streets for a bite of bread, he'd learned how to transform his tinker-toys into objects of useful wonder. They'd also gotten him chased out of more than one town by those fearing witchcraft.

Constantin sensed the beetle searching, darting through the large, cavernous rooms of the dormitories, into tiny closets, and even into the basement. He could follow the location of any of his objects once he linked to it. He could send brief messages or use it to find places or people he had seen with his own eyes.

Constantin drew his knees up and stared out at the mist as it crept to envelop the building. All the other times it had trapped him inside with no access to windows, and he'd never had the opportunity to study the phenomenon. It engulfed everything, massing so thickly that all the nearby buildings disappeared. Even the wall surrounding the orphanage and what was left inside was hazy and indistinct.

He shrank back as those black filaments webbed over the glass like a sudden frost. He drew away from the window, eyeing the sill. There were no drafts. It didn't appear like air was getting in, but it didn't pay to take chances. He slipped out of the niche and made sure the heavy drapes were in place.

He sensed when the beetle found Gabrielle, a distinct pinging in his head. She was in the southwest section, lower down. He sensed a large room and many other bodies. After a few minutes, he perceived her drawing nearer, so she must've received his message.

Constantin tightened the shadows around him and waited to be sure she was alone. No one came up to the dormitories at this time of day once the cleaning was completed, so they should be left alone. She appeared in the doorway at the end of the hall and looked over her shoulder before making her way inside at a run. Constantin smiled, his spirits lifting at the joy on her face. He eased back the shadows around him so she could see him and held out his arms as she threw herself into them.

"You came back!" she said, squeezing hard as if he'd disappear.

He chuckled. "You say that every time, *ma petite chouette*. I made you a promise, didn't I?"

"The mists are here. I didn't think you would come today." She glanced toward the shrouded niche and froze. "The hungry man is out there. He goes hunting when the mists come."

Constantin went still as well, an icy shiver running down his spine. He forced himself to go to the niche and peer out the window. The lanky figure of Andre Nightingale strolled into the shrouding gray as if it were a bright summer day. He'd known Nightingale went out into the mists. That's what led him to this place, but the sight troubled him. Whatever dangers the outside held plainly did not worry the creature. Constantin would dearly love to know what brought it out there.

"What does it hunt, *ma petite chouette*?" Constantin asked softly, and Gabrielle clung to him harder.

"More children," she said in a small voice. Gabrielle laid her head on his shoulder, idly playing with his hair, and then she relaxed as both of them lost the sense of Nightingale as it moved farther away. "He's gone."

Constantin set her down on a bed. "Are you hungry?" She was painfully thin, like many of the other children. He'd seen the dining rooms. He'd witnessed the children being fed slop while the masters and matrons had nourishing meals. Living under the eye of Nightingale took a toll on the hardiest even in the best of conditions.

"I'm always hungry," Gabrielle whispered. "Just like he is." She looked toward the window, her little face solemn. "He'll come back with more of us. He always does." She shivered. "They scream a lot. First, they scream to go to the music. Then it's like they wake up from a dream, and they scream for their families. Sometimes he tires of it, and the screaming stops."

Constantin cupped her chin. "You don't have to stay, Gabrielle. I don't have much, but you could stay with me."

Gabrielle shook her head, turning her frightened eyes on him. "I don't want to go to the ghostland."

He had tried wrapping her in the shadows once, and she had not cared for the experience at all. "It wouldn't be for long. Just until we are safe, but I understand."

Gabrielle's eyes widened when Constantin drew out the bread and roast beef. He'd leave the rest for her to share with her friends and take the silver bowl with him. It had to be worth a month's rent. Maybe even better lodgings where he could care for Gabrielle properly. She stuffed a roll into her mouth and reached for the slice of roast beef that Constantin held out to her.

"Are you still going to kill the hungry man?" she asked when the edge of her hunger eased.

"I am. I'm searching for a helper." Constantin thought of the chevalier the maids were discussing. If there was anyone who could help or would know of a way to kill a magicman, it was a chevalier. They were all rumored to be insane. Insane, but utterly dedicated to hunting down monsters. A chevalier wouldn't refuse him, even if Constantin had nothing to offer but his service, such as it was. "I believe one came into town. Have you heard of the Chevaliers de Rouen?"

Gabrielle nodded, her legs swinging as she nibbled on another roll. "Papa said the chevaliers had lost their way, but once they were the saviors of France. What does that mean?"

"It means they are as human as we are. They make mistakes, but they are our best hope." Constantin peeked out the window again. "I'm going to talk with him. If anyone can help us, it will be him."

Gabrielle paused in her scramble for food and stared at him with wary eyes that appeared too old for her face. "Why do you want to help us so much? What's in it for you?"

Constantin crouched in front of her. "When I was a little older than you, my papa sold me and my brothers to Nightingale. My *maman* and little sister had died of a fever, and he had no way to care for us. The creature had a place like this in Toulouse. We were with him many years before we escaped. We went through the same horrors you are. And like you, I could sense the monster's hunger, its feeding. I bet none of the other children believe you when you tell them about it."

She shook her head, her mouth turning down. "They say I'm touched."

"They said the same about me. I stopped talking about it because for the others who can't sense what it's doing, Nightingale gives them the bit of comfort that allows them to struggle on." It broke Constantin's heart again. He could harden himself against other adults, but not the children. "The ones that survive understand later on. Instead of giving peppermint sweets, it could've put a stop to all of this, but it didn't. They'll understand your warnings later."

The little beetle came back, flitting around Gabrielle's head, and Constantin caught it. It became inert in his hand, and he slipped it back into his pocket. "How do you do that?" Gabrielle asked.

"It's a bit of magic, like the shadow twisting." Constantin eyed the otherworldly quality about her. "One day you'll be able to do magic things as well."

"And then I'll be safe always?" Gabrielle tightened her little fists. "I can fight them?"

Constantin chucked her chin gently with a smile. She was a fighter to her core. "The world is a dangerous place, *ma petite chouette*. But *oui*, safer at least. Remember, you don't have to be alone. Which reminds me." He pulled the little mechanical cat out of another pocket. Constantin had finished the toy and was rather pleased with the result, as well as the avid gleam in Gabrielle's eyes. He brushed it with a thread of magic and the whiskers twitched. "This is for you."

"Me?" Gabrielle gasped, her hands reaching toward the creature that gave a whirring, soft purr as it batted her hands with its head.

"*Oui*. You'll have to keep her hidden." Even if the matrons or another kid tried to steal it, the construct would find its way back to Gabrielle, but he didn't want her to get into trouble.

"Oh, I will. I promise." Gabrielle carefully picked it up and slipped it into a ragged pouch in her skirts. "I won't be so afraid when they put me in the basement."

It was said so matter-of-factly, as if it was a foregone conclusion she wouldn't escape that punishment, that it made Constantin ache for her again. Children shouldn't be locked away from the sunlight and warmth. "There's something else special about that cat. If you ever decide you want to leave this place and I'm not here, you lift the cat to your mouth and whisper, 'Help.' It knows to find me, and I'll come right away."

"Promise?" Gabrielle's familiar query didn't have the same desperation that it once did. She'd learned that Constantin kept his promises.

Constantin smiled. "Promise. Let's go sneak this food to the neediest of your friends and get you back to your station so you don't get in trouble for being missing."

Gabrielle clung to his hand before he could wrap the shadows around himself. "You're not going outside while the mists are out, are you?"

Constantin shook his head. "I'll remain nearby until it's safe." Once she was settled, he'd seek out Nightingale's quarters to search for any weaknesses. He'd have to be quick. He had no way of knowing how long the creature would be out. Then he'd have time to create havoc for the human monsters that ran this hell.

Chapter Seven

MICHEL-LEON STALKED through the kitchen door of the *Château des Ombres*, seething with frustration. Another day of scouring the countryside around Paris and asking questions that yielded no useful answers, and he was no closer to solving their mystery. Coming back to this place did not improve his mood. He detested every stone of the château and was tempted to consign it to the same fiery fate as his ancestral home back in Sampigny.

Janvier glanced up from the long table where he worked on ledger notes and cleared a spot for Michel-Leon. At least the kitchens were welcoming. The Belangers had turned this place into a haven of warmth and light, banishing the neglect of the last decade. Salome set a pie on the counter, the scent making Michel-Leon's nose twitch.

She put her hands on her hips and eyed Michel-Leon with a stern gaze. "I see your look, my lord. I suppose it was you who got into the pantry this morning and left crumbs everywhere."

"Guilty." He gave her a look of appeal. "I couldn't resist bringing leftovers from dinner to fortify my day."

Janvier had been right to bring Hadrien, Salome, and their daughter Mahaut here. They gave the cold stones of the place some cheer, but Michel-Leon still worried and made sure they understood daily they weren't to stray from the proscribed areas. Which, for the moment, limited them to the kitchens, cold storage, and the rooms off of them for their quarters. When he had time, he'd look into expanding their space. Michel-Leon tended to his laboratory and study bedroom himself, and Janvier took care of their rooms, not that he saw them often.

"No luck, my lord?" Janvier asked and gestured to the table when Michel-Leon shook his head in disgust. "Sit, eat something, and we'll go over the maps of the surrounding area. Régine and Hadrien have not returned from Paris, but I expect her soon."

Michel-Leon sat down with a frown and pulled the maps to him. He marked out the area he had searched today. They had made significant progress, but there was still a depressing amount of countryside left to explore. There had been tales of a few strange sightings that occurred on the date they had seen the creature in the sky, but nothing yet that pointed them in a direction. They needed a landing spot.

Régine was compiling a list of missing people and the districts they had disappeared from, and he'd noted the dates and times and the approximate number. He'd studied the maps of Paris, hoping it would give them a direction to start in, but the depredations were too widespread. Studying the maps again left him with acute frustration and confusion. These mists were not following the patterns of old. Instead of flowing downstream, they radiated out in a sphere. He needed to figure out what caused the change, because he doubted it portended good news.

Not everyone who had been outside during the mists had been affected. Sometimes several members of a family had been taken, sometimes none, even if all had been caught outside. Witnesses reported the affected people talking about the song and being insistent on following it. They were calm when left alone, increasingly agitated to the point of violence if stopped. Some were found wandering afterward in a daze and remained that way for days before recovering.

Pieces of a puzzle with no solution in sight. Though one interesting fact—the disappearances seemed confined to the city and not any of the villages surrounding it, which differed from Metz. They couldn't be entirely certain that was true though. There were still villages left to visit and people to interview.

"You could ask the villagers if they have maps of the area or know of any cave systems," Janvier suggested as Salome set a full plate in front of both of them.

Michel-Leon spared the cook a brief smile. "*Merci.*" He contemplated Janvier's suggestion as he shoveled food in his mouth. He hadn't paused to eat since he raided the pantry this morning, and Salome was talented. "You and Hadrien look into that. Ask about any missing people. Warn them not to search any likely cave systems. I need to be sure they are taking necessary precautions. If anyone saw the creature land, that would be a miracle we could use. In fact, ask about any disappearances that happened that night before the mists started. Maybe it didn't leave any witnesses about."

"I will, my lord." Janvier beetled his bushy eyebrows. "However, you don't know the precautions you need to take."

"I promise not to be reckless." Michel-Leon shoved his curls out of his eyes. He needed to let Janvier take care of his hair for him. "I'm going on what we know: that a creature of considerable size has taken up residence in a cave near a city and a water source and has laid a nest. I'm going on the assumption that it will do whatever is necessary to protect that nest. Though, since none of the ancestors mention the creature, I'm assuming it never leaves its haven once it's found one. So what happens to it after the swam hatches?"

He set aside the maps and reached for a spare bit of paper to scrawl notes. "Step one, locate likely cave systems." He tapped the pen against the paper. "I might have to have a more in-depth conversation with the ancestors to develop a plan to combat the creature. We should have a combination of magic and weaponry, since we don't know that will affect it. We'll also need a way to combat the effects of the mists. I've been working on a filtering mask. In fact, I'll be in the laboratory. Send Régine up when she arrives."

"In the interest of saving time, set up a reward for information," Janvier offered. "Instead of you seeking others out, it should bring them to you."

Michel-Leon contemplated that. "Do it," he said shortly. "Screen the responders. Anybody who is credible, I'll talk to further."

"I'll set it in motion in the morning." The old man's eyes gleamed. "In the meantime, you have received another message demanding an audience about a magicman. I took the liberty of reading it in case there was any information in it we could use."

"Didn't we send Régine to meet with the man?" Michel-Leon asked as he took the ragged slip of paper with curiosity. There weren't many who knew that name. Magicmen tended to lie low. It gave them greater access to their prey. The message was terse, the handwriting as abominable as Michel-Leon's, and he winced as he read the words.

A magicman is preying on children at the orphanage on rue des Jardins. I asked to meet a chevalier, not a girl. S'il vous plaît, help. You can reach me through the tavern on the same street. Constantin Severin.

Janvier's lips tightened. "We did and she attempted to do so. She's not pleased with his attitude, and apparently the feelings were mutual."

Michel-Leon rubbed his aching temple and was glad he had not witnessed that meeting. He could sense the ancestors stirring, poking at him with whispered warnings of people watching. It was no wonder that so many of his brethren went mad. "*S'il vous plaît,* respond with my regrets. I will be more than happy to assist when we've solved the mystery of the mists. Until then, I'll be unable to help." He paused, distressed by having to refuse. But if he didn't fix the bigger problem, there wouldn't be an orphanage to worry about. Still, his sense of duty wouldn't let it rest.

"Meanwhile, I'll look into the history of the orphanage and search for a pattern of deaths. Every magicman feeds in a different way." The headache that had been threatening to blossom all day came to a head, and he rubbed his temples again. "It's what makes them so damned hard to identify."

Janvier cut off his ramblings with a wave of his hand. "Michel-Leon, there is only one of you, even with Régine and I to help. And because I know sending a refusal goes against everything you believe in, I already sent one. One problem at a time."

"That is taking liberties," Michel-Leon said with a fierce frown that didn't faze the old man one bit. "*Merci* for it. I'm off to my study and laboratory. I want to run some more experiments on the mist sample I have and work on that mask." He would search in his journals and books for any references to magicmen haunting Paris.

"Am I to assume that you are planning to retire in your study once again?" Janvier's eyebrows twitched in displeasure, and his mouth formed a stubborn line.

Despite himself, Michel-Leon smiled. Janvier would never change, and his manner remained a constant Michel-Leon could count on. "You assume correctly. Either the very comfortable chair there or the cot in my laboratory. I even put fresh bedding out, so there is no need for Mahaut to fetch more."

"Do attempt to get some proper sleep," Janvier said with a hard glower. "You can help no one if you waste away."

Michel-Leon laid a hand on his bony shoulder. "As always, dear friend, I strive to do your bidding." He left the warmth and comfort of the kitchens to Janvier's snort of derision and contemplated the scrap of paper in his hand covered in his own code.

He didn't know how Javier navigated the maze without a reminder. The last time he'd tried, he'd been locked inside the walls for two days before they had found him. A traumatic event at ten years of age. If he'd had his *grandpère's* tinkering skills, he could've created an automaton to help. His talent and passion lay in chemistry though, so no inventions for him. He was having enough difficulty with a simple mask.

Once he'd inherited the château, he'd made a systematic map of the lower levels. His initial ventures into the hidden walkways had been hazardous, and he'd come across more than one nasty surprise that his father's journals had neglected to mention. It was a wonder he'd survived his childhood. In the intervening years after he'd left to study in the rest of Europe, his father had become even more distrustful, and the changes reflected that fear. In the end, he had been right to be paranoid.

Michel-Leon had yet to figure out the labyrinth of rooms and passages on the upper floors, some that moved about like puzzle pieces on a whim. The château was as insane as its previous owners, yet he wasn't sure if he wanted to pull all of its teeth. There was a certain measure of safety, knowing that he could hide in the heart of the château and remain unmolested.

Unfortunately, leaving those in place also meant that when he was in Paris, he lived virtually alone except for the few he brought with him. He wasn't about to risk any others. In his mind, there were no acceptable losses.

The hallway outside the kitchens was dark and dank, heavy with dust and spiderwebs. Cleaned up, it could be beautiful, but at the moment it was heavy with an air of abuse and neglect. Michel-Leon skirted the grand staircase and hugged the wall near the windows as he made his way down another hallway littered with bits of fallen plaster. His footsteps showed clearly in the dust. The sense of eyes on him and the agitated mutterings in his mind had him looking over his shoulder once or twice, but he remained alone.

The back passages were safer than going from room to room, though Michel-Leon and Janvier had left one or two surprises. Caution demanded they leave some defenses in place. Michel-Leon popped open a hidden door in the main hall paneling and lit the lantern hanging on a hook inside the hidden stairwell. He would dearly love to have gaslights installed throughout the place, but that was a nigh impossible undertaking. He skipped the seventh stair and its hidden trap and then opened the door to his laboratory.

A stair creaked in the hidden passage, and Michel-Leon glanced back with a frown. "Régine?" The stairway remained empty.

Michel-Leon shook his head and left the door open to circulate the air as he entered his laboratory. If there was any room in the château he loved, it was this room. He'd spent many happy hours here when it was his *grandpère's* workshop. When his *grandpère* had discovered his love of science and experiments, he'd carved out a space for Michel-Leon's work and defended that interest to his father. As he said, they all needed activities to keep them grounded.

They had furnished the room with multiple tables for experiments. He had a microscope and chemical hearth and all his materials laid out in a disordered row on one table with another table that held his notes and books. Two more tables contained parts for the last invention his *grandpère* was working on when he died. Michel-Leon hadn't had the heart to remove it. One of his *grandpère's* clocks graced the wall over the cot Michel-Leon slept on. Another door led to his study. This was his haven.

Michel-Leon hummed in contentment and bent over his latest

test. There were interesting trace elements contained in the mists, and he wanted to know more. He'd need more samples than this and from other locations. Still, it was a start.

*

THE NIGHT WAS getting later, and still Constantin continued to study the chevalier as he puttered about the laboratory, muttering to himself. Perplexed, he watched while the man set up a series of beakers with a snippet of cloth at the bottom. He laid a journal and pen nearby and made notes as he went. Constantin had no idea what the man was doing, but with his preoccupation, Constantin deemed it safe enough to examine the more interesting aspects of the room. It had more appeal than the rest of the château, and it might give him some information he could use.

He'd heard the chevaliers were strange. This place confirmed it. Parts of it appeared as if it were about to fall apart. It was a huge rambling structure, and yet the people here confined themselves to a few rooms.

Tables lined with the most interesting diagrams and half-finished projects called to his soul. Mechanical bits littered the surface of one table neatly laid out in piles, and his fingers twitched to examine them. An ugly mask with thick lenses over the eyes and an apparatus over the mouth sat at another end, but too close to the chevalier. He longed to examine them further, but he had a job to do. He needed to find some information he could use as leverage to get the chevalier to agree to help.

As he eyed a wondrous clock avidly, the man turned his chair around, picked up the mask, and bent over the mouthpiece. He continued to mutter to himself, but too softly for Constantin to make out words. He had a head of burnished red-brown curls. His cheeks were stubbled as if he forgot to shave, and his mouth looked like he smiled often. He appeared far nicer than the stern-faced woman who visited him and, frankly, less capable of taking out a magicman. There at least had been a fierceness about the woman.

The chevalier was more focused on his experiments than on helping. Children were dying, and he was fiddling with a mask after sending notes of dismissal through a girl barely into womanhood. Constantin had been utterly disillusioned when he'd received the message denying his request, and he'd come here with a more dire purpose in mind. There had to be some way he could force the chevalier to aid them.

He'd changed his mind when he overheard the conversation in the kitchens. It wasn't that the chevalier didn't want to help. He'd sounded frustrated with his own lack of progress over the mists, though Constantin didn't understand how holing himself up here would help, no matter how intriguing the surroundings. Besides, there was something about the man that drew Constantin to him. He reminded him of a boy that Constantin once loved, though the chevalier didn't have Blaise's frail air. Still, his eyes were kind, and there was something innocent about him. He did not look at all like what Constantin expected a chevalier to be. He appeared more like a scholar than a warrior.

This room was full of items that challenged the mind. When the chevalier retreated to an adjoining room, Constantin found it stuffed with journals, maps, and books, all piled about haphazardly with no attempt at organization. The chevalier appeared to know what each stack contained because he never searched for long before returning to his lab.

Constantin stared at the books with longing. There could be information in there he could use. He could read and write. He'd learned that much in the orphanage, but he was no scholar. The chevalier mentioned there may be information in here concerning the magicman. He could search when this strange household was asleep.

Constantin took the chance of opening a journal when the chevalier left, and his heart sank. It would take days to search through this room for anything useful. There was no rhyme or reason to the notes and not everything was in French. He needed another way. Blackmail was a possibility. Everyone had secrets to hide. He hated to resort to that because it reminded him too much of the ugly time when he was first on the streets, but some of those children were getting weaker and Nightingale was bringing in new victims every few days. It made it all the more likely for tragedy to hit them.

In the meantime, he'd send another note and ask if the man could at least request a different chevalier to aid him. There had to be a way to convince him.

Constantin returned to the workshop. It was unlikely he'd get any other information at this time. The chevalier appeared content to focus on his strange experiments instead of doing something active of actual worth. It was infuriating. Constantin wanted to shake the man out of his preoccupation and haul him off to help.

He studied the chevalier a moment longer, flexing his fingers. The thought had possibilities. Constantin may appear young and slim, but he was far stronger than he appeared. He had years of living on the streets behind him. There were no guards, only one old man, another who preferred the stables, and a few women here.

"Stop nattering at me!" the chevalier snarled, making Constantin start. He stared at the man with widened eyes and a pounding heart, sure he'd been caught. But the chevalier waved his hand in the air, while examining something through a microscope. "I can't concentrate. All you do is natter."

Mystified, Constantin glanced around the room to be sure no one else had slipped in, but the only occupants were the two of them. The chevalier was crazed. He definitely needed to find someone else to aid him. This one didn't have a firm grasp on his sanity. Maybe he didn't comprehend the evil of the magicman.

"What do you mean 'the watcher is watching?' What nonsense is that? It doesn't mean anything. What else would a watcher do? Sweet Saint Jeanne!" the chevalier snapped, and then he straightened, his eyes narrowing as he examined the room. All traces of the preoccupied scholar were gone. His gaze had gone cold and hard as he reached for a cane with one hand and drew a sword from it before grabbing a pistol from a drawer with his other hand. "Who are you? Watcher, show your-self."

Constantin froze. This was a man who would cut down any in-truder before they had a chance to explain themselves. Maybe he wasn't so much crazed. Something warned him that Constantin was here, and he'd better get out fast before they told the chevalier how to locate him.

He inched toward the open workshop door as the chevalier moved around the worktable, his eyes constantly searching the shad-ows. "Where are you? *Bon sang*, where is it? How do I make it visible? Is it a spirit?"

Constantin barely dared to breathe as he took another step back-ward, fumbling behind him for the opening. As the chevalier moved straight toward him, Constantin's heart jumped. He'd never been seen before. Not by any mark. Not unless they'd run into him first. Then he realized that the man was trying to cut off his escape route.

"Where is it? What is it?" the chevalier demanded, still talking to himself, and Constantin skirted around him and made his way toward the door in the study on silent feet. There was another door there. One that presumably led to a hallway instead of the secret stairway. The chevalier would hear, no doubt, and give chase, but it may give him the lead he needed.

To his intense relief, the door in the study was unlocked. Constan-tin cracked it open, and the hallway was clear. He eased it open more, his heart pounding again when it squeaked. A crash and a cry came from the workshop. "*Non*, you fool. Don't go there!"

Unnerved by the chevalier's conversation with people that Constantin could neither see nor hear, he abandoned caution and plunged down the hallway draped with shadows as ominous as the château's name.

"Wait!"

Constantin glanced over his shoulder at the outline of the chevalier in the doorway. He reached a stairwell and grabbed the oaken banister as he rounded onto the treads. The floor rumbled beneath him, and Constantin caught the balustrade as the stairs fell away. Catlike, he clambered up on the narrow rail banister. This was faster anyway. He slid down the slippery wood, racing so fast he barely heard the heavy crash behind him.

There was no way to stop at the bend and Constantin tumbled off, his body skidding along the landing and down the other flight. He felt bruised all over and his glamour fell away with the impact of his rough landing. He rose on unsteady feet and wrapped the shadows around himself again as people spilled out of the kitchens and into the hallway. They hovered in the doorway, making no move to come closer. He glanced up at the staircase to check if the chevalier had followed and seen him.

To his surprise, no one was there, but then he noticed that the top several risers had fallen in, leaving a gaping hole in the stairwell. Constantin swallowed around the lump of fear that rose in his throat. If he hadn't been prepared to grab the railing. He shuddered. He'd have broken his legs at best. That's if nothing had been lying in wait at the bottom.

What kind of a place was this? *Château des Ombres*. Constantin felt a chill trickle down his spine. He'd thought it had been so named because of the long row of cypress trees lining the way, but after this scare, it took on a more sinister aspect. The old man and the woman who called herself the Widow Bardin came closer, keeping near the wall. Constantin had thought that odd earlier. Now he worried about what other traps lay here.

"Stay back," the old man ordered, waving to the servants crowding the doorway as he pushed forward with the widow that Constantin met by his side. "It's not safe."

"Michie?" the widow called as she peered at the stairwell with anxious eyes. She wore trousers and held a pistol steady in her hand. She looked as if she knew how to handle that pistol she carried so competently. Perhaps Constantin had been amiss in not speaking to her. "Are you hurt?"

She started to step forward and stopped when the old man held her back. Then the hidden door swung open, and the chevalier emerged, still holding his weapons. "Did you see anyone go this way? We had an intruder."

Constantin limped toward the dubious safety of the kitchen as the old man and widow approached the chevalier. They began talking in fast, excited voices, but he couldn't risk staying to listen. He hugged the wall when he could, terrified with each step that he'd trigger more traps. He'd wondered at the strange mannerisms he'd observed earlier. Now the dangers were patently clear. It was past time he got out of there. He'd figure out what to do next when he reached his rented room. There was definitely more to this chevalier than he'd initially suspected, and he'd find a way to make him help.

*

MICHEL-LEON PAUSED at the bottom of the steps and stared at the gaping hole at the top. "Your memory is better than mine, Janvier. Is that the only trap on this stairwell?"

Janvier approached, moving as fast as he could, his bushy brows coming together in a fierce frown as he examined the staircase and the triggered trap. "I believe so. What happened?"

"We had an intruder." Michel-Leon gave Janvier a worried glance and met Régine's gaze. He should've left him back at the inn despite Janvier's objections. The mists were dangerous enough. The invasion of the château and the spying in his own sanctuary was another worry.

"Where?" Régine demanded, her mouth tightening in anger.

"My laboratory, of all places," Michel-Leon said as he checked his notes to be sure there wasn't any nasty triggers noted that neither he nor Janvier remembered. Michel-Leon shook his head and tightened his lips as he steeled himself to go up those stairs. If there was a body at the bottom of the trap, they'd have to figure out a way to remove it. "Blast it."

"How did they get all the way up there without one of us noticing?" Régine demanded.

"It's a miracle they didn't get killed before then." Janvier sighed as Michel-Leon approached the stairwell. "Whoever it is, they wouldn't have survived that fall. It's a nasty one. Goes down to a closed off room behind the cold storage."

"We're going to have to check and remove the body. Then figure out how to reset the traps. Father ought to have the plans in his notes. This pitfall is more his nature than *grandpère's*." Michel-Leon gripped the banister as he moved up the stairwell, testing each riser before he put his full weight on it.

"I'll have Hadrien fetch us rope and a harness," Janvier said.

"I'm going with you." Régine demanded. "What did the intruder look like? Did they walk in or were they already lying in wait?"

"I don't know how they got that far either or how they managed to make themselves invisible. The ancestors didn't act concerned after they saw fit to warn me that someone was spying. Whoever it was didn't do anything to harm me. It had an opportunity. But I don't like it."

"I should think not," Régine said. "Could it have been a spirit?"

They reached the top and peered down into the dark hole, but Michel-Leon couldn't make out anything at the bottom. "A spirit wouldn't have done that. The ancestors would've recognized one and warned me accordingly."

"The watcher is flesh and blood. He is fey kissed."

"Well, if you can tell me that much, care to say who it was?" Michel-Leon asked, but the ancestors remained quiet. He exchanged glances with Régine. "Whoever it was is human but with abilities I haven't heard of."

"You're going to have to lower me down there," Régine said as Janvier returned with Hadrien, rope and harness, and a lit lantern.

"Non, I'll go down," Michel-Leon said firmly.

"Be sensible, Michie," Régine said as she sat down near the edge and slipped on the harness. "Hadrien and I cannot pull you up and down as easily as you can pull me. *Grandpère* will lower the light. I've seen bodies before. I won't faint."

"You fainting is not my fear." Michel-Leon hated the sense in her words and looked to Janvier for support.

"There are no traps down there if you're worried," Janvier assured him. "I had them all cleared out when we took up residence. No sense in killing ourselves to fetch breakfast items. Besides, that room is an oubliette. This is the only way in or out."

"I don't like it," Michel-Leon fretted, but he couldn't find any other argument against it other than she was a woman, and he knew better than to mention that.

"She does have a point. She is considerably lighter than you," Janvier murmured.

"There's nothing dangerous down there for her?" He cast the thought to the ever-present ancestors, and they remained silent, so he took that as a good sign.

"Fine, you can go." Michel-Leon knew when to recognize defeat. Régine gave him a beatific smile. "Lower the lantern first. I want you to see what is down there before you get there so you can have us stop if needed. If the intruder can make itself invisible, who knows what other abilities it has."

"I will shout if anything looks untoward." Régine double-checked the harness and then attached the ropes to it. "I'm ready."

The lantern was a bright spot in a well of darkness. Suppressing his misgivings, Michael-Leon and Hadrien slowly lowered Régine. He kept his gaze on her slim figure.

"Hold," Régine called up, her voice calm. "I can see the bottom. I want a good look before I go any farther."

Janvier knelt on the edge and peered down. "Well?" Janvier asked gruffly.

"I don't see anything but the fallen boards. There's no scent or sign of blood," Régine replied after a moment. "Let me down the rest of the way."

Michel-Leon probed the quiet ancestors, but he had the impression they were as curious as he was. He exchanged glances with Janvier, who nodded. They resumed lowering her, and the release of tension on the rope signaled that she'd arrived.

"What is going on, my lord?" Hadrien asked in a tense voice, and Michel-Leon shook his head.

"I wish I knew."

"It's not a large space," Régine called up, her voice so far away. "Our intruder dodged the trap. There's nothing down here but the fallen boards, and they appear to be remarkably undamaged. Pull me back up."

Michel-Leon and Hadrien hauled her up more rapidly than they'd let her down. He wanted her back up here, where he could see her. "We'd best be on our guard. If it tried once, it'll likely try again," he said with a grunt. "We should reset the trap. I doubt the pitfall will catch it off guard again, but since we're dealing with an unknown, I want the château to have all of its teeth."

"Do you want me to send for some able-bodied men?" Hadrien asked. "There are bound to be men in the village searching for extra work. I've gotten friendly with a few there."

The top of Régine's head came into view, her hair shining in the faint light. Michel-Leon let out a sigh of relief as she tipped her head back and met his gaze.

"That would be helpful." Michel-Leon and Hadrien swung her up and Janvier caught her and steadied her on the edge. He was suddenly exhausted. It had been a long day. Tomorrow would be an even longer one if he went traipsing about the countryside with the villagers. He had been looking forward to an uneventful evening of research and experiments. Now he was going to have to search through his *grandpère's* diagrams and see if he could figure out how to reset this trap. He hated dealing with mechanics.

"I'll get this fixed." Janvier patted Michel-Leon's arm. "I believe I know which journal to look in. We'll have the boards hauled up and the trap reset in no time."

Michel-Leon gave Janvier a grateful glance. "*Merci.* You have a better understanding of these contraptions than me. I always get caught in them. Hadrien, limit the number who come in and keep it to the families that have worked with mine before. I trust them to be discreet."

Régine stared down, her legs dangling over the side as she shoved her hair back in place with a few pins that had come loose. "What are we dealing with this time?"

Michel-Leon clasped her on the shoulder as he also looked down and tried to quell his unsettlement. "I wish I knew."

Chapter Eight

CONSTANTIN PACED THE tiny space of his room, trying to walk off the fear clinging to him after his narrow escape. His body ached with innumerable bruises. Cold metal brushed against his ankle, and Constantin stiffened before glancing down. The black kitten he'd made for Gabrielle wound around his feet, then sat back and stared at him with unblinking amber eyes. His chest clutched. Gabrielle had never sent a message before. He crouched and scooped up the construct, his heart pounding as he held the kitten to his ear and willed it to speak.

"Help me!"

Desperate fear laced Gabrielle's whispered words and banished his own. She needed him.

Constantin slipped the construct into his pocket and took off toward the orphanage at a run, wrapping the shadows tightly around himself. It was getting close to dusk and the broadsides weren't calling for mists today. So he was safe from that threat, but it would make it harder to sneak in once the doors shut for the night. If Gabrielle was called to Nightingale's office, there was nothing he could do to get to her that wouldn't alert the monster. Frustration clawed at him. One problem at a time. First, he needed to get into the orphanage. Then he needed to find Gabrielle. He'd figure out his next step after that.

Darkness shrouded the orphanage when Constantin clambered the surrounding wall. He crouched and studied the quiet grounds. The windows of the dormitories were dark. On the uppermost level where Nightingale's study was located, a light gleamed, like a single malevolent eye watching the world. Constantin glared at that gleam, his hand tightening on his dagger. He yearned to snuff out that light and the magicman with it.

He prowled the grounds, keeping a careful eye out for anything out of the ordinary. His usual door was locked, as were the windows on the lower level. A few men, obviously hired as guards, patrolled the grounds. Nightingale had finally taken steps to protect its remaining staff. Constantin would have to be more careful than usual. His encounter with the chevalier had reminded him that appearances could be deceiving.

Constantin eyed the windows on the second level. They were ringed with ledges. If he could get up there, he might find one unlocked or be able to pick one.

Ivy grew thick on one wall, and when Constantin tested its strength, he found it clinging hard to the stone. The main branches were solid ropes that had dug in deep. The ivy rustled as Constantin climbed, and his shoulder ached from where he had fallen down the staircase. He hoped that was enough disaster for one day. He had to shift position halfway up when he came upon a dry and brittle section hit with a blight, but he soon pulled himself up on the first ledge.

He paused long enough to listen and was glad he did when the gaslights at the main doors came to life, and moments later, voices carried as they came around a corner. It appeared as if they weren't doing a serious search. Still, this was a new development, and the magicman only turned on the gaslights when it expected a visitor.

Constantin waited until the guards turned the corner again and checked the windows. They were all locked tight, but the third one had warped and there was enough room for him to slip his knife blade through the crack and pop the latch. He checked to make sure another patrol wasn't coming around and that the room stayed dark before he eased through and re-latched the window behind him.

He was in an empty room. The window was covered heavily with thick drapes. He slipped over to the door and eased it open. He was close to one of the long dormitories, not Gabrielle's. From the hallway came the tread of feet as children filed down the hallway to reach their narrow, hard beds. There were several new tear-stained faces, but the kids remained silent under the vigilant eyes of one of the many matrons as they changed into their nightclothes and clambered into bed.

Constantin's heart ached for them. Many could anticipate a night of tormenting dreams, one of Nightingale's many methods it used to inflict suffering. Others could expect to be hauled away to do impossible chores while exhausted. Still more would be beaten or locked away. And some very unlucky ones would have their innocence stolen by those that guarded them. The children who remained unscathed in the morning could only expect a temporary reprieve that never lasted long enough. He longed to rescue them all.

Once they settled, he made his way down the hall on stealthy feet to Gabrielle's dorm and bed, but it was empty. There was such a hushed quality about the place that Constantin worried they would spot his constructs if he used them. He'd have to do this the hard way. At this time of night, there were only a few places Gabrielle was likely to be. Given her most recent punishment, she was probably stuck in the basement. She was terrified of being locked in lightless places, so it was a favorite place to send her.

Constantin headed downstairs, noting the increased activity on the inside as well. They were definitely keeping an eye out for an intruder, and he had the sinking suspicion it was him. But searching was not finding. The kitchens were dark, and the fire banked, and there was no one in sight. He sensed the jaws of a trap hanging over him. He had to be more careful than usual.

He sent the beetle under the door to be sure Gabrielle was there and almost immediately received the ping. A trap and a punishment, but perhaps the magicman wasn't entirely sure what it was dealing with yet. Constantin pondered the lock and weighed his best options for rescuing her. He didn't believe he'd be able to sneak her out with pure stealth, not if Nightingale was on alert, but if he used a combination of stealth and trickery that might succeed.

Constantin crouched in front of the door and got to work with his lock picks as he listened for evidence of anyone approaching. The lock was old but well maintained, so it didn't take much fiddling. The tricky part would be setting the lock again on the other side since he couldn't take a light with him. Constantin slipped through and quietly pulled the door closed behind him. Absolute blackness enveloped him, and a chill drifted up the stairs. Perfect location for storing root vegetables, terrible place for children.

He banked his anger as he relocked the door, going by sense and sound. The minutes ticked down too long, but finally the tumblers snicked as they fell into place. He tested the knob and it didn't move. He groped for the railing, the darkness disorienting him as he made his way down with careful steps. The last thing they needed was for him to take another fall.

"Who's there?" Gabrielle called in a timorous voice, followed by the rustling movements of someone trying to hide.

"It's me, *ma petite chouette*," Constantin whispered. "*Je suis désolé* it took me so long to get to you."

Gabrielle let out a soft cry of relief. He heard her scrabbling toward the stairs, her breath coming in quick, frightened pants, and then she was there, clinging to him. Constantin sat on the steps and wrapped his arms around her shivering form. "What happened, Gabrielle?"

"The hungry man sent for me," she hiccupped, her words stuttering out in her distress. "He wanted to know who was comforting me. I told him it was an imaginary friend, but he didn't believe me."

Constantin cursed himself. He should've thought of that. If anyone would've picked up on the change in Gabrielle's mood, seen the renewal and strength of her hope, it would've been Nightingale. It had caught on to Constantin's emotional state when he'd fallen in love with another kid at the orphanage. For some reason, that event had sent Nightingale into a rage that had gotten him booted from the establishment in the dead of winter. It would've been less cruel for it to kill him outright.

"Someone will be down soon to check on you to make sure you're still alone." Constantin picked her up and carried her deeper into the cellar. "They will ask you about your imaginary friend. You need to tell them I'm here."

"I don't want to get you in trouble." Gabrielle's arms tightened around his neck. "The hungry man said if I didn't tell, he would have a gentlemen visit me, one that likes little girls, and he had the matron thrash me before they locked me down here."

Constantin went cold and prayed Gabrielle didn't know what Nightingale meant. Eventually, it would happen, when she got inured to the current abuses. She was too pretty, and Nightingale would want to exploit that to its advantage, but Constantin had hoped she had more time. It had done the same to Constantin and a few others. No matter what else happened, Gabrielle was leaving with him tonight.

"They won't see me, *ma petite chouette*." He hoped it wasn't Nightingale itself that came to check on her. He didn't know if his shadows would work under that thing's gaze. "But it may make them believe you are telling the truth about an imaginary friend."

He felt around in the dark until he came across the bins and shelves of foodstuffs. He set her down as footsteps pounded overhead. That hadn't taken long. Nightingale must've been waiting for her flash of joyful recognition. "I'm going on the other side of the room, but I'll still be here. I'll make sure you're safe. No one's going to hurt you again because I'm taking you home with me."

She let out a quick whimper of fear and then nodded against his shoulder. "Promise you won't turn mean?"

Constantin closed his eyes and laid his cheek against her springy hair. It broke his heart that she had to ask. "I'm sure there may be times you and I disagree, but I'll never lay my hand on you, or say cruel things, or try to make you afraid of me."

The footsteps stopped at the door, and a key turned in the lock. "Hush now. I won't be far."

Constantin took up a position far enough away to protect his glamour, but close enough to intervene if necessary, as a faint light lessened the gloom. Heavy footfalls descended the stairs, accompanied by the swish of skirts and the jangle of keys. Not Nightingale then. Constantin offered a prayer of thanksgiving. Gabrielle stood where he left her, her hands fisted in her worn skirts. Livid bruises marred the dusky skin of her collarbone and arms, though her face remained unmarked. Constantin seethed. No, they wouldn't want her prettiness marred.

"Gabrielle, you ready to tell us who's visiting you?" The hard voice of the matron preceded her. She paused at the foot of the stairs, studying the room and its vast array of shelves and nooks. "Is there someone here now?"

"Just my imaginary friend." Gabrielle pointed in the opposite direction of Constantin. "He's right there. He's mad."

Mad wasn't the word. Furious was more apt. Constantin longed to knock the woman out and leave her in the basement to get a taste of the fear she dealt out. But she would be expected back upstairs, and Constantin needed to give them as much of a head start as he could.

The matron walked over to the area Gabrielle indicated and then looked around the basement again, her expression unsettled. Constantin hoped she sensed the weight of his stare, and it kept her from sleeping this night. Let her remember her companions who had mysteriously died and worry she was next.

"You've got the master in a state, Gabrielle. I ain't ever seen him like this." She stalked over to the little girl and loomed over her. "Enjoy your spine. I suspect he'll break it soon enough, and no imaginary friend is going to help you then." She laughed harshly and headed back up the stairs, taking the light with her.

"He's gonna get you," Gabrielle shouted after her, racing to the bottom of the steps. "Just you wait. He's gonna get all the bad ones."

The door slammed at the top of the stairs, plunging the room into utter darkness again. Gabrielle whimpered softly and before she could ask if he was still there, he touched her shoulder. "What now?" she asked, clinging to him.

"Now we try to relax and wait until most of the place is in bed and they believe you've fallen asleep. Then we'll steal out of here, quiet as church mice."

He made himself a comfortable spot on the floor and she curled up on his lap, his arms wrapped snugly around her, to give her warmth. It made him miss his younger sister. She'd be a young woman now if she hadn't died of a childhood fever. He'd have to find a home for Gabrielle. A loving one that would take proper care of her. His own life was too uncertain, going from job to job, city to city, scraping for money and food.

There was a widow down the street who had lost a daughter a few years back. She doted on the children who came by, baking them little treats and in turn, they took care of tasks around her house without even being asked. She'd care for Gabrielle proper, and if Nightingale hunted Constantin down, she'd be out of harm's way.

"He might not miss me. There are lots of new kids and the matron says I'm nothing but trouble," Gabrielle murmured, resting her cheek against his chest.

Constantin patted her back and stared up at the darkness over them like he could divine where Nightingale was now. Oh, the monster would miss her. She still had a lot of strength and fire in her. It had been so furious when Constantin crossed the threshold into adulthood and robbed it of the chance of draining the last of his vitality. It would hunt for Gabrielle, Constantin had no doubt. The same way it had hunted Constantin and his brothers when he'd made off with them. But it had never found them.

"How many more kids?" Constantin asked uneasily. He remembered the crowded beds as he snuck through the dormitories. In the past, Nightingale husbanded the children it had, so as not to draw attention to itself, but the mists had made it bolder, greedier.

Gabrielle shrugged. "Lots. They keep crying at night about monsters in the mists with big eyes and weird mouths and wanting the music and home. The mist monsters don't do anything but herd them along and give them to the hungry man. The hungry man's the real monster, but they don't see it."

"It is. Hush now. Try to sleep." Constantin rocked her, his mind whirling. The chevalier was concerned about the mists. This was more proof of a connection. Perhaps that would be enough to make the man investigate. He'd go visit him in the morning and demand an audience. Notes be damned.

Gabrielle drifted off, her hand still fisted in his shirt. Constantin laid a glamour on her, sinking her into a deeper slumber. He couldn't put people to sleep, but he could encourage them not to awaken. He didn't want her frightened by the shadow traveling or wake up at an inopportune moment and cry out. This was going to be tricky enough.

He stood and moved deeper into the cellar, near the stacked bottles of wine, and wrapped the shadows around them both. His heart pounding, he waited. It didn't take long for the hue and cry to raise. As he'd hoped, the shadows masked Gabrielle's presence from the magicman. He held her close and clung to the shadows as the cellar door opened and the matron raced down the stairs, followed by several good-sized men.

Light flooded the room, illuminating every inch. The matron let out a shriek of outrage. "Search the grounds. She can't have gone far. Hurry! I'll report to the master. He'll want to look himself."

Constantin stole up the steps behind them, and to his relief, they hadn't shut the door. He wasn't sure if the glamour would hold under Nightingale's scrutiny, and he didn't want to risk it. More shouting and the startled cries of children came from upstairs as they searched the dormitories. He had to find a way to save all the children.

He slipped out the kitchen door, praying no one would notice it opening and closing on its own. More people scurried over the lawn, checking outbuildings and the main gate. Constantin hurried to the postern gate, and his heart sank when he saw a guard there, where one had not been before. He couldn't lift Gabrielle up onto the wall without assistance, and he didn't want her to fall, but he couldn't unravel the surrounding shadows without Nightingale immediately sensing her.

He pulled out his dagger, hesitating. He'd prefer to knock the man out, but his back was to the gate, and if he set the child down, he'd face the same problem. Constantin could stab him in the throat, but he'd never killed anyone before like this, cold-blooded, without a chance to fight back. Those others he'd gotten rid of had been tricked into accidents with a bit of glamour. That wouldn't work here with the guard on alert.

So he hardened his heart. The guard was one of those hurting the children.

Constantin slammed the pommel of the dagger against the man's temple, and he dropped to the ground in a boneless heap. Constantin sensed the life draining out of him and felt sickened by what he'd done. He unlocked the gate and slipped through, pulling it closed behind him. As he hurried down the street, he prayed he'd only imagined the sensation of the man's soul leaving his body. He fled with Gabrielle. Fled the monster behind him. Fled the sensation of the dying man and the certain knowledge he was a monster himself.

Chapter Nine

MICHEL-LEON EYED the men crawling over the staircase and worried his lip. "Are you sure that's the only trap there?" he asked again, unable to quell the anxious question Janvier had already answered several times.

"If there were more, they would've triggered it already." Janvier caught him by the shoulders and directed him toward the kitchen. "Salome has a luncheon packed for you. Have breakfast and go. I suspect your search of the countryside will take considerable time, and you still need to direct Régine in her inquiries for today. There is no point in overseeing this project."

Michel-Leon turned toward the kitchen on reluctant feet. There was nothing he could do here but wring his hands and feel responsible if anything did happen. At least with the search, he'd have a chance of being useful.

"Morning, my lord." Salome nodded toward a plate covered with a napkin. "Tuck yourself into something hot there."

"*Grandpère* finally chased you away?" Régine asked with a grin as Michel-Leon joined her.

"Most decisively." Michel-Leon twitched aside the napkin, and his stomach rumbled. She'd loaded the plate with eggs, thick bread, and a slab of ham. A mug of strong coffee steamed nearby. He'd been up half the night, trying to find answers to his many vexing questions to no avail. This was just what he needed to wake himself up. "*Merci*, Salome. This will do quite well."

"I should take a break from making inquiries in the city," Régine said, pushing aside the remains of her breakfast. "I'm not finding anything new with my questions there. I could be more useful eliminating areas for you to search, interviewing the locals and getting possible locations."

Michel-Leon eyed her trousers. She was all ready to go. He needed to give her more responsibility. She was intelligent, capable, and driven. Right now he couldn't afford to quibble over social niceties and, quite frankly, his deep-seated fear of losing people close to him. He would smother her if he did.

"Let's look at the maps and figure out where to start." He nodded toward the thick pile Janvier had stacked neatly to the side. "But for the sake of my sanity, bring Hadrien with you, *s'il vous plaît*. I know it feels like I'm sending a keeper, but that's not it. You'll be able to split up in the villages for your inquires and guard each other's backs while covering the countryside."

"And who will guard your back?" she asked with a grimace but nodded and pulled out the maps, knowing she wouldn't get a response. "I see you've marked what you've already searched. Where do you plan to look today?"

"I've been concentrating on the areas near the château and expanding outward. So far, we haven't hit on even a hint. Let's assign you in an entirely different direction. We have to speed up our searches."

As they poured over the maps and made plans, a knock came at the kitchen door. Salome moved to answer it and returned a moment later. "My lord, there's a Monsieur Constantin Severin here to see you. The one who's been sending you the notes. Shall I invite him in or send him on his way? He says to tell you, 'I know what you search for in your journals when you are alone at night, and I know why you allow no visitors. I have some of the answers you seek.'"

"Oh, him." Régine made a disparaging sound. "He's an odd one, if you ask me, impatient and rude. He's a con man, looking for a payout. What a ridiculous message."

Michel-Leon glanced up from the maps, intrigued by the cryptic message as the ancestors tried to call out through the barrier he'd erected. What were the chances that his intruder would return so boldly? That was the one person he could think of who would give such a statement. Michel-Leon suspected that at least one mystery from last night would be solved. He lowered the barrier in his mind long enough to send out one query, and the answer came before he'd even fully formed the thought.

"The watcher is here."

Indeed.

"Go ahead, invite him in and offer breakfast. I doubt another refusal will deter him."

Michel-Leon sat back and studied the man as he came in. He had the impression of a slim figure swathed in layered and patched clothes. A hat jammed low over his head shaded his face, and long, wavy, gold-shot hair tumbled halfway down his chest. He didn't appear like a man who could render himself invisible. He appeared to be a harmless vagabond. Someone with abilities such as that could steal whatever they wanted and live like a king. Now, this was interesting.

"There is no point in me staying since our guest has no use for women," Régine announced as she rose with a glare in their visitor's direction. "I'll let Hadrien know we'll leave within the hour."

Michel-Leon almost warned her that Severin was their intruder from the night before but stopped himself. He could handle the man, despite his abilities. They needed to move faster on what was happening with the mists. If she knew, she'd insist on staying. "Be careful," he urged, and she waved him off.

"I'm always careful, Michie."

Michel-Leon waited until she left and then turned to Severin. "You're a man who has an uncanny knack for uncovering secrets. Seems like that would be a very dangerous profession," Michel-Leon said as the stranger sat on the bench across from him. "Almost as dangerous as infuriating my sister."

"It has its hazards, same as any other." The voice was husky and then it lightened with rueful amusement. "As I have so recently discovered to my chagrin. My apologies to your sister. I thought you were trying to foist me off with some excuse." He took off his hat and Michel-Leon found himself staring, to his profound embarrassment.

Monsieur Severin was beautiful, with sharply chiseled features, a sensuous, soft mouth, and dark eyes too old and mysterious for his lovely face. The man gave him a cynical smile as if he knew what Michel-Leon was thinking.

Michel-Leon glanced away, caught off guard. He'd known for years that he was more attracted to men than women. Not that it mattered since he'd taken his vow to not wed, to concentrate on his duties as a chevalier and nothing more. It wasn't like he'd ever had much time for dalliances anyway, and his father never would've stood for his tendencies. His thoughts flashed to Lord Lennox, and he banished them as fast. No sense going down that road again. And there was no sense in allowing his attraction or curiosity to distract him from the fact this man was dangerous and had his own motivations for being here.

"So, you were the one spying on me in my laboratory," Michel-

Leon said as Salome laid another plate in front of Monsieur Severin. "*Merci*, Salome. *S'il vous plaît*, leave us. We have some private matters to discuss."

"Of course, my lord." She wiped her hands on the towel and cast their visitor a look. "Should I let Janvier know?"

"*Oui, s'il vous plaît*." Janvier wouldn't interfere, but he'd keep an eye out. Michel-Leon waited until she closed the door and they were alone. "Did you discover what you wished to know?"

"Not even close." Monsieur Severin dug into the food as if he had not eaten for a week. He was thin. Perhaps that was the case. "I had not reckoned on a place like this. The locals warned me it was dangerous. I thought it haunted, and ghosts have never bothered me."

"The *Château des Ombres* has many dangers, some I'm not even aware of." Michel-Leon had never met anyone like Monsieur Severin. His beauty was unearthly, he knew about magicmen, and he must have a talent for glamour.

"*Is he human?*" he asked the ancestors.

They stirred and murmured amongst themselves. "*For the most part,*" came the maddening answer with no further clues. The mystery deepened.

"I apologize if I've caused you any concern when I observed you," Monsieur Severin said. "I thought you might have sensed me, though I'd be curious to know how."

"Almost as much as I'd be curious to know how you couldn't be seen." Michel-Leon eyed Severin's set expression. "And I suspect we're both going to be disappointed. We don't know each other well enough to give up such closely held secrets."

Monsieur Severin smiled faintly. "Now that is a dilemma. Do we satisfy our curiosity at the expense of our safety?" He shrugged and continued eating. "But I suppose that is a conversation for another day and not why I came. I will be happy to share my tricks with you, but it comes at a cost and a condition."

"I am your captive audience." Michel-Leon rose and retrieved the kettle on the stovetop to refill both of their cups. "I am assuming the cost is my help in destroying a magicman. There are not many who know that name. Are you sure that is what you're dealing with? They appear very humanlike. The signs that they aren't are subtle."

"Oh, I am very, very sure." Monsieur Severin leaned forward and fixed his grim gaze on Michel-Leon. Those fine features twisted with old hate, pain, and fear. "I know this particular monster personally."

The ancestors hissed with disapproval, and Michel-Leon closed the link between them before they could start babbling. He studied Monsieur Severin with new understanding and a pang of empathy. If he survived a magicman as a child, he was far tougher than he appeared. He could almost understand why the man invaded his space. Almost, but not quite. "*Je suis désolé* for what you endured. You would know better than most the nature of the creature."

Monsieur Severin's shoulders relaxed. "You must help me. As a Chevalier de Rouen, you have the tools and knowledge I need to make sure this monster never harms another child. It is your duty. *S'il vous plaît*, baron, I will pay any price you ask."

The naked plea in Monsieur Severin's voice made Michel-Leon flinch with shame. His frown deepened as he clasped his hands together. There were too many monsters, and to have to prioritize one life over another was deeply painful. It went against everything he believed in. "They are difficult to harm, Monsieur Severin, you must know that. I have other problems facing me at the moment."

"The mists from the Seine and the missing people." Monsieur Severin set aside his plate and gave Michel-Leon his undivided attention. "I have some information which may help."

Michel-Leon tried to quell his excitement. There had been no leads, and he was running out of options. This may be a break, even if it came at a cost. He might not trust the man, but he couldn't afford to ignore him. "Let us start over again. You may call me Parisee, not my lord or baron. I am not one to demand you defer to me, and you do not appear like the kind of man who defers easily. If we are going to work together, we should be companions."

"Severin will do," he replied roughly. He hesitated and took a sip of his coffee. "You have read me right. I have been in Paris for a month now. I came in not long after the mists started, and I'd heard of the missing people and witnessed the growing unease. It almost caught me on my first day here. The broadsides you've sent out have been of immense help."

"If you know about the mists and what they portend, then you know I have my hands full." Michel-Leon glanced toward the closed door, his gaze far away. "Every time it rises, more people disappear. If this continues, Paris will be depopulated. And as you say, I am a Chevalier de Rouen; it is my duty to attend to this more pressing problem. As devastating as a magicman is, their ravages are usually on a smaller scale and rarely lead to the deaths of the children involved. At least not right away. I will turn to it once the swarm is destroyed."

"What of the other chevaliers? Surely, they can help." Severin gestured around at the empty kitchen. "Why are you here alone if the situation is as dire as you say? Where are your brothers in arms?"

Michel-Leon stared down at the coffee in front of him. At the question, the voices whispered as if in answer to a call. His sudden surge of loneliness, grief, and sense of isolation broke through the wall he'd erected. "My brother died at the hands of a *melusine* when I was a young man. My grandparents and many cousins died in the fire that consumed my ancestral home back in Lorraine. Demon marked, I believe, though I haven't taken the time to investigate the ruins." It was sealed for now, and that was enough for him. One day, he'd have the courage to investigate.

"There was another city before Paris. Have you heard of the decimation of Metz?" Michel-Leon glanced up and met Severin's startled gaze. He shook his head and Michel-Leon continued. "It happened in my *grandpère's* time. The chevaliers bungled it. Over thirteen thousand died, including all the chevaliers who were there. It put us in disfavor with commoner and noble alike. As you can image, an order such as ours collects enemies. Old enemies with fearsome abilities. They began hunting us once we fell out of favor.

"I could recite stories for days about what befell us, but the telling would depress us both. The main one being that devoting yourself to hunting down the monstrous and inexplicable does not make for a long and secure life. Those that survived their younger years often found their sanity crumbling from what they'd encountered." Add in the edged gift they all inherited, and Michel-Leon was surprised the order lasted as long as it had.

"What are you saying? There are not enough chevaliers left to aid us?" Severin caught and held his gaze. It was almost as if he refused to allow Michel-Leon to drown in the memories or fall prey to the screaming that wailed in his head once he began talking of the purge. His gaze kept Michel-Leon grounded.

"The remaining chevaliers died in a raid a decade ago." Michel-Leon paused and the silence between them grew taut. "Because of that, there is one chevalier who still fights on. But I am only one. You should've talked with Régine. She knows what she's doing and she's been helping me. It's still not enough."

Severin jerked up from the table and walked away, rubbing his hands on the dirty, worn fabric of his pants. "Is there any hope for Paris or are we consigning them all to hell? The children included?" He whirled around to face Michel-Leon, his eyes blazing.

"I always have hope. Even if right now my hope lies in Napoleon agreeing to evacuate. I can't afford to fail. Metz's death toll was in the thousands. If this continues, Paris's will be in the hundreds of thousands." Michel-Leon rose as well and gathered the lunch that Salome had laid out for him. "So, you must understand why I can't afford to help with the magicman. I've spent too much time here already when I need to be scouring the countryside. *Je suis vraiment désolé*, Severin. If there is anything you can tell me that will help, I'll appreciate it, and I'll return the favor as soon as I am able."

Severin paced, muttering under his breath, but when he faced Michel-Leon again, his expression was set. "I believe the magicman has information that will help you. I'm not saying this just to get your attention. *S'il vous plaît*, a moment longer of your time. In return, whether you help or not, I'll aid you with the mystery of the mists. I don't know what capabilities I have that will be of assistance to you, but if it will get your attention faster, I'll do it for the children."

Michel-Leon hesitated and then gestured toward the rough kitchen table. It couldn't hurt to listen a little longer. "*S'il vous plaît*, sit and tell me what you suspect."

Severin sat at the table and pulled out a small tool pouch and a mess of wires and metal. "May I? I organize my thoughts better when I am tinkering."

Michel-Leon paused long enough to allow the voices to give warning if they suspected treachery, but they remained silent. "Go ahead. As I'm sure you've seen, I do as well." He wondered how long Severin had spied on him at his experiments and research.

Severin shrugged and selected a tool. "Though I had no idea what your tinkerings did. I didn't pay any attention to the rumors of the mists because the foremen were hiring from the recent shortage." He glanced at Michel-Leon. "I didn't care, you understand. I needed work."

Michel-Leon waved his concern aside. "I doubt you were alone in that relief."

"It was bad enough that any hint of the mists rolling in had the foremen scrambling to send us away with the promise to return on the morrow. I found myself locked in a tavern with dozens of terrified souls, and that's when I sensed the magicman prowling outside, hunting."

"How did you know it was a magicman if you were inside?" Michel-Leon asked.

"It felt…familiar." Severin's clever fingers plucked wires out and twined them together as he bent over the pieces to attach small bits of metal. Michel-Leon found himself as intrigued by his actions as he did his words. "I didn't show up for work the next day. Instead, I hunted it."

"How have you been surviving without wages?" Michel-Leon asked softly. He had never heard of anyone who could sense a magicman before, but he'd also never talked with one of their victims either.

Severin froze, hunched over his work. "Stole some things, sold some others." His fingers began flying again.

"Using your abilities to hide?" Michel-Leon poured him some more coffee. "I make no judgments, merely curious."

"Mostly for the kiddies. They're starving. I suspect it's because of the magicman feeding off them as much as the rotten food." Severin turned back to his work as a little construct came to life between his fingers. "I tracked it to an orphanage. While I was there, I noticed it continued to go out during the mists and a child I'm watching over said it did it every time. She also said lately that it's been coming back with more children than normal. Those children cry out in their sleep about monsters in the mists and needing to follow the music."

Michel-Leon frowned. "There's nothing in the few notes I have that mention monsters. At least not at this stage. When the swarm comes, then there will be monsters, and it will be too late."

Severin stared at him with wide, apprehensive eyes. "I'd ask how bad can it get. How much more do these children have to suffer through, but I already know the answer. Maybe I'm reaching, and maybe these children are merely reacting to the horrors they faced and made up the whole bit, but I don't believe that. If there are monsters out there, it's meeting with them. So if anyone has answers, it's Andre Nightingale."

Michel-Leon blew out his breath and drummed his fingers on the table. "Perhaps. I'm intrigued, if not quite yet ready to jump. It would help if I could speak with one of the children myself. It might be useful to know exactly what happened to them when the mists appeared."

Severin rubbed his hands on his arms and looked away. Michel-Leon took the time to study his elegant profile. Clearly, he was a man who had learned to survive on the edges of society. He could've traded on his beauty, but Michel-Leon suspected he hadn't. He didn't have time to be intrigued by him.

"I have such a child. She has not been out in the mists, but she has spoken with ones who have. She is observant and intelligent." Severin cast a sideways glance at him, his expression shadowed. "I rescued her because she was like me."

"In what way?"

Severin hesitated. "From what I've been able to gather, both through my experience and from what I gleaned from other survivors, each magicman feeds on children in its own way. This particular one savors the slow loss of innocence. It feeds off pain and sorrow. So it causes it in many ways, then comforts its victims so it can repeat the cycle until there is nothing left of its victim or the child becomes a hardened adult."

A sick churning started in Michel-Leon's gut. "I can't imagine what you and the others have endured." He'd delve into the journals again and go into deeper contact with the ancestors. There had to be an answer in there that could help Severin. He could recruit the Belangers to assist with the research as well.

Severin lifted one shoulder in a careless gesture, though the spasm of emotion that crossed his face said differently. "Like me, she sensed when it fed. To the other children, Nightingale is the man who dries their tears, cossets them, and gives them treats. As nightmarish as their world is, many of them came from places just as bad, and the magicman gives them what little kindness they've ever known. For Gabrielle and me, it's another layer to the hell."

Michel-Leon rubbed his chin as he considered that. Severin and the child were in danger. A child like that who would have the double trauma would be too valuable to let go of. Bringing them here posed its own dangers, but those he could control, and once he'd spoken to the child, he could send her far away from the magicman's reach.

"Is it necessary to dredge up old horrors for her? Just give me the weapon that will work against it, and I'll dispatch the monster myself." Severin's hands clenched into fists. Michel-Leon believed he had the spine to do it and the patience and intelligence enough to recognize the dangers. If Michel-Leon had a dozen more like him and Régine, he would be more at ease.

"Severin, I don't want to cause any more wounds. I'll be gentle with my questioning. The more information we have, the better our chances. Besides, if she is like you, it will search for her. You both would be safer here."

"Forgive me if I disagree with that." Severin rubbed his shoulder with a pained expression. "I carry bruises from my last visit."

"You're lucky you weren't killed. Still, there are safe places and paths within the château. The people here know them. Even if the magicman tracked her here, it would have a hard time getting to her without alerting us." Michel-Leon paused, reluctance evident in the unhappy line of Severin's mouth. "We will discuss ways of destroying the monster when you have returned with her."

Severin's mouth turned down even more. "I don't suppose I have much of a choice. I'll fetch her, and then we'll talk. So this means you will help?"

"That isn't much of a link. It could be a coincidence." Michel-Leon's jaw hardened. "But it's enough for me. A magicman is too canny to not get as much information as it could about the other monsters that prey in its territory before it set up a new home. Even if it has nothing directly to do with the mists, I would hazard to guess that it knows something about them. And I'd like to know how it moves around in the mists without being snared by them."

Michel-Leon held out his hand, and Severin grasped it in a firm grip as they took their measure of each other. "I know it's only the word of a street rat, but you help me and I'll help you in return." Severin met his gaze and held it.

"Anyone, man or woman, urchin or titled, who is willing to take on a magicman to save others is someone whose word I'll accept." Michel-Leon gave Severin a stern look. "I expect you to extend the same courtesy to my companion. She knows what she's doing. She is not happy about the way you turned her away."

Severin jerked his shoulder, his eyes tightening in irritation. "I'm not used to dealing with women. I'll apologize to her."

Régine had a natural beauty about her and a forthrightness that often made men uncomfortable. Too many thought of taming her, and Michel-Leon was happy to know she wasn't at all interested in being tamed. She would not give Severin an easy time of it. The mark against him would be a stumbling point, but the fact that he was the intruder would be the bigger one.

"Well, I'll be off. It'll take me a few hours to get her and get back. I'll want to make sure I'm not being followed." He rose and jammed his hat back on his head. "You have your own investigation to conduct. Let's say we meet again around dinner and take our measure then."

Severin didn't trust him enough to reveal where he was staying. Michel-Leon couldn't blame him. He didn't trust Severin much either. The man had spied on him, invaded his sanctuary. *Non,* until Severin was ready to share his little trick, Michel-Leon would guard his own secrets. At least he trusted Severin to watch his back until the moment they killed the magicman; after that, he had little faith.

"Done then." Michel-Leon considered the problem a moment longer. He needed to catch up with Régine before she left. "I'm going to send the Widow Bardin with you. Taking the carriage will be faster, and she can help if you run into trouble."

Severin grimaced and then nodded, his eyes glittering with unhappiness. Well, that would make two. Régine would not be happy when he told her, but he wanted her to observe their intruder and get her honest opinion.

Chapter Ten

CONSTANTIN SHIFTED UNCOMFORTABLY as the carriage the chevalier insisted he borrow bumped over every rut. Though the discomfort had less to do with the jostling and more to do with the fact he felt like a fool in the contraption. His own two feet had always been more than enough to get him from place to place. This screamed for attention, and attention was the last thing Constantin wanted. It was faster though, which was the sole reason Constantin agreed.

Adding to his discomfort was the woman staring holes into him from the opposite seat. That she had a reason for her dislike was all on Constantin. "*Je suis désolé* for brushing you off when we first met," Constantin said to break the fraught silence. She had not said one word since they set off. She was harder than the chevalier, though they shared a resemblance. "I didn't realize the chevaliers allowed women to aid them."

The widow's eyes narrowed, and she leaned forward with a threatening expression. "The chevaliers had many blind spots, which I find ironic considering who their founder was. Michel-Leon is more cosmopolitan. He knows my worth. You spy on him again, and you'll also understand why he values me."

In the last several years of living apart, Constantin had forgotten how dangerous a woman could be. He would do well to keep that in mind when dealing with the Widow Bardin. "I did what I had to do to protect those who have no other option. You should understand."

"I do, though if you'd bothered to talk to me, you might not have been almost caught in one of our traps." The widow leaned back, more relaxed. "If this goes how you wish and the magicman is killed, what happens to your charges next?"

Constantin frowned and turned his attention back out the window. "I wish I knew," he said under his breath. He didn't have the means to care for so many on his own. "I hope most find families to return to, since Nightingale found them in the mists."

"That is a strong possibility. Strangely enough, not everyone disappears for good." Traffic congestion increased as they reached the outskirts of the city. "Where to now, Monsieur Severin?"

"Now we go on foot." Constantin tapped on the hood of the carriage. It slowed and the door there popped open.

"*Oui*, monsieur?"

"Drop me off here. I'll return within the hour," Constantin ordered.

An expression of consternation crossed the man's face. "But, monsieur, the baron ordered—"

Constantin cut him off. "I know well what he ordered. I was there when he did. I don't want to draw more attention to myself than necessary, and where I'm going this will attract attention. The baron has enough trouble on his hands." Constantin didn't want to assume the magicman would know nothing about the chevaliers and their reputation. It would be better if there were no connection between the two of them.

"This is fine, *mon oncle*," Régine replied. "We'll go together."

Constantin expected no less and yet it still irritated. He jumped out of the carriage before Hadrien lowered the steps and then remembered belatedly he should offer his hand to the widow. When he turned back, she was already alighting on her own.

The chevalier and the widow were not at all what Constantin expected. She appeared more comfortable in trousers than skirts and more at ease with the lower classes than most women of her station. She went so far as to address the carriage man as uncle. Still, she had been introduced as the baron's sister. They both had that fire in their hair, though hers was more pronounced.

Then there was the chevalier himself. After spying on him, Constantin thought the man might be a touch crazed. There was nothing about his initial appearance that made him appear dangerous in any way until he was cornered. That made Constantin nervous. If it wasn't for the fact the baron had access to critical information and spoke with cool authority, Constantin would've searched elsewhere for help, chevalier or not.

"Well, let's get moving," Régine said, pausing beside him. "The sooner we've accomplished our task, the sooner we get on with our other search."

"This way," Constantin said shortly and led the way deeper into the city. There was a pattern to the mists. Though they shouldn't terrorize the residents of Paris for another several days, there was a hushed quality to the streets, a simmering mess of fear and growing anger underneath the expressions of stoic resolve. The buildings became shabbier, piled up together as Constantin moved away from the newly opened up and renovated sections of Paris to the places left unscathed for now.

A new chill touched him as he neared the warren of winding alleys and crowded structures where he had his lodgings. The premonition was a warning, a skittering of ice along raw nerve endings, and Constantin fought the urge to bolt as nausea struck. Running would not help. He doubted he'd even be able to blend into the shadows to hide. He recognized this sensation.

He turned and caught Régine around the waist, pulling her into a shadowed recess in an alley. She twisted out of his grip and before he could say anything, pointed a dagger at his throat. Ignoring it, he brushed a finger to her lips with a warning look. Her eyes widened, and she nodded.

"It hunts?" she said in a bare whisper, and he nodded back.

Constantin slipped his hand into his overcoat and curled his fingers around the device he'd tinkered with during the conversation with Parisee. He concentrated, offering a tiny thread of his soul's energy, and felt wings whir against his palm. He focused on the sense of Nightingale, opened his hand, and the device took off in a blur of wings.

It shouldn't work. Constantin still didn't know how he did it. Ever since he found himself scrabbling on the streets for a bite of bread, he'd learned how to transform his tinkerings into objects of useful wonder.

"That is a neat trick." The widow released her hold on him and kept her dagger at the ready.

Constantin concentrated and breathed a sigh of relief when he sensed Nightingale lurking near his rooms. He called back the beetle and caught it as it whizzed toward him. "We're going to have to split up. I'll lure Nightingale away. You get Gabrielle and bring her to safety."

"She won't trust a stranger," the widow objected.

"She'll believe this." Constantin brought the beetle to his lips and inserted another whisper of magic. "Trust the lady who comes with this message. I'll see you soon, *ma petite chouette*." He released it, and the beetle hovered on silent wings as Constantin gave the widow directions and a description of Gabrielle. "I'll meet you back at the château if I'm able."

The widow searched his face with a grim expression and then caught his arm. "Be careful. I'll get her out."

"*S'il vous plaît.*" It stung to leave Gabrielle's safety in the hands of another, but he would take no chances he'd lead Nightingale back to her. He turned in another direction and slid his hand into his coat again to grip his dagger. The cold, hard steel was a false comfort. He looked over his shoulder, searching the dark recesses of the doors, and strained to pierce the shadows by the corner as he made his way toward his room.

When he neared, the sense of Nightingale's presence grew stronger. He wanted to run and hide but forced himself to continue on as if he noticed nothing. The widow had to get to Gabrielle. He had to buy time, whatever the cost.

"Constantin, you try my patience." The voice was smooth, mellifluous, and it froze Constantin where he stood. How strange a voice that sweet could awaken such dark memories. Constantin turned with an effort to face the creature who had done its best to destroy him from the inside out.

"Nightingale." Constantin gripped the dagger tighter. His guts twisted as he tried to keep a blank expression. He'd never been good at lying to Nightingale, but he'd have to use every bit of skill he'd learned since he'd been on his own. "I'd heard you were in town."

The magicman appeared from the shadows with a smile. "You were my favorite once. That's why I allowed you to live the last time you stole from me."

Constantin held his ground as the magicman moved closer. It took every ounce of his willpower to keep his eyes on it and not cower in fear. The last time he'd been this close with Nightingale had been when the thing had closed the orphanage door in his face, freeing him from more anguish even as he deprived him of the only shelter he had.

The following theft had been an audacious move, born out of desperation and love.

"They were my brothers. I would never leave them with you." Constantin spat. "I made sure they were safe from you forever."

"You didn't rescue them all, did you? You didn't rescue your love." Nightingale's smile turned cruel. "But you tried. Tried to get him to see my evil ways. Tried to convince him to eke out a living on the streets with you instead of staying under my roof. You cost me, pretty Constantin."

"He chose you over me. So you didn't lose a damned thing," Constantin rasped. Blaise had been fragile, but Constantin had been sure what he'd felt for the other boy would've been enough for Blaise to want to leave as well. Together, they could've survived. He had never been so wrong. He often tormented himself by imagining what had happened to Blaise after he'd ceased to be useful to Nightingale. Blaise never would have lasted a week alone on the streets without a protector.

"On the contrary, I lost you. The other boy didn't have your will. He burned out like a gutted candle. You were the one who always resisted, who maintained the hope that one day you would be rescued. Then you gave your heart to someone who wasn't worthy of you and were of no further use to me. Do you know he died soon after? He took his own life. Would you like to hear how?"

Once, that would've hurt Constantin far more than the twinge he felt now. He'd known Blaise couldn't still be alive and hoped he'd found a better place. "What do you want, Nightingale? I'm sure you didn't seek me out to relive the past."

Constantin's fingers tightened on the dagger as his eyes sought an escape route. The streets had deserted, as if the local denizens had sensed the impending violence and made themselves scarce. He was all alone out here and unable to use any clever tricks to escape. He had to stall Nightingale.

The creature moved so fast that Constantin had a split second to register the attack. He found himself driven back against the rough wall with his own dagger pressed against his cheek.

He stared into the merciless eyes and knew he was going to die, and Nightingale would make it linger. Constantin spared no prayers for himself. Instead, he begged an uncaring God the chevalier wouldn't give up the hunt for Nightingale and would rescue the children. He had to trust the widow would get Gabrielle out and keep her safe.

If there is any holy being listening… S'il vous plaît.

"You've grown cold and hard, Constantin," Nightingale hissed.

Constantin's gaze darted away before he forced himself to meet the magicman's eyes. They were worse than cold, the absolute uncompromising pitiless black of the river in the dead of winter. "What choice did I have? You gave me nothing after you shoved me out the door. After years of feeding you. Cold and hard was the only way to survive."

"I have a great many questions I wish to ask of you. I suggest we find some place quiet so there is no rush. Your rooms perhaps. I assume you have something nearby." Nightingale smiled, and Constantin fought the terror of being a boy all over again and utterly helpless. He had to keep it together while allowing Nightingale to believe he was falling apart.

"Don't hurt me." He tore his gaze away and cowered to hide his relief. This would buy her more time to escape. "I'll take you, but I haven't done anything."

"We both know that's a lie." The magicman stood back and shoved Constantin away from the wall. He turned toward his garret room, his steps dragging. "You've been watching me. Did you hope I wouldn't notice the presence of a soul that belonged to me?"

Constantin's hands tightened into fists. He should've anticipated that. But there were pitfalls. Nightingale hadn't noticed him right away or he would've been dead when he accompanied Gabrielle to the attic rooms. It had to expend effort. The glamour shield he'd put on Gabrielle's toy must've been enough that Nightingale picked up on him instead.

"*Oui*, I watched you," Constantin snapped, trying to control the shaking in his limbs as he climbed the stairs. "I wanted to know if you were passing through or here to stay. Because if you're staying, I'll find another city to make my home."

His heart raced as Nightingale shoved him into the tiny room he occupied. The creature looked around with a sneer at the narrow, dirty window and the cracked shutter stuffed with an old rag. A pallet hugged the corner of the room, his extra clothes piled on for warmth, and a stub of candle remained on an old metal plate.

"This is not much of a home, Constantin." Its lips twisted in a parody of a smile. "I left you your beauty, Constantin, *mon garçon*. Surely you could've lured one or two customers up into this nasty little box of yours. Most would overlook the squalor for a taste if you cleaned yourself up."

Constantin's hands shook from the effort it took not to attack. He had to be sure when he did, there was a chance to get away. He needed a distraction, but it would be his sole chance. The widow had to have reached Gabrielle by now. "I'm not interested in your sick games, Nightingale. What do you want?"

Nightingale's eyes hardened. "You know what I want. My property back. Where is she?"

"Where is who?" Constantin disassembled. "I'm not into shes. You know that."

The blow that came struck Constantin in the face, making him stumble, and the second clout between his shoulder blades drove him to his knees. "Now who's playing games, little Constantin?" The magicman's eyes pulsed with a dark light. The tip of the knife scored a fiery line under Constantin's eye, and he flinched. "I know you were at my place, and I know you saw her."

"I didn't take her, I swear." Constantin bit back a curse as the magicman struck him again. The hot, metallic taste of blood filled his mouth, and then Nightingale wrenched his head back. The knife cut deeper this time, slicing a gash in his cheek, and he screamed. He had to hold on, make it believe he was completely cowed. "I didn't do it. I just went to look, that's all."

"That's not all. You subverted her. Got her to trust you. Then you went to visit a chevalier. Do not deny it." The magicman's eyes blazed hot with fury. Constantin sensed the energy stirring in him as much as he felt the blood dripping down his cheek and the hot, throbbing pulse of his wound. He'd sensed that same stir of energy every time the magicman fed off his emotions and pain as a child. But he'd never seen Nightingale in this enraged state, and Constantin struggled against the iron grip holding him.

"I went, but it did me no good," Constantin admitted, hoping that by giving a little truth here, Nightingale might believe the lie to follow.

The magicman picked him up and shook him as if Constantin weighed no more than the child he'd once been. "Did you pray you would get rid of me so easily?"

Constantin jerked at the hands holding him, twisted, and kicked, but nothing loosened the creature's grip. It was too strong. "He wouldn't help. He's too wrapped up in some nonsense with the mists. That's why he's in Paris."

To his shock, the magicman laughed and dropped him. Constantin pushed himself up. He refused to be on his hands and knees in front of this thing if he could help it. He gingerly touched his cheek and winced. The cut was bad.

"Not so pretty anymore, are you, Constantin?"

Constantin clenched his jaw. The scar was a blessing in disguise. He could live with being scarred. Being pretty had never brought him anything but trouble. "I told you everything I know, Nightingale. I don't have the child you want, and I couldn't get the chevalier to help me rid myself of you. I've tried, searching for weeks before I found one, then arguing in vain. There's nothing I can do to get to you. To injure you. Just leave me be."

The magicman grabbed him again, almost lovingly, as it pushed Constantin back against the thin wall. Silence seeped into Constantin's bones. Though the door was ajar, and anyone peeking would grasp his situation, they would likely remain quiet to save their own skins. "Your chevalier is right to fear the mist. It is a herald for the swarm, and when the swarm comes, this city will be devoured. Keep an eye on me if you will, little Constantin, and when you wake up and notice I am gone, I would run, too, far, far away."

A rush of relief made Constantin's knees weak. "Does this mean you're not going to kill me?" He hated the weak, sniveling stance. He longed to tear the magicman apart, to reduce it to a curled-up ball, crying in pain and desperation. He hated it. That hate was the only thing that drove him anymore.

"Perhaps, not this time. I find I am still fond of you." The magicman laughed as it stroked Constantin's chin. A shudder went through him. The creature had amused itself by such caresses, as if it were playing a doting father. It had never gone further than that, which was probably the sole mercy the thing ever showed its victims. But Constantin knew it had been near, lurking when others had fondled him. "And I like the idea of you looking over your shoulder, always fearing the time when I'm going to appear to end your life."

Bien sûr, why end his life when it could prolong suffering? That had always been its game. It had fed off Constantin's emotions, gaining strength from his pain. It had been another kind of rape. For some reason he had never been able to understand, he eventually had sensed the exchange of energy, just as he sensed the stolen power the magicman carried. Power saturated with pain and fear, making his stomach uneasy.

"*Merci.*" Constantin forced the word out through gritted teeth, and the magicman laughed again.

"You still have such spirit. I want to watch you scrabble as you try to survive. I want the fear of me to eat you alive." The tip of the dagger traced down Constantin's face. "Look me in the eye and tell me again you do not know where *ma petite amie* is. I will know if you are lying."

Constantin prayed it wasn't true. He had deceived the monster before. He stared at it and did nothing to disguise his terror. "I don't. Look at your customers or the men who guard your place. This wouldn't be the first time one of your children has turned up elsewhere already dead."

The magicman tapped the point of the dagger against Constantin's chin. "And the chevalier?"

"His study of the mists consumes him." Damn the entire order for allowing itself to die out as it had. There had to be others who hunted. If Constantin searched in London or Rome, he would find other groups who could aid him. He'd learn how to do it himself.

"He will be consumed if he's foolish enough to continue his efforts." The point of the knife slid higher to the corner of his mouth with a small, stinging cut, and Constantin tried to draw back. "No chevalier has uncovered the secret of the mists, and their searches led to their doom."

"What do you know about it?" As soon as the words left his mouth, Constantin knew he shouldn't have pushed.

The magicman's eyes narrowed with cold calculation. "You're too curious, Constantin, you and this chevalier of yours. *Non, non, non.* I cannot let you talk to him."

Panic churned Constantin's stomach as he shoved at the magicman. The energy inside it pulsed again as Nightingale maintained its hold on him with humiliating ease. The energy called to a dark corner inside of him. "You said you wouldn't kill me."

Constantin reached for the shadows in the room, prepared to wrap them around him in a shroud. It probably wouldn't be enough to hide from it completely, not with its senses, but if it would startle the monster, confuse it, he could use it to get away. He needed that distraction.

"I'm not going to kill you. I'm removing your prying tongue." The knife dug harder into the corner of his mouth, and Constantin tasted fresh blood. His control over the shadows skittered away. "Open up, little Constantin. Open up for me."

The energy inside the monster surged with glee, and in desperation, Constantin reached for it, caught on, and yanked. Power poured into him, and the magicman shrieked, an inhuman cacophony of bending metal and twanging chords. Its grip on Constantin loosened, and he jerked away, twisting the shadows around him to render himself invisible.

"What did you do?" Nightingale looked around wildly, lashing out with the knife. If Constantin wasn't so damned terrified, he would've taken satisfaction in seeing that calm veneer broken. "Where did you go?"

Constantin edged his way toward the door, pressing a hand to his cheek to keep the blood from falling and giving himself away. If Nightingale found him, nothing would keep the monster from tearing him apart.

"Give it back to me!" the magicman howled, ripping the pallet apart and scattering Constantin's clothes.

Constantin slipped another beetle out of his pocket and sent it toward the shutters with a whispered word. The beetle darted through the crack in the shutters. "Nightingale." The name hung in the air, ghostlike, and Nightingale turned toward the window with another howl of rage. It ripped the shutters off the hinges to peer outside.

Constantin eased the door open wider, twisting the shadows tighter around him. A sick lump of fear had lodged itself in his throat. He made his way as quickly and quietly down the stairs as he could, while the monster tore apart his quarters, seeking to kill him.

Chapter Eleven

MICHEL-LEON LEFT the villagers and turned his horse back toward the hulking block of the château, brooding over the sunny countryside. Another fruitless day of searching left him frustrated. There were many cave systems. Many underground locations to scout. It would take a lifetime to search them all.

"Don't give up the hunt."

"Wasn't planning on it," Michel-Leon snapped back irritably and blocked them out. Tomorrow he'd go down by the river and collect water samples and test if anything matched the odd chemical traces he'd taken from the mists. With any luck. Régine and the vagabond were back from Paris with the child. Whether they could give him any answers remained to be discovered.

He glanced down the road toward Paris and frowned at the smudge on the horizon. Apprehension clutched his throat. That couldn't be the mists. It was off schedule. He lowered his mental shields enough to send a query. *"Why this anomaly? How?"* He threw the thought to the ancestors as he stood up in his stirrups to get a better look. Their response and voices roared through his mind.

"The boar! The boar! Ware the maddened boar!"

Michel-Leon reeled, struggling to keep his seat as the horse reared. His vision flickered as images appeared around him, the remnants of his blood who had passed before him. They shouted, each one striving for his attention, howling out their news.

"The soul eater is an abomination! Kill it! Kill it! The swarm comes!" Underneath it all was the crackle of flames and a woman screaming in agony and fear.

Michel-Leon tumbled to the ground, struggling to draw in a steadying breath as the ancestors yanked him onto their plane. He scanned the faces of those surrounding him, focused on one, and prayed they were lucid enough to give usable information.

The figure coalesced into a more solid appearance. An older man bowed with age. Burned and tattered rags clothed him. So many of them died by fire. It awakened terrifying memories of his home in flames, smoke filling the corridors, making it impossible to discern a direction. He could not allow himself to be overwhelmed by memories.

Michel-Leon concentrated on the man before him. Burns disfigured his face, but Michel-Leon knew him by the seared pocket watch he carried.

"Grandpère," he said with a painful wrench to his heart. He couldn't mourn him as he'd deserved. The grief had threatened to drown him. The man's hollow eyes focused on him. His soul had long since moved on, but his shadow remained with all the knowledge he'd gathered over a lifetime of fighting monsters. If Michel-Leon could get him to focus. *"You were alive the last time the mists decimated the villages along the Meuse River. Help me. They are threatening Paris. You have to know something."*

Hands grasped his shoulders and though they were insubstantial,

Michel-Leon felt the chill of their touch. For a moment, the other voices threatened to overwhelm him again, and Michel-Leon forced them back.

"The boar won't stop." He paused and gave Michel-Leon a penetrating look. *"You understand the nature of the boar. They attack anything that threatens without mercy."*

Michel-Leon considered his words. They didn't make much sense, but he knew better than to dismiss them. He'd never been boar hunting, but he was familiar with the dangers. A boar was deadly. If a hunter got in its way, it would tear him apart. There was no soothing a boar, no reasoning, it kept coming until it killed or was killed. Was the boar a metaphor or another monster he had not encountered yet?

"What does that have to do with the mists? Do you know anything about magicmen?"

"Everything…" his *grandpère* hissed. *"It's all part of a whole. The soul eater, the watcher, the swarm."*

His horse nuzzled his cheek and jerked him out of the astral plane. Michel-Leon grabbed ahold of its reins, gasping at another sudden reversal as his vision grayed again with disorientation. He needed to go back. He needed more answers.

The mists! Michel-Leon struggled to his feet with a new sense of alarm as he remembered the imminent danger. Régine had gone to Paris today with Severin. He looked toward the horizon again and the gray haze covering the city. The air was clear for kilometers around Paris, which made the shroud that hid it even more ominous. He swung into the saddle and bolted for the château. It was late in the afternoon. Chances were they made it back. He prayed it was so.

The horse sensed his urgency and needed no encouragement to set out at a dead run for the château. Michel-Leon kept one eye on the empty road and the other on the swirling dome surrounding the city. It didn't appear as if it were encroaching on the surrounding countryside, but it didn't belong here either.

The stable doors were open and to Michel-Leon's intense relief, he spied the carriage. One worry out of the way. Now he could concentrate on the second problem. He could have miscalculated and the mists weren't early after all. It would be a disastrous mistake and would undermine people's trust in him. However, not as disastrous as the mists abandoning patterns that traced back centuries.

Hadrien emerged from the stables with a look of concern on his face. "I heard you race in here? What's wrong?" he called out as Michel-Leon slowed the horse and slid out of the saddle.

"She'll need to be walked for a bit," Michel-Leon said. "Where are Régine and Janvier? The kitchen?"

"*Oui*, my lord." Hadrien caught the horse's reins, speaking soothingly as he patted the mare's neck. "What has you in such a state? Did you find the caves you were searching for?"

"*Non*." Michel-Leon strode toward the kitchen door and pointed toward the city. "That is the reason for my state."

"Sweet Mary, mother of God," Hadrien breathed. If anything, during the race here the mists had thickened, though they remained firmly locked around Paris. "This one wasn't on your schedule."

"Indeed." And those implications scared Michel-Leon. Régine and Janvier looked up with grim expressions as Michel-Leon walked in. At least he needed to make no explanations here. "I take it you know," Michel-Leon said, shrugging out of his coat and rolling up his sleeves.

"We need to redo the charts. Make sure our calculations are correct. Then we need to send out new broadsides. The complaints are going to pour in as soon as the mists recede, and we need to have some answers."

"What are you talking about, Michie?" Régine jumped up from the table, revealing a young girl who had been hiding behind her as Janvier paled.

"The mists covering Paris!" Michel-Leon flung his hand toward the window as Régine went to see for herself. "Where is Severin?"

Tears welled in the child's eyes, and she huddled away from him. "I want Constantin."

"He didn't return," Janvier said softly. "He sensed the magicman and sent Régine on to get little Gabrielle." Janvier spared the girl a kind smile. "She waited a bit at the carriage, then thought it best to bring her here. She was getting ready to go back out."

Régine looked at him with a stricken expression. "*Je suis désolé*. I shouldn't have left him."

"*Non*, you made the right decision." Michel-Leon put his hand on her shoulder and weighed his options. "It's the decision he would've wanted you to make. He has a care for this child over himself."

He eyed the girl for a long moment as she stared back at him. There was a similarity between her and Severin, something about the eyes and the perfection of their features. "I'll search for him," he vowed. He couldn't leave Severin to face the creature alone, and there could be a chance he'd made it out of Paris. Michel-Leon crouched near the table. "I'll find your Constantin for you."

Hope entered her soft, dark eyes and she groped for Régine's hand as she returned to the table. Régine took Gabrielle onto her lap with gentle words of comfort murmured low, "He is good at finding things, little one."

Michel-Leon wished he shared her confidence. He had been failing at finding answers to the many questions plaguing him.

"Do you think that's wise?" Janvier asked.

"The mists aren't extending beyond the city. I can check the roads leading out and maybe discover where they are generating from outside of town. It's an angle we haven't tried yet. Get the charts and the notes we've made. There's an explanation for this aberration somewhere." Michel-Leon turned to Régine as she rose. "Stay with the child. Protect her. The magicman can move about in the mists. It may take the opportunity to come for her. If anything strange happens, retreat to my workshop. That should slow it down."

Though it hadn't stopped Severin. They needed to go deeper into the château. Janvier could lead them if necessary. "I'll be back soon. Get those charts ready and the notes of our calculations. We're going to be busy when I return."

Michel-Leon left again with rapid steps, pushed on by his urgency. Mists, magicman, and now boars. How much was one man expected to deal with? He'd send out another telegram tomorrow. He'd heard magicmen haunted Prussia as well. His contact there could have information about one monster terrorizing the city.

Hadrien took one look at him and fetched Régine's mount. "Do you want me to go with you?" he asked as he quickly saddled the mare.

"*Non*, tend to my horse and keep an eye on the horizon. If it appears as if the mists might be spreading, tell the others to stay inside and head to the village to warn them." Michel-Leon swung up and glanced down at the man standing by his stirrup. Hadrien and his family had been of immense help, and it worried him that being here put them in harm's way. "If that becomes necessary, stay there after your warning until you are sure the mists have receded."

"You have my word." Hadrien stepped back and lifted his fingers to his brow. "God go with you."

The road remained empty except for a few people scurrying away from the city. Even the birds had hushed as if a pall hovered over the entire area. Michel-Leon studied the shifting, swirling mass, making out rooftops that appeared and disappeared again. He hadn't taken the opportunity to study the phenomena before, erring on caution and staying inside. Now that he had a prototype for his filtering mask, he should take up quarters in the city. He could learn much by closer observation.

"*The watcher is near.*" Michel-Leon slowed the horse to a walk, scanning the empty road at the whispered warning. *"A taint stains him."*

Michel-Leon laid his hand on his weapon, questioning what that meant. Before he could call out to the vagabond, Severin appeared near the horse's side, causing it to shy and sidestep. Michel-Leon's blistering reprimand died on his lips. Blood caked Severin's face, and his shoulders slumped with weariness. "Sweet Saint Jeanne, Severin, what happened? The magicman?"

"It was waiting for me," Severin rasped. "It suspected I rescued Gabrielle and came to fetch her back. Is she safe?" He clutched Michel-Leon's leg.

"Oui. She is at the château with Régine and Janvier." He held out his hand for Severin. "Come on, you'll need that sewn shut. How hurt are you?"

"A few bruises and this." Severin gestured toward his face. He grabbed Michel-Leon's hand and swung up. "It would've been worse if I hadn't escaped."

Severin was lucky to be alive. Michel-Leon wanted to ask how Severin accomplished the feat but bit his tongue for now as he turned back toward the château. He was acutely aware of the man behind him and the awkward way he held onto him. He had to remind himself that attraction was not an option. Besides, the ancestors had warned he carried a taint. Until he figured out what that meant and how to heal him, it was best to keep his distance.

"How did you get away?" Michel-Leon asked.

"I'm not sure," Severin replied after a troubled silence.

"Do you think it's following you to the child?" Michel-Leon risked opening his senses to the ancestors, but they were quiet except for the usual restless muttering. Good chance they were safe for the moment.

"Non." Severin shuddered. "It can't sense me when I'm wrapped in the shadows. I hid her in another location and shielded her as much as I could with a toy I'd given her. It must've worked because it tracked

me down first."

"That buys us some time to make a plan." They remained quiet until they rode into the stable yard. Hadrien met them with a relieved expression, and Michel-Leon waved him off. "I'll take care of the mare. Have Salome put water on to boil and get Janvier's medical kit. Ask for Régine and the child to come down if they're not in the kitchen."

Hadrien hurried off with a nod, and Severin slid off the horse. For a moment, Michel-Leon feared his legs would buckle, and he would end up on the ground. The bleeding had eased, but Severin's complexion was pale and waxy. "Sit on the barrel there and get your strength back."

Severin nodded and moved over to it. There was something about the way he moved that said the injury went deeper than the cut to his cheek. Either that wasn't his only wound or it had something to do with the new taint he carried. Questions filled Michel-Leon's mind as he stripped the saddle from the horse. Severin needed some time to steady before the child saw him.

Michel-Leon left the horse in the paddock and found a clean cloth. "Here, press that against the wound until we tend to it. Come on. Let's get you inside and fix you up."

He hovered next to Severin, trying to decide if he needed an arm to lean on or not. When he moved to support him, Severin stiffened. "I can do it. I don't want to alarm Gabrielle."

Michel-Leon backed off. "*Mon ami*, that wound is going to scare her. I'm sure you'll look better once you clean up."

They made their way into the kitchen and the waif let out a cry of delight—the first sound of happiness Michel-Leon heard from her. She ran to Severin and burrowed close, burying her face against his side as she kept one wary eye on Michel-Leon. Her skin was dusky and her eyes a fathomless dark brown. Michel-Leon smiled at her. "Why don't you take a seat next to your friend? I'm going to tend to his injuries and then get us all something to drink."

Severin held Gabrielle tight and looked over at Régine. "*Merci,* for getting her and keeping her safe." She whispered something and Severin shifted to murmur back at her. After a moment, she released her hold of him and slipped onto the bench beside him. An unearthly pretty child, she had all of Severin's fey ways. There was going to be trouble. A magicman wouldn't suffer so many insults from what it considered was its prey.

"I'm glad you made it," Régine said. "We were concerned."

"I'm not used to that."

Severin's soft admission hit at Michel-Leon's heart. There was a wealth of loneliness and isolation in those words. Severin sat at the table as Régine stacked the maps and journals out of the way. "*Grandpère's* bag is here. He is working on the calculations, though he hasn't found a mistake yet."

Michel-Leon was beginning to think there wasn't one. All three of them had triple checked the work before and had come to an agreement. *Non,* that was the simple answer, which left the hard one. He lifted Severin's chin with his fingertips and tilted his head so he could examine the gruesome wound. The risk of infection was high. Janvier had a steadier hand than himself when it came to this work, but his eyesight was not what it used to be, so Michel-Leon would have to do.

"You can tend to me after you've talked to Gabrielle." Severin moved to get up and Michel-Leon pushed him back down. There was a strange energy about him, an unnatural light to his eyes that worried Michel-Leon even as the loss of blood made Severin unsteady. However, no flush of fever stained his face. The voices in Michel-Leon's head whispered uneasily.

"I can do both." Michel-Leon rolled his sleeves up and poured steaming water into a basin as Janvier arrived with his bag. "Set it on the table, *s'il vous plaît.* Salome, would you bring me some clean cloths and a bottle of cognac? I suspect both Monsieur Severin and I will need it and something warm for the child, *s'il vous plaît*. Janvier, any progress?"

"Not as much as I would like. I suspect it's going to take some time."

"I'll help you," Régine said. "I'm useless here, unless you want me to take notes?"

"*Non*, I can handle it." Michel-Leon spared her a brief glance. "I'll be up once they're settled. Both Monsieur Severin and Gabrielle will want some rest after this."

"You plan on doctoring it?" Severin asked, his incredulity evident in both the lift of his eyebrows and the shade of his voice.

"I'm not without some training in the task. Though Janvier has had more practice stitching me up." Michel-Leon moved to the bag and rummaged through it. Janvier's bag was as meticulous as everything else he did. Michel-Leon found the packet of needles carefully wrapped along with sturdy thread.

Severin reassured Gabrielle in a low voice, though Michel-Leon couldn't make out the words. He would dearly love to know how Severin smuggled her out of the magicman's establishment, but he'd have to exercise patience. Severin was not a man who trusted, for excellent reasons.

Michel-Leon laid out his supplies and washed his hands in the steaming water. He splashed some cognac into two glasses and handed the larger one to Severin. "Drink up, *mon ami*."

Severin downed the glass and turned his cheek toward Michel-Leon. "Get on with it, then."

Michel-Leon swallowed some of the spirits himself before he cleaned around the gruesome cut and the other nicks on Severin's face to be sure he didn't need any other care. The wound held no dirt or debris. The little girl's fingers curled protectively into Severin's soiled coat and watched every move Michel-Leon made with utter ghostlike quiet.

Michel-Leon smiled in assurance. "I promise to take good care of him."

"She's big on promises." Severin slipped his arm around her protectively.

Michel-Leon cleansed and threaded the needle before handing Severin the bottle of cognac. "I'll try to make it as neat as I can. It might not scar too badly," Michel-Leon said as he steeled himself for the task ahead.

"I don't care about that. Just get it done." Severin took a deep swig of the cognac, met Michel-Leon's eye, and nodded. "Go ahead."

Such a strange man. Michel-Leon had the impression that Severin hated the beauty given him. But if that was part of what had lured the magicman to him, Michel-Leon could understand. Severin winced when the needle pierced his skin but remained still while Michael-Leon continued his ministrations.

"Does it hurt bad?" the little girl whispered.

"The baron is being gentle. Why don't you pull out your cat and play at the table," Severin suggested, his lips barely moving. "We are safe here."

Michel-Leon heard the doubt in his voice. "Safer, to be sure, and we'll work on making it safer still. The magicman wouldn't try a direct assault yet. Not with the reputation this place has, and that gives us some time to assure we have a plan in place for him."

"What weapon can we use to defeat the monster?"

"*Désolé*, but there is no weapon that can kill a magicman outright. At least not one I know of, and there are several references to magicmen among the chevaliers' journals." Michel-Leon paused in his stitching as Severin's jaw tightened. He would have to be a blind fool not to have noticed the desperation in Severin's manner. He suspected the mental and emotional wounds Severin sustained by his childhood encounter with the magicman had not quite healed. Michel-Leon did not want to provoke fresh pain.

"What do you mean, there's no weapon?" Severin snapped. "There has to be some way of fighting them."

"Each one has its own particular weakness. Unless you know this one's, we're going to have to eliminate it the hard way." Michel-Leon wished the hard way wouldn't be so damned difficult and time-consuming.

"It has none that I have been able to divine," Severin ground out.

"Then we have to cut it off from its feed source. If you keep it away from that, then it will weaken and starve to the point where normal weapons can kill it." The wound was deep, but the edges were even so it made the task easier as Michel-Leon tied off a stitch and moved to the next one. "We will have to lure and trap it at the château."

"That is the most foolhardy notion I have ever heard of. Do you know how difficult it would be to keep this magicman away from children? How would we capture it in the first place? They are monstrously strong. Much less hold on to it long enough for it to weaken?" Severin's questions tumbled over themselves to get out.

Michel-Leon held up his hand, and Severin quieted, though his glare was sharp enough to slice. "I am fully aware of how dangerous it's going to be. But our other alternative is to watch, wait, and hope we uncover this magicman's weakness. I do not believe you have any desire to wait. And I do not have the people to keep a constant guard for it."

Severin closed his eyes as if pained. "*Non*, I'll not wait," he said, his voice hoarse. "Every hour that passes is an hour too long. *S'il vous plaît*, tell me you have a plan."

"Not much of one, and if you have any other ideas we can use to further our chances, I'll be grateful." Michel-Leon examined his handiwork. It should heal neatly. He cleaned the area again and prepared a bandage.

"I don't like waiting. Baron, if you could see...if you knew..."

The starkness in Severin's voice reminded Michel-Leon of memories he'd rather forget himself. "I know the pain of a child betrayed. But we are going to have one chance. If the magicman suspects we are a threat to it, it'll move before we're ready. It's better to have a sure strike in a few days over trying and failing and leaving those children without hope. I'm contacting a colleague in Prussia to request any information that will help. I know they had trouble with a magicman in Hamelin a few centuries ago."

"This had better work." Though Severin's voice was grim, Michel-Leon didn't sense any threat in him, merely a desperate urge to see the job done. "How long do you believe it'll take for it to weaken enough to be hurt?"

"The older the magicman, the more addicted it is to its prey, and the quicker it will starve." Michel-Leon gave Severin a sober look. "Older ones are stronger as well, more canny. So let us pray it is very old indeed and be on our guard with every safety measure in place we can conceive of."

"So what do we do in the meantime? Sit on our hands? Wait for it to attack?" Severin put his body between Michel-Leon and the child as if he could shield her. "It will come for us."

Michel-Leon stared out the window with a frown. "The mists are out of their usual pattern. That will confuse the magicman as much as it's confusing me. We need time to set the trap here and move people to safety. I propose we confound the creature by leaving the child here with Régine to protect. She can help Janvier oversee setting the traps. You and I will take up residence in a townhouse in Paris. The magicman will likely focus on the two of us together and try to figure out what we're up to.

"I will question you endlessly about it. The more we know, the better we can figure it out." He gave Severin a look of compassion. "I'll delve into places you don't want to go, but it will be our only chance. If I discover its weakness from you, then I won't have to ask Gabrielle to open up those dark memories."

"So you want us as bait? What's keeping it from attacking us outright?" Severin rose from the table and paced, his fingers fidgeting as if he wished for one of the toys he tinkered with. "Don't you have other things you have to do rather than sit around waiting to be ambushed?"

"Oh, we will be quite busy. I have been working on a contraption that may allow us to move around in the mists without being caught up in their thrall. Testing it will pose a risk, so I'm grateful to have your aid. Not that I propose putting you at risk. My invention, my risk. There are many questions to be answered." Michel-Leon studied Severin's restless movements. He still moved as if in pain. He needed a night's rest, some food, a bath, and clean clothes — both him and the child after their ordeal.

"I'm also working on a concoction that might nullify the effects of the mists, but I need more samples from the heart of the city. I don't believe the magicman will attack us though. It'll want more information. You sensed it earlier when you sent Régine away. That will be helpful. You escaped from it once. I doubt it'll risk coming for you again until it knows where the child is and has a better understanding of what you can do."

Severin fingered the bandage as Gabrielle slipped beside him and tipped her head back. "Does it hurt?" she whispered.

"A bit," Severin admitted. "But the baron made it better. He's going to have some questions for you about the hungry man, questions that may help us."

"I don't want to stay here while you go away." Gabrielle curled her fingers into his coat, and Severin crouched beside her.

"I don't want to be apart from you either, *ma petite chouette*, but it won't be for long. Will it?" Severin shot Michel-Leon a questioning look.

Michel-Leon shook his head. "A week at most while we set the trap. Do you mind answering my questions?"

Gabrielle glanced at Severin for reassurance, and he nodded. "*Non*."

Michel-Leon sat at the table and smiled at her. She continued to watch him as if she wasn't sure if he were a guardian angel or not. He had no idea how to interact with a child. They were strange creatures, with odd games of their own and private jests. This one, however, had more in common with him and Severin, a damaged child. "I am working with Monsieur Severin to trap the monster that took you. I'm also looking to solve the mystery of the mists so other children are safe."

"The hungry man?" The girl's voice was tentative, and if it hadn't been so quiet in the room, Michel-Leon doubted he would've heard her at all.

"*Oui*, mademoiselle," Michel-Leon replied as she inched closer. "How did you end up at the orphanage?"

"There was a sickness last summer. It killed lots of people. My papa too. They took me to the orphanage with lots of others. The hungry man showed up not long after, and it got scarier." Gabrielle shivered and hugged her arms to herself.

"Severin told me the hungry man brought some of your friends over after it found them in mists." Michel-Leon paused as she nodded. "Did you ever talk to them about how that happened?"

"*Oui*." The little voice was like a shadow, and it tugged at Michel-Leon's heart.

"What do you remember? Every piece of information helps." Michel-Leon gave her an encouraging smile. "Did they notice a smell? Or have a physical reaction to it?"

"They didn't say anything about a smell. They talked about wanting to go to the bright place. The music. It made them all tingly and tired. That's what they talked about the most. They had to go to where the music lived." A puzzled line appeared between Gabrielle's eyes. "They get upset if you ask too many questions. Even the matrons and masters gave up asking about the mists."

Michel-Leon frowned. There had to be some compound in the mists, something that acted as a soporific and a pheromone. Was it naturally occurring or manufactured? He knew of several chemicals that would put a person in a trancelike state. He couldn't be certain, but he would hazard a guess that this particular compound affected its victims by their breathing in the vapor.

Why would it affect some and not others though? It had to be engineered to target a certain type of people. There was so much they still didn't know about human biology and chemistry. Like why one person could have a successful transfusion of blood and another die painfully.

"The hungry man took your friends, interrupting their journey to the song. Did they remember or say anything at all about what happened when they were forced to stop?" Severin asked in a voice so gentle and coaxing that it surprised Michel-Leon. He would not have believed that tone came from him if he had not heard it himself.

"They talk about it like it was a bad dream. They cry about the monsters." Gabrielle dug her fingers into Severin's coat again.

"Maybe it was a dream," Michel-Leon urged. "Tell us anyway so we may judge for ourselves. Sometimes our mind takes what we hear while we are sleeping and translates it into a dream."

"They talked about walking to the bright place. There were other people there, too, and then later monsters with long noses and big eyes that didn't talk. The monsters took them away from the song, and it made all of them angry. They hurt some people." She paused and shuddered. "Then the hungry man was there. It would pick a few favorites and tie them together and take them back to the orphanage. They cried and screamed the whole time, but it was stronger." Her voice dropped to a terrified whisper at the end.

Michel-Leon noticed Severin's sudden tension. The magicman was a sore topic for him, and it terrorized her. Little Gabrielle had given him enough to ponder. She needed rest and some proper food. If he thought of further questions for her about the magicman and its connection to the mists, and he was sure he would, it would be better if they came from her protector.

"That is enough for now, child. You must be hungry and thirsty after all that talking." Michel-Leon pretended not to notice Gabrielle's questioning glance and Severin's slight nod in answer.

"You did good, *ma petite chouette*," Severin said, and Gabrielle's answering smile brightened the entire room.

"I had rooms cleaned up for you. In the servants' quarters, I'm afraid. The rest of the château is not safe." Michel-Leon gave Severin and the child a stern look. "Don't wander off. When we return from Paris, I'll show you the safe way to the workshop and laboratory. There might be some gadgets there you'd like to explore, Severin."

A hungry expression crossed over Severin's face. "I'd like that, *merci*." He glanced down at Gabrielle, and that look softened. "*Merci*, for everything."

Chapter Twelve

"ARE YOU SURE she'll be safe?" Severin asked with an anxious note as the carriage rolled away from the château and headed toward the city.

"If you're in Paris, the magicman will concentrate on searching for her near you. Since you went to all the trouble to nab her, the creature will not expect you to leave her behind." Michel-Leon paused as he sensed a stirring of intuition among the ancestors, but it settled down. "Besides, she's in a safe section of the château. Her and the maid have plenty of food, water, and entertainment. You, myself, Régine, and Janvier are the only ones who know how to get to her. Besides, we shan't be gone long. I want to run a few experiments while we tease and lure your monster. We'll return within the week."

The thought of guarding the child had not amused Régine, but the task of continuing to search for likely cave systems mollified her. Michel-Leon didn't want anyone straying too far out. Not until they knew if the last occurrence of the mists was a onetime aberration or not.

Severin grunted and pulled out his usual mess of wires and metal bits and the tiny tools he used to manipulate them. Michel-Leon watched in silence. Mechanics were not his strong point, but Severin was clever with those tools and pieces. Michel-Leon would have to ask him for his help if the filtering mask didn't work the way it ought. He had often observed his *grandpère* tinker in such a way, and the reminder sent both a pang of loss and the warmth of sweet memories through him.

He studied Severin as the carriage rumbled and swayed. Despite an occasional grimace when they hit a bump, he appeared totally involved in his work. There was something different about him, something that gave the ancestors pause, but Michel-Leon didn't know him well enough to nail down what it was.

He'd taken advantage of Michel-Leon's offer of a bath and clean clothes along with the room last night. His hair gleamed even more golden, and Severin had pulled the soft waves away from his face by tying it in a club at his nape. Janvier had inspected his wound and freshly bandaged it. The drawn flesh of his cheek tugged down his eye so his features weren't as symmetrical as before, but it didn't take away from his appeal.

Hell, he'd earned that badge by facing and outwitting a monster in defense of a child. His appeal had grown in spades. The thought of spending time alone with him for the next week disconcerted Michel-Leon. He would be underfoot constantly. It was different with Janvier and Régine. That was comfortable. He suspected his time with Severin would be fraught with tension.

Severin glanced up as the carriage slowed, and Michel-Leon looked away, embarrassed Severin had caught him staring. "What experiments do you wish to run?"

"I have a theory based on conversations I've had with people snared by the mists and who survived." Michel-Leon tapped his fingertips together. "There's something in them that acts as a soporific and a pheromone. It lulls the senses and entices, so people drop everything they're doing and disappear into the mists. There have been no signs of foul play. No indication a fight took place. People bedridden and unable to move wept for days because they could not walk out there, even knowing it would mean their disappearance."

"That is terrifying. What about the monsters in the mists? Do they eat the people?" Uneasiness crept into Severin's voice. "I almost wish you wouldn't answer."

Michel-Leon frowned. "The monsters Gabrielle describes are a recent phenomenon." He'd searched among the ancestors for any reference of them and received silence. Nor could he find a note of them in the journals. "There are several aspects about the mists that are new to this cycle. Is it because Paris is so much bigger than the last targets or are there other factors in play?" Michel-Leon rapped his fist into his palm. "I have more questions than answers."

"Talk it out. That may help." Severin met his gaze, and Michel-Leon's pulse skipped. "Tell me more about these experiments."

Michel-Leon had attempted to talk it out to his companions, to the ancestors, to any poor fool who'd listen for ten minutes before calling him a ravening lunatic. But Severin was a new set of ears and he needed to know as much as he could about the dangers they faced. Besides, focusing on the problem took his mind off his growing attraction. "I want to test the chemical elements in the mists. One, to discover if I'm right about the properties in them and their effects, and two, to develop a countermeasure."

"What if it's magic based and not science?"

Michel-Leon studied Severin with surprise. "That's an astute question. The possibility is there, so I'm not discounting it entirely. However, there have been many chevaliers who were experts in that field, and they did not find any magic involved. Again, it doesn't mean it's not there, but I don't believe anyone has investigated the science of the phenomena. By going this route, I may uncover something new that will aid us."

Severin held up the device he'd been tinkering with. "That's a solid theory. Perhaps I can figure out a way to make these more useful."

"They are ingenious little things," Michel-Leon said, admiring the beetle. "What do they do?"

Severin lifted it to his lips and whispered something. Michel-Leon straightened as the ancestors spoke, *"The watcher has fey magic."* The beetle lifted on blurring wings and darted toward Michel-Leon. Despite the action, he felt no menace, only awe at what Severin had created.

"I can use it to send messages, short ones, or receive messages if I attune one right. For instance, I could link that one to you. All you would need to do is tell it to find me and whisper your message."

Michel-Leon lifted his hand, and the beetle settled in his palm. The craftsmanship was remarkable, but the things Severin could do with them were a work of wonder. Mechanics and magic…what an interesting world they lived in. When it wasn't trying to kill them. "That's how you remained in contact with Gabrielle? And you mentioned shielding her with her toy?"

"It is. I needed to know when she was in danger while she was still at the orphanage. She wasn't quite ready to run off when I first found her. As much as I wanted to snatch her away, I didn't want her to fear me after." Severin looked away with a troubled expression. "You have so few choices as a child."

"Oui." Their gazes met again with commiseration. "The ability to send messages is always useful," Michel-Leon continued. The beetle lifted off his palm and headed back to its master. Michel-Leon studied Severin as he scrambled for a way to broach the topic of his other abilities. "What else did you learn to do with your creations as you strove to stay alive on the streets?"

Severin caught his device and slipped it into one of his many pockets. "I can use them to locate people or places." He grimaced. "Unfortunately, I have to have visited that particular place or met that person. And I can't see what the device does. I haven't figured out how to do that yet, which would be useful. We could send several of these things out to explore the mists while we stayed safe."

The possibilities fired Michel-Leon's imagination. "You have the use of my *grandpère's* workshop. You'll figure it out." Michel-Leon smiled at him as they pulled up in front of the townhouse. "You're a resourceful fellow."

"What is this place?" Severin asked as he clambered out and gave the carriage a baleful stare.

"A chevalier hidey-hole." The townhouse sat in a quiet square on the *Rive Droite* not far from the Seine. It hadn't been occupied in quite some time, and they'd only brought the bare necessities to make it livable. Michel-Leon didn't plan on staying long. "Which way is the orphanage?"

Severin turned and glanced at the sky before pointing. "On the other side of the Seine. I had quarters about a thirty-minute walk from there."

Michel-Leon studied the surrounding area and then directed Hadrien to take down his trunk and bring it inside. "We're close enough to catch its interest. Magicmen are very keen on survival. Come, let's get settled. I want to show you my filtering mask and get your thoughts. I'm sure we can make a few tweaks before the mists roll in, and I send myself out there to test it."

"*Bien sûr.*" Severin fell in step beside him, his expression inscrutable. Michel-Leon didn't know what to make of him or what to expect moving forward when they were alone together.

It didn't take Michel-Leon more than a couple of days to figure out he was going to go mad. This time, he couldn't blame it on the ancestors' voices or the problems plaguing him. It had everything to do with the man he was currently living with. Michel-Leon felt his cheeks warm at that last thought. Living with sounded far too intimate for his comfort. Their rooms were separate, but the sense of Constantin was everywhere in the small townhouse without others to buffer them.

There, he'd done it again, thought of him more familiarly in his mind. He had to remember Severin. Though it was hard when they worked together in a companionable silence, Michel-Leon found it restful. At least, he did when he wasn't working himself up because their hands brushed or he caught the scent of Severin's hair. They ate together. Shared one bathing room. Michel-Leon's face heated again. Not at the same time; though, that put more images in his head than he needed.

"Baron?"

There it was again. That distant tone that dug under his skin. Michel-Leon knew if he glanced up, he'd see the wariness in Severin's gaze. The man thought Michel-Leon odd, no doubt. He was odd and given Severin's experiences, and the little Michel-Leon had gleaned from him, he had reasons for mistrust. Whatever growing closeness Michel-Leon felt was all in his imagination.

"*Oui?*" Michel-Leon concentrated on lifting one of the simmering kettles from the fire in the kitchen.

"What are you doing?" The note of bafflement had Michel-Leon steal a glance at Severin. He'd pulled his hair back into a tail so it wouldn't get in the way of his tinkering and the style sharpened his cheekbones and emphasized the healing slash. He'd rolled his shirtsleeves up, exposing sleekly muscled forearms.

Michel-Leon jerked his gaze back to the kettle. "Heating water for my bath."

"I'll help." Severin grabbed a thick pair of gloves for the second kettle. "Though why you want a bath in this heat, I don't know. I've never known a nobleman to cook his own food or fetch and carry his own bathwater before. You are an enigma."

Michel-Leon couldn't come up with a graceful way to turn down Severin's offer. He was stronger than he appeared, swinging down the kettle with ease, though it was the largest one they had. The bathing chamber was far too small with the both of them in it, the bath far too inviting with its steam rising.

"It helps me to think—both the drudgery and the soaking." Michel-Leon set the empty kettles to the side, then added some cold water he'd already drawn from the well so the temperature was right, on the edge of too hot. He couldn't look at Severin in here. It was bad enough he had his scent and voice imprinted in his memory. "*Merci.*"

"I'll leave you to your thoughts then, baron."

Michel-Leon turned his back, ran a hand through his curls, and shrugged out of his shirt. Severin. He had to remember that and turn his thoughts toward more productive avenues, such as what experiments to try next.

He stripped down and hissed as he stepped into the water. The shock of heat drove other thoughts from his mind. As he eased himself into the water, he realized he hadn't heard the door shut behind his houseguest. Even as his gaze flew to the slight gap, he knew Severin was gone. The ancestors would've warned him if the watcher was watching again.

As Michel-Leon laid his head back on the towel cushioning the edge of the bath, he couldn't say if he felt disappointment or relief. Whichever it was, it distracted him from what he should focus on. The man had his thoughts flitting about like so many bats in a belltower.

"*Undisciplined garçon.*"

Michel-Leon grimaced at the voice of his father, which effectively killed any lingering warm thoughts.

"Go to hell and let a man bathe in peace," Michel-Leon muttered. "Though I suppose you're already there. Degenerate shade."

*

THE BARON SET Constantin on edge. He'd already known the man was different from others of his class. He hadn't appreciated how different until they had been alone together this week. He didn't act as a nobleman ought.

The chevalier was attracted to Constantin. He knew when a man eyed him with admiration, but he never acted on the attraction. He could've easily used his position to cajole or coerce Constantin into some intimacy, and he hadn't. It didn't help that Constantin found the man to be intriguing in return. It was his mind that lowered Constantin's defenses. He was always thinking, endlessly probing at the problem, coming at it from different angles in ways that often mystified Constantin.

When the baron gave orders, it was always when they worked on an experiment. It was given as if to a colleague or equal and the times when Parisee was abstracted by one of his puzzles, he didn't order; he asked. Frankly, his behavior made Constantin's nerves taut. He felt himself softening, and he had to remind himself of who he was dealing with and what the stakes were. It was too high a cost to pay to ease his vigilance.

"It is utter madness!" The baron tossed down the journal he'd been perusing and ran a hand through his curls, already disordered from the same action. "We need a fresh start. Let's go for a walk."

"A walk?" Constantin asked, confounded once again as he set aside the filtering mask. "Where? Why?"

"We'll go across the river and collect some water samples along the way. I'd like to look at this orphanage as well." Parisee pulled a satchel over his head and slid a few empty vials into the slots made for them.

Constantin stared at him, stunned, seeing Parisee in a new light. He'd come to accept the chevalier wasn't going to do anything immediately to help with the magicman beyond providing them protection. He swallowed hard around the sudden hope. "It will likely sense I'm near and could spot you as well. We may provoke it to act."

Then, oh then, Parisee would be forced to action, and perhaps Nightingale would be wounded despite the chevalier's warnings that it was invulnerable at this time. The baron's voice cut into his feverish thoughts. "Unlikely, but we will keep its attention where we want it."

"*Merci*, baron," Constantin said, lowering his head respectfully.

Parisee laid his hand on Constantin's arm with a gentle squeeze. "No more. Parisee, if you must, but no more baron or chevalier. I have a name. If you cannot bring yourself to say Michel-Leon, then Parisee will do."

Constantin smiled faintly. It was another step toward bridging the distance between them, but Constantin was willing to take that step if Parisee was willing to work on the problem of the magicman as well. "I will try…Parisee."

Parisee smiled, the warmth clear in his eyes, and then a red flush crept up his neck, and he snatched his hand away. "Come, action will provoke a reaction, and then we will learn something."

Or get themselves killed. The thought didn't stop Constantin from following after Parisee as he grabbed his sword cane and headed out the door. The summer sun shone brightly enough that Constantin dragged on his battered hat. They'd been hemmed in the townhouse and the walls had closed in around Constantin. It was good to be outside and to stretch his legs. He should've thought of this before.

He fell into step beside Parisee, who appeared content to remain silent as he studied their surroundings as if each fresh sight was something to marvel at. It made Constantin look as well, curious to see what the chevalier saw, but the wonder eluded him. The sky held the familiar smudge of smoke as more old buildings burned away to make room for the elite. At least it wasn't the mists, a small mercy to those living in

Paris, though there was little mercy for the poor.

"What is it you see?" he asked gruffly, unable to maintain the wary distance he tried to keep up. Parisee often had him thinking in ways new to him.

Parisee shot him a startled glance, and then he pointed toward the snarling face of a gargoyle on a nearby building. "My father used to tell me they came to life on moonless nights and went in search of boys who misbehaved. They would turn them into creatures of stone too, forced to guard and gurgle. I always thought we could've been friends if I'd ever met one. My father threatened me with the gargoyles often."

It made Constantin uncomfortable to think the man might also have nightmares from his childhood.

Then he pointed toward a small courtyard with the branches of a tree spilling over the wall. "That tree there looks like a giant having a rest between his labors."

Frowning, Constantin studied the leafy canopy and cocked his head. "I don't see it."

Parisee smiled at him sadly. "You are a marvel who creates marvels, but I fear people have let you down so often you cannot see the wonder in the world."

Constantin pondered those words as they paused by the river for the baron to collect his samples, and then they continued on toward the orphanage. The building had not changed, nor had the pall of terror and grief hanging over it. "That is Nightingale's lair," he said in a grim voice.

The expression of awe disappeared from Parisee's face. Now, he was a Chevalier de Rouen with the cool danger in his eyes, his head half-cocked as if listening. "It is an evil place," he said finally.

Relief flooded through Constantin. He hadn't let himself believe Parisee would do something about the magicman before, but the steel in his eyes cracked the shield of mistrust. "That it is. The creature preys on those most in need of mercy and a tender care."

Parisee studied him for a long moment. Behind the implacable gaze of the chevalier, Constantin glimpsed the man who fought monsters and tended to others with his own hands. Parisee glanced away, but not before that telltale flush. "We should get back and continue our studies. I believe we've given the magicman enough to occupy its thoughts."

Constantin stared at the orphanage and Nightingale's window. He doubted it could fear, but that didn't stop him from wishing the feeling upon the creature. He caught up with Parisee, and they discussed their next steps as they walked back to the townhouse.

"Go on up," Parisee said when they came indoors. "I'll make us some tea and bring up the sandwiches Salome sent."

He set his sword cane to the side and moved toward the kitchen as Constantin stared, disconcerted once again. The baron didn't treat him as a servant. He'd expected he would have to handle all of those little chores when they came to the townhouse, but most of the time, Parisee saw to them himself.

Constantin considered that as he climbed the stairs. He would have to offer more often and take on an equal load of those pesky chores. When he reached the room they'd set aside for their studies, he stared aghast out the window. Fog rolled in toward the townhouse in a cresting wave. This was not the right date. He was sure of it.

"Parisee!" He shouted down the stairs and then went to the chevalier's worktable to find the printed schedule.

"What is it?" Parisee demanded as he came up, taking the stairs two at a time, judging from the noise.

Constantin flung his hand toward the fog rapidly advancing as Parisee came into the room. "Has it ever changed schedule like this?"

"*Oui*, once before. The day you brought Gabrielle to us. It was off-cycle then too." The baron clutched his hair as he paced. "It is utter madness! It is not supposed to be here today. What is going on?"

Parisee stopped and stared out at the window, his hands on his hips as he muttered to himself in a one-sided argument. Constantin still didn't know what to make of his habit of talking to himself, even stranger, how he often appeared to listen to an answer. As he muttered, the mists completely enveloped the windows. "I'm going out in it. Don't scream dire warnings at me! That's what we have the mask for. We need answers."

Constantin wasn't sure if he was trying to convince himself or Constantin, and he didn't plan on arguing with the half-crazed man. Intriguing, *oui*, damn, too intriguing, and if he was honest, appealing even if he was a noble. But sometimes he made Constantin feel as if he was the third man in the room.

The baron stalked over to the table where he'd set up his experiments in their laboratory and began going through his notes. He waved a stack of thin paper he called litmus at Constantin. "I'll run experiments from the vapor collected. My tests back at the château had yielded nothing, but this is the heart of the city. If there is anything to discover, here is where I'll find my answers."

He was serious. Constantin stared at him in consternation and then stared at the window again and the seeking black lines that constantly searched for a way in. He was right. This was madness, but for a whole different reason. He didn't believe he'd be able to talk him out of this scheme, but if he went along with it, he might get the baron to agree to some precautions.

"If you're going out in that, you're wearing this." Constantin went to his own table and held up a contraption of leather strips and buckles. He'd thought of it after they discussed the possibility of going out in the mists to test the filtering mask. They needed a backup plan for when this one went all to hell.

Parisee looked up from the equipment he was sorting. "What is that?"

"It's a harness since you're bent on this mad plan. You put it on like this." Constantin demonstrated with the buckles on the back. If the baron was snared by the mists, it would be harder for him to remove it. "We'll tie the rope to this and anchor it inside. I can observe from the safety of the other side of the room. If something goes wrong, I'll pull you back to safety."

"That's a sound plan." The baron's eyes gleamed with excitement and curiosity. "Help me put it on. Now is as good a time to test as any. As a matter of fact, it might be a good idea to collect samples every hour so we can have a wide range to work with."

"You are too excited about this," Constantin grumbled as he came forward. "Aren't you worried about the effects of the mists? What if the filtering mask doesn't work? What if there's some other way of being affected by it other than breathing in the vapors?"

"The thought had occurred to me, but even that might give us some answers. If I could understand what it is like, viscerally, it would help." He smiled at Constantin as if to reassure him, but his eyes still had an avid gleam that didn't ease his misgivings one bit. "I won't allow my curiosity to outweigh my caution. There is too much at stake. That's why I have you as a backup."

Constantin slipped the harness around Parisee, mulling that over. The man acted secure with the idea that he could count on Constantin, and they hadn't known each other long. "You trust me with your life, even knowing I was spying on you inside your dangerous fortress?"

Parisee glanced at him, his head cocked to the side for a long moment. Constantin even found that frank consideration appealing. Parisee looked at him like a man, like an equal. "I trust you're fully invested in getting rid of the magicman and to reach that end, you'll need me. Therefore, there's no one I'm safer with at the moment."

"That's a fair assessment," Constantin said with a wry smile. He finished buckling the back and attached a couple of strong, thin ropes.

"We'll anchor this inside and hope the mists don't seep too far in."

"We can light several of the braziers. The mists won't like such a dry environment. It'll be overly warm in here, but that should help." Parisee scraped a hand through his hair and settled the filtering mask over his head. It strapped tightly into place. He moved his head awkwardly, as if it felt unwieldy, and his breathing rasped.

"How does it feel? Can you see well enough?" Constantin asked. He crouched and lit the first brazier in the row they'd lined up for this eventuality.

Parisee slowly turned his head from side to side. "The lenses limit my field of vision."

"I was concerned about that," Constantin said and moved to light another. "I will work on the issue with the next prototype."

"Is everything set?" Parisee asked, pulling a pair of gloves on so his entire body was shrouded in some fashion.

Constantin checked the straps and ropes one last time. "You're ready. *Bonne chance.*" He anchored the ropes to a ring on the wall that he'd installed. Parisee made his way to the door, paused, then opened it and hovered in the doorway. His whole body was tense, and he didn't look back. Constantin retreated to the opposite end of the room to keep a careful watch.

"It's dense," Parisee said in a tinny voice. "I can't make out the railing to the outer stair only a few feet away." He stepped outside. The mist swirled around and enveloped him until a gray shroud covered him.

"Keep talking," Constantin called, desperate for some reassurance as the black threads reached out to Parisee with seeking fingers. "It's another way we can keep in communication with each other."

"It looks like an endless sea. It reminds me of the astral plane where I encounter my ancestors," Parisee replied. Constantin frowned in puzzlement at that strange statement. "The similarities are helping me regain my equilibrium."

"Ah, your ancestors?" Constantin couldn't even see the outline of Parisee now, but the rope moved rhythmically. The mists remained in the doorway and didn't venture in past the dry heat put forth by the braziers. That was reassuring. A good number of those threads abandoned the doorway altogether and converged on the baron's fading form. That was less reassuring. If something happened to the chevalier, they were all lost. Constantin took an anxious step away from the wall.

Next time, they'd tie bells to the harness as an additional precaution. He moved closer to the doorway and peered outside, hugging his arms to himself. The mists and swirls of gray moving in hypnotizing patterns blocked out all other sights. He forced his gaze away and paced the small room.

"They are quiet right now, but watching, always watching with a crazed curiosity. No wonder the entire lot of them went mad." The odd response floated out of the mists, and it made Constantin uneasy, but at least Parisee still communicated. "I am collecting samples from different areas."

Constantin listened to Parisee's rambling monologue with a growing unease as he conducted his research. He sounded off, as if he were arguing with himself again, but the tone was different. Constantin moved closer to the door, being careful not to get too close. "Talk louder. I can't hear you."

To ease his nerves, Constantin sent out one of his beetles, and it confirmed to him that Parisee was where he was supposed to be. He returned to the worktable and picked up a piece of glass. There had to be a way to make a construct he could use to spy through its eyes.

It would leave Constantin vulnerable, though. If he was tied up elsewhere, how would he know what was going on around him? He shook his head with a shudder. He wasn't about to leave himself vulnerable again.

"I can't breathe in this infernal thing," Parisee snarled. "*Non*, I'm not going in. I'm not done. It's like working in a dreamscape out here. I'd kill for a glimpse of the light. Do you hear that? It's beautiful."

Alarmed, Constantin hurried to the door. "Um, baron, it's time you come in. I'm sure you have enough samples." He stretched, fumbling for the end of the rope.

"This is pointless. I'm looking in the wrong direction. All the answers are in the mists. They always were. I'll find the song at the end of the mists," the baron said in a strident voice.

The rope went slack as if Parisee were returning. Relieved, Constantin tugged on it, drawing it inside to guide the chevalier to the door. "I've got you. Don't you worry." The rope went taut and then jerked wildly as if Parisee struggled against the lifeline. Constantin cursed under his breath and pulled harder, but the chevalier fought him with every step. Constantin was stronger. Foot by foot, he dragged him toward the door, trying to keep from tumbling past the invisible line himself.

"Come on, Parisee," Constantin shouted as he pulled the chevalier closer, hand over hand. He thought he spied a thrashing form in the undulating mists. "Fight the call, damn you, not me." The rope went slack and Constantin tumbled backward with a cry, striking his head against the wall. Frantically, he pulled the limp ropes until he spied their severed ends.

"Find him," he gasped, sending the beetle zinging out. He paused long enough to wrap a piece of cloth around his mouth and nose, took a deep breath and plunged into the mists after him. Holding his breath, he concentrated on the ping the beetle sent his senses. Constantin had to get to Parisee before the man reached the outer stairs. He couldn't hold his breath long enough to reach the ground and drag him back inside. He couldn't risk fighting him on the stairs either. They'd both fall to their deaths.

Black threads moved toward him and made his skin crawl, but they carried no sensation when they brushed against his skin. He glimpsed a figure and plunged ahead, the pinging beetle confirming it was Parisee. He grabbed the man's shoulder and spun him around.

Parisee stared at him with wide, unseeing eyes. He had taken the mask off. Constantin had a momentary impression of his slack features before he socked Parisee solidly on the jaw. The chevalier fell back stunned, and Constantin threw him over his shoulder.

"*Je suis désolé, mon ami.* It's got to be this way." He sent the beetle toward the door and grimly set his focus on that. One step at a time. His lungs screamed, black spots appeared before his eyes, and he wasn't sure he'd make it one more step when the outline to the door appeared. Constantin staggered inside with his burden, dumped Parisee on the floor, then slammed and locked the door behind him.

He slumped to the floor, drawing in deep, shuddering breaths as Parisee stirred. "The song. Must get to the song."

"Oh *non*, you don't, Parisee." Constantin drew in a welcome breath and reached for the rope. "You're staying put until I know you're sane."

Chapter Thirteen

"SEVERIN. SEVERIN!" THE urgent calling of Constantin's name reached through the layers of exhaustion and he stirred. "Constantin!"

Constantin jerked to full wakefulness and almost fell out of the chair he'd positioned near the chevalier's bed. Parisee half sat up amongst the rumpled covers and pillows, his struggle hampered by the bindings that attached his wrists to the headboards. He eyed the baron warily, taking in the clear gaze that no longer burned with a feverish light. Still, Parisee had proven himself to be wily and dangerous since Constantin had dragged him back here. The pleading to be let go into the music had been punctuated by violent arguments with people who Constantin could not see, but clearly Parisee could. He had considered sending for Janvier and the widow but thought Parisee wouldn't want them to see him in that state.

"Tell me, baron, who are you?" Constantin asked, coming to his bedside.

Parisee's eyes narrowed. For a moment, he fought the bonds at his hands and feet, and then he stilled. "I know who I am. An idiot chevalier who took one too many risks. How long have I been trying to get to the music?"

"Through the night and most of today," Constantin said gruffly, searching for the trick. Parisee had tried to reason with him a couple of times but could not hold back the rantings for long. He'd always had an uncanny gleam in his eyes that was gone now.

Parisee let his head drop back on the pillows as he considered that. "You saved my life, Constantin, if I may call you that? And potentially many more. There are not enough of us as it is to combat this menace."

"You may." There hadn't been many to whom Constantin had allowed that familiarity. But after their time together in the townhouse, after their harrowing encounter with the mists, it seemed rude not to grant that to a man who risked his life for no reward. He couldn't picture himself reciprocating though. The growing intimacy between them set him on edge. He did not want to be concerned about the man other than a means to an end.

"Now that has been settled. Would you mind letting me go?" Parisee didn't look at him as he asked, but he did tug at his bonds. "This is a trifle awkward."

Constantin hesitated, weighing whether this was a trick. Then he figured if Parisee was still under the spell, he'd try to break free the moment he was half untied. Constantin would have to bind him again, and this time he would send for reinforcements.

However, the chevalier didn't bolt when his wrists were freed. He sat up slowly, rubbing at the bruising on them. Constantin waited another wary moment longer and then sliced the rope binding Parisee's ankles. "I tried cushioning you as best I could," he said with a frown at the sign of more bruising there. "You wouldn't stop fighting."

Parisee ran a hand through his tangled, burnished curls. "The call was fierce. Even stronger than the call—" He broke off with a shake of his head.

He glanced up, and Constantin found himself caught by the naked emotion in his eyes before Parisee looked away again. "*Merci*, Constantin. I don't know if I can express it enough, but I can tend to those stitches. The itching must be driving you mad."

The slash on his cheek itched abominably. Constantin had been on the point of doing something about it himself, but was sure he'd cause himself more damage in the attempt. "Eat and drink something first. Then we will tend to each other. I want to make sure you didn't break your skin in your fight."

They didn't speak again as they went to the kitchen. Constantin got out the last of the provisions brought by Hadrien and set them on the table. The chevalier appeared troubled and withdrawn. It awoke a different itch in Constantin, one he hadn't allowed himself to feel in a long time. Desire was one thing. He could admit Parisee drew him that way. Desire was quick and fleeting. He didn't allow it to create bonds. Caring was different.

"Did you want to talk about it?" Constantin forced himself to ask as the silence continued throughout their meal and cleanup.

Parisee turned haunted eyes on him, and then he forced a smile. "Not yet. I need to ponder it more. And you should call me Michel-Leon. All of this Parisee, baron, chevalier, has me looking for my cursed father."

"Where are your supplies?" Constantin asked, rising to put distance between them. "I want to make sure you are well else the widow will slit my throat."

"She might not go that far, but she would thump your head. I'll get my bag if you will heat some water."

Constantin watched him go, to reassure himself he was retrieving his bag and not heading out the front door. Footfalls on the stairs eased him, and he swung the kettle over the small kitchen fire. He suspected the chevalier needed a few minutes to compose himself, as Constantin did.

Michel-Leon.

The name and his invitation evoked warm emotions, a connection he dared not accept.

The tread of boots pulled him from his thoughts, and Constantin retrieved a basin to put the hot water in.

"Your bindings did not break the skin," Parisee announced, setting the bag on the table. "And the bruising isn't so bad that it keeps me from wearing my boots. I would ask, however, that you keep this between us."

Constantin glanced up, but the chevalier wasn't looking at him. Instead, he busied himself by laying out what he would need on a cloth. "You mean the minor detail where you experimented on yourself, got caught in a trap, and—"

"*Oui, oui,*" Parisee interrupted him with a flap of his hand. "Régine and her entire family would have my head if they heard."

Her entire family. Not his. The phrasing intrigued him, and Constantin tucked it away to examine later as he poured the hot water into the basin. "My head would be right there with yours for allowing it, so our secret is safe."

"I suspect you're good with secrets." Parisee didn't say anything else as Constantin returned to the table with the basin and sat down. Constantin tied his hair back, and Parisee turned his head with gentle fingers, tilting it toward the light streaming in from the window. "It appears as if it healed well, though you've been picking at the stitches."

There was no reproof in his voice, only understanding. Constantin felt alive being so close to him, being touched by him as Parisee cleaned his cheek with a soft cloth. The hot water soothed the itching there, but it didn't help the deeper itch. "I am not yet ready to call you by name," Constantin said, surprising himself with the words and the meaning behind them: that one day he would be.

Their eyes met, and Parisee smiled. "Well then, until you are ready."

Constantin almost drew him down to kiss him, to break the tension between them. Physical yearning he could handle. Parisee's eyes darkened, and then he stepped back, breaking the spell. "This shouldn't hurt."

Constantin closed his eyes and tried to concentrate on anything but his nearness and scent, the pull and tug of the stitches being removed. It was near impossible, but he clung to the reminder that this made him a man, not a shadow. Then Parisee smoothed something soothing and pungent on his cheek. "That should do it," he whispered. "I'll be in my study for a few hours. I need to get my thoughts down over the incident before I forget."

Then he was gone before Constantin could gather his wits and thank him.

*

THE OPEN WINDOW brought in a warm breeze that dug under Constantin's skin and made him want to tear down the four walls surrounding him. Ever since he'd been kicked out on the streets, he had not spent significant time indoors. It was a beautiful summer day, not a cloud in sight, and he was stuck inside with a cantankerous chevalier who was far more interested in his chemical experiments than he was in engaging in conversation or eating, for that matter, if Constantin didn't push the issue.

Constantin glanced at the table where Parisee was once again bent over a microscope, muttering to himself as he studied and took notes. He could not take another afternoon of this. Even tinkering with his projects and the failed filtering mask wasn't enough to divert his interest.

It didn't help that Parisee constantly drew his gaze—from the way the sunlight picked out the red and gold highlights in his curls, or how his eyes lit up with excitement when he noticed something new in his experiments.

He was a chevalier and a noble, while Constantin was a vagabond. Besides, the man was on the edge of crazy, if not over the cliff. He had spent restless, agonizing hours keeping watch over the man as he'd ranted and raved about going into the music and argued with unknown tormentors. His sudden snap back to sanity had been as unsettling. He'd questioned Constantin relentlessly both about the incident and if there had been any contact with Nightingale. Afterward, he holed himself up in his study for hours. Today hadn't been much different.

"I'm going out," Constantin announced, setting down the mask.

Parisee waved a hand in vague acknowledgment, and then his head jerked up. "Wait. What?"

Constantin gestured to the sunlight streaming in through the windows. "I'm going out, talk to some of my contacts, investigate how many people went missing in the last unscheduled mess."

"You can't go out." Parisee glanced at Constantin's neatly arrayed worktable that contrasted with his own chaotic space. "You haven't finished working on the filtering mask. The mists could come back any day, and at this point we have no way of knowing when."

Constantin shot Parisee an exasperated look. "How can I fix something when I don't know what went wrong? I need to think the problem through, and I can't think anymore right here. I need space." He'd untied Parisee from the bed just yesterday, and the man still wasn't quite all there. The muttering had gotten worse and was constant.

"It appeared to be working fine. It crept up on me unawares." Parisee shoved a hand through his hair and glared at the mask, not quite meeting Constantin's eyes. "I can't rule out the mists affected me through skin contact either. I tried keeping myself covered, but what if some vapor slipped through?"

"I'm not sure it came through skin contact because I would've been affected too." Constantin picked up the mask and examined it. At least he had the man talking and maybe he could keep the flow of conversation going if he worked on the mask as Parisee requested so churlishly. This was better than the interrogation. At least he was talking to him and not some unseen phantom.

"But we don't even know why some are affected and not others!" Frustration screamed in his voice.

"Have you discovered any elements in your experiments?" Constantin asked before Parisee could go off on one of his agitated rants.

Parisee frowned fiercely at his array of beakers. "There are unusual properties in the water. I need more time though and to get more samples when the fog comes back. I need that mask fixed."

"Well, I need a break to clear my thoughts." Constantin set the mask back down again. "I'll be back in a couple of hours."

"Constantin, be serious. The magicman is still out there. You've sensed it sniffing around more than once. It's not safe for you to go out alone." Parisee's brows drew together in worry. "I suppose an hour away from here couldn't hurt either of us. I could go with you."

Constantin couldn't miss the expression of longing the chevalier cast toward his equipment. It would be hard to resist if the man ever looked at a lover that way. "I've been on my own, protecting myself since I was a boy. I'm not worried about Nightingale." Well, not too worried anyway. He'd stick to crowds and hide in the shadows the moment he sensed the bastard.

For the first time all day, Parisee let their eyes meet, and Constantin felt a spark of heat. Constantin knew men who had denied their desires to the public but revealed their true natures behind closed doors. Not this man. He gave his scientific equipment more attention than Constantin. It was backward from all the experience that Constantin had of men in power.

"You should be." Parisee brushed his scarred cheek with gentle fingers.

Constantin caught his hand. He greatly desired to say something that would cut this tension between them, but the words caught before he could form them. His name was almost on Constantin's lips. He didn't know what to say to a man like the chevalier. Their worlds were so different, and Constantin suspected anything he had to say wouldn't be welcome. To reinforce that belief, Parisee pulled away as if burned.

"I'll be back," Constantin announced, and this time Parisee did not try to stop him.

Constantin was not in the habit of conversing with many nobles, but he'd observed enough while skulking through their homes, hunting down mysteries. It galled him he needed one's help. But Parisee was different. It was his own problem that those differences crept under his skin. He shouldn't allow one man to have such a hold on his interest.

Constantin headed out on foot into the sunshine. Its warmth gleamed on his face, chasing away the shadows haunting him. He considered checking in on Gabrielle's friends at the orphanage before he discarded the plan. True, Nightingale hadn't been able to sense him when he'd twisted the shadows around himself. However, he didn't want to rely on that fragile shield or use it so much that Nightingale found a chink in the armor and exploited it.

It felt too much like a betrayal of the other children trapped by the monster. He had to find a way to lure Nightingale out. It wasn't enough knowing they were laying a trap for it at the château. It made no sense that the magicman hadn't confronted them by now. It had to know they were in Paris. They flaunted it in its face before the baron's brush with the mists. Maybe prancing around in the streets alone would draw it out.

Despite the sunshine, there were few pedestrians on the bridge to the *Rive Gauche*. Most people wanted to remain close to home these days. As he walked by the work gangs clearing out the debris of torn-down buildings, he heard his name hailed.

He glanced around, his eyes narrowing as his shoulders tensed. There was no sign of Nightingale lurking. Of course, it wouldn't announce itself first. Still, Constantin couldn't rid himself of the uncomfortable sensation between his shoulders.

"Monsieur Severin!" Foreman Lyon called his name again and waved.

Constantin debated for a moment. He'd be an excellent source of information if he wasn't too irritated about Constantin's disappearance. He waved back and headed in the man's direction. "Where've you been?" the man demanded, his hands on his hips. He gestured toward the workingmen. "You've been missing for weeks. I thought the mists got you."

"*Non.*" Constantin shrugged. "I got caught up searching for some children who went missing. Hooked up with the chevalier that's in town investigating. I should've told you after everything you tried to do for me, but it has been chaotic."

Monsieur Lyon studied him with an assessing gaze. "Working with the chevalier appears to be treating you fine. Can he do anything about it? Their reputation isn't what it once was, but I can't think of anyone else who could tackle it." He paused and spit at the ground. "The emperor has left on his tour, and the *police nationale* aren't even taking names of the missing anymore."

Constantin rubbed his chin, relaxing as the man didn't take offense at his disappearance. They could use more eyes and ears in the city. "The baron is certainly dedicated to his calling. He's working himself to the bone to find the cause. Have you had a lot more problems with people going missing?"

"Every time the mists roll through." The man grunted. "Mostly newcomers. The old hands know to take cover. There's always new people in the city. We have a fresh problem now that's causing more issues."

Intrigued, Constantin turned his full attention to him. "A recent problem? Specific to you or more widespread?" He thought of Nightingale with a grimace. "Isn't there enough going on?"

"You'd think." The man gestured to the worksite. "After every mist, we discover stolen materials, parts, supplies. I tried posting guards, but they either go missing themselves or complain about strange monsters roaming the mists. Is it related? At first I thought it was competitors taking advantage. But that's foolhardy to risk, especially since the broadside warnings are no longer accurate. I wouldn't usually hold credence with tales of monsters, but I'm about ready to believe anything."

"Strange monsters?" Constantin thought back on his desperate foray into the mists to search for Parisee. He hadn't been in them long, and he'd focused on locating Parisee. He hadn't noticed anything odd, but if Nightingale could roam through the fog to hunt, why not other monsters? "Does the monster look tall and lean, like a gentleman of means?"

The foreman shot him a look of disbelief. "That doesn't sound monstrous. *Non,* these things have overlarge eyes and a strange mouth that hisses. Or so they say. Personally, I think they're letting their fears get the best of them."

Parisee would want to know about this development. "Have you always had an issue with items going missing?"

"There's always some on any site, but not like this. In the last several weeks, it's gotten noticeably worse." The man scrubbed a hand through his hair. "How am I going to get these jobs finished?"

"Are you the only site that's plagued?" Constantin asked.

"Everyone is. Even people who scoffed at our other woes have been making complaints. I have no idea what anyone would need all this stuff for or what they're building. I'd notice if an unauthorized construction project was going on. I'd know if Haussmann had started something new." Foreman Lyon threw up his hands. "It doesn't make any sense."

Constantin eyed the site with an assessing gaze. "Wood, metal? Building parts or machine parts?"

"I'm more familiar with the tearing down and erecting buildings. I've never been much for machine work. Don't have the talent for it, not like you." Lyon's shoulders slumped. "If I were to hazard a guess, I'd say you had enough materials for a scaffolding. The rest is more suited for machinery than buildings, but it's hard to say for sure without knowing what else was taken from others."

"Interesting." Constantin exchanged a sober glance with the foreman. "I'll let the baron know. He might want to talk to you and your men."

Some of the stress faded from the foreman's eyes. "I'd appreciate it. If I hear anything new, should I send word?"

Constantin weighed the options. He wasn't sure of the baron's plans, and there was always someone at the château who would know their whereabouts. He was anxious to get back and check on Gabrielle. "*Oui*, send it to the *Château des Ombres* kitchen door. If I hear of anything, I'll let you know."

Constantin headed away, mulling the news over. There had to be a way to move around in the mists. If others could do it, then they could as well. They needed to figure out the how. He glanced back at the worksite, or the why. Parisee would be intrigued, and Constantin had better figure out what went wrong with the filtering mask before the man chose to do another one of his self-experiments.

*

MICHEL-LEON STRAIGHTENED as Constantin's familiar footsteps approached, and a frisson of awareness swept through him. They'd only been in this close environment for a week, but a week was enough. The townhouse was too small. The intimacy of the space was getting to him. Michel-Leon wasn't used to sharing space with anyone other than Janvier, certainly with no one as beautiful as Constantin.

Even his birth name was beautiful, and Michel-Leon had to remember not to address him so familiarly. It appeared to make him uncomfortable, and he never returned the gesture.

Besides, beauty he could ignore. What got under his defenses was the curiosity of Constantin's mind. The way he searched for answers like Michel-Leon did and wasn't satisfied until the answers made sense. His commitment to ridding the world of monsters was equal to Michel-Leon's. Though understandably, his determination was more focused.

"The watcher returns."

"You think I don't know that?" Michel-Leon snapped.

"Who are you talking to?" Constantin asked, and Michel-Leon winced as Janvier's warning came back to him. "Something warned you when I was spying on you that evening. Is that who you're talking to?"

Maybe Constantin would understand, wouldn't believe he was crazy. Most people assumed he was. Janvier assured him he was not. Some days Michel-Leon didn't know. Michel-Leon turned to face his curious gaze. The walk had done Constantin good. He appeared less worn, and there was color to his cheeks.

"It's like ancestral memory. The fragments of all the other chevaliers who have passed on, their knowledge and experience as voices in my mind. Only those born of chevaliers can hear it." The whispering agitated again with Michel-Leon's announcement. So what if Constantin knew their secret? The voices would die with Michel-Leon. "And sometimes they never shut up. Like now."

"What is that like?" Constantin asked, his brow furrowing. "It must be maddening. How aware are they of what goes on? Do you have any privacy?"

"It has its moments. I've learned to block out most of it for some peace." Michel-Leon met his gaze, reassured by Constantin's reaction. "It doesn't feel intrusive. Maybe it's because they are the spirits of my ancestors and I've known them since I was a boy. I never felt spied upon until you came into my laboratory. You intrigue them. They don't know what to make of you, but they don't believe you are dangerous to me at the moment."

"*Merci,* for your trust. It couldn't have been easy to tell me." Constantin stared over Michel-Leon's shoulder a moment before focusing on him again. "I owe you an exchange of trust."

Michel-Leon glanced at his experiments. He'd reached a wall. As Constantin suggested, time away might clear his mind. He could pick it back up again when they reached the château. It wouldn't hurt to leave a sheet of stretched canvas on the townhouse balcony and a trough underneath to collect the water that beaded up during the mists. He'd run a new set of experiments after the next cycle. "Why don't we talk about it over a glass of wine? I could use one while our belongings are packed."

"Pack?" A startled look crossed Constantin's face. "Why are we packing?"

Michel-Leon led the way to the small study and poured them both a glass of wine. "Janvier sent word with Hadrien and his daughter about the progress he made resetting the traps at the château. We need to get back to prepare our trap. They are gathering our things."

He handed Constantin a glass, took a seat, and held the glass up to the sunlight streaming in through the window to admire the deep burgundy color. It kept his gaze off Constantin. "You reminded me of how exposed we are here. I suspect the magicman is holding off because it's uncertain of both my involvement and how you escaped it. I suspect that caution won't last for much longer. If it attacked us here, the outcome wouldn't be sure, and I like to be sure when it comes to such things. We may have one chance."

"I don't know if this will be any help, but I'm prepared to tell you some of my secrets." Constantin took a sip of his wine and looked uneasy. "I've never told them to anyone. Not even my brothers. However, I think you might need some context for it, because I suspect my past plays a large part in how I learned the trick." He paused and gave Michel-Leon a penetrating look. "Why did you tell me about the voices you hear?"

"In part because I have the bad habit of talking to them aloud. I didn't want you frightened or to question my sanity. We're going to need to trust each other." Michel-Leon raised his glass toward Constantin. "Mostly, though, because you came into the mists after me at grave risk to yourself. You're not a man to be taken lightly, *merci*."

"I'd say I ran out there because you were my only hope. But that would be a lie." Their eyes met, and Constantin's gaze held him captive. "I went out there for you." He clinked his glass to Michel-Leon's and drank deeper.

Discomfited, Michel-Leon tore his gaze away and concentrated on the wine. He told himself it was a step closer. Constantin may keep him at a comfortable distance, but this was a sign he cared. "So you were about to tell me one of your secrets?"

"*Oui.* You know, I was one of Nightingale's victims. When my mother and sister passed away with a fever, my father couldn't face raising three young boys alone, so he gave us to Nightingale. I did what I could to shield my brothers. They didn't sense what I sensed, but even then, living there in the orphanage was absolute hell for them too."

Conflicting emotions played across Constantin's face. Dredging up the memories couldn't be easy. He had to be one of the bravest people Michel-Leon had ever met.

"The only thing that made it bearable was another young man there. His name was Blaise. We became close friends. Eventually, we became more. I fell in love with him." Constantin grimaced. "Our bond affected the link with Nightingale. It was enraged. I thought it would kill me. Instead, it left me out on the streets. Said it would be crueler. I have no idea why it still could use Blaise, but not me."

"I suspect your feelings for Blaise pushed you from childhood to adulthood for the magicman's purposes. It's a creature that feeds off the souls, off the emotions of children. Falling in love versus infatuation crosses a line you can't retreat from," Michel-Leon broke in quietly. "Blaise must not have had the same depth of emotion, which is why he remained."

"*Oui.*" Constantin sighed heavily. "I gathered as much when I tried to convince him to run off with me. He refused to even consider the notion. However, I convinced my brothers."

Michel-Leon smiled. "So you've stolen from the monster before. How it must hate you."

"That idea pleases me, though at the time I was heartbroken and terrified. Being in its hell was bad enough, but it was a devil I knew. On the streets was a different story, especially when I had my brothers to support. I got them apprenticeships. They were rather angry with me, but their anger cooled when they found themselves in situations to their liking. I would've preferred to keep us all together, but it wasn't possible."

"Why didn't you seek an apprenticeship of your own? You are intelligent and clever with your hands."

Constantin grimaced and finished his wine. "I didn't want to give anyone authority over me again or be stuck in one place. I wanted the freedom to disappear if I could. So I took the unknown dangers of the streets instead."

Michel-Leon couldn't imagine Constantin as a young, beautiful boy on his own. Every lecher and user would've considered him prey. "How did you survive?"

"By learning to do this." Constantin held up his hand and concentrated on it. The surrounding light twisted, warping the eye for a moment, and then his hand disappeared. "I wrap myself in shadows, which also has the effect of Nightingale being unable to sense me with its mind."

"That is a neat trick." Michel-Leon reached out and touched Constantin's hand. He could still feel it and at the brush of his fingers, the illusion shattered. "I suspect it's because of the fey in you."

Constantin caught his hand, their fingers clasping, and Michel-Leon's heart leapt before he pulled back. "There is some link between the fey kissed and the magicmen, but the answer eludes me at the moment." The comment was enough to get the ancestors to whisper again, but not enough for them to give him anything useful.

Constantin grimaced and shrugged one shoulder. "It wouldn't surprise me if we were their preferred prey. I came across something interesting while I was out. Someone is taking advantage of the mists to steal from worksites. Considerable tools and materials have gone missing in the last few weeks."

"Looters probably," Michel-Leon said with a dismissive wave. "Though they do so at grave risk to themselves."

"I'm not so sure. Have you ever been outside when the mists arrive?" At Michel-Leon's shake of his head, Constantin continued. He didn't think seeing it happen from afar counted. "It comes at you in a rolling wave. It doesn't move like any mist I've ever seen. The streets empty fast so someone might be tempted to try, but they wouldn't be able to raid anything quickly enough to not get caught. The mists clear up almost as fast as they arrive, unless there's natural fog mixed in. Then it might linger for a time, though no one risks going out. The people I talked with also mentioned strange creatures in the mists. If a magicman could move about, why not others?"

That was intriguing and something Michel-Leon would have to consider. He appreciated Constantin's mind. The man had a way of raising questions that made Michel-Leon give deeper consideration into aspects he hadn't before.

"We'll talk about this more on our way back to the château. Meanwhile, I'm going to attempt to contact Napoleon again. The court is at *Saint-Cloud* or is it *Fontainebleau* now? Perhaps Lennox wasn't invited, and I'll get through to the emperor." Michel-Leon grimaced at the wishful thought. "While we hunt down the reason for the mists, we still have a trap to set for a monster. We should get on with that."

"Parisee, *s'il vous plaît*, tell me, what was it like." Constantin's eyes caught his. "When you were out in it and snared. I know you've been reluctant to talk about it, but the more we know, the better the chance we have at combating it. Isn't that what you often say?"

Michel-Leon could not ignore the appeal in Constantin's eyes, nor his wisdom. He drank some more wine as he gathered his thoughts. "It was…alluring. Only that's not strong enough. It's like if you took everything that drew you, the scent of a loved one, or the aroma of a hot meal after a long hard day, the glimpse of the sun after a week of rain. It wraps around your soul and fills you with longing until you have to follow and go to the music."

As if his words cast a spell, both of them remained hushed. Then Constantin reached over and covered Michel-Leon's hand with his own. "That wasn't real, Michel-Leon. Here is."

Michel-Leon stared down at their hands, his throat tight, and then the spell broke at a light knock on the door. Constantin pulled away, though the warmth of his touch remained. "Come in," Michel-Leon ordered in a gruff voice.

Mahout came in and scanned the room as if searching for anything else that needed tending to. "Papa is almost done with your lab. I have your trunk packed and am getting ready to start on Monsieur Severin's things, as little as they are. We will leave before the hour is up."

"I'll take care of that." Constantin jumped up, but before he left, he turned to look at Michel-Leon. "This is real. Hold on to this life."

Michel-Leon pondered Constantin's words. As much as the call to the music still sang its siren song within him, there was another song in his life which drew him, and it was Constantin himself. Answering the first call would likely have led to his death, but he had no idea where the second would lead him.

The door to his study crashed open, and Michel-Leon jumped, spilling the rest of his wine on his shirt. Régine came through, her eyes alight with excitement as she hauled an older man behind her, a villager from the appearance of his clothes. "Michie! We may have a location."

"Where?" Michel-Leon demanded, leaping to his feet. As he came around the desk, the man with Régine bowed low.

"My boys, my lord, *s'il vous plaît*—"

"Bother that," Michel-Leon snapped, hauling him straight again. "We don't have time for that nonsense. Where?"

"Here," Régine said, spreading her map on his desk. Her finger stabbed at a location southeast of Paris, not too far from the Seine. "His boys described a creature that matches ours. Huge, they said, and it blended into the shadows. It appeared to have had many limbs."

"I… I didn't believe them," the man said, his voice agonized. "I punished them for telling tales. They snuck out that night to search for the creature. I… I haven't seen them since. *S'il vous plaît*, my lord. Help me find them."

Michel-Leon closed his eyes, his heart twisting. The boys had been missing for far too many weeks. If they were lucky, they had died quickly. "Are there caves near your home? Caves your boys could've searched?"

"What is going on?" Constantin asked, coming to the door. "Do we have a lead?"

Michel-Leon ignored him, focusing his gaze on the stricken villager who nodded, wringing his cap between his hands. "There are, my lord, extensive ones. They aren't supposed to go in there. They aren't always stable, but we have caught them there before."

This time Michel-Leon looked at Constantin. Finally, finally, they had a direction. "We have a lead. Have Hadrien bring the carriage around. We'll go immediately. He can retrieve our things later."

Chapter Fourteen

CONSTANTIN LIFTED HIS torch higher as he peered into the gloomy entrance of the brush-shrouded cave. "Is this big enough to hold your creature?" he asked dubiously.

"The man assured me it opens up farther in, and there are several enormous caverns. Big enough for our mother," Régine replied, ducking to go ahead of him. Over her shoulder were coils of rope. They all lugged climbing and digging equipment.

"Shouldn't we have a plan?" Constantin appealed to Michel-Leon as the infuriating man followed his maddening sister. They were both reckless in their need for answers, and he could only pray for more caution. "What do your ancestors say about this venture?"

Michel-Leon glanced at him, his eyes bright with intensity. "They are yelling so loud I had to block them. I need to think and not be driven mad with them trying to talk over one another." He paused and laid a reassuring hand on Constantin's arm.

"I want a quick look to observe what we're dealing with. I won't make the same arrogant mistake those at Metz did. We will be cautious. If we run into any sign of mists, we will retreat immediately. We're going to need to work on that filtering mask. We need—" He broke off with a sigh. "We have so much to do."

Some of Constantin's worry eased. "We'll get to the work we need to do. I want to be sure some thought went into this."

"I have been thinking about nothing but plans since I started on this venture. There's no lack of plans. I lack information." Michel-Leon gestured toward the cave opening. "I'm hoping this will give me some."

Constantin had to be content with that. He stepped back to let Michel-Leon pass. "Lead on, chevalier."

He ducked and followed Michel-Leon in. The narrow tunnel sloped and twisted down, though the ceiling raised once they cleared the entrance. Régine wasn't too far ahead. She was hammering rings into the rock wall and threading a rope through the rings.

Constantin and Michel-Leon moved with care, the footing uncertain in the light of the flickering torch. "Do you have any idea of what we're searching for?" Constantin asked in a tense whisper that hissed around the corners.

"A sign the creature came through here or signs of a nest. I'd also like a clue that would lead us to the fate of those two boys." Michel-Leon studied everything, the walls of their serpentine tunnel, the floors, and the ceiling before moving on to follow Régine's progress.

Constantin tried to picture what he was seeing, but it looked like a cave tunnel to him. On occasion, Michel-Leon paused, his head cocked, and Constantin wondered if he risked trying to open the channel to his ancestors. It seemed like such a part of him as Constantin's abilities were. It was like that of another sense, as innate as hearing or smelling.

The tunnel snaked again and opened into a low hanging, wide cavern. Constantin swung the torch and saw Michel-Leon's expression mirror his disappointment and frustration. Régine stood next to the far corner where a rockfall had rained down a jumbled pile of striated rocks.

"This is the sole exit out from this chamber," Régine said when they caught up.

"Another dead end," Constantin said under his breath. There was no way of telling how complete the collapse was. The walls and ceiling of the cavern were craggy, rough-hewn and appeared solid. They could probably clear the rocks away quickly, with enough volunteers to assist.

"Time is running out on us." Michel-Leon jammed his torch into a crevice, his expression set. Somewhere in the distance water dripped. One tributary had to be close. Constantin could smell the damp in the air of fresh water and underneath it the cloying odor of old death and rot. It had to be his imagination. The boys had been gone long enough that no smell should linger.

"We'll need help," Constantin said as Michel-Leon clambered on top of the fall and got to work. He took the rock Michel-Leon handed him and carried it off to another corner, out of the way. As he turned back, he met Régine hauling her own burden.

"Let him release some of his frustration and energy this way," she whispered. "Then we'll talk to the locals for assistance."

"What about the trap for Nightingale?" Constantin asked, his stomach sinking.

"He won't forget about that," Régine assured him. "It's another piece of the puzzle and another monster to end. The magicman is un-likely to accost us during the day. It will wait for night or during one of the dark hours when the mists shroud the streets. We'll set up shifts and cover both avenues of attack."

Régine had her own steady wisdom Constantin hadn't appreci-ated before. The division of Michel-Leon's attention concerned him, but he understood it. The mists claimed children too. Constantin hadn't considered it in that light before, but now he had two new names that haunted his mind. Henri and Phillipe, two boys who had gone hunting a wonder and never returned.

*

MICHEL-LEON SAT down in the comfortable chair of his study, every muscle aching. He longed for a hot bath and knew he'd have to make do with a basin of tepid water instead. The work in the cavern was proceeding with agonizing slowness, but it was proceeding. At least there was an end in sight for their work on the traps of the château. He glanced at the telegram in his hand and prayed it also would lead him in a direction.

> **Magicmen are corrupted fey kissed. STOP. Fey kissed have the ability to heal souls. STOP. Magicmen consume them. STOP. Sending my notes and a book in the post. STOP.**

Michel-Leon pursed his lips as he reread the message. That explained a few things, like how Constantin and Gabrielle could sense Nightingale feeding, but it left so many other questions. Questions his research hadn't been able to answer. He folded the telegram and stuck it in his journal on his cluttered desk, then closed his eyes.

"How do the fey kissed become corrupted?" Michel-Leon cast the question out and the rustling whispers rose up like a stiff wind among dry and rattling leaves.

"By feeding off souls instead of healing. Ask the watcher. He started down that path when he confronted the soul stealer."

An icy chill brushed Michel-Leon. *"Is there a way to reverse the path?"*

He waited in trepidation as they murmured. A hand on his arm jerked him out of his light trance. He looked up into the curious eyes of Constantin and felt another pang. No, he couldn't allow that to happen to him. Constantin would kill himself before he became what he hated, but Michel-Leon needed more answers. There had to be a way to stop it.

"You need something?" Michel-Leon asked, striving to keep his tone light.

"You wanted to know when the workmen finished. They just left." Constantin gestured at the château's walls. "Janvier is leading them out safely."

"Excellent." Michel-Leon rummaged around his desk and came up with his list of safe passages and traps. "I should make you a copy of this. In case I make a misstep. I'm sending Janvier back home with all the village children and whoever wants to escape the mists. At least I'll be able to save some people."

"I question your self-preservation instincts. You don't know me that well." Constantin gave him a wry smile. "Are you sure you want to give me all your secrets?"

"Nonsense. The ancestors would've warned me if you are dangerous to me." Michel-Leon studied the list and tried not to dwell on the warnings he had received. Constantin would not fall prey to the corruption. He needed to know how it happened so he could give Constantin the right words of caution. He suspected Constantin would have a terrible reaction to news he had been corrupted and was in danger of becoming like the magicman. Until he had a better idea of what Constantin would do then, he'd remain silent. "I say we check the traps and make sure they're set from the heart of the château then outward. I don't want to have to dodge them twice."

"Have those voices ever been wrong?" Constantin asked with a lifted brow.

"Vague? *Oui.* Wrong? *Non.* The trick is asking the right question. The wrong one will send a flood of information or warnings that do not apply to the situation at hand."

Michel-Leon remembered the telegram and retrieved a book of spells from the bookcase. Magic didn't give him the same satisfaction as science, but against certain creatures, it was much more effective. If the magicmen truly had fey blood, then there would be something in there they could use. He had to be careful that Constantin didn't get caught in the same trap, especially if he had already taken the first steps down the path toward being a magicman. There had to be a way to reverse it, and he would find it. He needed to know more so they could take the proper precautions.

"Tell me again what happened when you encountered Nightingale in your quarters."

Michel-Leon listened intently as Constantin relayed the tale. They'd gone over it, moment by moment, several times already. Constantin's confusion over what had occurred in his room appeared genuine. Still, Michel-Leon sensed he was holding something back, either because he didn't understand what happened himself or because Michel-Leon hadn't completely won his trust yet. He needed to be careful here until he knew more. Give Constantin a warning, but not say something that may push him on the wrong side.

"Come with me."

Constantin followed him, peppering him with questions as Michel-Leon led him up another flight in his hidden staircase and down a long unused corridor. "Beware the plain tiles, *s'il vous plaît*. I don't want to run the risk these traps remain intact. We'll check as we leave."

"I don't understand. You said mortal weapons won't hurt it." Constantin gingerly stepped around the tiles, giving them a wary look. "What is the point of traps that endanger us but won't hurt it? How do you plan on luring it, holding it?"

"With this." Michel-Leon waved the book in his hand. "And with your unusual abilities. The traps won't harm it seriously, but they will cause it to expel energy to protect itself. They will enrage it and distract it from our true purpose."

Michel-Leon opened the double doors to a once grand ballroom. Cracked and faded tiles covered the floor. Cobwebs and dust draped every surface and coated the chandelier under decades of neglect. The ceiling soared up two stories to the rooftop and a balustrade circled it a level above where musicians once played to the dancers below. They could use the balcony to observe the creature.

"Interestingly enough, the magicmen are also fey kissed, which is why you and Gabrielle can sense it." Michel-Leon cast a sideways glance at Constantin to judge how he took the revelation. He frowned fiercely but did not appear deeply upset. Good. Michel-Leon did not want to distress him, even if the man's very presence caused no end of disquiet to himself. He drew Michel-Leon to him. There was no other way to describe it.

"Interesting. Disturbing." Constantin clasped his hands behind his back as he examined the room. He had pulled his golden hair into a tail, revealing his elegant profile. "Though I don't wish to share anything with that monster, it explains how Gabrielle and I sensed its feeding when the others didn't. If I could physically cut out our connection from my own body, I would, even if it cost me my life."

Constantin's words alarmed Michel-Leon. The magicman had tormented Constantin in ways that left deep scars on his psyche. He could easily picture Constantin harming himself out of desperation. Michel-Leon needed to know more. He had to find a way to fix this before he told Constantin so he'd have the problem and a solution at once. There had to be a way.

"Does this tie into your plan to get rid of the monster?" Constantin asked, cutting into his worried thoughts. "Is there a way to weaponize it?"

"There are spells that contain fey. Since it relies on the magic in its blood to exist, it'll be vulnerable to them. We trap it far away from any hint of a child and let it starve. As it starves, it'll weaken, then mortal weapons will harm it."

"That is a suitably terrible fate for it." Constantin walked about in a slow circle under the balustrade. "Where do I come in?"

"You said the glamour you used made it possible for you to hide Gabrielle and your presence from him." Michel-Leon looked up from where he perused the book. There were many types of magic. The spells in the book and those inlaid in the stones of the château required precise incantations and certain elements. The results weren't always consistent. Then there was blood magic, which no one with any sense utilized. The price was too terrible. There was also the soul magic of the fey kissed that went beyond the glamours of the fey. It was apparent there were two sides of an edged sword there as well.

"I have a twofold question for you." Michel-Leon said. "One, can you hide the presence of iron, and two, can you project the essence of yourself and Gabrielle into this room? The feel of your minds and emotional beings? I don't want to use her as bait."

"We will not use her as bait." Constantin's tone left no room for an argument. It was a strange time to be amused by it, but Michel-Leon hid a smile. Constantin was a refreshing change from the others of his class. Régine treated him like a brother, and Michel-Leon wouldn't have it any other way. Janvier spoke to Michel-Leon as he pleased, though he was painstaking about doing it only when they were alone. Constantin ignored all niceties altogether, and on the occasions when he remembered, his responses were perfunctory.

"I agree." Michel-Leon went back to flipping through the book until he found the spell he wanted. If they reinforced it with iron, the magicman would deplete itself, fighting to escape. In the meantime, Michel-Leon would work on a backup scenario or three. The last thing he wanted was a vengeful monster on the loose. "In fact, she is going with Janvier and the others, so if you want to say goodbye, I'd do it today."

Constantin nodded, though his eyes were dismayed. "I think I can do what you request, but I would need to spend some time with her. Is Régine still with her in her rooms?"

"It is the safest place. I'm counting on her attracting the magicman's attention when we parade her and all the other children from the village through the streets on the way to the train station. If you project she's still with us when we return without her, I believe the magicman won't be able to resist coming after her. What about masking the iron?" That would be the tricky part. Constantin would be using his fey abilities on materials that were an anathema to fey.

"I can't say without practice. I've never attempted it on a nonliving thing." Constantin appeared more intrigued than daunted. "I'll also work on that and have an update for you tonight. Do you need me to help with the traps?"

"*Non*, what you're doing is more important." Michel-Leon closed the book. "I'll walk you to Gabrielle's rooms."

"No need." Constantin tapped his temple. "I have an excellent memory for dangerous things. I kept a close eye on everything you did."

"If you're sure." Michel-Leon watched Constantin go and the way he neatly sidestepped the traps. Janvier had the same knack. Michel-Leon was the only one in danger of being killed by his own house. He shook his head and went back to studying the spell. They may not have much time, and he wanted everything in place.

As if summoned by his thoughts, Janvier appeared in the double doors. "I wanted to see this room of yours to check if my memory is correct. The doors are solid enough. I don't care how strong the creature is. It would take a considerable amount of effort and time to break them down and the hinges are on the wrong side. Do you think it would be able to jump and climb up to the balcony? What if it discovers the secret entrance there?"

Michel-Leon shook his head even as he eyed the possibility. "It's too high, I believe, but even if it could, all the doors are reinforced and I will trap each one. I also plan on sealing it within a circle at the center of the room if I can." He pointed toward an unusual pattern on the ballroom floor. "Fey ward. If I find the right spell to activate it the creature won't be able to leave that space. The trick will be getting it to cross the line. I'm having Severin figure that part out."

Janvier regarded him for a long moment and entered the room, shutting the doors behind him. "May I speak frankly?"

Michel-Leon grinned at him. "I have never known you to resist. Why start now?"

Michel-Leon's teasing had no effect on Janvier's grave expression. "I have worried about you since the moment you first drew breath. Over the years, my concerns varied, but lately I've been struck with an increased anxiety you will live out your life alone and deny yourself the chance for love. My Marcelle, rest her soul, was my truest friend and ally until her passing."

Michel-Leon gave Janvier a regretful look. "Then I am doomed to disappoint you yet again, *mon ami*. You know the vow I've taken. I'll not pass this curse along to any child of mine."

"There need be no children. Michel-Leon, I am aware of your attraction to Monsieur Severin. Just as I was aware of your dalliance with Lennox, though I never breathed a word to anyone. If Severin returns the feelings, act on them. My impression of him is that he's loyal, and he cares deeper than he's willing to admit. About a great many things."

Michel-Leon's cheeks heated to an uncomfortable degree. "I do not know what you are talking about," he said stiffly.

"I am not your father," Janvier replied gently. "I don't care that he's a vagabond with no home. Nor do I care that you both are men. I've witnessed you engage in conversations with him for hours, and it's not always about the problems you both face. I care that you both share an interest in things outside of hunting monsters. You can work side by side with him in your lab and you both are content. He's a man who would plunge into known danger to rescue you and call you out for risking yourself later. You need that. As I believe he needs someone who gives him a sense of home, a reason to return. You can do that for him. So don't dismiss the idea."

"I have Régine for companionship." Michel-Leon wanted to look anywhere but at Janvier's expression. He hadn't grasped his old friend saw so much. "She gives me all the balance I need."

"Michel-Leon, you can fool yourself, but not me," Janvier's firm tone made him wince. "Régine is a wonderful woman, fearless and intelligent and determined to go her own way. But she is as obsessed as you with her monster hunting. You love each other as siblings. Monsieur Severin is different. Dwell on that while I am away. Humor an old man."

Michel-Leon laid his hand on Janvier's bony shoulder. "I'll miss you and your frank talk. You are more a father to me than he ever was."

Janvier smiled at him, a rare smile that lit up his wintery eyes. "I'll miss you as well, rapscallion. But I'll rest easier, knowing both Régine and Monsieur Severin are at your side."

*

CONSTANTIN PAUSED, A hand lifted to knock when the commotion of a scuffle, and Gabrielle's muffled cries made his blood freeze. He wrenched the door open to the rooms she shared with the Widow Bardin. The two of them were rolling around on the floor. Gabrielle's hand fisted in the widow's hair, and she was trying to shout behind the hand clamped over her mouth.

"What is going on here?" Constantin demanded, putting his hand on his dagger as he glared at Bardin. Gabrielle didn't appear frightened, and that was the only thing that kept him from hauling her away. "Explain yourself."

Bardin blew a lock of hair out of her eyes and shot Constantin a narrow-eyed glare. "Don't you know to knock before entering a woman's chambers? Ouch!" She snatched her hand away from Gabrielle's mouth and gave the girl an approving smile. "*Très bon.* Biting is always acceptable in a situation such as this."

Gabrielle wormed her way out of the widow's arms. She was a mess. Her hair had come loose of its pins and stood out in a halo around her face. Her dress had tangled around her legs and ripped. She stood up, dragging her hair back from her face. "Can't I have trousers like you? Skirts are hard to fight in."

"Don't I know it." The widow Bardin pushed herself up and shoved impatiently at her own hair. "But it's good to learn how to defend yourself in skirts since we are so often shoved into them, whether we want them or not."

"*Je suis désolé.* I heard the struggle and I was worried." Constantin held out his arms as Gabrielle raced to him with a bright smile. "You should've told me you were teaching her such skills. I would've allowed it."

"I wasn't sure." Bardin sat back in a chair, crossing her long legs at the ankle. "My parents were adamantly against the notion, and I had to learn from Michie on the side. He's always indulged me. And it helped him too. He prefers studying to training. It used to make the old baron livid."

"*Salut, ma petite chouette.* You act like I didn't have breakfast with you this morning." Constantin said as he hoisted Gabrielle up for a hug. He turned his attention back to the widow. This glimpse into Michel-Leon's past intrigued him. "What was that like for him? Growing up as a chevalier?"

Bardin's expression turned stony. "You'll have to ask Michie. I don't gossip about him."

"Did you hear we're leaving?" Gabrielle cut in, oblivious to the tension. She wiggled to be let down and ran to the bed where her toy cat was curled up. "On a train. I've never met anyone who's been on a train. Everybody's going. At least all the children from the village are and some adults. But not madame though; she's staying with her brother." She glanced toward Bardin, who gave him a mocking smile. "You're coming with me, right?"

"Gabrielle, I have to stay here." Constantin crouched by her as her expression fell. "The hungry man is going to be hunting us, and I need to help the chevalier fight it."

"But what if you get hurt?" Gabrielle's hands twisted in her skirts. "He is so mad at you. I can feel it. He wants to kill you."

"The baron won't allow that to happen. He has a plan." An insane plan in Constantin's estimation, but insane plans paid off at times. "I'm sure Widow Bardin will watch over me as well, and it's not as if I don't have experience in surviving it."

"I promise to guard your guardian," Bardin said, her voice warm with affection. "And when the hungry man is gone and the mystery here is solved, you can return if you wish, or you may find you like the Inn of the Mountain. It's a good place for children to grow up."

"*Non.*" Gabrielle shook her head decisively. "Not unless Constantin goes to live there too."

Bardin shrugged a slim shoulder, her eyes narrowed on Constantin's face in a weighing manner. "If the baron wishes it, he'll extend the invitation."

Constantin didn't know what to make of that or what she thought of the idea. Better to retreat. He held out his hand to Gabrielle. "Come, let's go for a walk down to the kitchen and beg a treat off cook. I have an experiment I want to run with you."

"May I, madame?" Gabrielle asked, and at Bardin's nod, she

tucked her cat in the crook of her arm and took Constantin's hand.

Madame Belanger was more than happy to give them each a slice of quiche and an apple dumpling. She had plied food on Constantin since they first met and couldn't resist a motherless child no matter their race or station. Gabrielle carried their food wrapped in a napkin, and Constantin carried her past the traps up to the baron's workshop.

"Is this where you make your magic animals?" Gabrielle asked as she looked over the table and then went to explore Michel-Leon's row of experiments. "What's this part?"

"That is where the baron tests what's in the mists. He's searching for a way to make us immune to them." Constantin pointed out the beakers with drops of liquid and the microscope.

Gabrielle stared at Constantin with wide eyes. "He can do that?"

"If anyone can, it will be him. I have a great respect for his intelligence and tenacity." Constantin crouched down to look at Gabrielle eye to eye. "He has a plan to trick and trap the hungry man, but he needs our help."

Gabrielle swallowed hard and then lifted her chin. "What do we need to do?"

Gabrielle's bravery always astounded Constantin. "Well, you know how I hide us in the shadows?" She bit her lip and nodded. "It's called a glamour. I've learned a few things from the baron. The glamour is like a shield that hides the sense of our soul from others. It's something that people like you and me can do because we're fey kissed. Like it's how only you and me can sense the monster and hide ourselves from it. I want to try out another glamour. I want to make an image of you that not only appears like you but feels like you to the hungry man's senses. So, in a way, I would make a mirror image of your soul to trick it."

Her brow furrowed in thought. "How do we do that?"

Constantin thought about how he twisted the shadows around

himself, which made him remember the situation he'd been in the last time he used it. Somehow, he'd caught ahold of Nightingale's essence and pulled at it. He fingered the puckered scar along his cheek. It was still red and raw, though it had closed completely. "You might sense something from me, but don't be frightened. I won't hurt you."

"I know you won't," Gabrielle declared, burrowing close to him.

Constantin closed his eyes and held out his hand, searching for the sense of her. He fumbled around until he comprehended it wasn't that different from how he attached the sense of a person to his little devices to search. He had the instinct. Now he needed the technique. He opened his eyes and looked into hers and then she was there to his groping senses, like a wounded bird who feared so deeply but trusted at the same time. It brought tears to his eyes. He could sense the areas Nightingale carved out, and he suspected he had similar marks on his own soul scabbed over and thickly scarred.

She called to him with a siren's song, awakening a thread of hunger, and an overwhelming need to fix. She gasped as he expanded his senses more, enveloping her. "*Non,*" she whimpered, shrinking back.

The fear turned to terror in a flash, and the call to heal increased tenfold along with the hunger. Constantin ignored the latter and found the light opposite the shadows. He filled her with it, easing the old wounds until they shrank to scars and disappeared altogether. Constantin fell to his knees as the sense of her vanished.

What the hell had he done? Covered in shame, he forced himself to meet Gabrielle's gaze. He'd scared her and that fear had called to him, stirring a terrifying hunger. What was wrong with him?

She stared at him, her eyes wide with wonder. "It doesn't hurt any longer," she whispered.

Tears welled in her eyes, and Gabrielle threw her arms around him, crying in relief and joy. "It doesn't hurt!"

Constantin's eyes stung as he sensed every bright emotion. There was no fear in her any longer, not for him. There was only love.

"*Je suis désolé.* I'm sorry I scared you, *ma petite chouette.*" Constantin pressed a kiss to her hair.

"I don't care." She beamed at him through her tears. "It's all better."

She broke away from him to dance around the lab, her curls and skirts flying. Constantin watched her as he went over what happened. There was a link between them now, a bright silver thread, and he sensed another thread, one dark and evil that connected Gabrielle to the magicman. He narrowed his eyes in concentration and severed it, feeling the echo and recoil from Nightingale before it disappeared. It would be coming. It was a matter of time before the monster stormed the château. The bait they laid on the way to the station would be the final lure.

With the sense of Gabrielle still singing, Constantin projected another image of her. One that danced and twirled in a mirror image of Gabrielle and cast onto it the same emotions. Nightingale could shatter it if it concentrated, but Constantin was confident he could hold it long enough to lure the monster into their trap.

"What's that?" Gabrielle asked, coming to a halt as she stared at her image, which still danced. She clutched the cat to her and retreated toward Constantin.

"That is what Nightingale is going to chase while you get away to safety." Constantin waved the image away with a sense of immense satisfaction. Now he had to figure out a way to mask the physical elements of Michel-Leon's spell. He had ideas. He needed to test them and tweak.

"Excuse me, monsieur." Janvier gave him a wintry smile when Constantin met his eyes. "The baron sent me to tell you we're almost ready to leave for the train. Régine has the belongings for young mademoiselle already packed."

Gabrielle threw her arms around him and clung. "I don't want to leave. Can't I stay with you?"

"*Non*, Gabrielle." Constantin hugged her back. "I wish you could. When this is over, I'll send for you or come get you myself."

"Then I can stay with you? Forever?"

Constantin looked down into her hopeful eyes. What did he know about raising children? He'd been a loner always. "Maybe you will have found a better home and wouldn't want to be with me anymore."

She shook her head vehemently and hugged him harder. "*Non*, I want you. *S'il vous plaît*, Constantin."

"If that is truly what you want," Constantin said gruffly and picked her up to navigate the hidden stairs. "How did the baron survive his childhood growing up in this house?" It was another reason to be grateful that Gabrielle was leaving, no matter how much he'd miss her. The thought of her lost or wandering here gave him chills.

"He had me," Janvier replied. "I have always taken care of him the way you take care of young mademoiselle. I don't like going off and leaving him alone. No matter his insistence. Not when the situation is this dangerous. You will keep an eye on him, won't you?"

"We'll watch over each other." Constantin shot the man a curious look. "I'm sure the widow has taken that duty on as well and has done so for years."

Janvier didn't respond until they reached the bottom of the stairs and emerged into the hallway. "Michel-Leon told me what you did for him while you were in Paris together."

Constantin shrugged and set Gabrielle down. "I did what I had to do. I need his help." He brushed his hand over Gabrielle's loosened hair. "Gabrielle and all the children need his help." He met the grim look in Janvier's eyes. "And though I'm loath to admit there are needs that supersede ours, all of Paris needs his help. I gave my word. I'll not abandon him. We are becoming friends." Maybe more. Constantin couldn't stop the wistful thought.

Janvier clasped his shoulder in a grip surprisingly strong for a man that old. "That is why I trust him with you. My biggest fear is dying and leaving Michel-Leon alone. I will depart with a clearer conscience."

Janvier left Constantin speechless until he joined Michel-Leon on the front step. They oversaw the trunks loaded and that Janvier and Gabrielle were safely nestled inside the carriage.

"Were you able to do it?" Michel-Leon asked, searching his face. There was a look of relief in his eyes as he signaled for their horses to be brought around. "There is something different about you, something healed."

"Masking and projecting Gabrielle was easy. The other is going to require more refining, but I think I can do it." It couldn't be much different from infusing his toys with magic.

Michel-Leon gave him a wolfish smile. "Then let's ride out for the first part of our plan. Nightingale will notice the progression of so many children together, especially with Gabrielle in the center. It wouldn't dare attack us, not in broad daylight and with no preparation. The villagers accompanying us will also be a deterrent, and Hadrien is armed."

Constantin clambered onto his own horse as he caught onto Michel-Leon's plan. "That will put the monster in a state of extreme anxiety. So, I suspect on the trip back you want me to project the sense of her in the carriage alone? It'll believe I want her to remain with me?"

Michel-Leon hesitated and nudged the horse into a walk as the carriage set out. "Magicmen are notoriously jealous. They don't easily let go of what's theirs. It'll view you as a rival flaunting your win. I expect to have it knocking down the main doors soon. All is in readiness there except for masking the spell and iron. It may not be needed if we enrage it enough. I hid it under a massive carpet. But I like layers of security."

Constantin shook his head with an admiring smile as they joined the other villagers. "You are a wily bastard, Parisee. I never would've taken you for a trickster." His gaze roamed over the road and the men surrounding the cart with the village children. This was a crazy plan, but it might work.

Chapter Fifteen

CONSTANTIN TRIED TO concentrate on pulling together the fine details of his latest construct, but his fingers fumbled with fatigue. The château felt empty without Gabrielle, though he could sense the illusion he maintained to lure Nightingale in. Even the Belangers had left for the safety of the village.

After they'd returned from the station, Parisee, Bardin, and Constantin spent hours perfecting the illusion, working on the traps, and shielding the iron ward. Then Parisee and his sister opted to catch some sleep while they could, since someone would always have to remain awake after they trapped Nightingale. Constantin chose the first watch because he wasn't certain he could maintain the illusion if he slept.

He set aside the project as useless and knuckled his eyes. He'd get some tea and check the time. There was no sense in waking anyone else up. Constantin wouldn't be able to sleep, no matter how exhausted he was. Not until Nightingale showed its face.

He made his way to the kitchen and grabbed the kettle. As he turned to fill it with water, a sense of unease trickled down his back. His fingers tightened on the handle as the hairs on the back of his neck stirred. Nightingale. He'd know the sense of it anywhere.

Constantin turned toward the kitchen window, his throat tight. Though his mind screamed at him to run, his limbs felt clumsy and weighed down. Nightingale stared at him. Its eyes black holes of cruel intent, its face white as death.

Constantin yelled and jumped back, dropping the kettle as the sense of Nightingale's fury struck him full force. It had never been so livid. Not the day it had booted Constantin out of the orphanage, not the day it had confronted him over Gabrielle's disappearance. It was coming for Constantin's blood and Gabrielle's soul. And it wasn't going to let anything stand in the way.

"Little Constantin," Nightingale hissed. "Recognize this?"

Something thudded against the leaded panes of the window, and it took Constantin a moment to recognize the bloodless twisted features. Hadrien Belanger. Constantin stumbled against the wall, his stomach twisting with horror and regret.

Hadrien's mouth moved as he mewled in pain. *Mon Dieu.* He was still alive. Constantin took one step toward him even as Nightingale lifted him, as if Hadrien weighed no more than a doll.

Constantin and Hadrien screamed in the same breath.

"*Non!*"

"Run!"

Hadrien's cry broke off in a scream of agony that abruptly ended as the magicman tore off his head.

With another shout of terror and revulsion, Constantin leaped for the bellpull to alarm the others and dashed out of the kitchen as the door shuddered under the impact of Nightingale's fists. As he scrambled for the dubious safety of the château's inner chambers, one thought kept hammering at him the way the magicman hammered at the doors.

It would take the monster no time to batter it down.

Wrenching open the hidden doorway, Constantin forced himself to take the stairs slowly. He couldn't get caught in one of the traps. It had been reset this time with a chemical agent of Parisee's devising. He didn't want to be the one to experience the effects first.

As he made his way toward the ballroom, he split his concentration between remembering the location of each trap and focusing on the sense of Gabrielle's presence in the room. This could all go to hell if he lost his concentration.

Any worries he had over the kitchen alarm not working and waking the others were laid to rest when the magicman triggered the first trap. Constantin smiled grimly at the clatter and fall of the treads on the staircase, followed by a shriek of outrage from the magicman that pierced through the walls. If the alarm didn't wake Constantin's companions, the magicman's progress would. The monster hadn't been expecting that. Maybe it would move more cautiously and give them time to get in place.

When Constantin emerged onto the balcony overlooking the ballroom, he found Parisee and Bardin already awaiting him. The chevalier studied the floor below with a tense expression. "Sounds like it's getting hit with every trap we set up. Do you have any sense these are hurting it?"

Constantin braced himself to brush up against that mind and shuddered. "Pissing it off more than anything. It's not thinking too straight. It might be scratched and bruised, but not enough to slow it down."

"I'll take it being distracted. Are you ready?" Parisee cocked his head as another shriek echoed, closer this time. He examined the map in his hands. "Huh, that one wasn't on the list."

"I'm ready." Bardin knelt down, the barrel of a rifle resting on the railing as she took careful aim at the double doors. When this was over, Constantin was going to have to tell them it had killed Hadrien. He had been kin to them. This would hurt them. He could no longer keep either of them at a safe distance from his heart. It was too late. They had crept in all unaware. Having them stand there with him, ready to face down a monster, destroyed his defenses. No one had ever stood for him like that.

Constantin would have to break their hearts, and he didn't know how to relay traumatic information. He was no good with people. He didn't even know what Hadrien had been doing there. The man was supposed to be safe in the village with his wife and daughter.

If they survived, he thought, as another scream of rage allowed them to track the monster's progress. The strength of Nightingale's fury battered his mind.

"As ready as I'll ever be." Constantin cracked his knuckles and stepped forward to the railing. He stared down at the rug on the floor and the construct of a hummingbird he'd placed there. Constantin found it much easier to attach the image to a physical object. He'd had so much practice at that. Gabrielle appeared, huddling in a pile of skirts, clutching her cat to her as she cried. He projected another image of himself standing in front of her with a weapon drawn.

"*Très bon*," Parisee said in a low voice and clasped his shoulder. Constantin let the warmth of his approval bolster him as he sensed the rage of the magicman draw nearer. He was about to face the nightmare of his childhood. Whatever the outcome, he would stand firm. Only this time, he wasn't alone. Out of the corner of his eye, he saw Parisee pull out his revolver as Bardin remained steady. If the worst happened, that might hold the monster off long enough for them to escape, but Constantin doubted it.

"For the record, if we die, *je suis désolé* for dragging you both into this." Constantin gave Bardin a grim smile as he stepped away. Light and shadows warped around him and the world around him grayed as he shrouded himself. "But I'm glad you have my back."

*

MICHEL-LEON STARED at the spot where he knew Constantin still stood, but there was nothing to indicate he occupied the space. No bend in light waves or ripples. He resisted the urge to reach out and touch him, knowing the illusion would shatter, and they were running out of time.

"That's uncanny," Régine said, never taking her gaze off the doors. "But I agree with our disembodied voice. I'm glad you're both here. I've never seen a magicman, but this one sounds insane."

"We won't die. I have it on good authority the traps in this room will hold most monsters." Michel-Leon paused and threw the thought at the ancestors. *"Right?"*

"If you get the creature in the circle, it will hold."

Michel-Leon held onto that assurance as another howl erupted from the hallway, this one tinged with pain. "Régine, I think the iron-tipped arrows you suggested did some damage. I will have to add that to my notes."

The doors flung open, and Nightingale appeared, seething, bleeding in several places. It glanced at Gabrielle and Constantin near each other on the ballroom floor, then up at Michel-Leon and Régine. "You will beg for death before I'm done with you, just like that mewling servant of yours, and then I'll suck your soul dry though it gives me no power. I'll do it to savor your screams and deny you an afterlife."

"Michie?" Régine's voice hitched with sudden pain as Michel-Leon's thoughts spun. He'd gotten everyone away. Who had it hurt?

"Stay steady, Régine," Michel-Leon said softly to her. "We'll figure it out. Maybe it's lying."

The projection of Constantin reached back to offer a hand to Gabrielle, and Michel-Leon marveled at how lifelike it was. It moved with a natural grace. "Get ready to run, Gabrielle." It even had Constantin's voice.

"Not one more step foul creature," Michel-Leon thundered as the magicman tensed to spring forward. "Or you will regret it."

"The Chevaliers de Rouen go extinct today." Nightingale sneered and lunged toward the pair on the carpet, moving impossibly fast. Gabrielle screamed, and the illusion shattered.

Michel-Leon intoned the last words of the spell and light flared in a circle through the carpet. Constantin appeared beside him as he banished the surrounding shadows, and Nightingale blinked up at them in momentary confusion.

"Where is she?" the magicman howled and rushed forward, only to bounce off an invisible cage around it.

"I warned you you'd regret it." Michel-Leon stared down at the monster, who ignored him. It shrieked and pounded, testing every inch of the prison that surrounded it. "Who did you hurt?" The magicman howled louder, beating its fists against the barrier and screaming threats.

Constantin gave him and Régine a look filled with regret. "It's Monsieur Belanger. I'm not sure how it got to him, but he's dead. *Je suis désolé.*"

"*Mon oncle* Hadrien?" Régine scrambled to her feet, her face white. She gripped Constantin's sleeve. "Are you sure?"

"*Oui*," Constantin said gruffly, patting her on the hand as her eyes glistened. "I didn't see his wife and daughter, so maybe they're still safe."

Régine glanced at Michel-Leon and he nodded. "Go. Check on them and be careful." He stressed the last words as she took off at a run.

"Are you—?"

Michel-Leon waved off Constantin's query. "I'm fine." He stared down at the howling monster with flinty resolve. He prayed Salome and her daughter were safe. Either the magicman had hunted them down, knowing it would hurt them, or Hadrien had not remained in the village as he'd been ordered. That was the more likely scenario. He'd fussed over being sent off to safety, leaving the three of them to guard the keep.

He closed his eyes as memories flooded through him. Hadrien's patience with the horses. How he'd known the peculiarities of each one and how to pair a rider with the right mount. He had been the one to teach Michel-Leon and Régine how to ride when they were young.

"*Je suis vraiment désolé*, Michel-Leon," Constantin said softly, touching his hand, and Michel-Leon's eyes flew open.

"*Merci, mon ami.*" Another barrier had been crossed between them. Michel-Leon wished it hadn't been over grief. "The chevaliers and those who serve them know the risks. So few make it to an old age. Hadrien would consider his sacrifice worth it if children are saved. His soul can rest now that the monster is caged."

"I can't believe that worked. At a terrible cost though." Constantin studied Nightingale with a grim expression. "Now we have to wait for it to starve?"

"I discovered something that might make it move faster." Michel-Leon crouched and picked up the tome at his feet. "I'm not the only member of my family to think this room would be a good place to trap a monster. I shudder to imagine what might've accidentally gone off during a vigorous gigue in the château's heyday."

He caught the sudden quicksilver of Constantin's smile, and the genuineness in it made him smile back. He hadn't had the privilege of seeing that expression on Constantin's face before, and it made him appear so much more approachable. It shot a light through the tragic turn their triumph had taken. "What?"

"I like your sense of humor. I expected a chevalier to be a grim fellow, entirely fixated on the job, which you are to a terrifying degree." Constantin grimaced and shrugged. "I suppose we are two of a kind there. But I enjoy your quippy observations. It's refreshing."

Constantin disconcerted him. Michel-Leon didn't know how to

respond as inexplicable shyness settled over him. True, he could be a bit of a loner, but he could handle people even if they didn't know how to respond to him. Constantin was different.

"Um, what was I saying?" Michel-Leon glanced down at the book in his hands and then at the magicman who had ceased shrieking and stood there staring a promise of death up at them. "Oh, the traps, *oui*."

He paged rapidly through the book, searching for the spell he sought. "I'm not sure exactly what this is supposed to do. The words to set it in motion are clear enough, but the explanation…" Michel-Leon shook his head. "The man's Latin is atrocious. *Mon grand-oncle*, I believe. There are certain details missing. Fear of this falling into the wrong hands, I suppose. Ah, *oui*, here it is."

Michel-Leon slammed the book shut and intoned the words. Runes built into the walls around the room began to glow, and the temperature dropped until their breath steamed out in white puffs. Frost formed on the walls and floor, spreading out and thickening into ice. "Well, that's interesting, not sure how helpful it is."

"Is that the best you have?" Nightingale taunted.

Michel-Leon reached for the book again, and Constantin stopped him with a hand on his arm. "*Non*, leave it like this. It feels the heat and cold as much as you and me, even if it won't sicken." Snow began to fall from the ceiling in fat flakes, and there was a hint of a knife-edged wind that swirled the snow in little eddies. "Does this bring back any memories?" Constantin asked. "You know, I believe it might get colder in here than it was the night you shoved me out the doors. Enjoy, Nightingale. I doubt you will find a man to keep you warm as I had."

With that parting shot, Constantin turned on his heel and left. Frowning at the tragic implications, Michel-Leon studied the room again and the still glowing runes for any sign of weakness in their structure. It would hold. Ignoring the magicman's imperious shouts for release, Michel-Leon followed Constantin and caught up with him on the stairwell.

"How old were you?" Michel-Leon asked after an awkward pause.

"Old enough to survive," Constantin replied in a grim tone. "Do you judge me for selling myself?"

"*Non.*" Michel-Leon caught his arm and met Constantin's gaze so he could see the truth. "I regret you were forced to do so, and I admire your will. If this eases that memory in any way, there is an orphanage in need of leadership. I had Janvier investigate purchasing the place before he left. I'll send a telegram in the morning, and perhaps you could explore finding someone worthy of caring for the little ones who remain."

Constantin's expression relaxed, erasing some of an old pain. "*Merci*, that does ease me." He glanced up toward where the ballroom would be. "That was a neatly executed glamour up there. Your family might have some fey blood as well. The interesting thing about illusions, they can still harm you once you get taken in."

"That's good to know. I believe your magicman is in for an interesting time. The frost was one of several torments built into the room." Michel-Leon's sense of triumph fell away as he thought of Hadrien with a wrench of sorrow. He would have to arrange matters for him and his family, check on Régine. She would be grieving. The shadow of his old sorrow welled up in response. Monsters disguised as men had taken his birth family and now other monsters stalked his new family. It was better to go through life alone.

"Go, get some rest," he said, turning away from Constantin and the temptation he provided. "We'll talk again tomorrow."

Chapter Sixteen

"WHY IS IT taking so long?" Constantin growled as he entered the kitchen and found Michel-Leon and the Widow Bardin there, eating their lunch. Michel-Leon wrote in his journal, and she pored over the maps she was marking up with their progress in the caves. They had cleared one rockfall to uncover a series of branching tunnels that spider-webbed the area. Investigating them was time-consuming, and they had yet to find evidence of the missing boys. At this point, Constantin believed they would find nothing because the boys had been devoured whole. Still, that wasn't his only frustration. "Nightingale should be weakening."

Michel-Leon glanced up with that familiar abstracted expression. Too many times, he acted as if he didn't even see Constantin. He then felt as unreal as when he cast the shadows around himself. There were times when he thought Michel-Leon was as attracted to him as Constantin felt in return. But those moments were far and fleeting.

Bardin gave him a brief smile that didn't touch her red-rimmed eyes. "I share your impatience. Come, sit." She pulled aside the maps to give him room.

"The magicman is tough. A creature like that doesn't survive without being resilient, but its increasing desperation is a good sign. It spent a good number of hours last night expending its energy to claw at the barrier." Michel-Leon put a cap on the inkwell and rose to dish a plate for Constantin. It smelled like leftover stew again. They subsisted off whatever the villagers brought them. Michel-Leon had given Salome and her daughter leave to go home to grieve if they wished, but for the time being, they opted to remain in the village.

"So far we've subjected it to cold, lightning, and drowning in blood." A distressed expression crossed Bardin's fine features. "A particularly gruesome glamour I wouldn't care to repeat."

"It doesn't act desperate." Constantin threw himself down on the bench and tore off a piece of bread from the board in the table center. "It gloats over its imprisonment and the pain it's caused."

It particularly enjoyed tormenting Bardin over the murder of her uncle, recounting details with hellish glee until she attempted to shoot it. Constantin sided with her on that point. He also wished to dispatch the monster and move on.

"Because it knows it gets to you. Pay closer attention next time you visit it. It's aging. It's going to worsen the longer it doesn't feed and is forced to expend its energy with these attacks." Michel-Leon set the bowl in front of him. "Eat and tell us the news. I'd hoped the time outdoors would've made you cheerier."

"The orphanage is still in a state of turmoil, but at least every one of those wretched people in charge is gone, and the children already appear more relaxed." Constantin dug in, sopping his bread into the broth. The state at the orphanage did cheer him, but the impasse with the magicman and the mists drove his dark mood right back. He shrugged and stabbed his finger at the maps. "I surveyed that area as you requested. It led to a cavern with no other exits as far as I can see."

"Show me," Bardin demanded, shoving the maps in front of him.

Constantin traced an area, and she made careful notes in a precise hand. "This makes no sense, Michie," she said. "We have scoured the caves and still find more tunnels and dead ends. The mists affect not one town or village outside of Paris. I didn't find any indication there are nests hidden within this cave system. We can keep searching the caves, but my instincts say we are wasting time there." She folded her hands on the maps and gave Michel-Leon a searching glance. "I know the ancestors insist the answer is there, but maybe they are wrong."

Michel-Leon's gaze went far away while he spoke to those voices in his head. It was uncanny. An irritated expression crossed Michel-Leon's handsome features as he waved his hand. "Always doesn't mean forever," he muttered under his breath. He got up and paced the room with his hands behind his back. "This could be the second anomaly. The erratic nature of the days the mists appear is the first. However, the answers have to be down there somewhere. If the boys had just gotten lost and died, we would've found some sign of them."

Constantin watched him, at a loss for how to help. He knew nothing about this world of chevaliers. "There are a lot of construction sites. Maybe one abandoned in favor of other projects? Could the creature have nested there instead?"

Bardin pulled out another map. "It would be helpful for you to go back to the palace and contrive to get a map of the construction and of the cave systems southeast of Paris. We need to know what's ongoing, what's coming. Even if the court left for *Château de Saint-Cloud*, there will still be functionaries at the palace and Haussmann is still working on his rebuilding."

Michel-Leon scratched at the stubble on his chin. "That's a thought. My concern about the nest being somewhere in the city is that we would've heard of something by now. It wouldn't be easy to hide that many eggs, which I assume is why they've always chosen to lay them in caves. Easier to hide and defend. In a city, anybody could stumble over them. And the creature isn't small."

Constantin eyed the consternation in Michel-Leon's eyes and decided it was time to shift direction before the man worried himself into a knot. "How goes your chemical tests? Did you get the breakthrough you wanted?"

Acute frustration crossed Michel-Leon's face. "Maybe, I'm not sure." He sat down heavily across from Constantin and pulled out a sheaf of papers from under his journals. It was covered in notations and formulae, a language Constantin did not understand, but found compelling. "I hope we may be able to counter the effects of these mists. And I do believe the tweaks you made to the mask should be of significant benefit. I'd like you to construct another for yourself."

"We have enough materials for one." Constantin nudged his chin toward the formula. "You ready to test that concoction of yours on me?"

Michel-Leon stared at him aghast. "You are not my test subject, Constantin." He colored and looked away. "*Je suis désolé*. I shouldn't have addressed you so familiarly. Though you said I could, but you didn't reciprocate, except that one time. I shouldn't have presumed."

Constantin merely raised an eyebrow. "We're all living under the same roof. You and I share the same suite of rooms since I've taken over Janvier's space. We are all fighting the same monsters and trying to track down the same answers. I have no need for formality if you don't. I put up walls, but they aren't as important anymore, Michel-Leon."

Michel-Leon glanced down, coloring even more as Bardin looked on with fascination. She turned and studied Constantin, her gaze cool with consideration. "I agree. You may call me Régine."

"You were going to test it out on a live subject, weren't you?"

Constantin cut in to ease Michel-Leon's embarrassment. "I'm as good as any other, hale and hearty, and forgive me for saying so, more expendable than you."

Michel-Leon's face settled into stiff lines and their eyes met. "You are not expendable." He set aside the formula. "I am sure it will work and will be nontoxic. However, I'm not sure it will work for every nest. What if the pheromones in each nest change? There won't be another for fifty-two years, and I have no way of testing it." He pounded his fist on the table.

"If this works and it does change, you will have laid the groundwork, Michel-Leon. Others can pick up where you left off." Constantin tapped the sheaf of papers with his forefinger. "Worry about Paris now and another generation in another location later. But we won't know if it works if we don't test it."

"I'll consider it," Michel-Leon said in a tone Constantin was coming to recognize that meant he was finished with a conversation. "Any new and interesting rumors in the city? How about you, Régine? Anything else we can use from the villages?"

It was gratifying to know Michel-Leon trusted him with the information gathering. He often lamented that he was wasting time chasing down rumors when he could be working on more promising leads, but they both knew it had to be done. Constantin had vast experience chasing down rumors, so it was logical for him to do it while Michel-Leon worked on his experiments.

"There are an inordinate number of people going missing when the mists aren't out." Constantin frowned as he relayed the conversations, and Michel-Leon listened intently. "There's always some, unfortunately, especially in the cities, but this appears excessive even with the influx of outsiders. Do you think it's related?"

"The villagers from Henri and Phillipe's home have complained about the same, but not on the same scale and not in many weeks. I've only made a list of names of those who had been in the city when the mists came, but never returned." Régine shuffled through her notes. "But there have been mentions of those who disappeared from the city on a sunny day. I didn't consider it to be a factor at the time, but I could be wrong."

Michel-Leon threw up his hands. "It's late June. The mist cycles should be moving farther apart, not closer together. There shouldn't be strange creatures roaming about during it. There is nothing about this that isn't abnormal. So, *oui*, I'd say there is a link though I have no idea how."

"There is another aberration. It appears some folks who have disappeared into the mists have been returned," Constantin added.

Michel-Leon's gaze focused on him in a way Constantin would have found pleasing if the man wasn't focused on the mystery plaguing him. Even if Michel-Leon wasn't utterly consumed by his dedication, Constantin didn't have a chance in hell of capturing his attention. Their stations were so far apart. He had been content to be alone for so long, but now he was finding the idea untenable.

"How so? How many? What are their conditions? What do you mean, returned?"

Constantin held up his hand before Michel-Leon could bombard him with more questions. "Exactly how I said. People who were reported to have disappeared into the mists, but they reappeared on their doorstops overnight, befuddled. Apparently, this has been happening with the elderly, now it's including the very young. As for their conditions, it's hard to say." Constantin pinned Michel-Leon with a look. "They appeared to be as disinclined to talk about it as you were."

"It's like a culling." Régine frowned. "Like with farm animals. Perhaps the young had also been culled out before, but the magicman took them instead of allowing them to be returned."

"I suspect so." Constantin shot a glare toward the ceiling. "The creature knows more than it's saying and today I'm going to get some answers."

Michel-Leon laid a hand on his arm. "Give me a moment to organize here, and I'll go with you."

"No need." Constantin shrugged his hand off. "You've been alone to converse with the monster many times. It's my turn. Maybe our history will allow me to get something out of it that you can't."

Constantin left Michel-Leon behind, but he couldn't leave the frustration. Despite the fact the château was a four-story rambling monstrosity, they occupied an intimate space together. The kitchen was safe to inhabit as was their workroom, Michel-Leon's study, and where they slept in rooms next to each other.

Constantin had the impression that Michel-Leon wasn't comfortable in that big, lonely bed by himself. More often than not, when Constantin went to collect him for his shift to watch over their prisoner, Michel-Leon was fast asleep on his cot in his workshop, muttering to himself. Constantin had speculated more than once, questioning if the voices gave him any rest at all, or if it was a lifetime of habit that had the man talking to himself.

No one had ever captured his imagination like Michel-Leon, and it annoyed the hell out of him.

*

MICHEL-LEON STARED hard at the door Constantin disappeared through. They were both on edge from lack of sleep, too many questions without answers, and the tension of waiting for the magicman to break. The creature was old. Older than Michel-Leon had first suspected, wily and strong. It had more surprises in store for them, and they couldn't let down their guard. Constantin shouldn't be alone with it. Not with their history.

"Michie." Régine grabbed his hand as he started to go after

Constantin. "I suspect he wishes for some time alone."

"He's been alone all morning." Michel-Leon shook off her hand. "You know what a bastard that creature was to you, and it had only had one memory to wound you with. It has had years to hurt Constantin. It will use anything to lash out."

"What does he mean to you, this vagabond you've taken in?" Régine's eyes were concerned. "He doesn't strike me as a man who sticks around after a job is done."

"I'm not looking for him to stick around." Michel-Leon rubbed his knuckles against the ache in his chest. "He's going to help as he promised, and that's all."

"Somehow, I have trouble believing that is it." Régine also rose. "I'm going into the village to check on *ma tante* Salome. Tomorrow we should take a chance and head into the city, depending on what Constantin gets out of the magicman. We need to start taking turns guarding it. It can't always be you confronting it. I've come to terms with *mon oncle* Hadrien. He'd still be alive if he'd listened to you instead of coming back to help."

Michel-Leon rubbed a hand over his aching eyes. "I should've anticipated that. He shouldn't have died. That was my fault."

"*Non*, Michie. It is the monster's fault." She came to him and slid her arm around his waist. "He did it with cruel purpose. Even if Hadrien had remained at home safe where he was supposed to be, the magicman might've sought him out just for the opening blow it would give us."

Michel-Leon knew she was speaking sense, but he was tired of losing people. "I'm going to check on Constantin, then we'll make our plans for tomorrow. Two of us to go into Paris, one of us to keep an eye on the monster."

Régine looked as if she wanted to say something more; then she merely patted him on his arm and let him leave. Questioning his own motives, Michel-Leon followed Constantin. Was he concerned about the man because of the growing friendship and deeper feelings between them? He couldn't get him out of his mind. What would it be like to experience passion, however fleeting, with someone, especially someone he cared for?

Occupied by his churning thoughts, Michel-Leon almost missed the trap on the inner stair. Swearing under his breath, he paused to collect his thoughts over his pounding heart. No, his concern for Constantin had nothing to do with his desire and everything to do with the fact that both the magicman and Constantin himself were an unknown with a connection between them that went beyond tormentor and victim.

After all, a magicman was a corrupted fey kissed. Michel-Leon needed to remember that.

Just as he needed to remember Constantin had enough men in his life who had wielded power over him to use him. Michel-Leon would not add himself to the list.

There had to be something they could do to speed up the deterioration of the magicman. Michel-Leon was not one to enjoy the suffering of any creature, even one who fed off children. It was better to have it over and done with cleanly. Not this slow starvation. He'd have to check the village again and the surrounding village to be certain no more children and anyone who could be taken for a child lingered nearby. He doubted the magicman's reach could extend beyond the château, but he wasn't about to take any chances either.

"Wait." The warning came as Michel-Leon's hand settled on the door to the balcony. He paused, cocking his head. *"The souleater seeks to subvert the watcher."*

Michel-Leon went cold. He would not allow that monster to sink its mental claws any deeper into Constantin. It would not corrupt this fey kissed, not after how Constantin managed to rid himself of the last taint.

He opened the door, moving on quiet feet. Constantin stood at the railing, his hands white-knuckled where he gripped the railing, his posture tense to the point of shattering. The magicman caught sight of Michel-Leon, and its mocking grin widened. "Blaise misses you, Constantin. He's sorry he never told you he loved you back. Here's your chance to right that mistake."

"Magic!"

The voices howled, sending Michel-Leon reeling back as the glamour settled over him, trapped him in the cage of the magicman's vision. He fought against it even as Constantin turned toward him with a stricken expression.

Chapter Seventeen

CONSTANTIN STARED AT Blaise, his heart catching anew. He'd grown in the intervening years and the fragile quality about him had steeled. This Blaise wouldn't hide from what they felt. He could see it in his eyes, still as open and guilelessly blue as they had been before.

"Go on, little Constantin. Take what you want. What you've always wanted."

Constantin shook his head, trying to shake off the power of Nightingale's voice that sank into his brain, setting fire to his thoughts. His heart ached with the renewed pain of rejection. If he'd convinced Blaise to run away with him, then he'd still be alive. They'd still be together, and Constantin wouldn't forever be alone.

"Constantin." Blaise smiled sweetly at him and reached out his hand.

Constantin caught it and pulled him close. "You're still alive? How? Nightingale told me you died after I left."

Guilt clawed at him. He should've tried harder, been more

persuasive in his arguments. There had to have been something he could've done that would've convinced Blaise that being with him was safer than staying with the monster. He buried his face against Blaise's neck. "I won't let it hurt you."

"It lied to twist you up," Blaise said, giving him a shake. "Everything it does is to cause pain. You know that. Snap out of it."

The voice was right. The words were wrong. Blaise had never believed in Nightingale's evilness. Constantin pulled back to view him, and Blaise smiled sweetly again. His lips moved, but no sound passed by.

"Take him. Make him yours again. Punish him for pushing you away." Constantin heard Nightingale well enough though. That hated voice telling him to take what he wanted. The words pushing and prodding, tugging at every string that tied them together.

This wasn't right.

Constantin pulled Blaise close again, cupped his cheek, and closed his eyes, seeking the sense of his soul. He knew what Blaise felt like. He'd been the first one Constantin could sense after Nightingale's feeding opened up the ability within him. Constantin would know the fragile sense of his spirit anywhere.

The oily corruption of Nightingale hung over him like a shroud, but Constantin pushed through it to the man beneath. There was no fragility there, but a strength and purpose of will that blazed through. Constantin's breath caught as the sense of Michel-Leon hit him. He was beautiful. With a sweet innocence that had remained intact, despite the horrors he faced as a chevalier.

That is what Nightingale wanted. He wanted Constantin to hurt him, to tarnish him, to destroy that innocence so he could find some sustenance from it. Constantin's throat ached. He'd come so close to falling into that trap, twisted by his own desires for a man he couldn't have and haunted by the death of a sweet youth from his past.

He pulled back, not looking at him even as he held onto the sense of Michel-Leon. He didn't want to see what Blaise would never become. "*Je suis très désolé.*"

"Constantin, it's me." For a moment, the voice hovered between Blaise and Michel-Leon as the magicman fought to keep the glamour on him.

"I know." Constantin stared into Michel-Leon's eyes as the glamour shattered. He appeared so concerned, his eyes dark with worry, that Constantin moved before he thought. He cupped the back of Michel-Leon's neck and kissed him.

Michel-Leon went rigid with shock, but he didn't pull away. His heart beating faster, Constantin drew him closer, slanting his mouth to deepen the kiss. Michel-Leon made an odd little sound and clutched at him. His lips parted and Constantin took the invitation for a taste.

Sweet heat swept through him as Michel-Leon kissed him back, shyly at first, as if he had not been kissed in a long time. Constantin threaded his hands in Michel-Leon's thick, soft hair, his breath coming faster. He hadn't been wrong. Michel-Leon wanted him as much. The single question remained: How far would Michel-Leon let him go?

He wanted to take off the clothes that separated them and explore every inch of him in the big, lonely bed Michel-Leon occupied. He broke the kiss and pressed his cheek to Michel-Leon's, needing to savor the contact a moment longer.

Mocking laughter came from below and reminded Constantin where he was. Who was observing them.

He pulled away. Stricken, humiliated that Nightingale put him in a situation where he'd been forced to reveal his growing feelings for Michel-Leon. He couldn't look the creature in the eye.

"Now the chevalier knows you for the rutting beast you are, Constantin."

"Silence," Michel-Leon said in a venomous voice, and the shame was too much. Constantin left before he could hear any more. Once in the hallway, he began running from the specter of his past and his fear of the future that was now tainted.

*

MICHEL-LEON STARTED to follow but then turned back to the magicman. Constantin needed space to get himself back together. He'd further embarrass them both if he chased him.

He turned to the railing to stare down at the monster below. The creature was pleased with itself, but its use of magic to trick Constantin had cost it. New lines had etched into its face, bags sagged under its eyes, and its hair had gone snow white. The deterioration would speed up from here.

"You torment him to your own detriment, and still he's stronger than you." The magicman's eyes went flat with rage as Michel-Leon's words hit home. "How it must burn to have a child like him escape your clutches, to survive and thrive without you. You weren't expecting that, were you? Or his audacity to challenge you now that he's an adult."

"I can crush Constantin's mind anytime I wish to." Nightingale's finger stabbed the air, and then it straightened with a sly smile. "It amuses me to make him suffer. He deserves to suffer after what he has stolen from me."

"An interesting conceit, considering you stole from him first." Michel-Leon braced himself on the railing and opened his mind further to the ancestors and their unceasing whispers. Those who had fought such monsters in the past vied for his attention.

"Do you apologize to the lamb when it graces your table?" Nightingale sneered. "The children are prey. Those who should shelter them cast them out, and I take them in. They are unwanted, unloved. If you valued them so much, you'd ensure their care. So spare me the lecture."

Michel-Leon couldn't deny the partial truths the magicman threw at him. If it hadn't been for Constantin, no one would've ever noticed the children's sufferings. There were too many in need of shelter, food, and love. They had to do better.

"Can the magicman crush Constantin's mind?" Michel-Leon sent the silent question to the ancestors.

"The answer is uncertain. There are too many variables. The watcher is stronger than he appears, but there are still ties between them."

Michel-Leon didn't believe the magicman could fulfill its boast, not unless they gave it an opportunity. He didn't intend to do that. Still, it wouldn't hurt to keep the two apart.

"Hungry?" Michel-Leon asked with a solicitous smile. "I suppose you could do with a meal."

"We both know you're not going to allow me to feed." The hunger that crossed Nightingale's face chilled Michel-Leon's blood. Whatever humanity it once had burned away long ago. "Mark my words: I saw the birth of the chevaliers, and I'll witness their whimpering end with you."

The magicman's words sent the ancestors whispering with recognition, but Michel-Leon concentrated on the monster before him. If they came up with anything useful, the voices would tell him, but he couldn't allow himself to be distracted. He'd dig down the mystery of Nightingale's words later.

"I'm open for negotiation." Michel-Leon gestured toward the circle that bound the magicman. "If the information you give me is sufficiently valuable, then I'm willing to free you. Provided you leave the city and hunt elsewhere. Of course, that deal is void if I catch wind of your name again."

"You lie." The magicman stabbed a finger in Michel-Leon's direction. "You won't be satisfied until I'm dead."

"*Non*, Constantin won't be satisfied until you're dead. Constantin is not here. I am. I have deeper concerns." Michel-Leon cocked his head as a name came to him. "Etienne Corrilaut, the man known as Poitou, who aided another monster in the murder of children. That's who you once were."

A spasm crossed the magicman's face. "That name no longer has any meaning for me. I am Nightingale."

"Weren't you burned at the stake along with your master?" There had to be a way to use this information to his advantage. All the pieces clicked together as the ancestors whispered again. "Oh *non*, you used a glamour to escape."

"No one who served Gilles de Rais was innocent." The magicman smiled up at him. "Do you want to know what he did with the children when he had them?"

"All that pain." Michel-Leon closed his eyes, sick to his stomach as the whispering continued detailing crime after crime. Hundreds of children slaughtered when Etienne was starting out and how many hundreds more since then? He was grateful Constantin left.

"Forgive me if I don't believe then that you'll free me or let me feed." The magicman swept a mocking bow. "I'll have to rely on my ingenuity to escape and wallow in your blood for revenge when I do."

Michel-Leon leveled a hard stare at the magicman. "Thousands will die with the mists. Hundreds have already gone missing. And that is before the swarm hatches. I'm willing to make a deal with a devil to stop that, even for a devil that tried to cause me personal harm. You answer all my questions about the mists, and I'll set you free. That's the deal. Consider it."

He left in search of Constantin without triggering another glamour, though he longed to. It would give Nightingale time to consider his offer. He couldn't give vent to his need to punish, no matter how much the monster deserved it. Time was running out. And the sole gamble he had to go on was that Nightingale's sands were moving faster to its own destruction. The need to survive would win out in the end. It had to.

Now he needed to figure out what to say to Constantin. Michel-Leon checked their workshop first. Constantin was enough like him that he often tried to lose himself in a puzzle, but the workshop was empty. He'd eaten, so perhaps he was trying to catch up on the sleep that eluded them both.

He sat down at his desk, reluctant to barge in on Constantin while he was in the bedroom. The intimate space would've made him nervous without the added element of a bed being there. Michel-Leon felt his cheeks heat painfully.

This was ridiculous. He'd taken a vow of abstinence for a valid reason. Even if that reason was moot, according to Janvier, he didn't need the distraction of a relationship. Chevaliers did not make good husbands or fathers or partners of any kind. Duty consumed them. Too taken up by the voices in their heads that drowned out conversations with living people.

He'd explain to Constantin that he was flattered. Well, more than flattered. He had not engaged in a dalliance in ages. There was nothing about Michel-Leon that had inspired passion or interest in men before. Not unless they wanted to use him. Constantin probably hadn't wanted to kiss him at all. The magicman had pushed him into thinking he was somebody Constantin had lost.

That thought was depressing. Even if Constantin had grasped who he was kissing, Michel-Leon wasn't the person Constantin wanted. He had to be as embarrassed as Michel-Leon was. There was no sense in tormenting them both further with a difficult conversation. He wouldn't say anything.

Even if he wanted to kiss Constantin again. Even if he might want something more, they couldn't, and that was that.

Chapter Eighteen

"ARE YOU SURE about this?" Foreman Lyon said in an undertone as Michel-Leon pulled a box out of the carriage. "I've never heard of a medicine that works against mists. Chevalier or not, it seems foolhardy."

"We've tested it multiple times," Constantin assured him. Experiments that stretched his nerves, but Michel-Leon had not fallen prey to the lure of the mists as he had in the past.

"I have tested it on myself, Constantin, and my sister. It works." Michel-Leon held up one of the little bundles of snuff. "But in an excess of precaution, if you go out into the mists after taking this, I'd make sure you are well tethered and you have a strong friend to pull you back if you start feeling peculiar. A sample of three people is not odds that would reassure me, but this is what we have."

"Well, now you have an entire crew," Foreman Lyon replied. "Maybe it works for us all, maybe it doesn't. But it's something more than we had before. If you have tested it on yourselves, that eases my skepticism."

Michel-Leon frowned at the men gathered around them. "Are you sure you want to do this? Constantin told me you are willing, but I want to be certain."

Lyon stepped forward. "I've lost two crews' worth of workers in total, as well as my sister's son. I'll try any damned thing that helps. Work has completely halted. We can't make any headway, which means we're not getting paid and food is not going on the table. And if this aids you in your investigation, then I'm willing."

"Let them," Constantin cut in and exchanged glances with Michel-Leon. He didn't understand the man's hesitancy. "They want to help, and we need the help. We are tied to the château more than we want, and we need eyes in the city. The information we've gathered from him has already proven valuable."

Michel-Leon's mouth turned down in reluctance. "Well, I can hardly deny that. I don't want to lose anyone else in the foul mists, which is why I concocted these, but don't allow your immunity to go to your head. There are still dangerous things out in the mists from what you tell me."

The foreman nodded and took his little bag before allowing the men lined up behind him to do the same. "You take it the same way you would snuff." Constantin demonstrated and waited while the doses were taken. "I'll check in with you after the next cycle."

"Do you have any idea when the mists will be back?" a man in the back asked. "We had it plague us for two days in a row and nothing for three now. Everyone is anxious when we step foot outside our door."

Acute frustration crossed Michel-Leon's features. "I am attempting to track down a pattern, but so far, the answer has eluded me. The moment I do know, I will send out new broadsides so everyone is warned."

"And I'll come by the worksite and let you know," Constantin added, hoping the personal interaction might ease some of their fears.

"In the meantime, we are working on more of these." Michel-Leon held up the redesigned filtration masks. "I intend for it to be another layer of protection. My theory is that there is something in the mists that acts as a drug and luring agent. The dose I gave you should counteract that. In case that fails, this should filter the air so you do not breathe in what's infecting people."

"How does it work?" the foreman asked, leaning over for a closer peek. "Did Monsieur Severin help you with that?" He traced a finger over the nose and mouthpiece, then glanced up at Constantin. "It looks like your work."

"I did," Constantin replied, well satisfied with the results. "We tested it before the inoculations to be sure it would filter out the vapors and it did. That was the problem with the prototype. It delayed, but didn't block it all."

"You use it like this." Michel-Leon slipped the mask over his head and strapped it into place to demonstrate.

"It's the demon in the mists," a man in the back shouted as the crowd murmured in fear, drawing back. Even Foreman Lyon took a step away. Constantin took a closer look at Michel-Leon. He could imagine how terrifying it would be to have him coming at you in the mists with the mask on. Maybe they weren't dealing with new monsters, merely men in masks taking advantage of the situation to steal. That would be a welcome relief for them if not for their victims. One less problem to deal with.

"What do you mean?" Michel-Leon demanded. He tore off the mask, scouring the frightened, tense faces in the line.

"Your mask." One man pushed forward, his face leeched of all color. "It reminds me of the creatures that roam the mists. The ones that I swear were taking things."

Michel-Leon frowned and looked at Constantin. "As usual, any answers lead to more questions. The damned magicman needs to be questioned again. That is one creature who has been out in the mists and who could answer decisively what the hell is going on. Especially since it must've dealt with them for the children."

"You won't get any argument from me." Constantin had observed the decay in Nightingale's face and body. Some men might enjoy the slow ending and delight in their adversary's downfall and torment. He wanted it over and Nightingale behind them. He didn't trust the monster for a moment. Every second it remained alive was a second it could use to retaliate and get free.

"They wore constructs like this?" Michel-Leon turned to the crowd and lifted the mask.

"*Non!*" The man who had screamed in fear pushed forward this time, his face a study of terror. He coughed, a wet tearing sound, and his lips were stained with the blood of consumption. "It weren't no mask. I was out there. I was taken by the mists." He shuddered and rocked. "Those monsters took me from the others, made me go back from the music."

"Aren't we all crazy?" Michel-Leon muttered under his breath in the irritated tone Constantin recognized. He was responding to the ancestors. Knowing that eased much of the uncertainty of being around him. Michel-Leon was saner and more stable than many.

"He was taken, my lord," Foreman Lyon confirmed. "Two weeks past. He was on guard duty. Too weak at the time for labor, but he could keep an eye out for us. We found him the next day wandering the ruins and crying to himself. This is the most coherent he's been since then."

That was the clearest confirmation Constantin had that it related the missing items to the mists. Like he'd theorized. He just wished he knew what it meant.

Michel-Leon caught the man by the shoulders. "I was denied the music too and made to go back."

The man's eyes focused on him with startling intensity. "Let me go back. I'll be worthy."

A wild light entered Michel-Leon's eyes, and it made Constantin uneasy. He still had not talked to him any further about what it was like out there. Now he wondered if that had been a mistake. "Do you know the way? Can you show me?"

"Michel-Leon, is that wise?" Constantin cautioned, laying his hand on Michel-Leon's arm.

"I had not been out in the mists long enough to get a proper sense of direction, but this man had been out in it for hours." Michel-Leon met Constantin's concerned gaze. Constantin recognized it was the first time they'd really looked at each other in weeks, and it struck him how much he'd missed it. "What choice do we have? I'd follow a madman if it took me where I needed."

A bewildered expression crossed the man's face. "You don't know either? I can't find it. The trail is gone."

Bitter disappointment filled Michel-Leon's gaze. "*Je suis désolé*, I do not, but maybe we can help each other find the way. Tell me about the monsters who turned you aside. You said they weren't wearing a mask, but they looked like this?" He held up the mask again, and the man shuddered.

"Their eyes were covered, black and shiny and big and their mouths gaped like gasping fish. They made sounds, horrible hissing noises." The man covered his ears as he rocked. "They lined us all up in the ruins. Most of them they took away with the stolen stuff, but they said I wasn't worthy. They hit me on the head, and I went to sleep."

"Before they caught you and lined you up, where were you headed?" Constantin asked gently. "Across the river? Away from Paris to the southeast?"

"I…I don't think so. I don't know. Everywhere there were mists. But I didn't hear the river." The man covered his ears. "Just the hissing. No words. And the call to the music. It was everything."

Constantin worried his lip. Their brief forays out into the mists had shown how impossible it was to find any landmark that would help with their bearings. It had forced him to use one of his gadgets to lead them home again. "You'd know better than I," he said to Michel-Leon. "When you were caught out there, did you have the presence of mind to know where you were going other than the music?"

Michel-Leon sighed, his shoulders slumping. "*Non*, the call overwhelmed everything."

"We found him not far from the site." Foreman Lyon faltered when Michel-Leon met his gaze. "If that's any help, my lord."

"Any piece of information is another clue in the puzzle, even if I don't know how they go together." Michel-Leon sighed and let the man go. "*Merci* for coming all this way. We will check in with you after the next cycle. *S'il vous plaît*, exercise caution."

Foreman Lyon pulled Constantin aside, his gaze grave. "Is there any hope? I looked into what happened at Metz as you told me to. The details were sketchy, but I heard enough. That's what we face, isn't it? A swarm of demons?"

"I believe if they were demons, the chevaliers would've found a way to find them, but there's always hope." Constantin grimaced. Michel-Leon was influencing his outlook. "I'd gather my belongings for an evacuation if I were you. It never hurts to be prepared for the worst-case scenario."

"We have nowhere to go." Foreman Lyon's hand fell away.

"There's a village near the château. They'll take you in. So when I say go, take your family and go." Constantin eyed the cloudless sky. "Paris will need help rebuilding if this goes badly."

"If the snuff works, what about inoculations for my family? I fear for them every time they leave our rooms." Foreman Lyon gestured to the rest of the dispersing group. "Most of them have loved ones who rely on them."

"The chevalier is working to make more." Constantin carefully stowed away the filtering mask. "And I'm making more of these. We have some business at the château, but I'll check on you in a few days and let you know where we stand."

Michel-Leon waited until they left and then climbed onto the carriage bench and took up the reins. Once Constantin settled next to him, they set out. "This all fits. I just cannot put the puzzle together. The creatures this man talks of sound like nothing the ancestors have ever encountered. They either must be something new or something ancient that hasn't surfaced in a millennium."

Constantin drummed his fingers on his thigh. "Based on what we have so far, I'd hazard it's something new, and it's linked to the aberrations that have you in such a tizzy. Or it's a crime of opportunity. If we could make a mask that filters out the mists, why couldn't someone else?"

"If it's a crime of opportunity, why not take items of real value?" Michel-Leon navigated the congestion of people and wheeled vehicles with competent ease. Once again, Constantin was struck by how different he was from others of his class. He was used to doing for himself. That was something Constantin understood. "I wish I could disregard him as a madman, but the other men agree there were strange-looking creatures out in the mists."

"Some of the children described the same. How much longer until we're done with Nightingale? I want that over with. As you have said, we have other more important things to concentrate on. If it were gone, we could go back to the townhouse and conduct more conclusive experiments and search the mists ourselves or delve deeper into those caves. Even using the compasses to explore the open passages heading toward Paris hasn't helped us make much headway." Constantin pounded his fist into his palm. "There has to be a way to push it further along."

Michel-Leon glanced at Constantin. "That creature holds on for spite, but it can't hold out much longer. There is something it is using to hang on, and I need to figure out what it is. Are you sure it is no longer tied to you?"

"I thought I severed it when I healed Gabrielle, but after it tricked me with the glamour, I investigated again." It still made Constantin's skin crawl. "Some links were back, weak but there. I might always be susceptible to it because I was with it for years. I don't know. I'm keeping an eye on it."

"What do you mean, healed?" Michel-Leon asked in a strangely neutral voice. "Can you do it for yourself?"

"When I was working with her to test if I could do the reflection you requested, I sensed the wounds on her soul." Constantin frowned as he tried to put into words what he'd done. "Her pain called out to me. I had to respond. But I don't know if I can do it for myself."

"It would be worth exploring." Michel-Leon urged the horses to a faster walk as they left the city. "I read that fey kissed had the ability. I'm glad you could do it for her. I hope you could do the same for yourself. You've carried those wounds around long enough."

Constantin studied his profile. He wished he could get a read on the man. He sensed Michel-Leon had wounds of his own. "Do you think it can be hurt with mortal weapons yet?" Constantin asked.

"I know you're impatient. I am too. But we have a chance here to get answers out of it. Nightingale knows something about these mists." He growled in aggrieved frustration. "We have scoured the cave system and have found no evidence of the nest. This inoculation has to work if Nightingale won't bend. We'll be able to track infected people once we're out in the mists with them."

He paused and gave Constantin a self-deprecating smile. "If it works. We don't need the creature."

"Let me talk to Nightingale again," Constantin urged. "We share a history. Maybe that will give me the opening to get something out of it."

"Your shared history is what concerns me." Michel-Leon started to reach out to trace the puckered scar on Constantin's cheek, but jerked his hand back as his cheeks flamed red. He turned his attention back to driving. "I don't want it to have the opportunity to hurt you again."

"That won't happen until it's dead and burned to ash." Constantin bit back his disappointment and concentrated on the countryside. "I'm going to talk to it when we return. Guard my back if you want, but I'm going."

Chapter Nineteen

"HOW'D IT GO in Paris?" Régine asked as she met them in the château's courtyard. "*Ma tante* Salome and Mahout returned. They insisted," she cut in when Michel-Leon protested. "Let them stay, Michie."

"The murderer of their husband and father is still inside!" Michel-Leon flung his hand toward the château as Constantin climbed down from the carriage. "What if it gets free?"

"If it gets free, there will be enough warning with traps going off for them to get into a hiding place," Régine replied while she unhitched the horses from the carriage. "It will be searching for sustenance, not revenge, not yet, not until it has fed. Besides, I'm not sure it can break free. It's weakening more every day. They need this, Michie."

"I'm going to have that conversation with Nightingale," Constantin said. "Maybe I will jog something useful from it."

Michel-Leon turned worried eyes on him. "I cannot stress this enough. Be careful. Remember what happened last time."

Constantin's gaze dropped to Michel-Leon's mouth, and the man flushed. "I'm not likely to forget. We should revisit the situation under different circumstances."

Michel-Leon reddened further as Constantin turned away, and he overheard Régine's curious whisper, "What happened that you didn't tell me?"

He smiled as Michel-Leon made a noncommittal response. Dealing with Régine would occupy his attention and perhaps force him to think a little more on their kiss.

The kitchens smelled of fresh baked bread and not the usual stew. Salome stood at the table, rolling out piecrust with her sleeves pushed up past her elbows and her hands floured. She glanced at Constantin with red-rimmed, tired eyes. "Don't you start in on me. We're back and we're staying."

"I'm not the one you need to argue with." Constantin paused, awkward with everything he wasn't sure he should do or say. But her pain reached out to him, and he moved toward her without thinking. He slipped an arm around her shoulders and laid his scarred cheek on the top of her head. "Welcome home, Salome. We missed you."

With a choked-off sob, she turned her face into his chest and held on a moment before straightening and pulling away. "Go on. You have things to do. Dinner won't be served for a few hours yet." She dabbed at her eyes with the end of her apron and went back to her piecrust.

Constantin paused, struck by the sense of her pain being momentarily eased. He wasn't sure what he had done, but maybe there was something to Michel-Leon's claims about the fey kissed. He headed deeper into the château, the evil presence of the magicman filling his mind. Régine was right. It was weaker, but the heart of it remained strong.

He paused outside the doorway to the balcony and laid his fingertips against the barrier. It was foul beyond there, the kind of evil that stained everything it touched. He heard a familiar footstep behind him and turned his head. "You didn't have to come."

"Neither did you," Michel-Leon said. "I would not have the magicman hurt you more."

"*Pourquoi?*" Constantin's lip curled as he shot Michel-Leon an angry, defiant stare. "Because you care so much about a rootless, dangerous man. Let me handle this."

Nightingale waited for him, facing the doorway with all of its arrogance. The creature had prided itself on its appearance, taking care its clothes were well-kept and in the latest style and that it was groomed to appear respectable. Now it was disheveled and dirty, its exterior reflecting the monster within. More of its fey nature was apparent in the sharp features and red-stained hands and mouth.

"Looking seedy there, old man." Constantin glared down at Nightingale. It had been a man once from what Michel-Leon had told him, but whatever was human in it had died long ago.

A cutting smile crossed Nightingale's lips. "I'm still strong enough to take you out, little Constantin. Why don't you come down and join me? Let's share in old memories."

"When I come down there, it'll be to stab a knife through your withered heart." Constantin rested his forearms on the railing, conscious of Michel-Leon lurking in the passageway. He was convinced Constantin needed a guardian angel, and it shamed him that he was grateful for his presence. "So what are you feeding on if there are no children around for you to torture?"

"Memories, Constantin." Nightingale's smile fell away. "I especially have sweet memories of how well you fed me. I can still hear your screams. And how you fought everything I devised for you, fought to the bitter end. It made you taste that much sweeter."

Constantin's vision tunneled onto the hated figure in front of him as the pit in his stomach went ice cold. "Those memories won't sustain you forever, and I have the pleasure of watching you rot in front of me."

A hand gripped his shoulder, and Constantin felt Michel-Leon's comforting aura. "I told you to let me handle it."

"We are stronger together, Constantin." Michel-Leon squeezed his shoulder and let go of him to stand by his side. "Have you thought about what we discussed, Poitou? Do you wish to tell us what you know about the mists? I'll make it worth your while."

"I don't need your deal, chevalier." Nightingale's cold, inhuman gaze flicked to Michel-Leon before concentrating on Constantin again. He sensed an old, bitter sensation as Nightingale's mental fingers stroked his soul. Constantin's hands tightened on the railing as he shoved back at the magicman's invasion. "I will take what I need right here."

Memories slammed into Constantin's consciousness, fueled in a powerful flood from the monster below. Bits and pieces carved out of him and soiled were being forced back into him helter-skelter in a sick parody. With each one the memory came so sharp and clear that Constantin could taste it, could feel it.

With a howl of rage and fear, Constantin struck back. He banished the boy he'd once been, even as Nightingale sank its claws and teeth into his spirit as the creature tried to feed on him and tear his soul free at the same time.

Two could play this game.

Constantin reached out as he had the day he'd wounded Nightingale. It was easier this time, his path surer as he put together what he did with Gabrielle and reversed it. No healing light for the magicman. After this many centuries, there was nothing left to heal. Only fire and pain for this monster.

The magicman screamed, and the shrill sound filled him with the sweet taste of victory. He hungered for more of Nightingale's fear and pain. And then it was there, coating his tongue and enveloping him in a tainted embrace.

"How does it feel, Nightingale?" Constantin rasped. "How does it feel to be fed off of?"

*

MICHEL-LEON STARED at Constantin in horror as the ancestors' voices shrieked at him. His face was drawn into a mask of rage and vengeance. "Shut up!" he snarled, struggling to think with so many talking at once. He pushed the ancestral voices away and locked them behind the wall Janvier had helped him create when he was a child. One that allowed him to keep his sanity at times like this.

Michel-Leon muttered the words to a glamour, and the electricity hummed in a ring around the monster. Lightning arced out, slamming into Nightingale and throwing it to the floor. Michel-Leon didn't like the hungry, feral look in Constantin's eyes or the way the magicman shrieked as it diminished before Michel-Leon's eyes. Its hair thinned to wisps. Its skin became like paper. And as it changed, so did Constantin, appearing more fey than he had before. His features sharpened, the scar on his cheek standing out in puckered relief as color drained from his face.

Lightning arced into Nightingale as Michel-Leon grabbed Constantin and shook him. "Let go of it! Constantin!"

Constantin's lips peeled back in a parody of a smile, and though he was facing Michel-Leon, he was staring right through him. Michel-Leon narrowed his eyes, gauging Constantin's awareness of what was around him. Violence would make him fight back harder.

He cupped Constantin's face in his hands. "Come back to me, Constantin." He kissed him, and Constantin stiffened in surprise as Nightingale's shrieks cut off to whimpers. Constantin trembled, and Michel-Leon slid his arms around him as Constantin clung to him.

"The watcher is twisted. Corrupted." The ancestors broke through the wall to give him a warning he didn't want. *"He had taken a step away*

from the dark path and then turned right back down it."

Michel-Leon closed his ears to the whispers. *Non*. He refused to believe it, refused to believe Constantin couldn't turn this around again. He'd witnessed what had caused it. He had some answers he sought, enough to give a proper warning.

"Michel-Leon?" Constantin whispered against his lips in a shaken, dazed voice.

"It's me." Michel-Leon pulled back enough to search Constantin's face. The kiss had accomplished what he'd intended for it to do. It had snapped Constantin out of his link with the magicman, but a part of him longed for a proper kiss. One born from each of them seeking it out and not a moment they were pushed into.

He traced his finger over the scar on Constantin's cheek and forced himself to meet his gaze. To his immense relief, it was Constantin who looked back at him, the fey, feral mien fading. The stain of it remained with a cold taint in his eyes, but Michel-Leon had hope it could be healed.

It would be healed.

"Welcome back." Michel-Leon grasped Constantin's shoulders. "It's dangerous for you to be here. This is the second time Nightingale has linked with you."

"But I hurt it this time." The coldness grew stronger with Constantin's fierce smile.

"At a cost, *mon ami*." Michel-Leon didn't know how he was going to tell Constantin that if he kept going down that road, he'd become what he hated. The seed had already been planted. He wasn't entirely human anymore, but he wasn't a magicman yet either. He would find the words and the way, but not here in front of the monster, who would consider it another weapon to use against Constantin. And Michel-Leon feared Constantin would be especially vulnerable to that weapon. "Promise me you won't try to hurt it like that again. It leaves a shadow of it in you, and you deserve to be free of it. Healing eases that shadow. Heal, don't feed."

The fierce smile fell away, and a question appeared in Constantin's eyes. "Do you care, Michel-Leon?"

"I do," Michel-Leon admitted and felt a chink in his armor give way.

"*Pourquoi?*" Constantin pulled away. "I'm a vagabond with nothing to my name, no home, and one goal." He flung his hand out toward the magicman. "To witness that thing destroyed."

Now was not the time for vague half-truths or to fob Constantin off with a trite answer. Michel-Leon dug down for a way to express his feelings for Constantin. "Because you took a wounded child and made them a force for good instead of evil."

"Gabrielle? Anybody would've—"

Michel-Leon shook his head and pressed his fingers to Constantin's lips. "I'm talking about you, Constantin. I have a great admiration for you. And you remind me I cannot forget the little costs in the face of the grand picture."

Constantin flushed, and Michel-Leon squeezed his shoulders again. "Promise me you will not feed off the magicman. Promise me. I'll believe your word. This is serious, Constantin."

Their gazes locked for a long moment, and then Constantin nodded. "I promise."

"*Merci.*" Michel-Leon let his hands fall away. "I'll check on Nightingale, but for the moment, I believe it will be safer if you two are several floors apart. I'll meet you back in the kitchen."

"Do you think it's safe for you to be here alone with it after what it tried?" Constantin stiffened as if he longed to look at Nightingale but dared not to as well.

Michel-Leon gestured to the magicman who had collapsed in a wizened heap, unaware of what was going on around it as energy crackled again. "It isn't in a position to harm anyone. It won't be long. Days at the most. Don't come back here. I'll let you know when the end is near. If you want to be there, then you may. But we cannot risk you being with it again. Understand?"

Constantin hesitated, measuring the steel in Michel-Leon's words. "I hope you get the information you want from it first."

"If not, we'll find a way." Michel-Leon waited until the door shut, and then he went to the railing and stared down at Nightingale. Despite its collapse, there was a gleam of uncanny alertness to its gaze. "I know you hear me, Poitou."

A tic appeared in the creature's cheek. "I am Nightingale."

"*Non*. Names have power, and I will deny you the power of the monster you turned yourself into. Though I suspect you've always been one. I wouldn't attempt feeding off Constantin again. He is not a terrified child anymore. His will to survive is stronger than you, and he will fight back to your detriment as you've learned." Michel-Leon just didn't want him to have to pay the consequences. "Are you ready to talk?"

The magicman pushed itself up to a sitting position and shot Michel-Leon a baleful glare. "This isn't over, chevalier."

"*Non*, it's not," Michel-Leon agreed, staring down the creature with dispassion. "But it soon will be. You attempt anything, and the lightning will strike again. It's your sole warning."

He left, pondering what to do next. His contact in Hamelin had sent him a ream of notes and an old book regarding magicmen and their link to the fey kissed. He'd read through it carefully again with what he'd learned today. Maybe there was something they could do to reverse the process. Michel-Leon wanted hard facts before he told Constantin what he'd done when he'd fed off the magicman. He wouldn't take it well, but if they had answers…a direction…that would help.

There had to be a way. After all, Constantin had already accomplished it once when he had healed Gabrielle. Despite Constantin's belief, he couldn't do it for himself, Michel-Leon chose not to accept that. There had to be a way. Someone else he could heal from the wounds on their soul.

If there were no answers there, then he'd have to delve deeper into his ancestor's memories. It would be dangerous, but Constantin was worth it.

Chapter Twenty

CONSTANTIN EYED THE stables and determined his own two feet were good enough. He could seat a horse decently. He'd had practice from time to time, but he'd never been confident on them the way Michel-Leon and Régine were. The village wasn't that far away. If all went well today, Michel-Leon wouldn't be nearly as alone as he feared.

"Constantin." Régine called after him, and when he pretended to ignore her, she ran after him. "Constantin! A word, *s'il vous plaît.*"

"I don't have time for words." Nightingale was close to succumbing, and Constantin wanted to be there when it happened, or he'd never believe for certain the monster was gone.

She growled low and fell into step beside him, dressed once again in her trousers and scarred boots, her hair pulled back in a plait that was neat for now. By the end of the day, the curls would escape in a crimson halo. Constantin finally understood her and her moods. She flipped between cool disdain when she was defending herself and passionate fury when she was defending others. The fire in her eyes today told him everything he needed to know. She was going to badger him about Michel-Leon.

"You will make the time to speak to me," she said between clenched teeth.

Constantin gestured to the road. "We can talk on the way, then."

"Where are we going? You were rather vague at breakfast." She shot him a fulminating glare. "He might not have noticed, but I did."

"To the village."

"I thought you might've been trying to go off to the cave system alone," Régine said. "You know, he always wants at least two of us there at a time. He doesn't want to risk anyone getting snared unwittingly. To be honest, I don't know how much farther we can delve there. We encounter more rockfalls than open passages. It's not safe."

Constantin made a noncommittal sound in response. He agreed with her summary of the situation, but the fate of the two lost boys pulled at him. He knew what happened to the people who disappeared into the mists. They were fodder for the growing swarm, but that didn't stop him from wanting to try. If he had known the boys, he could've used his beetles to find a trace of them, though he wasn't sure if his abilities would work on finding the dead whose soul has gone on.

"Why the village?" Régine persisted.

Constantin thought of Michel-Leon's words, how they were in this together, and sighed. He wasn't used to telling others of his plans. "You know how much he worries about being the singular one in this fight."

Régine made a disparaging sound. She was good at that, conveying her thoughts without words. It was a skill. "He's not alone. He has me and *grandpère* and I suppose you."

"Does this mean you trust me?" Constantin asked.

"You did spy on him." Régine eyed him, weighing and measuring. "But after the initial contact, you treated me like an equal, so I have to give you some measure for that. You've stuck by his side. I know something happened between you, him, and the magicman, but he won't say what it was."

"The usual, threats and jabs that hit at the heart of who we are. The same things it attacked you with." Constantin's conscience nagged at him. Régine couldn't help either of them if he lied or withheld the truth. "Though it used our old connection to try to have me harm Michel-Leon on one occasion, but I fought back." There was no need for her to know about the embrace. At first it had infuriated and humiliated him to have Nightingale witness it. Now he was coming up with reasons to pursue a second embrace.

"Has it been able to attack him directly or just through you?" Régine persisted.

"Just through me. I'm the weak part of this plan." As much as it galled Constantin to admit it. "One of the many reasons why Michel-Leon ordered me to stay away." For now, he'd listen.

"Michel-Leon is planning something," Régine said unhappily. "But he won't tell me what, probably because he knows it will upset me."

That was intriguing. Constantin would ponder that while they were out and then corner Michel-Leon later to discover what he could get out of him. "Well, if you're coming along, you might as well help. We're meeting a group from Paris and the villagers this morning. I sent out messages yesterday."

"What for?" Régine asked, baffled. "We've asked for volunteers for the caves already, but we've moved beyond the area they know. We've gathered what information we could from those who survived the mists."

Constantin shook his head. She was as stuck in the old ways as Michel-Leon. He supposed that was understandable. "Michel-Leon needs more people, not just me, you, and your *grandpère*. He needs more chevaliers, so I've recruited some."

Régine stopped in the middle of the roadway and stared at him with an open mouth. "But he doesn't want more chevaliers. The curse—"

"Exists through the blood," Constantin interrupted. "He wants a new way to pass along the information the chevaliers have gleaned, through the books he's creating, if he ever has the time to work on them. These people will help buy him time."

"Well, *oui*, that's part of it." Régine hurried to catch up, her voice curious. "But he also doesn't want to get people killed. He's too soft-hearted."

"But we're not." Constantin glanced at her out of the corner of his eye. "They know the dangers. They are not going into this blind, and we will train them to defend themselves. We'll give them the knowledge that will give them the edge."

"You're going to stay," Régine said in a soft voice, and when Constantin glanced at her, she was eying him again, the weighing and measuring back. "You care about him."

Constantin shrugged uncomfortably. "I suppose you could say I care about you all. My family is long gone. I keep in contact with my brothers, but they have lives and needs of their own, and I don't get to visit them as often as I like." He paused, uncomfortable with Régine's steady regard and giving voice to the welter of his emotions. "I suppose you could say you and Michel-Leon are like family to me. I'm not going anywhere, not after the magicman is gone, not after the mists." He didn't comprehend he'd made that decision until the words were out of his mouth.

Régine looked as if she wanted to say more but clamped her lips shut and remained silent until they reached the outskirts of the village. There were a good two dozen of them, men Constantin had spoken with and gathered information from since he'd started working with Michel-Leon.

Régine scanned the faces. "I recognize many of them. Good choices. Where are the women?" She turned and lifted a brow in his direction. "Women have a stake in protecting their homes as well."

"Ah, well." Constantin scrambled for a way out of this. "I thought I'd leave the recruitment up to you. You'd be the better judge of who can handle it. Michel-Leon would want to coddle and while I know a woman can be capable of defending herself, I think you'd be better at this."

Régine clasped his arm with a warm smile. "Smart answer."

"*Bonjour*," Constantin said as they approached. "For those of you who haven't met her yet, this is the chevalier's sister, the Widow Bardin. Do you have anything new to report?"

Constantin studied the group of assembled men and, if he judged rightly, he'd have names to add to the list he'd created. Everyone here had a vital stake in the situation unfolding in Paris. They had shown resolve and intelligence. Michel-Leon could use men like that at his back.

"The inoculation worked like a charm. Not one of us had any issues," Foreman Lyon said. "Though, if you don't mind, we'd like some of those filtering masks as an added precaution."

"That will be arranged. Especially since we will require your help soon. We plan on hunting those creatures you spied in the mists sometime soon. Hopefully, within the week." Constantin clasped his hands together. "May we count on your help?"

"You're not really an itinerant worker. Are you?" the foreman asked, narrowing his eyes.

Constantin didn't know what he was anymore. "I am a monster hunter, not a chevalier, but a man who is interested in keeping those I care for safe. To that end, I seek others like me."

The men exchanged uneasy glances, though Foreman Lyon stuck his chin out at a stubborn angle, and a glint of resolve appeared in his eyes. "I've never heard of the chevaliers recruiting before."

"There has never been a need before. They recruited from within, but the chevaliers are a relic of our past. If we are going to have a hope of fighting the monsters of our future, we need to band with the baron and his sister and learn what they know." He gestured to Régine. "Did you want to add a few words?"

She stepped forward, her bright hair shining in the summer morning sun. "Monsieur Severin is right, as much as it pains me to admit. What made the chevaliers strong is also what led to their downfall. Constantin has this radical idea of recruiting and training, and I believe it's a good one with one caveat. There are all kinds of monsters. You from the city understand the threat of the mists and you from the village have had to contend with the presence of a magicman as well. Your streets are empty of children until it is safe for them to return. The streets of Paris are also heavy with fear and sorrow. If the chevaliers pass on, then there will be no one left to defend France."

"Eloquently put, my lady," Constantin said with a bow of his head. "What say you all?"

Constantin wanted Michel-Leon to have permanent backup. Not just him, Régine, and her family. That man would never lay down and quit, not until he was dead. He knew it haunted Michel-Leon. He knew the man was reluctant to bring others into this, which is why Constantin intended on presenting him with men and women already committed to the idea.

"It is a dangerous thing you propose," Foreman Lyon said slowly, his brow furrowed with concern. "Some of us have families, other careers."

"Because we have families is why we must consider it." Another man stepped forward. "This is something that can be done in degrees. Whether we participate like we are now, as needed, or if we go with Constantin and become one of them."

"Exactly so." Constantin nodded at him in a gesture of respect. "I'm not asking you to give up your lives and follow me. I'm asking for aid when we need aid. I'm seeking to build a network in every town and village, so when there is a need for help, we find it there. And if there are those who are willing to devote their lives to this hunt, then they would be welcome. You need not decide today or tomorrow. Consider that and go with your gut. That's how I've survived, and if you know of anyone else who would be interested, then *s'il vous plaît* let them know to talk to me or to Widow Bardin."

"Which brings me to my caveat." Régine cast a stern glance around at the men gathered. "I fight alongside the chevalier. If you have women among you who wish to learn how to defend themselves, who wish to learn how to defeat the monsters stalking them and their children, I urge you, *s'il vous plaît* let them join."

Constantin and Régine conversed with them a while longer and collected several names of those who were interested. "Why didn't you take the horses or carriage?" Régine asked as they headed back to the château. "It would've been faster."

"My own feet have always worked well enough for me." Still, in this instance, Constantin wished he had. They'd been gone from Michel-Leon for several hours already. It made him nervous to leave him alone with the magicman, even if the only ones Nightingale had harmed had been himself and Hadrien. "This has been a good morning's work though."

"I agree. And I'll leave you to tell Michie about it since it was your idea."

Constantin eyed Régine. He longed to ask her about Michel-Leon. He didn't understand him, but he wanted to. It was patently clear Régine and Michel-Leon had a love for each other, even though they were not the siblings they claimed to be. He knew Michel-Leon had no intentions of ever marrying or having children. So what happened between himself and Michel-Leon was of no concern to anyone but each other. Still, Michel-Leon acted reluctant to open up any further about his emotions.

He wasn't comfortable dragging Régine into it, and she appeared content to walk in silence. Constantin brooded over it, afraid it was their class difference that bothered Michel-Leon, but he finally decided he needed to talk with him. Because he was falling in love. Better to know his chances than live on false hope. He'd done that before.

He closed his eyes, picturing the expression on Michel-Leon's face when he said he cared. That alone made it worth the chance.

By the time they walked into the château's courtyard, clouds had rolled in, heralding rain. The deepening shadows of nightfall and the dark and brooding edifice reflected Constantin's mood. The château's outside mirrored the dangers within, but it still had a grace and charm all its own that he often overlooked.

The château was silent, but the oppressive gloom of a dying magicman clung to the aura. Constantin felt a twinge of pity for the creature and hardened his heart against it, counting all the dead he could lie at its feet. Even counting the names he knew from his childhood added to the names of its most recent victims, Constantin knew there were so many more corpses piled on like cordwood behind them. *Non*, no pity for that thing.

Salome met them with hands on her hips. "Neither of you had returned for a noon meal, and my lord has not pulled himself away from his study all day." She pointed to a neatly packed basket. "I was about to bring this up to him."

"I'll take it up," Constantin said, remembering his promise to Janvier to keep Michel-Leon fed.

"And I'll eat here, then check on our prisoner." Régine gave Salome a smile of contrition. "Is there anything I may help you with?"

"*Oui*, eat." Salome pointed to the table. "Especially if you're going to deal with that thing."

Constantin headed upstairs after Salome added his dinner to the basket. He hoped the man was overworking in the lab or study and not once again trying to pull information out of a monster that would rather die first before giving them any aid. The workroom was dark, but light spilled in a warm glow from the study.

Constantin paused in the doorway and took a moment to scrutinize Michel-Leon. The lamplight brought a warm, rich glow to his untidy curls, and his expression was intent as he noted details in one of his many open journals.

Michel-Leon paused, and a smile flitted across his face. "How fares your inquiries?" he asked without taking his eyes from the journal.

"How do you always know when I'm here?" Constantin asked. There were many times when it wasn't apparent Michel-Leon heard voices at all and other times when it was quite clear. He had been witness to many a one-sided argument, which was often startling and sometimes entertaining. "Do your ancestors announce me?"

"Like a hundred Janviers with half his charm." Michel-Leon glanced up with an inquiring expression. "I hope it doesn't disturb you. Janvier warned me many times to not answer them out loud. It is another instruction of his I've failed to master."

"You should talk more of your successes and less of your failures," Constantin reproved, and Michel-Leon grimaced. He held up the basket. "Let's eat and I'll tell you of my inquires, but before we start, since I don't want to lose my appetite, I sense Nightingale is still with us?"

"I dislike that you can sense it, but *oui*. I suspect that it lives off malice and memory as it once boasted." Michel-Leon stacked his books to the side to make a cozy spot for them to eat. "*Je suis désolé*, Constantin."

Constantin shrugged and unpacked the basket. "The monster

may have its memories and rot with them. When this is over, I'll not think of it ever again."

"A fitting punishment."

As Michel-Leon rose to help him, their hands brushed together, and a tingle of heat went through Constantin. He caught Michel-Leon's hand. "I…" He trailed off as words failed him. He brushed his thumb over Michel-Leon's pulse and felt it skitter. He was not as immune as he tried to appear.

"I believe I know what you're going to say, and it cannot be." Michel-Leon pulled away with a smile of apology. "I've taken a vow of chastity."

Of all the responses Constantin expected, that was not it. "Why on earth would you do that?"

Faint color appeared on Michel-Leon's cheeks. "I swore I wouldn't pass along the curse to any children. I watched people be consumed by it. I can't knowingly give that burden to another, especially one of my own, without their knowledge or consent… I won't do it."

Constantin considered him, trying to gauge the real reason, as Michel-Leon wouldn't meet his eyes. He understood his excuse was a factor, and he couldn't blame him for not wanting to have his children deal with the voices. But that didn't explain it all. "You carry too much alone, Michel-Leon."

"Well, who else is there?" Michel-Leon met his eyes and smiled again. "Other than Régine and you."

Constantin's heart skipped and he longed to reach out to him and pull him into his arms, but he sensed Michel-Leon was still skittish. "You do not fight alone. I know you worry about the chevaliers dying out."

Michel-Leon gestured to the scattered books. "I worry the journals will not be enough."

"What about volunteers?" Constantin cocked his head as Michel-

Leon's gaze sharpened. "Those who train as chevaliers trained, without the burden of the voices, those who join with full foreknowledge of what they will face. So it is their choice."

Michel-Leon's brow wrinkled in a troubled frown. "It's a dangerous choice. It's not a question I want to have to ask."

"I've done it for you." Constantin pulled the list of names from his pocket and handed it to Michel-Leon. "These are people from the village and Paris who want to help. Most of them only want to be involved as long as the mists are here, but there are three who are interested in fighting alongside us for the long road."

Michel-Leon scanned the list with a stunned expression. "I don't know what to say."

"Consider it, and while you're at it, think about why you're alone when you don't have to be." Constantin caught and held Michel-Leon's gaze. "Neither one of us will ever have children. You and I both err on the side of choosing to remain alone. But even I know the power of allowing yourself to be held. It helps you to remember why you fight."

Chapter Twenty-One

MICHEL-LEON STUDIED the list long after Constantin left him. What a gift he'd been given. By a man who was incredible in every way. He ached with the need to tell him what was in his heart, but he didn't know how to approach him — didn't know what to say or how to act. He was completely clueless when it came to relationships, but perhaps Constantin was right. There was no need for him to lock himself away.

He fervently wished Janvier was there. He'd give Michel-Leon his honest opinion, though he suspected the old man would agree with Constantin on every point. Michel-Leon couldn't talk to Régine. He loved her, but there were some things he couldn't discuss with the woman he considered his sister.

He listened to Constantin working at his table as Michel-Leon continued his research. He had some thoughts on how they could approach the nest if they ever found it. Time was slipping away so fast. But tonight, he'd get some answers. He waited until Constantin said goodnight and acted as if he'd be a while still in his research.

Then Michel-Leon studied the names, once again marveling at Constantin's gift until he was sure Constantin was likely asleep. He carefully tucked the list away in his journal. In the next few days, he'd have to make it a point to talk to each of the volunteers. But for now, he had a promise to Constantin he needed to fulfill.

He rose and retrieved his sword, checking the blade to ensure the engraved inscription was intact. It had been a while since he'd needed to use it, and he wanted to be sure the spell still worked. The magicman had to be vulnerable at this point, and Michel-Leon didn't trust it wouldn't have a last trick or two to play. He wasn't going to allow Constantin to be hurt by it again.

Michel-Leon had one final lever to use to get the creature to speak. If that didn't work, he was done with stringing this out. Constantin deserved closure. He stopped by their rooms on his way up. Light spilled from underneath Constantin's door. Good. He needed the rest and didn't need to witness what was coming. It would distress him.

He quietly shut the door, headed to Régine's rooms, and knocked.

"Come in." Régine sat by her dressing table, running the brush through her long red curls. Her brows lifted at the sight of Michel-Leon's sword. "What is it?"

"I need you. Get your rifle and the bullets we've spelled." Michel-Leon glanced toward the ballroom. "It's time this is over."

Régine's expression firmed as she rose, and a steely light appeared in her eyes. "Where's Constantin?"

"In his room. With any luck, by the time he recognizes something is changing with the magicman, we'll have what we need." He held open the door as Régine grabbed her weapon and headed out with him.

"Shouldn't he be a part of this?" Régine asked in a hushed voice.

Michel-Leon shook his head. "Twice the creature was able to target him. I'm not going to risk a third time. Not when Poitou is this desperate." Besides, Michel-Leon had some words for the magicman that

Constantin would never allow him to utter without a fight.

They went up to the next level. The hallway was a shambles from all the traps the magicman had set off. It was past time Michel-Leon pulled the teeth of the place. Reputation alone would keep people away from the *Château des Ombres*. He didn't want anyone to get hurt coming in here after he passed.

"Go up to the door of the balcony and keep guard. I'm going to offer Poitou a deal for more information. Let's discover what we can jar loose from it. If it tries anything, shoot it." Michel-Leon thought of Constantin with a pang. "Constantin might sense something. He is connected to the monster. If he does, try to keep him from interfering."

"Understood. Keep yourself safe, Michie." She squeezed his arm as he gave her a grim smile.

"You too. There is no one I trust more to have my back." Michel-Leon could know that and still be grateful she was in a safer position. She knew the monsters and risks as well as he did, and she was as diligent in fighting them. It pained him he could not trust Constantin in this. He had no doubt of the man's heart and soul, but he was the weak link when it came to the magicman. The thought of him being hurt pained Michel-Leon more.

"Give me ten minutes to get into place." Régine took off without a backward glance, resolve apparent in every step.

Michel-Leon waited, gathering his arguments and offers together. This would end tonight. He opened the double doors to the magicman's prison and heat poured over him, drying the spit in his mouth and making his skin tighten. A blazing sun pounded down on the withering monster in the center of the room. Poitou had curled into a tight ball to protect itself, and it didn't notice it wasn't alone any longer.

With a word and gesture, Michel-Leon banished the glamour and Nightingale moaned, a wretched and pain-racked mewl. This was torture, and it went against everything Michel-Leon believed in. He preferred a quick and clean kill if it was necessary. But there was nothing clean about a magicman, so he hardened his heart against pity. "Are you ready to talk?"

"Leave me be with your pestering questions," it rasped as it uncurled its long limbs with painful slowness. "I'll not tell you anything, chevalier. Nothing! I'm not dead. None of your torments will kill me."

"*Non*, I suspect not." Michel-Leon paused outside the hidden circle. The glamour of a harmless old man the magicman had surrounded itself with had finally fallen away, showing the monster within. "You appear as if you didn't entirely escape the flames that sought your life when you were executed after de Rais."

The magicman was a shriveled husk, its skin blackened and burned, weeping with blood and other fluids. A livid bruise ringed its neck from where they tried to hang it first before it faced the fires. The soul magic it used to sustain itself was nearly spent, and it had reverted to how it looked before it shed its humanity. A creature too old and depleted to survive what was coming, and they both knew it.

"I have one last offer to make in exchange for information." Michel-Leon crouched so he stared at the magicman in its burning yellowed eyes. A chill touched his heart. This here was true evil. As dangerous as the swarm was, there was no malice in it, solely hunger. A magicman's hunger could never be satiated. Michel-Leon felt tainted just by being near it. "One last chance."

"Bah." The magicman spit blood at him, staining Michel-Leon's rumpled coat. "There is nothing you may offer. Nothing that will entice me. You plan on killing me."

"Oh, I do," Michel-Leon said softly, the words laced with menace. "And I'll take great relief in it, I assure you. But as much as it goes against my nature, I'm willing to give you one last sweet memory before you go. That's how badly I need that information."

"Constantin to play with?" The magicman went still, studying

Michel-Leon with a crafty gaze. "*Non, non*, you won't give him up. No deal."

There was something about the man who Michel-Leon had come to care for that called to the magicman. He hoped it had to do with their fey-kissed blood. That was the sole lure that made sense. There was something about it that was more potent for this monster. "What about the little one who Constantin stole? She's still a child, still innocent."

A scuffle broke out on the balustrade, and Michel-Leon went cold. He glanced as Constantin muscled past Régine, his face pale and pinched with horror. "*Non*! Michel-Leon you can't!"

The magicman cackled and Michel-Leon turned his stony gaze back on it. *Bon sang*, he hadn't wanted Constantin hurt, and now he would be. Only this time, Michel-Leon was the cause.

"Stay out of it, Constantin," Michel-Leon warned, keeping his eyes on the magicman. At this moment, it was truly dangerous. "This is the only way. We are running out of time. Summer is coming to a close. The mists are erratic and the swarm is getting closer to hatching." He glanced up, met Constantin's stricken gaze, silently willing him to understand. He stood on the balcony, gripping the railing like it was a lifeline. Michel-Leon hardened his heart against the pain he saw etched into Constantin's face. Régine stood behind him, blocking the door. "I warned you when this started. One life is not worth thousands."

"*Non*, you can't! She's in Lorraine. She wouldn't get here in time."

It killed Michel-Leon to know he would have to dash the desperate hope in his eyes.

"I lied," Michel-Leon said softly, and Constantin reeled back as if struck. "I had Janvier come back with her after everyone was safe. In case we needed her."

"And you say I'm evil." The magicman laughed softly as Constantin dropped to his knees with an expression of horror etched deeply into his face. No sound uttered from his lips, yet Michel-Leon could feel his pain. "You've hurt him worse than I ever could."

"I know." And Michel-Leon would live with that regret, with the memory of Constantin's anguish. "Whatever it takes. Do we have a deal?"

*

HE WOULD KILL them all for this betrayal. Constantin seethed as he spun around for the door.

Régine pointed her rifle at his head, her expression stern. "Stay right there, Constantin," she warned.

"Treacherous, lying, monsters," Constantin hissed, crouching low and holding out his hands.

Régine's mouth firmed, but before she could say anything, Constantin twisted the shadows around himself. Régine cursed and lowered the rifle to poke the butt at the air, searching for him. Constantin retreated down the balustrade and walked the entire length around to slip behind her. He'd stop this. No matter what it took.

"We have a problem," Régine called down. "He pulled his disappearing trick."

"I'll deal with him later," Michel-Leon said, keeping his eyes on the magicman. "Get the child. Come back with her, but don't come up here yet. I'll let you know when a deal has been made."

"Understood."

A part of Constantin hadn't believed in their treachery, but when Régine disappeared through the door, he wanted to howl in pain and rage. He would carry them all to hell first before he let them harm another child. *And how many more children will die if Michel-Leon doesn't stop the swarm?*

Constantin's steps faltered, and he almost stumbled. No one should have to make that choice. It couldn't have been an easy choice for him to make. But the deception burned. Knowing Michel-Leon had lied. That he'd held Gabrielle aside to use her for leverage. He wasn't the man Constantin thought he knew. The man he loved.

Constantin clambered over the balustrade and swung down to the floor, banishing the glamour as he went. He fell hard, pain shooting up his legs. Nightingale cackled, and Constantin sensed it trying to reach for him as he recoiled from that evil mental stroke. "Your agony is so sweet, little Constantin. Will the chevalier leave you to watch as I take back what you stole from me? I hope so."

"*Non!*" Constantin fought off the attack as hunger called to him to grab what remained of Nightingale and consume it. Michel-Leon spun around to face him, and the resolve on his face hurt Constantin anew. "I won't let you take her! Damn the consequences. We'll find another way."

He swung at Michel-Leon, and he dodged. All traces of the scholar disappeared as Constantin faced the chevalier. He caught Constantin's arm and before he could blink, Michel-Leon was behind him, his arm around Constantin's throat in a viselike grip. Then they were tumbling to the floor, Michel-Leon's legs wrapped around him so Constantin couldn't struggle.

Constantin fought, trying to pry his arm loose, trying to find leverage. Though the pressure was uncomfortable, it didn't cut off his air as Constantin expected it to.

"Trust me, *s'il te plaît, mon cher.*" Michel-Leon breathed in his ear. Stunned, Constantin slowed his struggles as he assessed everything he knew of Michel-Leon and Régine.

He did trust Michel-Leon, a completely novel experience for him. He was so used to being betrayed, having to guard his back, to search for the other angle. But his thoughts kept going back to the sorrow in Michel-Leon's eyes when he heard of the magicman's crimes. His flinty determination to protect as many as he could. The way he took each death as a personal failure.

Constantin slowed his struggles more, projecting helplessness along with the rage that had consumed him. Nightingale still lurked, trying to break through and feed off his emotions. Michel-Leon relaxed fractionally. "Time to go to sleep," he said, his voice intent.

His thoughts spinning, playing on that implied command, Constantin went limp. He remained careful to block Nightingale out, so he appeared unconscious. He wasn't sure what game Michel-Leon was playing, but he was willing to let it spin out for the time being. Michel-Leon held him a moment longer and then released him, easing Constantin to the floor.

"He'll be out for a while, so it's just you and me. Do we have a deal or not?" Michel-Leon asked.

Silence stretched out, and Constantin forced his breathing to remain slow and even and disciplined his emotions, exerting his will to calm and his thoughts to still. After an interminable wait, he sensed Nightingale probe him again, but it was weak, so weak. Constantin didn't think it could even latch on and feed unless it was in contact with its victim.

Constantin bit back a surge of muddled emotion as Nightingale withdrew.

"We have a deal," it rasped. "Fetch the child."

"I am no fool," Michel-Leon responded. "I want the information first. The child will be within the château momentarily, but I'll not have her brought up yet. You may start by telling me where the swarm's nest is. I suspect you know."

Nightingale laughed sardonically. "I am no more a fool than you. You are worse than foolish, so sure of your knowledge, so sure of your reasoning. All the swarms are in caves, so you've been concentrating your searches there. I've been observing. Fool. Fool. Fool. The swarm is not outside the city."

"I've gathered that much, though it makes no sense," Michel-Leon said, his voice urgent. "Then where, if you know so much? Where would that mother be able to hide and lay her nest? She is not a small creature."

"It is underneath it." The magicman began laughing again, and there was an edge to it that chilled Constantin as if any vestiges of humanity had finally snapped. The mocking jeer crawled along his nerves. "No more will I say. Not until I have the child. Then you may ask any question you wish."

"Very well," Michel-Leon said, and Constantin tensed, prepared to fight him if necessary. "Constantin, does it tell the truth?"

Constantin sat up and stared at Nightingale. This was the monster that plagued his memories and nightmares. He didn't know if he'd ever be free of it, even after it was dead. Nightingale narrowed its eyes at Constantin and hissed. There was fear there in that inhuman gaze and consternation. Constantin drilled that memory into his mind as well. A magicman could know fear.

"I believe so." He glanced at Michel-Leon as he stood up. "Is it enough?" *Mon Dieu, let it be enough.* He couldn't take any more.

"It will have to be." Michel-Leon drew his sword as Nightingale struggled to its knees, panting, its rage almost palpable.

"We had a deal, Chevalier!"

"I lied." Michel-Leon said and glanced at Constantin. The care he saw in those eyes almost brought him to his knees. Michel-Leon held out the sword. "Do you want to be the one to execute it?"

Constantin stared at Nightingale again, remembering all the times he'd dreamed of this moment. Now that it was here, he no longer longed for revenge. He just wanted it over. He wanted to know Nightingale wouldn't harm anyone again.

"I don't care. You or me, just do it. You do it," Constantin said, ashamed of his doubt, that he'd thought for one minute Michel-Leon would deliberately harm someone he'd sworn to protect, that he wasn't as committed to taking down the magicman as he'd said.

"*Ainsi soit-il.*" Michel-Leon faced the magicman. "Etienne Poitou Corrilaut, you have haunted the children of France for centuries. You've stolen their innocence and well-being. You've tortured and killed untold numbers and twisted others to aid you. For those crimes and many more we do not know about, I, Michel-Leon Parisee, Baron de Dagonville and Chevalier de Rouen, do sentence you to death. May God have mercy on what's left of your soul."

Nightingale scuttled back until it hit the invisible barrier as Michel-Leon crossed the line into its prison. With a bestial cry, the magicman launched itself at him in a blur of motion and latched onto Michel-Leon.

"*Non!*" Constantin sensed the magicman trying to feed off Michel-Leon as he struggled to get the creature off him with his arms pinned to his sides. He couldn't let that happen. He crossed the barrier to face his nightmare.

"Michie!" Régine came through the double doors, her rifle raised, and Constantin flung up a hand.

"Wait, we can't hurt Nightingale without hurting Michel-Leon too." But there was one way. Constantin grabbed the creature, sensed its rush of fear as its lips peeled back in a horrible grimace. "Let go of him, or I'll suck out what's left of your miserable existence." He longed to do it anyway. The desire welled up, the hunger stronger this time, but Constantin gritted his teeth and ignored it. He'd promised Michel-Leon he wouldn't do it again, and he'd keep that promise unless it was necessary.

"Constantin, don't." There was a terrible fear in Michel-Leon's eyes, and he wrenched himself free of Nightingale. "You can't."

Constantin kept his tight grip on Nightingale as it fought him like a feral thing, even though it was nothing but bone and skin and sinew. "Don't you believe it deserves that end? Bah, I'm done with you."

Constantin threw Nightingale away from him. He felt fouled by handling it.

Nightingale leapt at them with a snarl, and terror slammed back into Constantin's throat. Michel-Leon's blade flashed, piercing it through, and it collapsed into a heap, clutching its chest, as blackened blood oozed out. "You believe you won." It turned hate-filled eyes on Constantin. "You're like me."

Its body began crumbling in on itself, starting with its feet.

"I am nothing like you!" Constantin spat.

Nightingale's lips curved in a terrible, mad grin as its legs turned to ashes. "Oh, *oui*, you are."

"Shut up, Poitou," Michel-Leon ordered, and the grin widened as its collapse quickened. Régine came up beside him, her gaze horrified.

"One day you'll understand," it whispered, sinking down, its gaze fixated on Constantin in a way that shook him to his core. "When you feed off innocents too, you'll remember me."

"I would never." Constantin staggered back, sickened, and horrified at the thought. "I would never do what you do."

"You'll seeeeee..."

Constantin wrenched the sword from Michel-Leon's grasp and struck off the monster's head from its crumbling body. It rolled away, the terrible grin remaining until that too turned to dust. Constantin sank to his knees, unable to pull his eyes away from the desiccated remains.

It was over. It was finally over. Emotion heaved up, choking him. Constantin buried his face in his hands as sobs shook him. Years of pent-up anger and grief racked his body. Arms came around him, and Constantin leaned into Michel-Leon's embrace.

Chapter Twenty-Two

MICHEL-LEON HELD Constantin as the storm of emotion shook him. He'd carried so much, in memory and duty, for so long. As much as Michel-Leon hated to witness him in such distress, he sensed Constantin needed to get this out or else it would fester inside him.

Régine entered the ballroom with a stricken expression. "Will he be all right?"

Michel-Leon wished he knew. The magicman's words kept circling in his head. Nightingale had known Constantin had the potential to turn into a magicman. And Constantin had been about to tear the creature's twisted soul apart. The ancestors had confirmed his intent and warned him so he could intervene. The edge Constantin walked scared Michel-Leon more than he wanted to admit.

He had to speak to Constantin, warn him of the danger. Be sure he understood the stakes this time. *Bon sang*, he didn't want him to be hurt anew by his hands tonight. It was bad enough he'd overheard his lies to Nightingale. Still, he had to do it. He wouldn't risk dooming

Constantin because of a misguided need to shield him. He needed to have faith in Constantin's resilience as much as he believed in his ability to stay on the healthy path.

He gave Régine a helpless look, and she patted his shoulder, then knelt on Constantin's other side. She smoothed back his hair, exposing the scar on his cheek. "You did it, Constantin. You saw it through to the end. Gabrielle is safe. Neither of us would ever hurt her, under any circumstance, no matter how much we needed this information."

"I know. I know." Constantin lifted his head, his face ravaged. "My doubts about you both almost ruined your ploy. *Je suis désolé*."

"I believe you strengthened it. Your outrage was the tipping point. I will add my assurances to Régine's. I never intended for you to overhear that. Come," Michel-Leon murmured, helping the other man to his feet now that his tears and shudders subsided. "We could use a stiff drink."

"I'll leave you both to the drinking," Régine declared. "I need to let *ma tante* Salome and Mahout know it's over. We should be together tonight and soothe each other. Have a drink to *mon oncle* Hadrien for me."

"Let her know we leave for Paris in the morning," Michel-Leon said, and she nodded.

He clasped her hand in gratitude and support. Then Constantin caught it and held it to his chest. "If you ever need anything, I am there." His gaze switched between Régine and Michel-Leon. "Both of you."

Régine smiled and kissed his scarred cheek. "It isn't necessary, but *merci*. I have two brothers now."

They parted on the stairs, Régine to go to her family, while Constantin and Michel-Leon retreated to the haven of their workshop. "I'd hoped that all those souls he'd consumed would finally be released," Constantin murmured in a lost voice when they were finally sitting down with cognacs. "But I sensed nothing like that with Nightingale's death."

"*Je suis désolé*, Constantin, but I don't see how it would be possible." The more Michel-Leon learned of the monsters, the more he committed himself to hunting them. At least they were rare creatures. He had to ensure he passed along what he'd learned. "What's destroyed stays that way, but the magicman will never harm anyone again. You made sure of that. Against all odds. You wouldn't give up. You should be proud."

"It will have to be enough." Constantin gave his glass a grim glare, then tossed back the contents. He set the glass down and fixed his gaze on Michel-Leon. "I don't think I'm in the mood for drinking or talking."

The direct stare and words flustered Michel-Leon, filling him with heat. He took a hefty swallow of his drink, but the heat only increased, and then Constantin was moving toward him. He should protest, put a stop to Constantin's intent, but his tongue remained tied as Constantin pulled him up and into his arms. Constantin tasted like cognac and reckless heat, always ready to dive in without thought of the consequences, and Michel-Leon allowed himself to be pulled along in his wake.

He slid his hands into Constantin's hair, his heart pounding faster with Constantin's rough, urgent kisses. His senses felt alive and all of them locked on the man with him. "Constantin," Michel-Leon whispered. His thoughts whirled as Constantin's lips traced a path along his jaw to his ear, revealing sensitivities Michel-Leon didn't know he had. He clutched at him, trying to form a coherent thought.

Constantin pulled back and took Michel-Leon's hand. "Let's seek more comfortable quarters."

Michel-Leon dug in his heels, and Constantin shot him a confused look. He scrambled, trying to find the words to fit all of his tangled emotions. He wanted to throw away caution and say yes, but his concern for Constantin wouldn't let him. "I don't want to take advantage of you." He flushed at Constantin's surprised expression. "You've had enough men in your life who have done that."

"How would you be taking advantage?" Constantin asked. "I want you and you want me. It seems straightforward. Sex is a good way to distract ourselves from our problems for a time."

His body yearned for him to shut up, but Michel-Leon persisted. "What happened earlier would be upsetting to anyone, but you lived with what it both did to you and had done to you. I don't want…" Michel-Leon's words failed him.

Constantin's eyes softened. "I think you may be the first lover of mine to express such a sentiment. Once again, you surprise me. I am not used to someone like you." He slid his work-roughened fingers over Michel-Leon's cheek and buried them in his hair. A glint appeared in his eyes that made Michel-Leon's knees shaky. "However, you are the virgin here. Perhaps I am taking advantage of you."

Michel-Leon's cheeks heated. He hadn't appreciated his inexperience had been so evident. He had the impression, though, Constantin wasn't put off by it. "Well, there is that. If you're sure."

"Oh, I am." There was a wicked glint in Constantin's eyes, and the weariness etched across his features had eased.

Michel-Leon laced his fingers with Constantin's, jittery with nerves as Constantin led him along the hidden passageways. The voices nattered at him in an indistinct murmur, but Michel-Leon couldn't concentrate enough to get the gist of the message. It didn't seem important, so he shut them off. This was a private moment. And though there was too much riding on their success, too many strings they needed to follow up on, this was important. Or else, as Constantin pointed out to him, why were they fighting so hard if not to live?

His nerves increased tenfold as Constantin shut the door to his room and slid the lock home. Memories came to him of other stolen moments that left him filled with longing and frustration before they ended with such finality. Constantin was not Lennox though. He was not a man who thought of himself first and others second. And when he did think of himself, it was usually in survival terms.

"What are you pondering so hard?" Constantin asked, tipping Michel-Leon's face toward him.

Michel-Leon's heart caught painfully. He could trust Constantin with this. "It is a novel experience to be here like this with someone who isn't seeking to use me either. To him, I was merely a distraction to toy with. I thought I cared for him, but care dies quickly when it is one-sided."

"Ah, that explains a few things. Your reluctance with intimacy." Constantin rubbed his thumb over Michel-Leon's jaw. "*Je suis désolé* someone did that to you. I won't."

"I know." Shyly, Michel-Leon slid his fingers through the silken weight of Constantin's hair. "You already have what you want from me."

A quick, naughty smile crossed Constantin's sensual mouth. "Oh, my innocent chevalier, not even close." He kissed Michel-Leon, swamping him with emotion again as his mouth taught him how lips and tongue could play and tease with both tenderness and hunger. "I've been thinking of you in this big and lonely bed," Constantin said as he pulled away and tugged Michel-Leon toward it.

"You have?" Michel-Leon asked, bemused, as Constantin sat on the edge of the high bed and urged Michel-Leon closer.

"You mean you haven't been thinking of me?" Constantin said with an amused light in his eyes, and Michel-Leon blushed again. Then his expression became serious, and he slid his hands into Michel-Leon's hair again. "You are a balm to my soul."

Before Michel-Leon could respond to the startling admission, Constantin was kissing him and unbuttoning his shirt. Michel-Leon went hot and cold, tingles rippling over his skin, and then he was doing the same. They pulled back long enough to strip off their garments, and

Constantin's mouth was on him again.

Michel-Leon shivered as he pressed hot, urgent kisses along his throat and collarbone. Constantin awoke a hunger in him that he'd buried for so long he'd forgotten it was a part of him. He slid his hands over Constantin's smooth torso and the lean body that still showed evidence of so many years scraping for food. Constantin's hands on his belt sent another shiver through him.

He pulled back and knelt before Constantin to remove his boots. He knew it was a delay born of shyness, but Constantin didn't appear upset by his withdrawal. "I've never had a nobleman at my feet this way, acting as the servant."

Michel-Leon wanted to ask if he'd been with any other noblemen but held his tongue. "I'm just a man. Titles in France can be dangerous, given the mood of the people and the indignities forced on them. Sometimes I wonder if we've learned anything."

He tugged off one boot and let it thump to the floor before moving on to the next. "It gives me the funds to pursue my calling, but I would prefer to only have the title of chevalier."

"Despite the pain and loneliness it causes you?" Constantin asked with a cock of his head.

"It is what I am." Michel-Leon slid his palms up Constantin's thighs and let Constantin pull him back up into his arms.

"It's not all you are." Constantin reversed their positions and kissed Michel-Leon tenderly before pushing him back on the bed. He quickly stripped out of the rest of his clothes, standing unabashedly naked in front of Michel-Leon. The lamplight burnished his skin, emphasizing his fey-like quality. He looked so beautiful, like he didn't belong in this world.

The scar on his cheek reminded him that Constantin was a man, the same as him, and that he'd much rather be treated that way. Both of them had been so caught up in the roles given to them. The changeling vagabond and titled chevalier who had no business forming a friendship, much less even more. But here alone in their room, they could just be. Longing welled up in his heart as Constantin smiled at him.

"I will be right back, and I expect you to be naked as well when I return."

Michel-Leon stared in stunned disbelief as Constantin strode naked across the room with no apparent discomfort for his state of undress. He disappeared into the adjoining room, where he slept. Michel-Leon pulled off his boots and the rest of his clothing. He didn't want to disappoint Constantin when he returned, and the longing to be with him overcame his shyness about getting naked as well.

Constantin returned, bouncing something in his hand. Michel-Leon's curiosity about it swept away with Constantin's smile of approval and the long, hungry gaze he gave him. Michel-Leon's heart beat faster as Constantin crossed back over to him. Both of them carried scars visible against the skin in the lamplight. Each scar told a story, and he wanted Constantin's, but not tonight.

Constantin clambered up beside him, and they drew the bedcurtains around them, enclosing them in hushed darkness. Michel-Leon slid his arms around Constantin as they came together, and his breath caught at the sensation of naked flesh against naked flesh. He'd been partially unclothed with a man, come to completion with their fumbling explorations, but it was not like this.

They kissed, urgent and hungry. All the upheaval of emotion they'd gone through that night translating into passion. Constantin's lips branded his skin, and Michel-Leon moaned as he skimmed his fingertips over Constantin's smooth body, seeking touches that pleased him. Constantin made him ache in so many ways. He distracted Michel-Leon from his tasks, made him ponder things other than monsters or his quest to leave behind a written legacy. They had so much in common, the way they viewed the world and their duty that went beyond the differences in their station.

Michel-Leon found himself wanting to spend more and more time with him, confide in him, and steal away times like this when they could lock themselves behind closed doors and love each other. He wanted Constantin to find a home with him.

They laid back on the thick pillows and the taste of Constantin was on his lips, the scent of his hair as it fell around him when Constantin lay over him. Michel-Leon groaned, sliding his hands down the muscles of his back, tracing the outline of his ribs and hips.

"How do I please you?" Michel-Leon asked, trying to gather his wits as Constantin scattered them with every touch.

"Let me show you," Constantin whispered. Then his mouth moved lower, finding a sensitive spot right under his ear that made Michel-Leon shiver. Every time Michel-Leon got used to a touch or the brush of his lips, Constantin moved on until Michel-Leon was swept up in the haze. The feel of Constantin's mouth on his nipple had him clinging to the headboard, his body writhing as he panted.

Who knew a touch, a kiss, could have so much power?

Michel-Leon's mouth was dry, and all he could do was make little whimpers that encouraged Constantin as he explored. He urged Michel-Leon's legs apart and settled between them. The sensation of Constantin's hardness against his own sent a fresh wave of heat through him. He was on fire, and for once, he didn't fear it.

He found a spot on Constantin's neck that made the other man shudder and circle his hips against Michel-Leon. There was madness in this rush of desire and Michel-Leon didn't want it to stop.

Constantin grasped his cock with slickened fingers, and Michel-Leon groaned, his hips rocking as he pushed into his hand. It felt so unbelievably good, better than his own touch, more potent. The circle of his fist moved up and down on his shaft, and Michel-Leon thought he'd go out of his mind with the pleasure. Just when he thought it might be too much, Constantin backed off, leaving Michel-Leon trembling in reaction.

"Let's see how well you learned your lessons," Constantin challenged as he shifted to lie back on the pillows beside Michel-Leon.

"I…" Michel-Leon trailed off, at a loss for what to say. He reached for Constantin instead, wanting to give him the same feelings, the slow buildup to the edge. He started by kissing him, marveling at how such a simple meeting of lips could feel so right. Constantin let him take the lead, and at first, it filled Michel-Leon with shyness, but the way he kissed him back sparked his curiosity more. He craved to know what it would be like to have Constantin writhing and panting as well.

Constantin's nipple pebbled against Michel-Leon's lips, and he experimented with kisses and nibbles. Constantin threaded his fingers in Michel-Leon's hair, pressing gently in encouragement. He took it into his mouth, remembering how electric it had felt. Constantin's breath caught, and his cock throbbed against Michel-Leon's stomach.

If it excited Constantin that much with this spot, how much more of a reaction would he get if he experimented lower? Michel-Leon broke away and kissed down Constantin's stomach. His scent grew stronger. Michel-Leon both wished he could see Constantin better and was grateful for the masking darkness. He fumbled for him, wrapping his fingers around Constantin's shaft.

Constantin hissed, his fingers tightening in Michel-Leon's hair, and he froze.

"Is this bad?" he asked.

Constantin chuckled, the sound ghostly in the dark, and his grip eased. "*Non*, it feels good."

Michel-Leon dipped his head and ran his lips over where his hand was. Constantin's shaft burned against his lips, the skin silky and inviting.

Constantin gasped. "I have not given you that lesson yet!"

Michel-Leon smiled, pleased at the reaction, and it emboldened him to do more. "Well, I am a scientist. I learn by experimentation."

Constantin groaned and lifted his hips. "Who am I to argue with science?"

Michel-Leon bent over him again, making a silent vow that the next time they would do this in the light. It was one thing to feel Constantin's reactions; it would be another to witness it. After all, observation was key.

He ran his fingers over Constantin's straining cock and followed with his lips. It felt vitally alive against his mouth and left a unique taste heavy on his tongue. He kissed, nibbled, and sucked, experimenting with everything Constantin had shown him until he tensed and pulled away, panting hard.

Before Michel-Leon could ask if he'd done anything wrong, Constantin was kissing him, hungry and urgent, sweeping him up in his fire again. He turned Michel-Leon, laying him on his back. "We'll experiment more later," Constantin said as their lips parted.

Constantin straddled him again, settling over Michel-Leon's hips. Before he could ask him what new game this was, Constantin grasped him and sank down onto his cock. Shocked, Michel-Leon went still, and that incredibly tight heat enveloped him.

"*Oui*," Constantin groaned, settling down against him and rocking. A delightful constriction around his shaft made Michel-Leon break out in a sweat. His fingers dug into Constantin's hips as his heart pounded. Then Constantin began to move on top of him, riding him, breaking him in, and all Michel-Leon could do was hold on and attempt to keep up to the final, reckless end.

"*Mon seigneur*." Michel-Leon stared up into the darkness, his brain spinning, his body humming as Constantin folded over him. He slid his arms around the other man, and Constantin chuckled.

"Not yet." Constantin kissed him and slid off him. He kissed

Michel-Leon's shoulder. "But give me a few minutes, and we'll see if I can do better."

"Better?" Michel-Leon lay his head on Constantin's shoulder. "I'm not sure I could survive better."

Constantin chuckled again. "Let me show you, slower this time."

They kissed. Then Constantin proceeded to give truth to his words. Finally, limp, exhausted, Michel-Leon dropped into sleep right away with no thought of the dangers and deadline looming over them.

Chapter Twenty-Three

MICHEL-LEON STIRRED next to him, muttering in his sleep in agitation. His long, naked body moved against Constantin and stirred his interest all over again. They'd dallied deep into the night until both of them were spent and sated. He slid his arm around Michel-Leon, loath to wake him, and Michel-Leon's muttering died off.

There was still so much Constantin had to learn about him. He wasn't sure if his troubled dreams manifested from the confrontation with Nightingale, or their looming deadline, or if his ancestors hounded him in his sleep as well.

He hoped not the latter. The man deserved some respite from his duty. The dreams probably weren't because of the end of the magicman either. It was a goal finished for the chevalier, nothing more.

To Constantin, it was everything.

He didn't have to worry anymore about Nightingale targeting his brothers' children or any of the other little ones. He could move forward with his life, find new goals. Like helping Michel-Leon teach a new brand of chevaliers. Finding ways to blend magic with constructs. And if he was fortunate, building on the growing relationship between them. Constantin pressed a kiss to Michel-Leon's naked shoulder as his thoughts continued to wander.

He should be elated and energized, but Constantin couldn't quite get Nightingale's parting shot out of his mind. He knew that's what the monster intended—to get in his head, to cause him further sleepless nights forever.

Restless, Constantin clambered from the high bed and yanked on his breeches. Dawn wasn't far off, and there was the faintest hint of light on the horizon. Michel-Leon would insist on relocating them to the town house today. There was no point in staying at the château now that it was no longer needed as a prison. All the answers to the swarm were in Paris.

Constantin leaned against the embrasure and studied the horizon as streaks of color appeared along the east. He brooded over Nightingale's last words. *"When you feed off innocents too, you'll remember me."*

It was nonsense, utter nonsense. He'd never hurt a child. But the uneasiness remained. Gabrielle's memory haunted him as well, the hunger that struck with her fear. It hadn't been as strong as the call to heal, and he'd been distraught when he recognized he'd scared her. But what if there was some merit to what the monster had said?

Constantin pushed away with a shake of his head. No, no more. Nightingale had haunted him his entire life. He wasn't about to let the monster haunt his future too. He had a future, a purpose. If he let Nightingale taint that going forward, then that was on him. He sat on the edge of the bed and pulled on his boots.

He sensed Michel-Leon right before his arms slipped around Constantin. "What are you thinking about so hard?" he asked softly.

Constantin shrugged as he laid his hand over Michel-Leon's. "I am troubled. It's probably nothing. I feel like I should know what

Nightingale was talking about." He gestured toward the window. "About Paris, I mean, and where the swarm is."

"*Moi aussi,*" Michel-Leon said with a heavy sigh. "It is right there, tantalizing, but the answer eludes me."

Constantin hesitated. He didn't want to address his concerns. He didn't want to give them any weight. It was insanity…but what if Nightingale's story had a germ of truth in it? He couldn't take the chance. Michel-Leon would tell him what he needed to know, and if he didn't know the answer, he would track it down. He wouldn't let something like that slide away without confronting it.

"Do you think there's any merit to what Nightingale said?" Constantin glanced over his shoulder at Michel-Leon in the early morning light. He would smile and tell him not to let the monster concern him. And then Constantin could put it behind him. "That I'm doomed to be like it?"

Michel-Leon went still, and his eyes reflected his concern as fresh denial and pain hit Constantin. *Non, non, non. I won't be like that monster. I can't be.*

"There is a danger," Michel-Leon said slowly, carefully. "But it's a danger I fully believe you can fight, and as time goes on, that danger should lessen."

Sickened to his soul, Constantin pulled away roughly. "What are you saying? I am nothing like Nightingale. Nothing!"

"*Non,* you're not." Michel-Leon's quiet, instant affirmation eased some of the tumult inside of him. "The magicman was a monster in every sense of the word, and it was a monster long before it fed off souls. It served a man, Gilles de Rais, who lured children to his home with the promise of a better life. He preyed on those whose station wouldn't give them a chance to fight back. Once he had them, he butchered them. The man that Nightingale was then helped de Rais with every part, from the tricking to the burning of the bodies. You are a protector of children, not their nightmare."

Constantin shoved away from the bed, weighing Michel-Leon's words. "Then why do you believe there is a danger if I am nothing like it?"

Michel-Leon hesitated again, and Constantin felt another stab of fear. "The danger lies in your origins. You are fey kissed. As far as I have been able to tell, all magicmen are corrupted fey kissed. The key here is corrupted, Constantin."

Constantin paced, absorbing that information and its implications. "So all I have to do is keep from being corrupted." He found his shirt and pulled it on with jerking motions, trying to make sense of it. He didn't even know what that meant. Constantin was not an innocent man. He had not been innocent in a long time. He'd killed. He'd sold his body. He'd stolen. What did corruption mean for a man like him? "I have done things in my life I'm not proud of, things that kept me alive."

Michel-Leon waved that concern aside. "We've all done things we're not proud of. That's not what they mean by corruption."

A gnawing fear wouldn't let Constantin be. "Then what do they mean? *S'il te plaît*. Michel-Leon, you must tell me."

"I need to look further into it, and I am. I'll do whatever is in my power to keep it from happening." Michel-Leon studied him soberly and rose to slip on a robe. "It's why I warned you not to steal power from the magicman. From what I can tell, what happened is you fed off his soul. Soul feeding is addicting. I'm still piecing it together from a book loaned to me."

The room spun on a wave of lightheadedness. Constantin gripped the bedpost for support, physically sick. "Are you saying I have some of that monster in me? Get rid of it!"

Michel-Leon hesitated. "I don't know how. Not yet, but I will. Constantin, I—"

"No more." Constantin waved him to silence, his heart pounding.

He was a monster, doomed to become what he hated the most. He had that thing fouling him. Constantin would always be fouled. The scars where Nightingale had carved out bits of him were bad enough. "I cannot hear anymore."

"Constantin, don't, *s'il te plaît*. There is hope." Michel-Leon reached for him, and Constantin twisted away. He couldn't bear to be touched right now, touched by him. Michel-Leon was the farthest thing from a monster. "You are a protector at heart, not a leech."

"The ancestors should've warned you about me," Constantin rasped and froze in place as something flickered in Michel-Leon's eyes. He was laughably easy to read once Constantin had gotten to know him. "They have. *Mon Dieu*, they have."

Before Michel-Leon could respond, he wrenched the door open, ignoring Michel-Leon's call. He raced down the hallway, running from Michel-Leon's increasingly frantic cries. Constantin ran from his past, from his future. He clawed at his chest as if he could physically remove Nightingale's taint from him. Between one step and the next, he wrapped the shadows around himself, twisted, and disappeared.

Whatever else Michel-Leon said was lost as Constantin slipped into the hidden staircase, careful of the traps he'd memorized. Though what would it matter if the château killed him? Other than Michel-Leon would go to his grave blaming himself. *Non*, it had to be by Constantin's hand. He could not bring any danger of this to Gabrielle. It had to end. He'd take what remained of Nightingale with him and make sure this never happened. He'd die free with no chance of more corruption.

His heart despairing, Constantin climbed to the top floor, entered one of the abandoned rooms, and crossed to the window. The sky was stained a gorgeous flood of reds and pinks as he flung open a window. He stared down at the paved ground impossibly far below.

He closed his eyes, bracing his hands on the sill, and doubt swamped him under. He pictured Michel-Leon's face, the way he felt last night when they'd made love, the timbre of his voice. His heart caught. He did not want to put Michel-Leon in the position of having to hunt him down one day. He had to do this for him too.

Constantin swung his leg over the side and soon perched in the open window. Michel-Leon would care for Gabrielle when he returned to Sangipay.

If he returned.

Constantin sagged against the window, pressing his scarred cheek against the rough stone. Was he going to leave Michel-Leon alone to solve the mystery of the mists? After he'd given his word he'd help if Michel-Leon destroyed the magicman? Here he was hours later, seeking to break that promise.

Non, he wouldn't be alone. He had Régine, and she was more than capable. *I have two brothers now.* Régine's words floated back to him. He'd lost his sister when she was barely more than a babe, and he'd like to believe that if she'd lived, she would've been as fierce and fearless as Régine.

Constantin rubbed his chest and the stinging marks he'd left there, and his fingers curled into claws again. He couldn't let Nightingale take root. He had to end this.

On the heels of that argument came another. He had time. Michel-Leon's ancestors would warn him if Constantin was becoming a danger. He couldn't leave Michel-Leon and Régine alone. What else did he have anymore but his word of honor? Constantin still needed to organize the volunteers. Needed to use his constructs to help Michel-Leon search for the swarm's nest now that they had a direction.

But if even one child was hurt by his hand… Constantin couldn't bear the possibility. He slammed his fist against his chest. There had to be a way to get the corruption out!

He wasn't sure how long he sat there arguing with himself, fighting the waves of despair and anger mixed in with cutting hope. The door to the room opened, and Constantin stiffened until he remembered Michel-Leon couldn't see him. He kept quiet and still as footsteps approached, cringing inside. He longed to glimpse Michel-Leon's face one more time and yet was terrified of doing so.

"Constantin?" Michel-Leon said softly, his voice brittle.

His hand brushed over Constantin's back, and the illusion shattered. Before Constantin could react, he was wrapped in muscular arms and pulled away from the sill, back into the safety of the room. Michel-Leon held him, murmuring his name over and over.

Constantin sagged against him, all fight gone. He was stuck at a crossroads, but he didn't have to drag Michel-Leon with him. "How did you know I was there?" Constantin asked after Michel-Leon fell silent.

"I didn't. Régine and I have been searching for you everywhere. When I saw the open window, I feared the worst." Michel-Leon shuddered and pulled back. "*Bon sang*, Constantin. It doesn't have to be this way."

"I can't have that thing inside me." Constantin clung to him, staring into Michel-Leon's stark expression. Then he forced himself to let go. He couldn't be with Michel-Leon, not when they had no chance at a future. "I can't. I won't become what it was. I'll stay long enough to help you with the swarm, and then I'm ending it."

"We will find a way," Michel-Leon swore. "You won't be doomed. You can fight this."

"You don't know that!" Constantin flung an arm out. "You are a man of hope. I am not. You see the good in things even when none exists. I can't take that chance. I can't harm a child. You don't know what it was like. I can't become that." He turned away before Michel-Leon could reach for him again. It hurt too damned much. "We should leave for Paris. Get this over with."

"Constantin."

Constantin could not ignore the plea in Michel-Leon's voice this time. He looked at Michel-Leon and saw for the first time he'd neglected to change. Michel-Leon stood there in nothing more than a robe, his feet bare, his hair sleep rumpled. He looked like home. "The fey kissed are corrupted when they turn from their purpose. They are meant to be soul healers. So do that. Heal, don't destroy. You think on that these coming weeks."

They stared at each other, challenging, neither willing to give way, both aching. Then Constantin nodded. "I'll keep your words in mind."

Michel-Leon tightened the belt around his waist with a sigh. "That's all I ask."

They left, side by side, but with a widening gulf between them, one Constantin dared not cross, no matter how much he longed to. It had to be this way.

Chapter Twenty-Four

MICHEL-LEON OBSERVED Constantin as he supervised the unloading of the carriage. He had withdrawn in on himself, communicating only when pressed. He wasn't sure what to do or even if there was anything he could do. Constantin believed himself to be a monster, and there was nothing Michel-Leon could say that would disabuse him of the notion. Constantin had to come to the realization on his own.

He hoped that by giving him some space, Constantin would work through his demons. A goal and tasks would give him a sense of purpose. He suspected that much of Constantin's life had been spent running from his past, and now that Nightingale was dead, he was adrift.

"I wish you would tell me what happened between you two," Régine said as he turned from the window. A worried frown marred her brow. "He is worse, not better after the magicman died."

"I cannot tell you." Michel-Leon met her gaze and sensed her frustration. They had never kept secrets from each other. "It is deeply personal to him. If he chooses to tell you, then I can discuss it, otherwise my hands are tied."

Régine's frown deepened. Cocking her head, she went to the window. "It's because of what you've told me before, isn't it? Because he is fey kissed. Answer me this, is he a danger to you?"

"*Non*." Michel-Leon also highly doubted Constantin was a danger to others now that he knew what the risks meant. He would kill himself before he harmed a child. Constantin could find a way out of this, go in another direction, and reverse the damage. He had to believe in himself. "He is a danger to himself." And that grieved Michel-Leon.

Michel-Leon retreated to his study as Constantin came up the stairs. The rustle from Constantin moving around in the workshop was a comfort. He would be occupied and safe. It still made Michel-Leon cold when he remembered where he found him, perched on the windowsill. He'd come so close to losing him right as he was coming to comprehend how much Constantin meant to him.

He couldn't lose him. He wouldn't. Constantin had too much to offer to the world.

"Brooding isn't going to solve your problems," Régine said from the doorway, and Michel-Leon sighed. Of course, she had followed him. Was it too much to ask for peace to think?

"I am not brooding." Michel-Leon unrolled his maps of Paris and studied them. "I'm trying consider all the angles. Come, tell me what I'm missing." He moved to the side to make room for her at the desk.

"We have been over these maps hundreds of times." Régine came to his side. "Perhaps talking to Monsieur Haussmann may help. He has been the architect of the city for quite a while."

"I might do that." Michel-Leon frowned and opened his senses to the ancestors. Maybe they would see something he was missing. There was no pattern to the mists. No pattern to the missing people. There was nothing to indicate where under Paris he should start. The swarm had never made their nest so close to a city, but that might've been because the access wasn't there. But the potential size and scope of this nest terrified him. That could be why the patterns were off. The nest needed to feed more.

He wasn't entirely invested in the theory though. He was still missing an element, and it had to do with those creatures roaming the city. The next time the mists rolled through, he was going to hunt them down. He longed to confide his fears to Constantin, but he was already struggling, and he didn't want to lay an additional burden on him.

"The Lou Carcolh."

"Idiot!" Michel-Leon clutched his hair until his scalp stung. The realization hit him like a bolt of lightning as the ancestors whispered to him. The answer had been right in front of him the entire time. "I'm a blinded idiot. The tunnels linking the quarries. I've never considered them. There are tunnels underneath Paris."

"What tunnels? Do you mean the catacombs?" Régine asked as Michel-Leon scrambled through his maps, searching for one of the quarries. If anyone had ever mapped their length. Many were too dangerous to traverse, prone to flooding or with unstable walls and ceilings. "There is nothing to indicate that on the maps."

"My memory is sketchy on them. *Grandpère* told me the story. Paris was having a problem with their graveyards, so the decision was made to re-inter the bodies under Paris." Michel-Leon tapped his temple, trying to recall the details of the story. "The church forbade visiting the ossuaries for decades. They didn't believe it should be a public spectacle."

"Why under Paris? Why didn't they build out?" Régine asked as she took half the stack from him.

"The tunnels were already there. They used the rock they mined from there to build the city. Then it started sinking under the weight, so they sent architects down to shore up the walls. A chevalier had to be called in because a *Lou Carcolh* had made its way north and settled down in the warren of tunnels and was impeding progress. Nasty creature, lethal. When they started moving the bodies down there, the stories came back."

The map wasn't in the stack.

Michel-Leon turned to the trunks he'd brought with him from Paris. It had to be in here. He specifically remembered culling it for the trip. When he finally pulled it out, he groaned. It was an absolute maze. They'd need to search systematically, and it would help to have a more up-to-date version.

"How would the monster have gotten underneath Paris without being seen?" Régine asked as she peered over his shoulder. "We saw it. It's huge. How would it fit? Could it have come all the way from the village southeast of Paris?"

"*Oui, oui,*" Michel-Leon countered impatiently. "How did it get into any number of caves where the swarm nest was? We can only theorize because a body is never found. I suspect their mother is the swarm's first victim. But I believe it has an ability to squeeze into places that defy its size. Look." He traced one of the tunnel lines.

"There is an entire network of these. It could've worked its way closer until it found a likely nesting spot and no one would know. For all we know, it may have a way of hiding itself. Anybody who went down into the tunnels would not have emerged again. I'd be curious to see a list of missing people who disappeared down there, but I believe the visits into the catacombs are still restricted to a handful of times a year."

"Mademoiselle Belanger," he shouted until the maid appeared in the doorway. "Send a message to Haussmann's office. Ask him to send me a copy of the maps of the tunnels beneath Paris. No wait, I'll go myself. I need to impress upon him the urgency. If anyone will have one, it'll be him." He thought of Janvier and groaned again. "Lay out something somewhat respectable for me and your cousin."

He loathed the idea of taking the time to change, but he didn't know enough about Haussmann or what he may have heard about the chevaliers. He'd need all of his aura of respectability given by his class.

"Come," he said to Régine. "We need to talk to Constantin."

He took the stairs two at a time and burst into the workshop. Constantin looked up, startled, the first genuine emotion he'd revealed in days. "What's wrong?"

Michel-Leon crossed to him and grabbed him by the shoulders. "We're going to need more of your constructs. The ones you use to search and more masks." He let go of Constantin and turned away, dragging his hands through his hair as he tried to collect his thoughts.

"How many more?" Constantin asked with a quick, curious glance at Régine.

"As many as you can make." Michel-Leon spun to face him. "How many can you concentrate on when you send them out?"

"I suppose as many as I need to. I've never tested it. Once I've sent them on their search, they require nothing else from me until they've located what they're seeking. Why? You know where to look? Remember—"

"The tunnels beneath the city. There's no other answer. I'm an idiot for not considering it before. I'd forgotten all about them."

"Michie, don't abuse yourself. It's been a long time since you've been in Paris," Régine chided. "And you never had to deal with any issues in the catacombs or the tunnels. If anything, the ancestors should've thought of it if they'd stop panicking every time the swarm is mentioned."

"There are catacombs beneath the city? How macabre." Constantin shook his head with a grimace, and the sorrow returned to his gaze. "There's still one problem, Michel-Leon. I can't search for what I can't picture. *Je suis désolé*, my constructs will be useless."

"Bullshit."

Constantin blinked at Michel-Leon's profanity. Régine shot him a quelling glare and laid her hand on Constantin's arm. "What he means is—"

"Don't tell me what can't be done," Michel-Leon interrupted and caught Constantin's gaze. "Let's see what can be done. Let's find solutions. We have a description. I'm not sure how good it is. The man who'd seen what was left of the nest was going off memories that were fifty years old. But it's a start. If I give you that description, do you think you could find it? Or narrow down our search."

For a moment, Constantin's eyes reflected his despair, and then his expression firmed. "It is worth a try. Tell me what I'm searching for."

Michel-Leon seized on the hope and exchanged a smile with Régine. "Give me a moment." He raced back down to his study and pawed through his books until he found his journal. He leafed through it while running back upstairs, narrowly missing tripping on the risers. "Here." He found the section and turned it toward them. "We met a man on the train down here. He was a survivor at Metz. He found the remains of the nest in a nearby cave, including some unhatched specimens."

Michel-Leon would've dearly loved to have one of those. "Everything he said is here, and we worked on a couple drawings together based on his memories and what Régine and I saw of the mother in the night sky. You can thank Régine for the notes. We'll add what Henri and Phillippe described to their father."

Constantin studied the page, his expression set as he muttered to himself. "I'll let you know what I find. I'm going to invite the foreman to come with some of his men. We're going to need more hands to make the masks and constructs. We're going to need more materials."

"I'll see that you have the money and materials. I'm on my way to see about getting a map of the tunnels. If we can rule out sections with your constructs, narrow down our search. That will be less for us to do. We can start with the tunnels on the southeast edge of the city."

"I'll go to the telegraph office instead," Régine cut in. "Monsieur Vautrin said he was settling in London. I'll see if I can track him down and see what else he may remember. I'm sure it has been on his mind. Perhaps new details have emerged."

The three of them exchanged a look filled with tense excitement. "We may pull this off," Michel-Leon murmured.

"I admire your optimism." Constantin straightened. "Off with you both. We have work to do. I'll warn Salome to expect several more people, at least."

"And I'll let Mahout know to open more rooms. We might have to double up if you get enough volunteers. I can stay with my aunt and cousin. If you share a room, we'll have enough space for a crew." Régine gave Michel-Leon a bland look. "I'll meet you out front on the hour."

"I can sleep on the floor," Constantin said as he turned away, killing Michel-Leon's wistful wish for a kiss.

"That won't be necessary," Michel-Leon said, and Constantin stiffened. "If you're uncomfortable with me, I can have a couch brought in," he continued and hurried out before Constantin could say something to reject him further.

*

"*MERCI* FOR SEEING me. I know the demands on your time are enormous," Michel-Leon said as he was ushered in to Haussmann's crowded office. "I am Michel-Leon Parisee, and I need your help."

"I'd heard of your mission." Haussmann smiled faintly. He was a round man with dark receding hair and a kindly face. "I'm afraid it was being mocked in certain circles at court." His smile fell away. "Those dissenters, for the most part, have fallen silent and more of those with money to spare are fleeing Paris in greater numbers. The emperor is quite desperate."

Not desperate enough to call for Michel-Leon, though, or to offer aid to his people. He was still safely away from Paris at the summer court. "I've narrowed down the location of the nest. I believe it's under Paris, not outside it."

Haussmann's eyes brightened with understanding. "The ossuaries."

"Indeed, or even the greater area of the quarry tunnels. I'm praying you have maps that are more up to date than mine." Michel-Leon took the seat offered him. "Mine predate the catacombs when the tunnels were still being shored up, and I fear they are not complete. From what I've gleaned, the system is quite vast."

"You are in luck. The tunnels under the city intrigued me on an engineering level. Therefore, when I began the reconstruction of Paris, I had new maps made as I wanted to be sure they'd wouldn't cause any issues with my vision." Haussmann called for an aide and spoke briefly with him. "We ended up interring more bones from cemeteries as we expanded the renovations."

"How many entrances are there?" Michel-Leon asked.

"Well, one official one. Near the *Barrière d'Enfer*. I've considered closing off the entrance after an entire party went missing down there. I had concerns they had wandered into an unstable area. From what I understand, everyone who went hunting for the missing party also disappeared. However, given the extent of the tunnel network, there are many other places where it can be accessed."

"Closing the main entrance is a good idea if you have the authority to do so." Michel-Leon tapped his fingers together as he considered the issue. Michel-Leon wished he had heard about the missing people sooner. They might've been buried among the other lists of the missing. He was closing in on the nest. He sensed it. Now he had to figure out the battle plan. "The missing people were probably enticed into the nest. The mists are alluring, like bees to honey. Anyone caught in it would be unable to resist. I doubt the creature is near the main entrance. It would want people to come down, but not too many at once. It would want to space out its feedings."

"That is a terrible thought." Haussmann grimaced.

"By any chance, was your missing party in the southeastern side of the city?" Michel-Leon asked.

"How did you know?"

"There were a couple of boys who had seen the creature land near a village southeast of Paris. They went searching for it and never returned. I know the tunnels are extensive, but I'm not sure how extensive." For all Michel-Leon knew, the creature could burrow itself into rock.

"Hundreds of kilometers," Haussmann replied. "Something needs to be done about the mists, and I for one am willing to offer whatever aid I can. I'm behind schedule, and there's so much more to be done. The Paris project keeps expanding, though, I'll admit, that's partially my fault as I have new ideas. Still, we need to get back on schedule."

Michel-Leon refrained from damning his schedule. People were dying and more would come. Haussmann was cooperating, and he couldn't jeopardize that with ill humor. The aide returned, carrying a bundle of rolled papers.

Haussmann thanked the man as he accepted the bundle and dismissed him. Michel-Leon took the bundle with trembling hands and unrolled them. He stared at the honeycombed lines, mapping out likely routes and possible nesting sites. "Let's start by closing all the entrances that we can determine. I suspect the creature has made its way to the heart of the city. Then it could send its lures over the entire city for sustenance."

"How do you plan on searching if people are lured in when they get near?" Haussmann asked.

"I've developed some equipment with a local genius, Constantin

Severin, that helps filter out the effects. I've also developed an inoculation that so far appears to work. I'm trying to expand on it. We have volunteers helping." That had always been the problem before. They had the knowledge to track down the mists, but not the equipment. "With more manpower, we can expand our search. We're getting close and none too soon."

"Do you know how to destroy the nest when you find it?" Haussmann asked as he marked accessible entrances for Michel-Leon's benefit.

"I am still studying the best way of doing that." Michel-Leon examined the notes, making plans to explore. "We've never gotten this far. In the past, we've relied on evacuation."

"Which will not work in Paris." Haussmann straightened with a grimace. "I'll have more copies made of these for you, but you can use this for now. You must understand. These are incomplete. I don't think anyone has done a survey of all the tunnels. Some are too dangerous to explore. It's easy to get lost down there."

"I do understand. It is a start." Michel-Leon rolled up the offered maps, his heart pounding with purpose. He'd pick up Régine, meet with Constantin and his team, and they would get started immediately. "If you will excuse me. I must go. There is no time to waste."

Chapter Twenty-Five

CONSTANTIN BLOCKED OUT the murmur of other voices and concentrated on the constructs he'd sent out. One by one, he sensed their continuing search underneath Paris, but not one pinged back at him with the familiar sense of having found something. He bit his lip in frustration and despair. He needed to report some success back to Michel-Leon or he'd be useless on top of being a liability.

He bent over his copy of the maps and tried to translate his sense of where the constructs were to their placement on the map. "It looks as if they have penetrated this far," he said, tracing a line down several corridors.

Michel-Leon leaned over next to him and nodded with a grunt. "And nothing so far?"

Constantin's shoulders slumped. "*Non. Je suis désolé.* Though I have no way of knowing if it's because there is nothing there or because it's not able to interpret what I want it to find. I need a clear picture of what we're searching for!"

Michel-Leon clasped his shoulder with a warm squeeze. "Don't give up. This is only the section nearest to the southeastern border. If fate were kind, it would be there, but it's been my experience that a kind fate has a hidden catch. We wouldn't have this much if it wasn't for your insistence the magicman knew something. This is progress."

Constantin wished it felt more like progress. They were in the midst of the hottest days of summer. Tempers were short. And if Michel-Leon's timeline was right, the swarm would hatch next month in September. That didn't leave them with much time.

Michel-Leon left his side, and Constantin missed his presence. Their workshop was full as they produced more of the masks, and Michel-Leon refined and created more of his inoculations. Constantin turned from the maps and began double-checking the completed masks. Any gap or hole was a potential danger to the one wearing it.

"The mists are coming more frequently, but it's as if they are fragile. They don't last as long. We will need to move quickly when the next one rolls through. I expect sometime today." Michel-Leon glanced at the clock with a frustrated frown. "Where is Régine? She should be back by now."

"She has a mask if the mists return before she arrives." Constantin paused and closed his eyes, searching for the sense of the construct he'd left with the intrepid woman. "She isn't far and is moving toward us. She should be here in a few minutes."

Relief crossed Michel-Leon's face. "I hope she has news about Haussmann's missing team. I told him not to send another one down into the catacombs after the first one went missing, Napoleon's orders or not. She should be able to at least pinpoint where they entered."

"She wouldn't have gone down there," Constantin assured him. "She has more sense than that."

Michel-Leon's shoulder jerked in acknowledgment. "Maybe, but getting close could provide its own dangers. Who knows what triggers the mists now? Nothing is certain anymore. Nothing is going the way it's supposed to!" The last part came out in a near shout of frustration.

Constantin studied Michel-Leon and considered if he was going about this the wrong way. The man had a way of concentrating single-mindedly on one aspect of the problem. They'd already deviated with the magicman, and it had given them some answers. It might be worth diverting Michel-Leon's penchant for coming up with theories in another direction.

"Have you considered other forces might be at play?"

"What do you mean?" Michel-Leon demanded as he paced around the tables. "Don't you think we're dealing with enough? Is Paris so ill-lucked that it has to contend with a magicman, the swarm, and another threat?"

"Why not? Luck, good or bad, isn't justice. A city this size is bound to have multiple supernatural problems, even more so if they are connected. We already know Nightingale was using the mists to hunt. We have evidence something else is moving around out there, strange misshapen men. Let's ask ourselves what are they doing and why?"

"You pose good questions," Michel-Leon said with a sigh. "And I cannot deny I believe there is merit in them, but I'm not sure we have the time to explore another mystery."

"We'll get some answers and direction soon," Constantin assured him and eyed the stockpile of masks. "We can equip about twenty of us."

Twenty of them to go searching through the mists, risking getting caught up in their lure if they failed to make them correctly, searching for monsters. As scary as the notion was, it felt good to do something.

Michel-Leon nodded as he continued to study the horizon. "Your volunteers are ready? They know how to defend themselves?"

"They can. I'll distribute these to the volunteers who are not here." Constantin loaded the masks he was taking into a bag. "When the mists do emerge, where should we meet? Here?"

Michel-Leon considered that for a long moment. "*Non*, let's meet at the foreman's site. We know they were targeted many times for materials. It appears to be more in the heart of things than we are here. We'll go to them. Maybe that will give us some of those answers we are fumbling for."

"I'll spread the word." Constantin studied Michel-Leon's back as he turned away. He knew the man was unsure about where they stood and was hurt by Constantin's rebuff. Michel-Leon would be receptive if Constantin went to him, and Constantin longed to do so. He'd had a taste, and he wanted more. He wanted to win Michel-Leon's heart, but he couldn't subject Michel-Leon to his demons. Not anymore. "If it comes while I'm out. Be safe."

Michel-Leon turned back, his gaze grave. "You as well."

Constantin left before he could give into the urgings of his heart and say something. Michel-Leon had been right to keep his distance. He knew the risks and dangers of this life. Once this was over, Constantin was done. There was no sense in breaking two hearts.

*

THE MISTS MUFFLED everything, cloaking the work site in a fluid gray that shifted and swirled. The black threads were weaker and broke apart as they moved through them. It put Constantin on edge. How were they supposed to find anything in this damned mess? He'd be surprised if Michel-Leon could locate them at all.

Constantin paced around the small guard shack the foreman had built and kept peering through the window shutters. He did not like the idea of Michel-Leon and Régine navigating this entrapping haze. He should've been the one going out in this. Constantin had the constructs to lead him.

"Something comes!" one of the guards hissed and everyone put their hand on their guns.

"Hold, *bon sang*," Constantin snapped. "Either it's the baron and you'll be shooting at our allies, or it's the creatures stealing from the worksites, or it's some poor lost soul snared by the mists. We would like to discover what the creatures are up to, and we'd like to follow the mists' victims. So hurting any of them would be at cross purposes to what we want to accomplish."

"It's the monsters," the guard snapped back, pointing out the window. "See over there in the shadows of the wall? There's a light."

"Make sure your masks are secure," Constantin replied, checking his own straps. If it was the mist monsters, he'd have to go on without Michel-Leon. They couldn't waste this chance to discover their purpose.

A gleam of orange and yellow set the mists on fire so they reflected back a multitude of colors. "Did your monsters carry torches?" he asked the guards.

"*Non*, not sure how they saw a damn thing," Foreman Lyon said, his voice tinny behind the mask.

"Probably magic," the guard responded.

Constantin glimpsed figures moving steadily toward them, torches at the front. Ignoring the warning hiss from the foreman, Constantin stepped out and sent a construct out with orders to hunt for Michel-Leon. It pinged back at him immediately. "It's our friends," Constantin said over his shoulder to Lyon. "Michel-Leon? Régine?" he called.

"Constantin." There was relief in Michel-Leon's voice. The mists swirled around the shadowy figures, backlit by the torches, and then they emerged. "I was beginning to think my compass had led me astray."

Constantin clasped his arm, conveying without words the depth of his relief. "I thought you may have gotten lost."

Michel-Leon's returning grip eased his aching heart. "It is a danger. Have you seen anything while you waited?"

"Nary a soul until you arrived," Constantin reported. He turned toward Régine and clasped her hand. "Did you see anything along the way?"

"The streets are empty except for a few souls that the mists have enraptured. We caught one." Régine jerked her thumb over her shoulder and Constantin peered past her to the men hanging on to a struggling, gagged woman. "We should release her, see where she leads us. She should take the quickest route to the nest."

"What if she slips loose from us and gets lured to her death?" Michel-Leon said with the exasperation of a man who had heard this argument before. "Or pulls off the gag and begins screaming for the music again?"

Constantin recalled Michel-Leon's struggles and shouts when he'd been rescued from the mists. If given the chance, she'd probably quiet down once she was allowed to continue on her single-minded mission. "I think it's a risk we should take. You're using one of my harnesses. That'll make it difficult for her to escape us."

"See." There was triumph in Régine's voice. "Besides, we're bound to encounter something else."

"I agree." Something Constantin both welcomed and dreaded. It would give them answers. He only wished he knew where those answers would lead.

"Fine, we'll go with your plan. Traveling in a group like this has me on edge," Michel-Leon said and shrugged irritably. "We become a target. Let's go. There is nothing we can do about this."

"I suggest we douse the torches," Constantin said. "They don't help us to see that much, and they are the first thing we noticed as you approached. We'll do a headcount every so often. If anyone loses the group, stay put and I'll send one of my constructs after you to lead you back to us."

Foreman Lyon nodded his head as the workmen muttered uneasily. Foreman Lyon hastened to reassure them, "I've seen how those things work. Better than a compass."

"That is a good plan," Michel-Leon said. "These mists aren't going to last for much longer, and we need more information than we have."

"Hold on, let me get a sense of her." Constantin moved toward the woman and caught her shoulders. She struggled against his grip, crying out behind her gag. He closed his eyes, fumbling for her spirit, for enough of her presence that if he had to send out one of his constructs, he should be able to find her again. Her confusion and longing battered at him, and he released her, stepping back to nod to Michel-Leon.

"Sweet Saint Jeanne preserve you," Michel-Leon said softly to her. "I want you to lead us to the music. Can you do that?" Michel-Leon coaxed and waited until she nodded her head, and then he undid her gag and hands. She immediately set off as if the rest ceased to exist for her.

She moved at a fast walk, muttering to herself the entire time. Constantin caught words now and then, reminding him of the time when Michel-Leon had been caught in the mists and how agitated he'd been.

They set off after her, Régine in close step, holding on to the harness, ready to grab her again if needed. Constantin stole glances at Michel-Leon, trying to gauge how the woman's reaction was affecting him, but it was impossible to tell with the masks on. Michel-Leon glanced at his compass.

"We should be nearing the river. I hope she doesn't walk us right into the water. We don't appear to be heading toward the catacomb entrance. Wouldn't that be a rather prosaic end? Everyone drowns and is drawn out to sea instead of lured into a nest. All the theories of generations of chevaliers proved wrong."

Constantin strained to hear the wash of the river, but the mists muffled everything. The shroud surrounding them stifled even the tolling of the bells from Notre-Dame. Black threads crept over his mask, seeking a way in, and his skin crawled. Régine kept a forceful grip on the tether connecting her to the entranced woman, though she strained to move faster. A trickle of unease upset Constantin's stomach as if the unnatural shadows that swirled and faded in the mists sought to do them harm.

He shook his head. Now was not the time to get fanciful and spooked. He slowed to take a headcount, but it was hard to make out all the figures swimming in and out of the mists. "Do you hear that?" Constantin asked, halting and holding up his hand. He strained to listen again. It came, the scrape of leather on stone and a soft, hissing. "Someone is out there."

"I don't hear anything," Régine said, also coming to a stop. Michel-Leon looked around, his eyes narrowing.

"The song! The music!" The woman reached the end of her tether and fought it, straining to move forward again.

Michel-Leon swore and Régine caught her as the surrounding shadows erupted with movement. Constantin glimpsed a man with a deformed face. His eyes bulged. His mouth locked open in a puckered grimace that emitted a low sound like a teakettle before a full boil. Lyon shot and the creature went down. "*Putain*, what was that?"

"Don't shoot unless you're sure. We might hit ourselves." Constantin knocked his gun aside as Michel-Leon and another creature crossed their path, locked in battle. Then one caught him, crushing his arms to his sides.

He lashed out, kicking as a wave of sickness washed over him. There was something dreadfully wrong with these men. Beyond the misshapen faces and the utter silence with which they fought, except for that low whistle. They didn't grunt when blows connected or cry out in pain. It was unnatural. He fought harder, panting as panic clawed at him until he finally broke free. He straightened, whirled around to confront his attacker, and was met with empty eyes.

Constantin gasped and fell back, reaching out with his other senses. They had no soul. It was as if something had neatly excised it from them and the wound cauterized. His stomach heaved, and he gagged. A hard hand yanked him back up and Constantin fought it until he recognized it was Michel-Leon.

"Let's go." Michel-Leon gave him a shove, his gaze constantly moving, searching. "She walked off in that direction, and the creatures followed. Do you think you can find her?"

Constantin looked wildly around him at the others already gathering to follow and the bodies of the creatures lying in the street. He wanted to examine them, but they didn't have time. "We'll have to check to see if these are still here when we're done."

Michel-Leon nodded. "One of them ripped the mask off the foreman."

Constantin went cold. He considered Lyon a friend. "How is he? Was he affected?"

"The inoculation held." Michel-Leon met his gaze. "Can you find her?"

"*Oui.*" Constantin pulled out one of his constructs. "Are we all here?"

"By some miracle." Régine emerged with an irritated expression. "*Je suis désolé*, Michie. I let go of her."

"I expect you to defend yourself," Michel-Leon replied. "We'll find her again."

Constantin blocked out their conversation and concentrated on the construct as it winged off. "She's not too far," he reported. "A couple of blocks away. I think she stopped again."

"Or was stopped," Régine said ominously.

They picked up their pace, half running through the mists as the woman cried out again, begging for the song. Her cry was echoed by others trapped deeper into the darkness of the street, their voices disembodied and eerie. They slowed as the mists thinned, and they saw the creatures surrounding her, herding her away from the direction she wanted to go.

Michel-Leon hissed as one of their volunteers raised a rifle. "*Non,* let's follow. We need to know what part they play in this."

"But what about the location of the nest?" Régine asked.

"One problem at a time. If others escape and head toward the song again, we can split up and follow. But for now, we stick together." Michel-Leon motioned for silence.

They crept along behind the creatures, using the voice of the woman as a guide. The footfalls of others became clearer, though muffled. They inched closer until the outlines of figures appeared. A couple dozen of the soulless creatures had gathered a group of people and were busy tying and gagging them. They pulled a toddler from its mother's arms and stuffed it squalling into a sack.

Michel-Leon laid a hand on his arm as Constantin stiffened and growled. "We'll rescue them. It appears as if they are culling out the able-bodied. But to what purpose?"

Constantin considered the scene and had to agree. They herded the most fit into a group, roped together while the others were bound hand and foot and left on the ground to try to crawl away without much success. Black threads covered them more thickly, trailing off in the direction they wanted to go. Constantin marked it in his mind and hoped he'd remember when the mists cleared.

The man next to him coughed, and as if ruled by one head, all the creatures straightened and turned in their direction like puppets on a string. Ice trickled down Constantin's spine even as Michel-Leon shoved at him. "Scatter! Hide!" he ordered in a fierce whisper.

They came at them in a whistling rush. Constantin reached for the weapon Michel-Leon had foisted off on him even as he fell back hunting for something to shelter behind. The weapon felt awkward in his hand. He was more used to hiding than fighting. Twisting the shadows around him, Constantin stepped into a doorway.

One of the creatures went down to gunfire, and then they were on the group who hadn't moved fast enough. Constantin stepped out of the shadows and grappled with one that had born a volunteer to the ground. He struggled, trying to knock it out or restrain it as it tried to do the same. They were impossibly strong, cold to the touch, and the sense of wrongness emanating from them made his stomach roil anew.

The mists around them tattered, and as abruptly as the monsters had attacked, they froze as sunshine peeked through the fading mists. The opponents stared at each other. Constantin struggled to his feet and shuddered at his first good view of them. They looked like wax sculptures of humans who had stood too long in the sun. They melted back into the shadows and disappearing mists, taking their wounded and dead with them, leaving behind the people they had gathered.

Michel-Leon bolted after them, swearing under his breath, and Constantin followed. But they moved impossibly quick, flowing like fast-moving water, and were soon gone. "Can you sense them? Follow them?" Michel-Leon demanded.

"*Non,*" Constantin gasped, trying to collect his breath. "They don't have souls. There's nothing to follow. I could try using my constructs the same way I am for the nests, but I expect we'll have the same results. There is nothing for them to home in on.

Michel-Leon swore again and kicked a loose stone. He stopped, hands on his hips as he studied the surrounding warren. They could've gone anywhere. "We'll spread out in a grid and see what we find. They can't have holed up too far away. And we'll study Haussmann's maps again and see what entrances are in the direction that our victims were trying to go. We might as well inoculate them while we have them. Perhaps it will help them to shake off the effects."

"What were they?" Constantin asked as they headed back toward where Régine was managing the crew and victims left behind.

"Men," Michel-Leon said shortly, his mouth tight with frustration. "Or men once."

Constantin shuddered. "They didn't look like any man I've ever seen. Their souls were ripped out. I haven't sensed anything like that. Not even with Nightingale."

"They've been altered with blood magic. Whoever did it probably used their victim's soul energy to make the changes." Michel-Leon sighed as they reached the others. Régine straightened and gave them both a sharp look.

"Any luck?" She frowned as Michel-Leon shook his head and gestured toward the crying group they'd rescued. "We'll have our hands full dealing with them. We need to make sure those affected by the mists will return home."

Constantin considered their options and the people they had left. "Régine, why don't you take a few of the men to help handle them and the inoculations for those who want it. Michel-Leon, you study Haussmann's map and take a few others to search for likely entrances. I'll take the rest and see if we can figure out where the creatures fled."

"*Non.*" Régine came over and studied Constantin's expression. "I'll follow the monsters. You help here. You're better with frightened and devastated people than I am. You're more reassuring. Besides, getting close to those monsters made you ill."

Constantin couldn't argue with her logic. "If that is how you want it. We lost them near *rue de Église*."

Michel-Leon clapped his hands together. "We have a plan. Let's take a few hours at our task and then meet back at the house to piece together what we've learned. Something is bound to shake loose."

Chapter Twenty-Six

"I BELIEVE WE should enter here," Michel-Leon said, circling his finger around a spot on the map. "It's not too far away from where we first encountered the creatures."

Régine tapped her fingers on the table. "As of today, how many other entrances have they blocked off?"

"The main one near the *Barrière d'Enfer*. All the ones in the renovated parts of the city." Constantin leaned over next to him and, despite his best efforts to ignore his nearness, Michel-Leon felt the tingle. He laid chess pieces he'd raided from the study onto the maps in selected locations. "And these as well. Which leaves several dozen locations for us to search. Though we have to assume, given how extensive the network is, we'll miss some. Not to mention it connects to the village somehow unless a tunnel collapsed behind it. We had penetrated far, though clearly not far enough."

He had the impression Constantin was emerging from his dark mood. The fight with the monsters had invigorated him, but he still didn't act interested in picking up where they'd left off. Michel-Leon needed to stop thinking about that. He had survived without a relationship before. He would survive going forward.

"Remind me why we're going down there when we're essentially blind?" Régine asked, meeting Michel-Leon's gaze. "Everyone who has gone into the quarry tunnels has not emerged."

"They did not have the inoculation or the masks." Constantin straightened. "The constructs may not have found the nest, but they could lead a team back out to safety if they get lost or if they find anything."

"We're changing the experiment and seeing what new data emerges. I'm sure those who went down were caught up in the mists. I suspect going down near the nest might trigger them, which would explain the aberration in their frequency. However, it doesn't mean there still isn't a danger." Michel-Leon frowned at the map. "True, we had no luck with the constructs, through no fault of your own, Constantin. You warned me of the limitations. I want to know what happens when we get closer to the nest so we'll know what to anticipate. I'd like to go in force, sweeping through the entire network, but before we risk anybody, we have to have some idea of what to expect."

"I think we should take triple precautions," Régine urged. "Let's not rely on your constructs or your compass. We'll need extra torches, something to mark our way, like chalk."

"There is sense in that." Michel-Leon glanced over at Constantin to check if that bothered him. He was prickly lately, but Constantin was nodding.

"There is a carriage here for you, my lord," Mahout announced from the doorway in tones of hushed reverence.

Michel-Leon glanced up in confusion. "I didn't order the carriage."

"You are being summoned." Mahout clasped her hands together,

her eyes wide. "The palace sent it. The emperor himself. He has returned to Paris early."

"Now? He returns to Paris now? Is he mad?" Michel-Leon threw up his hands and gestured to the map. "And why does he summon me? I don't have time for a summons. There is never enough time. I've sent him enough messages that he ignored."

Mahout's eyes widened even more in stunned dismay, and she glanced at her cousin for support. "I already laid out suitable attire for you and Régine. You want me to dismiss him?" Her voice dropped as if she didn't dare utter such a suggestion out loud.

"*Non*," Régine cut in and shot Michel-Leon a firm look. "Michie and I will attend. I'll need you to help me with my dress. Constantin, you talk to him. You can start organizing the teams while we're out."

"You can't ignore this, Michel-Leon," Constantin cut in quietly after she left. "You have a chance here to reestablish the reputation of the chevaliers."

"What chevaliers?" Michel-Leon muttered. This was a waste of his time to coddle those with power and no wit or sense of responsibility.

"*Michel-Leon.*"

He sensed the voices stirring, his father's in the forefront strident with anger as always. Michel-Leon attempted to calm his thoughts before they resolved to comment more on the issue. "I have a hundred things I could be doing instead of getting dressed up and going to court."

"The rejection stung your pride and sense of civic responsibility. I understand, but as you say, we don't have time for pride." Constantin caught his elbow and steered him away from the table. "We do have chevaliers, the ones you and I are going to build. Go. I will make sure we have all the equipment we need for a survey of the catacombs and talk to our teams to see who wants to volunteer for this assignment."

Michel-Leon clamped his lips against further complaints. This was the first time Constantin had offered anything regarding their future that wasn't clouded with doom. He didn't want to spoil that.

Alone, Michel-Leon struggled into the clothes Mahout laid out for him. He missed Janvier, though his aged valet would've had several choice things to say at this moment. Michel-Leon occupied his thoughts on the demands he'd make of the emperor. He needed to remember to couch them in terms of suggestions rather than demands. Strong suggestions.

"I hope we get useful assistance out of this meeting, and not a lot of hand wringing and half hysterical accusations," Régine said as they met again in the hallway. She was resplendent in a full-skirted mint and cream gown and with her hair drawn back in an elegant twist that tamed her curls. She adjusted his collar and nodded. "We'll do."

"I see your *grandpère* managed to leave some frippery for you." Michel-Leon kissed her hands. "I know you hate this getup more than I. You have my eternal gratitude for accompanying me. What made you decide to come?"

"The more arguments, the better. I had Mahout send a message to Haussmann. We need allies. And there is another reason. I want to watch your back." She gave Michel-Leon a searching look. "Before we go downstairs, you should be warned. He sent Lennox to escort us."

"Good thing I brought my cane in case I need to skewer the rat." Michel-Leon grimaced. "More like Lennox sent himself when he realized Napoleon was going to insist on this meeting. He's doing damage control so he doesn't appear incompetent."

"You no longer have that bitter grief in your eye when you say his name," Régine observed with a shrewd examination of him. "Good, it's about time. Constantin is the better man for you." She headed down the stairs at a regal walk, leaving Michel-Leon sputtering after her.

"My apologies for leaving you waiting, Lord Lennox," she said smoothly, holding out her hands to Michel-Leon's nemesis. "Michie didn't tell me they sent an old acquaintance of his to fetch us."

Michel-Leon had to admire Régine's ability to bluff an opponent. If she wanted to cozen Lennox instead of going for his eyes, then Michel-Leon was happy enough to take the other role.

Lord Lennox took her hands and bowed over them, hiding his confusion. "I was not aware Parisee had married."

"You are mistaken as usual," Michel-Leon said coldly, taking Régine's hand back and tucking it through his arm. "This is my younger sister, the Widow Bardin."

"I did not know you had a sister." Lennox's gaze slipped to Régine again, appraising as she lowered her gaze demurely.

"There are many things you do not know about me." Michel-Leon gestured toward the door. "Let us be off. I'd hate to keep Napoleon waiting."

"This is not the end between us," Lennox warned as Michel-Leon handed Régine up into the carriage.

"This war with our families is worthy of a Molière play. There are more important concerns at hand," Michel-Leon murmured. "We cannot make peace. Not at this point, but we can work together."

"Do not think to mollify me. Not after what your family did."

Michel-Leon caught his arm. "My family targeted your monster. Not your father and uncles, though what they were doing was wrong. I used to wonder if you deliberately used me that summer, but I no longer care. Fight with me. If for no other reason than to save your own hide."

"You would have me believe you no longer care about what happened to your home and family?" Lennox's nostrils flared. "I don't."

"Answers will not lessen the grief." Michel-Leon let go of him with a sigh. "I choose to believe you were as much a pawn as I."

Lennox's eyes narrowed. "You've changed."

"That may be. Unfortunately, I don't believe you have." As

Michel-Leon turned away, Lennox cleared his throat.

"I learned later after my uncle's death. All those who were behind the attack are gone."

Michel-Leon's throat tightened and then eased. They'd never be friends again. It was enough that Michel-Leon knew the truth, and he could put it behind him. "*Merci*," he said tersely and clambered into the carriage, taking a seat by Régine. She gave him a quick, searching look, and he smiled slightly.

Between the two of them, they kept Lennox off balance during the carriage ride to the palace, with the coachman clearing the way, booming in his deep voice as he drove. Michel-Leon preferred to get his information straight from the emperor and not have it tainted beforehand. Every time Lennox attempted to draw him out, Régine diverted his attention. He couldn't count on Lennox's support, even if they had cleared the air between them.

At the palace, Lennox cut through the formalities, which told Michel-Leon more than words the summons was serious. Perhaps Napoleon would listen. He quickly led them through a series of rooms kept stifling hot and as opulent as an array of gilt boxes until they reached one of the grand salons. To his relief, he noted Haussmann among the courtiers and advisors. He'd have an ally.

All conversation ceased, and even the low music came to a stop as the courtiers noticed them. Lennox moved past them and bowed grandly. "Your Imperial Majesty, as you have requested, I've brought the chevalier. Allow me to present, the Baron de Dagonville, a Chevalier de Rouen, and his sister the Widow Bardin."

Michel-Leon bowed low as Régine curtsied gracefully next to him, then straightened to get his first impression of Napoleon III. "Welcome back to Paris, Your Imperial Majesty."

Napoleon had broad, drooping shoulders and wore a military uniform. A pointed mustache and curling beard dominated his long face, and his small eyes were kind as he studied Michel-Leon in return. "The Chevaliers de Rouen have a long history of serving France."

Michel-Leon had questioned many people about what to expect from Napoleon in the off chance he would have this opportunity. The emperor tended to vacillate before making a decision and was more of a man of feeling than principle. If Michel-Leon appealed to his emotions, to the kindness he saw, they might receive the aid they desperately needed at this hour.

"We have dedicated ourselves to the protection of the people since 1431."

"Do you really believe the same monsters that destroyed Metz threaten us?" Napoleon lit a cigarette, though the room was already blue with smoke. "You are not the only one seeking answers. My councilors have assured me this phenomenon differs in many ways. Public opinion seems to think there are a number of supernatural forces at work."

"I know they are the same menace, discrepancies aside. I have made several breakthroughs I hope will allow us to eliminate the swarm before it hatches." Michel-Leon clasped his hands behind his back. "And I have a theory about why this incident differs from the others."

"We witnessed the creature arrive ourselves, Your Imperial Majesty," Régine said. "There is no doubt the swarm has returned to France and settled in Paris."

"You speak before your brother, madame," Napolean said with a steely note and Michel-Leon stifled a wince. He was so accustomed to Régine speaking her mind he had forgotten that the court was not as invested in women's rights as he.

"Bear in mind who founded the chevaliers, Your Imperial Majesty," Michel-Leon broke in smoothly and was relieved as the emperor inclined his head in acknowledgment of that fact. "The women among us have a great deal of wisdom and insight to offer."

"I was also told you came seeking help, though I regret I was not told immediately." Napoleon nodded toward Haussmann.

Months ago, Michel-Leon thought sourly with a hard glare at Lennox, who returned it with an expression of equal venom. No, they would never be firm allies. "My apologies. I mistrusted the message, given the chevaliers' reputation for failure and madness," Lennox said between gritted teeth. "Their failure at Metz caused unspeakable tragedy, and the Dagonville family, in particular, is known for their odd ways."

"It is a good thing I did not mistrust," Haussmann cut in. "I have been working with the baron. I would not have sent my urgent message if I didn't believe he could help. It is my opinion he knows what he's doing."

"Your dreams of vainglory have deluded you," Lennox spat. "You are an architect. What do you know of such matters?"

Napoleon's expression did not change, and Michel-Leon could not deny the failures they'd had in the past. "The chevaliers' mistakes doomed Metz. The city is still recovering from its decimation. Lennox brings up a good point, though churlishly said. Why should we have any faith in you?"

Michel-Leon looked around the gathered courtiers and turned his attention back to Napoleon. "Historically, the chevaliers dealt with creatures based in magic and lore, which is a science in its own right. Each one has its own reason for existing. Magic follows rules, like science. You know the creature, the rules, then you can deal with it. The swarm has eluded us for centuries because we could never study it. Only try to glean what we can after the monsters have hatched and moved on, which hasn't left us with much. In the past, the best and surest way of dealing with the creatures was to evacuate and return when the danger had passed."

"Evacuate?" Napoleon blanched. "You cannot be serious." He

gestured helplessly around him. "Do you have any idea of the size of Paris? Where would we put all of those people? For how long? Do you have a date for when the swarm will hatch?"

"Soon, very soon. Sometime in September, though the discrepancies cause me concern." Michel-Leon glanced at Régine, and she nodded in agreement. "I don't believe we'll have time to wait until it hatches. I have come up with an inoculation that has proven successful against the effect of the mists, and it has allowed us to do more than any of the chevaliers of the past."

Régine gestured toward Haussmann. "With the aid of his maps and men, we believe we're narrowing down the location of the swarm's nest."

"*Oui.*" Napoleon leveled Haussmann and Lennox a look of grave concern. "Haussmann reported that you believe it is in the quarry tunnels. However, all the teams sent down there to investigate reported that the tunnels filled with mists within minutes. Some disappeared. What happened to them, Chevalier? What is happening to the people who disappear off the streets of Paris?"

"Their presence in the tunnels triggered the reaction. The nest needs food to hatch. The mists intoxicate the senses to lure their prey to the nest. I am afraid anyone caught in it walks willingly to their death." Michel-Leon rubbed his chin. "I tested the reaction on myself, and I can assure you the effect is quite potent."

Napoleon moved to study the map of Paris that hung on the wall. "And you've found a way to stop that effect? Does it work?"

"So far it has. We have tested it several times on a number of people who volunteered. A companion of mine also helped me to design and construct these." Michel-Leon nodded toward the box he'd brought, and Régine pulled out the filtering mask. She handed it to Haussmann, who handed it over to Napoleon. "We use that as a first line of defense."

"Who is this 'we' you keep harping on?" Lennox demanded as the emperor studied the mask with an intrigued expression. "I thought you were the last chevalier. Your family died in disgrace."

"The gentleman who helped me come up with that, Monsieur Constantin Severin, has quite a talent for such things. He has recruited others to aid us in getting rid of the swarm. We went out during the last cycle and rescued some poor souls who had been caught out in it." Michel-Leon gestured toward Régine. "And my sister, the Widow Bardin, has always aided me in all my endeavors. I would not have gotten this far without her by my side."

"Surely, madame, you do not accompany Parisee everywhere." Lennox cut Michel-Leon a withering glare. "We have had our differences, but I cannot see you allowing a woman to go into danger."

"I assure you, I do," Régine replied in a crisp voice with a warning in her gaze. "I have helped him with many a dangerous task, such as hunting down a lich as a case in point, and investigating demon marks. The wives and daughters of chevaliers have not been idle, and there are women among our volunteers as well. They wish to protect their homes and families too."

That quieted Lennox and half the court, though Michel-Leon suspected it was for different reasons. Lennox had gone pale and wouldn't meet his eyes. He hadn't suspected others might know of his family's crimes.

He eyed Napoleon, trying to gauge whether he would be receptive to the entire story and decided it was better to err in being forthcoming than not. "We encountered strange creatures in the mists. I don't know if this is part of the recent phenomenon or not. They appeared to be caretakers of a sort for the nest and were herding people. They die as easy as any human, but we could not recover the bodies of the ones we slayed."

Another layer of frustration for Michel-Leon. He would've paid dearly to examine one closer or even to capture one to discover if he could communicate with it. "We need more people."

"You want us to risk ourselves?" Lennox glared at Michel-Leon. "Once again, the chevaliers fail in their duties. This lies on your head."

"This lies on us all," Haussmann thundered.

Michel-Leon didn't spare Lennox a glance. He met Napoleon's gaze and the concern he saw there. "The manpower I speak of is scientific in nature. I need people to replicate my inoculation and distribute it to all the people. That should be the first priority. My people and I will concern ourselves with tracking down the nest."

"You will also need men to help eradicate it when it is found. That seems imminently reasonable. I trust your assurances the concoction is safe." The emperor waved Michel-Leon silent before he could answer. "I will get the aid you require and others to construct more masks. I'll assign soldiers to you. We will have them inoculated first and given masks."

Michel-Leon bowed low. "*Merci*, Your Imperial Majesty. This will be of immeasurable help."

"I'll require you to keep me posted of any developments," Napoleon added sternly.

Michel-Leon noted the quick gleam in Lennox's eyes and spoke quickly before he could offer to be a liaison. "Of course. I'll send them through Haussmann. In fact, we would like to speak with him again before we go." There was more than one way to cage a rat. "If we could go over your reconstruction plans, monsieur. We believe we can pinpoint some troublesome areas where we can investigate further."

"You have me intrigued, baron. I am at your immediate disposal."

Much to Michel-Leon's intense relief, Napoleon dismissed them. "I think that went rather well," Régine commented as they headed down the echoing hallways. "I hope to never see that Lennox creature again."

"Your lich and demon mark comments shut him down rather nicely. I hope so as well. That chapter is over. It is time for a new one." Michel-Leon gave her a tight smile and urged Haussmann on, moving as fast as he dared. "Forgive my haste, but we are at a crossroads. Every minute is precious."

"I understand." Haussmann quickened his steps. "It won't take long to reach my office from here."

They emerged from the palace, blinking into the bright sunlight. The blue sky was always a reassuring sight these days, with the mists being so erratic. Michel-Leon would dearly love more time to study everything. Despite the success of his inoculation, there were still so many unanswered questions.

Everyone who was caught outside couldn't be taken in by the mists, or Paris would be half depopulated. Maybe it had something to do with the reason some people thrived after a blood transfusion and others died.

"It was the same at Metz. And with Angers too. If an entire family was caught out in it, one or two would be called. The rest were left alone." The voices rolled on with other tales and bits of information, but nothing new tangled out.

He needed to examine one of the creatures that attacked them. He had never heard of a monster like that before, and it mystified his ancestors as well. Which could mean two things: either they were dealing with a monster that had never been seen before, or some mutation that happened because of the mists.

That was an intriguing thought.

"The mists have never altered people before. Blood magic is at work. Don't forget about the blood. The boar is to blame. Remember the boar."

"Baron, have you heard me?" Haussmann's voice cut into his thoughts as he clambered into his carriage.

"My apologies. I was considering one aspect of our current

conundrum."

"You have to forgive him," Régine said with a smile. "It's an unfortunate habit of his."

"Understandable. I was asking what you hoped to glean from the reconstruction plans," Haussmann asked as the carriage rolled off.

Michel-Leon tapped his fingers on the knob of his cane. "The creatures I spoke of have been raiding construction sites for various materials. I have no idea as to what end, but I thought you might've received reports, and we could pinpoint the most troublesome areas. That might help confirm where I've narrowed our search."

"Now that you mention it. People have gone missing all over Paris, but the raids appear to be limited to the *Rive Gauche*. Perhaps a look at the plans and reports will reveal other oddities."

By the time Michel-Leon was in Haussmann's office and poring over the plans with the architect, Régine at his side, he was sick with impatience. He flipped through the plans, noticing how progress had slowed after the mists arrived at a time that should've been ideal for construction. He had sympathy for Haussmann's own delayed deadlines.

As he scanned through them again, he frowned and circled a spot on the plans with his finger. "Why did you stop your plans here?"

"That's not far from where we ran into those creatures," Régine observed. "Isn't there an entrance to the catacombs there as well?"

Haussmann studied the plans intently. "I believe there were reports of a haunting." He turned toward the reports, neatly stacked, and went through them. "It wasn't a priority project, and with everything else going on, we set it aside to pick up again when matters calmed down. I was thinking of having a priest do an exorcism in case it was spirits."

He muttered to himself as he read. "Ah *oui*, here's the first incident. The entire team disappeared this spring and the team after that.

We blamed it on the mists." He handed over the report as he moved on to the next one. "Afterward, everyone who approached it complained of a strange sensation of being spied on or followed if they got too close. There were a few more disappearances, some in broad daylight. People have been avoiding it since and find excuses to leave quickly."

"I will talk to people in the neighborhoods surrounding the area, but I believe this is a good place to start." Michel-Leon peered at the notes. "A fire destroyed this area?"

"*Oui.* Many of the structures are quite unsound. I thought this would be an easier project. No one to evict but squatters."

"If you don't mind, I'll take these with me." Michel-Leon rolled up the plans. "I want my friend to take a look. I'll send you an update tomorrow."

"Be careful." Michel-Leon glanced over at Haussmann's solemn tone. "Both of you. I don't like the feel of this."

Michel-Leon exchanged glances with Régine. "I am always careful."

Chapter Twenty-Seven

"WAKE UP! WAKE up! The boar is here!"

Michel-Leon jerked out of a solid sleep and almost toppled out of his chair, exhausted by his efforts to hunt down the swarm and the creatures that had attacked them in the mists. He glanced around his study, piled with books and notes, trying to locate the danger as the voices howled at him with increasing intensity. He couldn't think or even hear the state of the household over the din in his mind.

"Quiet!" Michel-Leon snarled, rubbing at his aching temples. Mercifully, the ancestors listened. The house was mostly silent, and the gaslights still gleamed warmly in the hallway. The activity in the workshop had slowed, but a few remained awake and at work. He'd check in upstairs first and see if either Constantin or Régine were awake and then take a peek outside.

He reached for his cane and drew the sword from it before locating the revolver among his papers. As he took the stairs toward the workshop, the house filled with the tinkle of breaking glass from below and above. Michel-Leon spun around on the staircase and rushed down as cries of alarm echoed between the walls.

Dark figures with distorted faces, enlarged eyes and frozen, twisted mouths clambered into the foyer from the broken window. A strange hissing noise came from that gaping maw. Michel-Leon shot at one of the mist monsters and it went down, but others were unlocking the front door to let more in. The thudding and splintering of the kitchen door breaking down warned him that others were coming in the back.

Mahout screamed behind him on the stairs. Her eyes were wide with horror, and her hands were white-knuckled where she gripped her sleeping robe. "Get upstairs. Get your *maman*," he ordered. "Find a room and barricade yourselves inside. Don't come out unless I, Régine, or Constantin say so."

She rushed away as Michel-Leon took more shots and then paused to reload. He didn't have enough bullets to take them all down, and they were coming in too fast to pick off. He fell back as they swarmed toward him and held them at bay with his sword. The ones from the kitchen were now in the hallway, and he was trapped between the two forces.

"Michie!" Régine called. "Constantin? Where are you?"

"Downstairs hallway," Michel-Leon called back, reeling as one came under his guard and caught him in the ribs with a crowbar with a glancing blow as he twisted away. Pain racked his body, but as he fell back, he was fairly certain he had narrowly missed having some ribs broken. The clamor of fighting increased upstairs. Michel-Leon slashed at the one who attacked him and retreated another step back, aiming for the stairs.

"He's here! He's here!" Another figure darkened the doorway as the voices shouted in warning. The light in the hallway had broken, and all Michel-Leon could make out was a silhouette.

"Enough," they commanded in a vaguely familiar voice, a man's voice.

"The Boar." The voices hissed in his mind as the creatures attacking Michel-Leon drew back a few steps. The boar was a man, not a creature as Michel-Leon had supposed. He straightened but didn't lower his sword as the man approached. The noise of battle faded upstairs, and Michel-Leon worried over the other members of his household. He eyed the man as the intruder crouched in the shadows over one of the fallen bodies of its creatures. So this was the one the voices considered to be as dangerous as the mists.

"Did you have to kill them?" he asked in a voice heavy with bitter sorrow, and again the sense of familiarity tickled.

"They invaded my home and sought to harm us. What did you expect me to do?" Michel-Leon asked evenly as the man straightened. "Step into the light so I can see you."

"You attacked them on the street when they were doing their job. You killed three of my children." The man stepped forward, his eyes gleaming red in the dark before the stairwell light slanted across his harsh features.

Michel-Leon's breath caught. Auguste Vautrin.

"You've been using blood magic since we last met." Michel-Leon stared at him, sickened by the evidence of his eyes. Then he studied the creatures surrounding him, who were unnaturally still. The only evidence that they were living was the hiss of their breath through their twisted mouths. "You've warped these things, tearing their souls from them to fuel the changes you wanted. How many humans have you altered to do your bidding? How could you damn yourself this way? Vautrin, they were human. You've destroyed that."

"I had to," Vautrin snapped. "I will never allow the swarm to hatch. Never. These changes make them immune to the mists. They don't mind."

"Sweet Saint Jeanne, you ripped their souls from them. There's nothing left for them to mind. They're puppets! Not people." Another thought sickened him further. "Where's Raul? You didn't do this to your grandson, did you?"

"Raul has been changed, but his soul is intact." The response from the ancestors surprised Michel-Leon. They rarely named those they encountered, unless…

"Raul doesn't understand what I'm trying to accomplish." An expression of frustrated sorrow crossed Vautrin's face as he neared. "You cannot understand if you weren't at Metz when the swarm hatched. He will understand before this is all over."

Vautrin caressed the back of one of his altered humans as he pushed through their ranks. "Their souls are serving a higher purpose. France will remember each one of them as heroes. The saviors of Paris. They will have accomplished something unlike you! Damn all the chevaliers."

Vautrin's expression distorted into rage as his finger stabbed toward Michel-Leon. He raised his sword to hold him at bay and the creatures stirred restlessly, closing in at the implied threat. Vautrin resembled the boar he was named for with his reddened, mad eyes. "Do you know where the swarm is? We can end this. Destroy the nest together."

"Do you even know how to destroy the nest?" Vautrin paused and searched Michel-Leon's expression. "If I told you where it was, what would you do next?"

Excitement gripped Michel-Leon. Vautrin did know, and there may be enough sanity left in the man that Michel-Leon could reason with him. "I am looking into that. I have theories—"

"You've had months to come up with a plan. Months! Theories?" Rage suffused Vautrin's features again. "Useless like the rest of the chevaliers who had generations upon generations to solve this plague. I regret having to kill you. You and your sister showed me kindness.

But I cannot allow you to get in my way. All the rest of the people you've recruited can be made into my children or held in wait in case we need more fuel for my ship."

Michel-Leon lifted his sword toward Vautrin's throat. The stairs creaked and then silenced. *"The soul sister is near,"* the ancestors whispered, and some of Michel-Leon's anxiety eased. Régine, at least, was alive. The sounds of fighting escalated upstairs, and he was sick with worry about everyone else. He believed Vautrin would make good on his threat.

"You will not harm a single soul in this household," Michel-Leon warned. Vautrin muttered under his breath, lifting his hand into a claw as a red light coalesced between his fingertips. Michel-Leon tensed to thrust his sword home.

"Don't kill him!"

Michel-Leon reeled from the echoing roar in his mind. He fought to return to his body as the ancestors yanked him onto the astral plane. For a moment, he glimpsed Vautrin there as well before he clawed his way back to consciousness.

He and Vautrin stared at each other with equally stunned expressions. Michel-Leon's sword fell from nerveless fingers, and Vautrin's hand dropped as the creatures milled about in confusion. Régine appeared on the last few steps, her gun trained on Vautrin. He met her gaze and shook his head.

"You're a chevalier too." Michel-Leon reached to grab Vautrin's shoulders, and the man shrank back.

"Non, non. I'm not like you." He gripped his hair with a cry of distress. "Why won't they let me kill you?"

Régine eased a step closer, her expression mirroring her shock and envy. Neither the creatures nor Vautrin noticed her approach. They were all caught up in his mental agony. What one shared, they all shared.

"Chevaliers can't kill each other. You can keep the voices from taking over. Let me teach you," Michel-Leon offered.

Vautrin must've been one of the children left behind and forgotten in Metz, assumed dead in the slaughter. He'd been forced to grow up with no understanding of his heritage, consumed by the chevaliers purpose, with the memories of the horror he'd witnessed to fuel it, and no way to make sense of the voices in his mind. No surprise he had become so twisted. Michel-Leon didn't know if there was a way to cure him of the taint of blood magic, but he would try.

"Stay away from me," Vautrin raged, pointing a shaking finger at Michel-Leon as he backed away. "Let me do what I'm destined to do. It'll all be over soon. Stay away. I will slaughter anyone who comes near me or mine on sight. Even you!"

As Vautrin backed away, so did his creatures, slithering back into the darkness of the broken doorway. "Wait!" Michel-Leon followed as Régine fell into step beside him. "What do you plan on doing with the nest and a ship? Let me help."

"Do you think this is wise?" Régine muttered under her breath. "We can't hold them all off if we extend ourselves out here. The ancestors might not be able to stop someone this far gone."

Vautrin's eyes glittered with madness. "You want to sacrifice yourself? Steer the ship to the stars? That's the only way you can help."

"How did you find the nest?" Michel-Leon asked, stepping closer as the creatures hissed in warning. "I must know."

Vautrin's eyes went distant. "You see a swarm hatch once, and you can hear the call of them forever. That's how I knew they returned. That's how I found them."

He whistled sharply, and more commotion erupted overhead. His creatures picked up the bodies of their fallen. Then Vautrin disappeared into the night, his creatures following, leaving the front door listing on its hinges. Michel-Leon and Régine chased them, but they moved eel-like through the shadows and they soon lost them.

"What is going on, Michie?" Régine asked, brushing back the tangle of her hair that had loosened from its braid. For the first time, Michel-Leon noticed her feet were bare and she had on her nightclothes and robe.

"We have some answers only to have more damned questions. We'd better check on your family and our crew in the laboratory." His blood was cold. "Constantin was up there. I'm sure of it." Frustrated, he raced back to the townhouse with Régine to check on everyone.

Salome had emerged and was railing over the state of her kitchen. Michel-Leon left Régine to deal with her and raced up the stairs to the top level. The workshop was in chaos, tables overturned, and three bodies were laid out under shrouds. Lyon and Pariseau were setting things to right. Michel-Leon's heart clutched. Neither survivor was Constantin.

"Are you unhurt?" he asked as he forced himself to head toward the sheet-covered bodies. He couldn't lose him. Not now. "Weren't there more of you up here?"

"Those bastards killed Favager, Olivier, and Renaud." The foreman spat. "Severin is following after them."

It was all Michel-Leon could do to keep his hand steady as relief swept through him. Constantin may have better luck with his unique ability to blend in with the shadows. "I should've foreseen this," he said softly as he studied the features of the fallen men. "Do they have families?"

"*Non*, my lord. They were alone in the world." Lyon exchanged glances with Pariseau. "We were their family."

Michel-Leon pulled the sheet over their faces again. "I'll make sure they have a proper burial and aren't forgotten in a pauper's grave." It wasn't enough, but it would have to do. He desperately wished Janvier was there. He wanted his council. He needed it. Vautrin's involvement changed so much.

He was going to have to go onto the astral plane for answers. He'd have to go deeper than he'd ever gone before, and the thought scared him. What if he couldn't pull himself back out? If anybody could reach him, it would be Janvier.

He would have to figure out a way of doing it without him. Michel-Leon rose and began helping the survivors put the house back together again while he waited for Constantin to return.

Chapter Twenty-Eight

CONSTANTIN PAUSED AT the entrance to another city square and tried to get a feel for the quarry he chased. He'd followed them all the way to the other side of the Seine, and they were deep within an area of reconstruction. To Constantin's eye, it looked as if a conflagration had swept through, gutting the surrounding buildings. His heart quickened with excitement. This was the area Michel-Leon was interested in exploring, but his prey was getting farther away, and Constantin turned his attention back to them.

It was hard to follow the soulless creatures. There was nothing to latch onto. Every time he brushed up against them mentally, he encountered something else so vile and corrupted his stomach heaved, and it forced him to break contact. Constantin moved off in the direction where he last sensed them and took a risk of reaching out again.

The unnatural evil he'd first detected rolled over him, closer, stronger. Constantin collapsed against a wall, retching in reaction. He tried to break off contact, but it caught him in its web of blood, pain, and power. The dark thing inside him stirred and the horror of that gave Constantin enough impetus to wrench himself free.

Constantin used the wall to steady himself as he took deep, cleansing breaths. He had to keep hunting and refused to give in to his dark side. He would cut it off and starve it the way they'd starved Nightingale.

When he straightened again with a foul taste in his mouth, there was no trace of his quarry. It was as if they'd ceased to exist. The soulless men and even the foul stench of blood magic had vanished like smoke on the wind.

Constantin studied his surroundings with narrowed eyes. In the distance, his ears caught the clop of horse hooves on cobblestone, the rattle of carriage wheels. But those familiar sounds were far off. Paris was never silent, but here it was different. A stillness overlaid the section like a smothering wool blanket. Constantin wrapped the surrounding shadows tighter, feeling uncannily exposed. He moved in the direction where he last sensed the unnatural presence. He'd advanced half a block before he found himself turned around and heading back the way he'd come.

He frowned and glanced over his shoulder. He didn't remember turning, or even thinking about it. Facing the street, he walked forward in deliberate care with one foot in front of the other, and the same thing happened. Between one step and the next, he had turned around and was moving away.

Constantin marked his location and tried approaching this section from another direction. The same thing happened. It was nearing dawn by the time he finished mapping out where the interdictions began and ended.

The effort of keeping the glamour on himself had worn him out. Wearily, he turned back toward the townhouse. He'd report to Michel-Leon and Régine, and catch a couple of hours of sleep. When he awoke again, he'd attempt sending some of his constructs within the invisible barrier that turned people away.

Every light in the townhouse blazed when he caught sight of it, and Constantin noted the guards on the roof. If only they'd had the foresight to consider doing that before. The townhouse was too exposed. He'd have to convince Michel-Leon and Régine to retreat to the château. He hoped they were safe and hadn't been harmed in the attack. The creatures had overwhelmed them and then stopped on some hidden signal before disappearing again. He didn't have time to check on them without losing the trail, and it weighed on him. He wasn't used to caring for others.

Constantin dropped the glamour with a sigh of relief and trudged toward the front door. It opened before he arrived, and Lyon stepped out. "It's good to see you, Severin."

Constantin smiled and clasped his hand. "And you as well. How many did we lose?"

Lyon's gaze clouded. "Three. They were closest to the door and were swarmed. The chevalier and his sister are making arrangements for them."

Michel-Leon and Régine were safe. Constantin relaxed even as he felt a twist of sympathy for the fallen. He'd seen them go down and he'd feared the worst. "How are the baron and his sister?"

"The chevalier is getting quite anxious. He's walled himself up in his study and is talking to himself. Some are starting to question his sanity. I've convinced them he is fine based solely on the fact the widow doesn't appear to be bothered by his ways."

"He's as sane as you and me." Constantin entered the townhouse to the comforting aroma of brewing coffee and cooked eggs. "He talks to himself as he works through problems. The bigger the problem, the louder he talks and after last night, we have some huge ones on our hands."

"If you say so," Lyon replied with a bit of dubiousness in his voice.

Constantin glanced up the stairwell. "Do me a favor. Have Salome send up a tray for the two of us. I'll go talk to Michel-Leon in his den. Be prepared to pack up. I'm going to try to convince him to head back to the château. I doubt I'll be able to, but if I do, I want to be ready."

"But that place is haunted." Lyon drew back in alarm.

"Dangerous *oui*, haunted *non*." But right now it was more dangerous in the townhouse and the only person, place, or thing that was haunted was Michel-Leon himself. Constantin wearily trudged up the stairs and entered Michel-Leon's den without knocking.

Michel-Leon's head jerked up, a scathing expression in his eyes that quickly changed to stunned relief. "You're back." To Constantin's surprise, Michel-Leon came to him and threw his arms around him. "I was worried about you."

Constantin allowed himself the luxury of being held by him before he remembered his reasons for staying away and pulled back. "You weren't hurt in the attack, were you? I thought we were done for, but then suddenly they retreated for no reason. Another press and they would've swarmed us all under."

"It was getting hairy. My ribs are going to feel the bruises for days. Régine was about to come to my rescue when they left. Sit, I'll catch you up and then you can tell me where you've been." Michel-Leon paced as he relayed what happened to him and who was behind it all. Judging from his stride, any wounds he'd taken were minor.

Constantin sank into a stuffed chair with a frown as he tried to make sense of it all. "So we're dealing with another chevalier? Does this put you in more danger?"

"He's not a chevalier." Michel-Leon rubbed his temple and muttered under his breath in an argumentative tone. "Even if he has the blood and the abilities, he doesn't have the training or the understanding of his responsibility. But because he has the damn blood, the ancestors are keeping him from killing me. He's crazy enough, though, that I cannot trust it would last."

"We should regroup and return to the château," Constantin said, and Michel-Leon turned on him with wide eyes.

"That is the last thing we should do. We are so close to an answer." He strode over to his desk and stabbed a finger at the layers of maps. "Here is the key. It's dawn now. We should go investigate as soon as we can muster the men." A knock came at the door. "Go away," Michel-Leon snapped.

"*Non*, don't. Come in." Constantin rose and went to the door. Salome stood there, tray in hand, loaded down with their breakfast. "Bless you, madame."

She cast a worried look over him and then at Michel-Leon. "At least one of you has sense. Régine is sleeping. I suggest you do the same after you eat."

"I am yours to command." He took the tray over to Michel-Leon's desk and set it down. "Sit and eat, and we'll discuss our plans."

"Not if your plans involve moving to the château. It's too far away." Michel-Leon sat down across from him, his face shadowed with weariness. "There's too much to do. We need to discuss if this area truly is the locus of our issues. We need to find the nest below. And we need to discover a way to destroy it. And we needed all of this yesterday. The good news is that Vautrin is under the same deadline. He said something about building a ship to the stars, which is insane."

Constantin glanced up from his study of the maps, intrigued by the idea. "A ship to the stars? Is that why all those materials are disappearing?"

"I suppose so, though how such a thing would be possible, I don't know." Michel-Leon accepted the cup of coffee with a grateful smile. "I believe the key to finding out what to do with the nest when we locate it will be with the ancestors. They've been pestering me more and, conversely, have been harder to understand. I fear I'm going to have to go in deeper."

Constantin took his first sip of coffee and felt the warmth go through him. "That scares you. Do you fear not being able to find your way out again?"

"Always," Michel-Leon replied softly. He looked up with a small smile. "But that is the hazard. Did you have any luck following the creatures?"

"It was difficult." Constantin drank again to wash away the memory of that taste. "The creatures are impossible to sense. There's nothing left of them that can be called human. Nightingale left more of a trace than they did. And there was something else. Based on what you said, I'm assuming it's Vautrin. He made me ill every time I brushed up against him. How does blood magic work?"

"Human sacrifice." Michel-Leon appeared troubled. "I'm assuming he murdered some to get the power to take the souls from others, which he turned into these creatures of his that are immune to the effects of the mists. He also said something about using them for fuel, and I have grave concerns about what that means. The swarm is a danger true, but Vautrin has already caused irreparable harm, and he is incapable of seeing it in his present state. He will not stop until he destroys the nest. We're going to have to focus on him as much as the swarm."

"I suspect we'll find all the answers here." Constantin traced the area Michel-Leon was interested in. "I tracked them this far, but there is something that blocks me from continuing."

"An uneasy feeling?" Michel-Leon asked. "That's what Haussmann's people reported."

"It's stronger than that. It's a force that turns you away, and you don't even comprehend it until you are moving in the opposite direction. I'm sure that alone would make people uneasy. I'm not sure if it's some type of blood magic, as you say, or a glamour. Frankly, I'm too tired to figure it out. I'm going to sleep for a few hours and then attempt to send one of my constructs through to see what happens."

"That is a good plan. I need to sleep as well if I'm going to wrestle with the ancestors. Régine will be awake soon and will oversee repairs and organizing the men. I'll leave her a note. She can prepare the report. We should let the palace and Haussmann know we are making progress." Michel-Leon met his eyes. "We can take turns guarding each other's backs. I'll watch over you when you send the constructs in, and you watch over me when I delve into the ancestors' memories."

"I'd like that." Constantin found he couldn't look away from Michel-Leon as warmth filled him. He'd been avoiding intimate contact with the chevalier, and his reasons for doing so seemed fuzzy now.

Michel-Leon broke their gaze, color appearing in his cheeks. "I'm going to retire to my rooms." He fiddled with a pen, staring hard at his maps. "Would you, uh, join me?"

Regret filled Constantin at the shy, sweet offer. He longed to say yes, to lie down with him and hold him, but until he figured out what he was and how to deal with it, he didn't trust himself. He'd sensed it stir with hunger earlier, and he could not take that chance. Not with Michel-Leon. "My apologies, I cannot."

He reached out to touch Michel-Leon's hand to ease the sting, but Michel-Leon pulled back, his cheeks scarlet. "Well then, I will see you in a few hours."

Constantin studied the door after Michel-Leon left. He'd been wishing for Michel-Leon to turn to him. He'd finally seduced a sweet response from him, and they'd been tiptoeing around each other ever since. Mostly because of Michel-Leon's shy inexperience and Constantin's fear that he was a monster.

Michel-Leon's words came back to him, reminding him he was a healer, not a monster. And Constantin remembered how he'd urged Michel-Leon to hold on to what was important or else they could lose what they were fighting for. Didn't the same apply to him? How could he hope to hold onto his humanity if he didn't grab ahold of what he loved and cherish it?

They were going to be diving deep into hell soon as they searched for this nest. They had no way of knowing if they were going to survive. Michel-Leon was going to have to face his nightmares and delve into his ancestors. Constantin would have to do the same, face the hunger if he wanted to hunt Vautrin. Michel-Leon had reached out to Constantin, and Constantin had spurned him.

Constantin closed his eyes with a heavy sigh of regret. Michel-Leon had unlimited bravery when it came to risking his body and mind, but he was far more cautious when it came to his heart. He couldn't leave things between them like this.

He leaped up and headed toward Michel-Leon's room. The house had quieted, and he suspected they weren't the only ones attempting to grab some rest. He paused long enough to make sure they were still guards on duty and then rapped his knuckles against Michel-Leon's door.

"Go away."

Constantin's lips twitched at the surly reply, and then his heart ached. He'd humiliated Michel-Leon, though unintentionally. He opened the door and slipped inside before locking it behind him. Michel-Leon glanced up from the divan where he'd been sitting as he took off his boots. He studied Constantin with a hooded gaze and pulled off the other.

"Did you need something?" he asked, looking away and setting his boots to the side with deliberate care. His coppery hair gleamed in the early morning light that streamed from the window. The sight of him made Constantin's buried heart stir. They were fools, taking turns spurning what was between them when they could use it to strengthen themselves.

"I do," Constantin replied, striding over to him. Michel-Leon looked up, startled, as Constantin caught him and hauled him to his feet. Before Michel-Leon could form the question in his eyes, Constantin kissed him. Michel-Leon made a muffled sound of surprise, and then he wrapped his arms around Constantin and kissed him back with urgency.

"You, that's what I need," Constantin replied as he eased back enough to pull off Michel-Leon's shirt before removing his own. Discoloration marked Michel-Leon's side where bruises were forming. Constantin skimmed his fingertips over his ribs, reminding himself that he should take this slow if Michel-Leon showed any signs of pain.

Michel-Leon's gray eyes gleamed. "Me too," he said and reached for Constantin again. His mouth was hot and demanding, stoking that burning fire they'd tried to keep banked.

The sunlight streamed over the bed as they made their way over to it, stealing kisses and shedding the rest of their clothes. The shy expression in Michel-Leon's eyes Constantin found so sweetly endearing was quickly replaced with the avid curiosity that was as engaging. He sat on the edge of the bed, wandering his fingers over Constantin's bare skin. "I recall you enjoyed the touch of my mouth here."

Electricity sizzled, and Constantin's breath caught as he captured Michel-Leon's roaming hand. They'd explore later, when they had the time and energy to do it properly. He kissed Michel-Leon's work-roughened knuckles and bore him back on the bed with an urgent kiss. He longed to feel Michel-Leon inside him, to ride him rough and fast.

Michel-Leon caught onto his mood and followed suit, returning his kisses with nips and soothing swipes of his tongue as he arched underneath him. He tasted the wild energy running through the chevalier, and it called to the same energy inside of him. They were two halves that fit together to make a whole.

Constantin's hands raced over his long, lean body in an explosion of heat and need and hunger. They'd waited for too long, both of them, and to what purpose? Michel-Leon broke away, panting, and framed Constantin's face in his hands. "What you did last time, I want to try." At Constantin's confused look, he blushed. "I want to feel you in me. I want to know what it's like."

Constantin groaned. Michel-Leon was a never-ending surprise and delight. "Your love of experimentation may be the end of me."

Michel-Leon laughed, a delighted sound that filled him with wonder. "I've learned you are a survivor. I doubt I could hurt you."

The words struck a chord with Constantin, and he recognized Michel-Leon had the power to hurt him far more than Blaise ever had. He held Constantin's heart in his hands.

"You're wrong, Michel-Leon," Constantin rasped as he slid his arms around him. "You could slay me."

Michel-Leon held Constantin in return with a quiet intensity, as if his emotions ran as deep. Constantin wasn't good with words, but he could show how much Michel-Leon's unwavering support had meant to him. It had helped him get his feet underneath him and gave him the will to fight.

Michel-Leon slid his hand in a long caress down Constantin's back. "You have that power as well."

He undid him. Constantin kissed Michel-Leon again. He'd give Michel-Leon the chance to act out all the experiments he wanted when they weren't bouncing from one crisis to another. "Another time, I forgot to grab the oil before I came."

Michel-Leon pointed to the vial peeking from under the pillow and blushed deeper when Constantin raised his eyebrow. "I had hoped you would agree, and I wanted to be ready because I needed to be with you. I was scared I'd lost you. What made you change your mind?"

"I reversed the discussion we had the last time before we ended up naked." Constantin smiled and traced his finger down Michel-Leon's cheek. He laid a soft and sweet kiss on Michel-Leon's lips. "When we have more time, I'll let you experiment all you want."

Michel-Leon groaned as Constantin rolled under him and reached for the vial. He pressed it into Michel-Leon's hand and dug his fingers into the bright warmth of his hair. He pulled his knees up to cradle Michel-Leon's hips and fisted his hand, dragging Michel-Leon down for an urgent kiss. "Rough and fast."

He felt the instant response in Michel-Leon's body. It didn't take him long before Constantin felt the sting and insistent pressure of Michel-Leon's cock. He welcomed the sensation with a sigh of pleasure, hooking his legs around Michel-Leon's waist to make it easier for him. He flexed his fingers in Michel-Leon's hair and rocked up to meet him.

Michel-Leon caught onto the rhythm quickly, their hands clasped, fingers twining together. Caught up in their closeness, distracted by the physical sensations, Constantin reached for him and sensed Michel-Leon's pleasure and wonder.

Michel-Leon gasped with a shudder. "I can feel you."

Constantin froze and started to pull back, but Michel-Leon shook his head. "*Non*, I like you there. Don't leave."

Constantin kissed him, reaching for the feel of him again. Everything he loved about Michel-Leon was there on the surface, his curiosity, fierce determination, and deep love for the people he fought for. As their bodies came together, Constantin sensed the touch of their souls and the pain and fear Michel-Leon had buried and tried to forget.

The hunger was different this time, translated into a sexual need. Constantin groaned, sweat slicking his body as he met Michel-Leon's powerful thrusts with increasing intensity. He eased the wounds in Michel-Leon's soul, the terror of fire, the pain of a child who couldn't meet his father's expectations. As he healed, Constantin sensed some of his own scars fading.

Michel-Leon shuddered again, his orgasm hitting him in several long waves that caught up Constantin as well. Still twined together, body and soul, Constantin followed, holding on to him until they were spent. They curled up around each other and drifted off.

Chapter Twenty-Nine

MICHEL-LEON WOKE up as Constantin stirred next to him. Light and warmth from the noonday sun flooded the bedroom. His thoughts immediately jumped into what he had to do, even as his body protested with the need for more sleep. Shouts of alarm caught his attention, but they were from outside, not inside, and must've been what awoke him. Though he suspected the cause, he rose to be sure.

Through the window, he observed people scurrying about, closing shutters and hiding behind closed doors. Already the light was dimmer. His window faced the wrong way, but Michel-Leon knew the mists were coming.

As he pulled on his breeches, Constantin pushed himself up. "Do you want to send another party out? I can be ready in a few minutes."

"*Non*," Michel-Leon replied after a moment's thought. "Vautrin will expect that and be ready for us. We don't need more bloodshed. As much as I want to go out and rescue every mist-spelled there is, the quickest way to save them is to destroy the swarm. That's what Vautrin wants as well. Then we can figure out a way to keep him from causing more harm."

"This may be cold, but why not shoot him?" Constantin sat up, his golden hair flowing around his naked torso. He appeared more fey than man. Michel-Leon constantly marveled that they had found each other.

The voices in Michel-Leon's head hissed their disapproval at Constantin's suggestion. "I'm afraid I can't." Michel-Leon tapped his temple. "They won't let me. But we'll figure out a way to deal with him."

"Well, I don't have the same restraint." Constantin pulled back the covers, rose naked, and stretched luxuriously. "What he's done, there's no coming back from. You didn't sense it the way I did. Blood and agony saturated him. *S'il te plaît,* understand, I do not kill lightly. It would be a mercy for him as well."

"I'm going to ask the ancestors to see what we can do. In the meantime, why don't you try sending your constructs into that zone? If that works, we will figure out what to do next. There has to be a way around the barrier, or better yet, through it." Michel-Leon shrugged into his shirt and ran his fingers through his curls as he decided against getting dressed further. For what he had to face, he wanted to be comfortable.

"I have some thoughts." Constantin stamped his feet into his boots. "It could be something similar to my glamour. In which case, I can dispel it easily if we find the right pressure points. If the construct goes through, I think I can experiment further with that."

"Do you need me to keep a guard while you do that?" Michel-Leon asked, and Constantin shook his head.

"We are pressed for time, and if I'm correct, I should be safe. Vautrin can destroy the constructs, but he can't harm me through them." Constantin gave him a humorless smile. "He can only do that in person."

Michel-Leon settled himself into a comfortable chair near the window and rested his hands on the arms, his head against the back, and lifted his legs onto the settee. "I'll come find you when I'm done, and we can compare notes."

Constantin gave him an odd look and crouched near his chair. "Do you need me to keep an eye on you? Didn't you say Janvier used to do that for you?"

"He did when I got pulled in unexpectedly. Kept me from falling over and bashing my head." Michel-Leon smiled at him. "I should be fine. I've been dealing with this all my life. If you don't hear from me in an hour, come in and shake me. That should pull me right out of it."

"If you're certain. You did say we would look out after each other." Constantin covered Michel-Leon's hand with his own. "Don't take risks."

"Only calculated ones, I assure you." Michel-Leon stared up into his brown eyes with a new sense of security and comfort. "I have many reasons why I will fight to remain whole and sane, and you are one of them."

Constantin smiled and kissed him. He remained near as Michel-Leon closed his eyes and relaxed. This differed from when he was yanked in. This time, he was seeking admittance. Once his thoughts settled, he focused on the plane where he'd find all the ancestors. "Take me in."

A roar of voices came at him like a rushing wave and Michel-Leon let it flow over him, concentrating instead on spacing his breaths until they were even. When the tumult subsided to a manageable level, he opened his eyes and focused on the first wavering form in front of him. The ruined face of his brother stared back, and Michel-Leon's heart ached with remembered grief.

"How do I counter Vautrin's blood magic?" Michel-Leon asked, reminding himself this was just Gregoire's shade and not his fallen brother.

"The watcher is the key."

Constantin. Michel-Leon's heart caught again. "Where does the watcher's soul hang in balance? Is he in any danger of becoming a magicman?"

The air swirled around his brother, and he disappeared to be replaced with another familiar face. Michel-Leon's father did not appear any less disapproving in death than he had in life. *"The watcher is on the side of the healers. But he is not one to dally with as you have done. You need to rebuild the chevaliers. You need to attend to your duty."*

There were far more important concerns on Michel-Leon's mind than making more chevaliers and inflicting his father upon them. "We believe we've located the swarm. How do we destroy it?"

His father grabbed ahold of him with phantom fingers that dug into his arms despite their insubstantiality. He loomed before Michel-Leon as he had so many times before when Michel-Leon was a child. *"Are you listening to me, garçon?"*

Years of training and discipline settled over him, dispelling the ice filling his veins. Michel-Leon pushed back and his father vanished. He took a step deeper into the void and latched on to another shadow with a face he didn't recognize. "How do I destroy the swarm?"

"The swarm destroyed Metz. So many dead. So many lost to the shadows."

Michel-Leon side-stepped the wraith's attempt to latch onto him. "I know about Metz. I don't know how to destroy the nest. Can you help?"

The man shook his head regretfully, and Michel-Leon took another step. He sensed the ancestors gathering around him as he passed, opening a pathway for him to go in deeper. He glanced back over his shoulder at the shining cord connecting him to the real world. It disappeared into the shadows, but it was still there. The only thing he could do was go farther, and as he did, his sense of time faded.

Eventually, a light appeared ahead, flickering orange and yellow.

The clamor of the ancestors' misery, their screams and moans waned, replaced with the tormented screams at the heart of this place. He paused. Michel-Leon had never gone in so deep. He'd never heard of anyone speaking to the Burning Maiden. He'd wandered back through centuries of chevaliers.

If anyone would have answers, it would be her. Michel-Leon stiffened his resolve and locked his gaze on that unsteady glow. The ancestors melted away, leaving him alone. The flickering light became a pillar of fire, and as he neared, he saw the pile of logs that fueled its base. A slender form twisted and writhed within that pillar. Her screams pierced the air, and his heart wrung with pity and awe.

Michel-Leon fell to his knees and bowed his head with the profoundest respect, his fist pressed to his heart. "My lady."

The screams of agony retreated into the distance, though still audible, and then the roar and crackle of flames faded too. Light approached him. *"Look at me, my chevalier."*

Michel-Leon lifted his head. One moment she was a blackened corpse, her body twisted in torturous pain, the next she was a young maiden dressed in armor with her helmet tucked under her arm. The vision wavered back and forth between the two images. "I need your help, my lady."

"You are the first to have risked coming this far back in a long time." Her eyes narrowed in thought, and she cocked her head as if listening to voices only she could hear. It had been rumored angels talked to her, though those who killed her would've argued it had been demons. Michel-Leon saw nothing demonic in her eyes, only an unwavering determination he understood.

"I had to. So many lives are at risk. We've already lost too many to the swarm."

"How long has it been? How do my people fare? Do many chevaliers remain?"

"It has been centuries, my lady. Centuries filled with bloodshed as the people of France battled ourselves. But a new time is coming, a time of science and progress, and I have hope it will unite everyone." If they could survive. "I am making a book, recording everything the chevaliers have learned about the monsters and creatures that inhabit our world. The book will last when the chevaliers are gone."

She stared down at him sternly. *"You did not answer my last question. How many of my chevaliers remain?"* She looked away, her gaze distant as the flames flared again. *"They were witnesses to my end. I saw each one in the crowd. They remained loyal after my death."*

"There are two bloodlines I know of remaining. Mine and Vautrin's if his grandchildren survive his madness. He never had the benefit of our training. The tragedy at Metz warped his mind. Everyone remained loyal to you until the last chevalier." Michel-Leon closed his eyes. *"Je suis désolé,* my lady, but the chevalier bloodline will end with me."

"Look at me," she commanded again, and Michel-Leon could not deny her. She touched his chin with charred fingers and heat seared him, making him cry out in pain. *"The chevaliers will not end with you. You will usher in a new era. Swear this to me. Swear you will not lose faith. You will recruit and teach to make sure all of France's children remain safe."*

Michel-Leon thought of Constantin's efforts to bring others in. He thought of the shrouded bodies laid out this morning, fallen soldiers in an endless fight. He thought of the farmers' lost goods when dealing with the goblin raids; the orphans tormented by the magicman, all the missing people of Paris and those who returned, scarred from their experiences in the mists. It was a brutal, never-ending fight and one he could not abandon.

"I swear it, my lady."

She smiled, though there was as much steel in that gesture as there was when she was at her most stern. *"I believe you. Why did you seek me out, Chevalier? The need must be dire."*

"The swarm has returned, and this time the death toll will be in the hundreds of thousands. In the past, it has forced us to evacuate until the danger has passed. Even then, so many were lost. We have narrowed down the likely location of the nest, and we have found ways to counteract the effects of the mists it produces. Before I go down with my team, I need to know how to destroy the nest. We may only get one chance at this."

"You say we, though you are the last chevalier." Her eyes went distant again and the voices of the ancestors murmured. Michel-Leon heard bits and pieces of conflicting advice about the watcher, and he stiffened. *"Your sister in spirit, the watcher, and the people he has found — you will be the new order, one not tainted by my gift that became a curse."*

For once, Michel-Leon wished Régine had the capacity to be here. She put in the work of a chevalier, lived and breathed it, but always considered herself as less. He'd have to tell her the Burning Maiden saw her as one of them.

"The watcher has dangerous abilities. You know the risk he carries."

"I do," Michel-Leon said hoarsely. "I also know his heart and the strength of his will. He won't go down the wrong path. Not when he knows what the cost would be. He has dedicated his life to saving people, whether or not he admits it, not harming."

She peered over his shoulder, cocking her head again as more voices murmured. *"He has fed off souls before."* She caged him between her burning fingers again as he tried to shake his head, and they seared deep into his skin. Michel-Leon bit back the cry of pain. *"Unwittingly. He has also healed unwittingly."*

"I believe in him," Michel-Leon insisted. "He will not falter."

"And if he does? Would you have the strength of will to do what you must?" Michel-Leon's heart broke at the idea. He'd have to. Constantin would want him to, but it wasn't a situation he'd ever want to

contemplate. It would kill him inside. *"I can see you would. However, I do not believe it will be necessary. He is strong and his heart is as pure as yours."*

Relief flooded through Michel-Leon as the ancestors whispered. *"Merci,* my lady," he said reverently.

"There is strength in your unity. Hold to that. Love sees us through our trials. Love of our country and our people. Love of family and individuals. My chevaliers have forgotten that part, and it's the most important. We fight because of love. Don't forget."

"I won't." Michel-Leon watched in bewilderment as she stepped back. The burns disappeared, leaving her whole and almost childlike. "My lady, what about the swarm? How do we destroy it?"

"The answer is fire. It is always fire, our weapon and our bane," she whispered and faded into the shadows as Michel-Leon's heart lurched. *"Goodbye, last of my chevaliers. Go build a new world. A better world."*

Michel-Leon reached out toward her, but she was gone. He rose on unsteady feet and turned to go back, only to find his path blocked by row upon row of shadowy wraiths.

Chapter Thirty

CONSTANTIN LOOKED UP from his sketches, but Michel-Leon still had not stirred. He sat as he had for the last several hours, his hands relaxed at his side, his features composed. Occasionally, he'd mutter, but even those had ceased. Constantin had tried waking him when the deadline had passed, to no avail. All he could do was stand vigil and wait and worry.

Régine hadn't had any luck getting him to wake up either and considered sending a telegram to Janvier. Her *grandpère* might have a trick they could try. She said they might be overreacting, and the fact Michel-Leon didn't appear distressed gave them both some comfort. She thought both of them hovering would be counterproductive, but she was close at hand if needed.

Constantin longed to tell Michel-Leon the breakthroughs he'd made. He'd pinpointed the location of Vautrin. He'd been an idiot not to think of using his sense of Vautrin right away. Constantin would never forget the touch of that man's soul. It was as fouled as

Nightingale's if that were possible. He did not wish to be close to him again, but he had to be taken down like the maddened boar he was named for.

He studied Michel-Leon's sleeping features again. He appeared younger, more relaxed like this, with the mantle of the chevalier stripped away. Young and vulnerable. Constantin's heart ached with a tenderness he had not allowed himself to feel in a long time. Michel-Leon might not be able to kill one of the last of the bloodline, so Constantin would do it for him. He didn't know what it would take to win Michel-Leon's heart, but he'd find a way because Michel-Leon already had his.

Constantin returned to his sketches, the scratch of the pen on paper the sole sound in the room besides their even breathing. He had no idea what a ship to the stars would look like. Constantin had filled the paper with various ideas, but he wanted to know what Vautrin had come up with. He longed to take it apart and put it back together again.

He also longed to take his relationship with Michel-Leon apart and stick it back together again. Some days, he still wasn't sure how he'd ended up here. Constantin Severin, the vagabond who flitted from city to city, working on whatever job he could find, in love with a titled gentleman who bore too heavy of a burden. Constantin had a future now. He had learned things about himself he'd rather not know but was grateful he had discovered them before he caused harm. He had a mission, one that would probably keep him traveling as much as he had in the past.

He paused with a slight smile and looked at Michel-Leon again. He had a home, wherever that might be, because Michel-Leon was home. It filled him with a sense of awe.

Michel-Leon stiffened, and his features tightened. One of his arms moved, coming across his chest either in a salute or to ward off something Constantin couldn't tell.

"Michel-Leon?" he said softly and set aside his sketches.

The muscles of Michel-Leon's face twitched with emotion Constantin couldn't name. He rose and went over to him, drawn by curiosity and relief. He laid his hand on Michel-Leon's shoulder and gave him a shake. "Are you coming back?"

Michel-Leon made a sound of pain, and his head jerked as wide, angry red lines appeared under his chin. Constantin grabbed him and shook him harder, his heart pounding with fear. "Michel-Leon, wake up!"

The bedroom door opened and one of Lyon's men stuck his head in. "What's wrong?"

"Get the Widow Bardin," Constantin ordered. "See if she has any smelling salts." If that didn't work, he'd dump a bucket of water on him.

Michel-Leon made another small desperate moan, this one of denial, and then cried out again in pain, his body arching as the scent of burned hair and flesh filled the room. Constantin caught him before he could fall and eased him down to the floor. "*Non, non, non.* Wake up, damn you, wake up."

His heart raced as he closed his eyes, clasped Michel-Leon to him and reached out for the sense of him. He was far away, so far away, and Constantin couldn't reach him. Silently, he shouted, willing Michel-Leon to hear his call and follow him back home.

"What is going on?" Régine hurried in and knelt beside Constantin as the men hovered in the doorway. Her hand rested on the hilt of her dagger as she searched the room. "Is he being attacked?"

"I think so. I thought he was done with his meeting with the ancestors and was waking up." Constantin laid Michel-Leon down. His worry increased as he saw the livid burns against Michel-Leon's temple and the furrows going back through his hair. Michel-Leon had never said anything about being attacked while he was with the ancestors in their realm. He appeared more concerned with falling down and hitting his head.

"Let's see if this works." Régine waved the smelling salts under Michel-Leon's nose after Constantin laid him on the ground. Michel-Leon turned his head away, wrinkling his nose, and Constantin sensed a spark from him getting closer. "Come on, Michie, remember the words *Grandpère* used with you. Help me sing, Constantin. It might help if he hears our voices. *Frère Jacques, Frère Jacques…*"

Constantin picked up on the words with her, closing his eyes again to reach out for that spark. He called out mentally, stretching as pain bloomed across his forehead, and then the sense of Michel-Leon rushed toward him.

Michel-Leon heaved, drawing in a breath like a drowning man who had found land and air. Constantin searched his face and found awareness there. He sank back on his heels in relief. He hadn't lost him.

"There you are," Régine said in an approving voice as she tucked the smelling salts away. "You scared the hell out of me, Michie. I think we could all use a sip of the good stuff." She clambered to her feet and shooed out the curious onlookers. "I'll bring you up something and a salve to soothe those burns. And then you'd better tell me what happened."

"I thought I'd lost you." Constantin helped Michel-Leon sit up and move over to the chair as she left. "What went wrong?"

"I went in too deep. All the way back to the beginning." Michel-Leon clasped Constantin's hand. "I couldn't find my way back, but then I heard you both, and I sensed you searching. The ancestors mobbed me. They were drawn to my interaction with our founder and wanted answers of their own."

He broke away as Régine returned with a tray. He let her fuss over him while Constantin poured them all cognacs. His fingers trembled as he drank.

"I thought I'd lost you," Constantin repeated as Régine dabbed ointment on Michel-Leon's burns. "Was it worth it? Worth the risk to your hide? What would've happened to us if you'd died? We couldn't hope to face the swarm without you. They hurt you. I can see that plain, and let me tell you, you're not going back to meet with those crazy bastards again."

Régine gave him an approving look. "I agree with Constantin. I can't believe they did this to you. What were they thinking?"

"I'm not done yet," Constantin continued to rail, pouring out all his worry and fear for him as Michel-Leon listened in patient silence. Finally, Constantin rounded on him. "Say something!"

"*Je t'aime.*" A brilliant smile crossed Michel-Leon's face. He appeared tired and battered, but the smile lit him up, and Constantin blinked as Régine turned to hide her smile.

Staggered, Constantin sat down hard in the chair opposite him. "What did you say?"

Michel-Leon reached across and took his hand again. At a loss for words, Constantin tightened his fingers around that grip. "I said, 'I love you.' *Merci* for coming for me." He reached for Régine's hand. "*Merci* to you both."

"That is my clue to leave." Régine gathered her ointment and cognac. She leaned over and brushed her lips over Michel-Leon's cheek. "Try to stay out of trouble. You can tell me what happened after you both have this overdue conversation. We need to make a plan."

"I...I..." Constantin stared at him at a loss for words as Régine left.

Michel-Leon waved his hand. "You don't need to say anything or reciprocate. I thought you should know, considering what we face."

Constantin set down his cognac and leaned forward to rest his elbows on his knees as he studied Michel-Leon. He was lucid, and all of his attention was on Constantin as if he were the only thing that was important when he knew damn well he wasn't. No one had ever looked at him like that before.

"I've been in love once before and losing him hurt worse than being put out on the streets, even knowing he didn't return the feelings the way I wished. I didn't want to love you because I feared the same thing with you. Didn't stop me from falling in love with you anyway, Michel-Leon."

Another sweet smile crossed Michel-Leon's face. "My reasons for resisting had far more to do with my duty as a chevalier than it did with you. You're the one who reminded me there's more to life. And the lady at the heart of the void reminded me that the reason we fight is because of love. I'd be a fool to ignore either one of you."

"The lady? Is that who you went to meet?" Constantin needed to step back to examine all the emotions Michel-Leon stirred in him, all the dreams that wanted to awaken. This conversation seemed like the best way to do that.

"I didn't mean to go that far, but no one I spoke with had any concrete answers." A flicker of frustration crossed Michel-Leon's face. "I don't ever plan on going that deep again, though it was illuminating."

"How did you get your burns?" Constantin asked, gesturing to the livid marks on Michel-Leon's face. "They appeared as you sat there. I thought you were supposed to be safe."

"She touched me. Like the ancestors, she sometimes appears as she was at her death. She's the Burning Maiden." An expression of awe washed over Michel-Leon's face again. "She created the chevaliers and the link to our past."

"Who is she?" Constantin asked.

"Sainte Jeanne d'Arc." Michel-Leon levered himself to his feet as Constantin froze in awe. "She has faith in us."

Constantin shrugged, still struggling with the idea Michel-Leon had spoken with the Maid of Orleans. "Faith in you perhaps," he said, falling in beside Michel-Leon on the stairs.

"*Non*, all of us. She mentioned you, and Régine, in particular." Michel-Leon canted his head in Constantin's direction. "She also says your heart is pure, so remember that when you consider yourself a monster."

Constantin swallowed hard and shook his head with a slight smile. The idea humbled him. "Who am I to argue with Sainte Jeanne?"

"I wouldn't. Her sword is sharp." Michel-Leon gave him a wry smile and then opened the door to the frenetic activity in the workshop. The men and women they recruited worked at the tables, constructing and double-checking the masks to equip them and Napoleon's soldiers. Another group checked weapons and ammunition under the watchful eye of the emperor's representative. Constantin's constructs filled another table in neat rows.

Régine stood at the desk with the commandant and Lyon poring over the maps. "Glad you could join us," she said in a bland voice with a teasing glint in her eye. "We were going over our attack plans. By this evening, there should be enough masks for us all with spares. We have weapons and torches at the ready. I think we should wait until first light before we move out. This campaign is likely to take a while."

"I agree." Michel-Leon studied the map as Constantin took the measure of the others at the table and saw the same resolve in their eyes. "Taking out Vautrin will be the first half of the battle. After that, we descend into the catacombs."

"Did the ancestors have any suggestions for dealing with the swarm?" Régine asked as she set pieces on the map around Vautrin's stronghold. "I think we should surround them on every side we can. We have the men. He's relying on that barrier to keep him out."

"Fire," Michel-Leon said shortly. "Hence the request for the torches, though I'll be relying on magical means. I'll need to bone up on my spells and conserve my energy. We're going to have to burn them out. It's a good thing we'll have the masks. The smoke alone would choke us into unconsciousness."

Régine's gaze landed on him, her eyes swimming with sympathy and concern. "Oh, Michie."

He waved that aside and cut a glance at Constantin. "My fear of fire is not as paralyzing as it once was. The memories are still there, but I'm not worried it will make me a liability. You can thank our watcher here."

Régine caught Constantin's hand and squeezed it in gratitude. "Well then, we'll need two teams. One to deal with Vautrin, the other to go into the catacombs. As much as I'd like to flood the place with soldiers and torches, we'd end up tripping over each other and doing more harm. Commandant, would you pick out a few of your most stalwart men to go into the catacombs with the chevalier and me?"

The commandant appeared ill at ease and glanced at Michel-Leon for confirmation. "I can do that, madame," he said at Michel-Leon's nod. "But surely, you are not going with us."

"She goes," Constantin said before Régine could retort. "The first opportunity you have, you should take care of the swarm. There's no one I want at Michel-Leon's back more than you, Régine."

"Where will we be?" Lyon asked.

He thought of the blood-soaked presence he sensed. "We will deal with Vautrin."

Chapter Thirty-One

STEELY DAWN LIGHT crept over the buildings as they gathered in the street the next morning. Constantin eyed Michel-Leon as he swung up on his horse and checked his weapons. He hadn't slept well, tossing and turning and muttering all night, which kept Constantin awake as well. Michel-Leon had risen early enough to ensure he inoculated every one of their entourage, and still he fretted over whether they had enough masks and constructs.

He'd needed to sleep after the ordeal he'd gone through yesterday and the night before. But he'd driven himself to accomplish everything that needed to be done for this morning's raid. The burn marks stood out in angry lines on his face. Constantin suspected Michel-Leon would be marked for life from his encounter. Just like Constantin was. He fingered the scar Nightingale left him and banished the memory. He was alive and Nightingale wasn't.

Jeanne d'Arc. Constantin shook his head, still in disbelief. It made a certain logical sense, given what he knew of the chevaliers, but it still stunned him. He had so many questions, but they would have to wait for another place and time.

"Stop worrying about me," Michel-Leon ordered calmly with a glance toward Constantin. "I am rested enough. Once this is over, I'll rest more soundly than I have in months."

"Let's not waste any time, then." Constantin eyed the wagon and the crates of constructs packed inside filled with as many as he'd been able to churn out. "And let's pray the barrier is merely a glamour."

"You think your theory will work if it is?" Michel-Leon asked as they left side by side.

"Glamours shatter easily if you trigger the right pressure points. I've been careful not to alert Vautrin I've been able to penetrate his barrier. One of these things crossing the barrier when I'm in another location is not enough to break the spell. However, my hope is, if I send a couple hundred from several directions, all zeroed in on him while we're surveying the barrier, that'll be enough to take it down."

"It's going to leave you vulnerable," Michel-Leon warned.

Constantin grimaced. "For a brief time. I'm more worried about what we'll discover when it comes down. And that's not even mentioning the swarm nest." The warping of Vautrin's soul painted an ugly picture. Constantin braced himself for a brutal scene.

The streets deserted as the company marched down them. People watched and whispered from doorways and windows. Some stood wide open and empty from past depredations of the mists. The closer they got to the barrier, the more those empty holes stared back at them.

Constantin held up his hand and pulled his horse to a stop as they reached the street that branched off toward Vautrin. "It is around the corner." He swung down and clambered into the back of the wagon, where Lyon was already pulling the tops off the crates.

Régine approached with the commandant. "We'll take the north end. I'll meet you at the catacomb entrance. Don't you think about going in without me, Michie."

Michel-Leon smiled faintly. "I wouldn't dare."

She hugged him and then turned to Constantin and did the same. "If anyone can do this, it's you." She gestured to the commandant and his men and strode off to take up her position, a long, leggy figure with a bright tail of hair.

"She could replace us both." Michel-Leon tied his horse to a post and went to the corner of the building to peer around. "The best glamours are those that are so innocuous you don't even realize there is the slightest thing off. This one is good and is fueled by blood magic."

"That explains my reaction to it." Constantin laid out his army of constructs with the help of Lyon as the volunteers gathered torches. "Is everyone ready? If this goes down, things are going to happen fast. I'm sending half through Régine's side. They'll all move at the same time, and that will be the signal."

"I'm ready," Michel-Leon replied with a pistol in one hand and his sword in the other. "Follow my lead. We have to neutralize Vautrin before we go after the nest. If a creature doesn't appear human anymore, kill it. They will keep attacking until we do. Otherwise, let's try to contain them. Once it's under control, I'll meet with Régine and her men, and we'll go down."

Constantin noted Michel-Leon didn't give the order to kill Vautrin. Fair enough. He'd do it for him. He closed his eyes, concentrating on the mass of small mechanicals in front of him. A gasp rose from the watchers as they hummed to life and the air filled with the whir of hundreds of little metal wings and the roll of wheels. He sent half to Régine, conscious of the waiting expectation. "They're in place."

Michel-Leon gave him a grim smile. "Take it down."

Constantin nodded and relayed the sense of Vautrin to the constructs. He made sure they were in a wide formation and then sent them arrowing toward the barrier and the monster hiding behind it.

When he'd sent constructs singly to Vautrin to test them, he'd never sensed the barrier. He did this time as hundreds bombarded it at the same moment. He felt the ripple of reaction, the momentary desire to turn away as the barrier resisted the sense of his mind, and then the glamour shattered.

"It's down," Michel-Leon shouted as alarmed cries rose from down the street. "Go!"

A sense of satisfaction filled Constantin as Michel-Leon rushed off with his volunteers. Constantin began to pull the constructs back as they reached Vautrin and then broke off with a gasp.

"*Mon Dieu.*" His mind filled with the agony of souls being ripped from their mortal frames. Not one or two, but dozens. The pain of it amplified by the hundreds of signals bouncing back at him. Lyon grabbed him as the edges of his vision went black and he swayed. He clung to him, struggling to regain his sense of self.

"He's killing them!" Then the sense overwhelmed him completely, and he went under.

Chapter Thirty-Two

MICHEL-LEON TOOK in the nightmare scene revealed behind the glamour. Burned buildings provided a shell around the cleared out inner area. A construct soaring several stories attracted his attention. It appeared to be made of metal, and its top tip narrowed to a point. The sides were smooth with no windows. The squat bottom had double doors open to a dark maw. Figures scurried down the ramp from that opening, all of them with the altered features of the soulless and the familiar hiss of their breathing.

The shape reminded him of rockets used in battle, but this was so much larger than those, and he didn't see any sign of gunpowder. Vautrin was insane enough to consider blasting the nest into oblivion, never mind what it would do to Paris in the meantime.

"My Lord Chevalier!" Michel-Leon glanced over at the urgent call. One of the volunteers he'd left with Constantin raced up. "What happened?"

"Monsieur Severin collapsed!" The man looked around at the

chaos with wide, frightened eyes. "He's still breathing. The foreman is with him."

Michel-Leon glanced back toward where Constantin should be, torn between concern and duty. *"The Boar escalates his attack. The watcher cannot bear the pain of those dying."*

Michel-Leon could not go to him. He had to trust in Lyon to keep him safe. "Return to Severin and Lyon. Guard them on your life." He shoved the man away to safety and turned to the soulless as they attacked.

They were hard pressed, but the soulless appeared torn between the assault and some other duty that had to do with the strange building. Michel-Leon pushed the advantage, driving deeper into Vautrin's haven. When the battle turned in their favor, Michel-Leon stepped to the side, scanning the fray as he searched for Vautrin. That's who he needed to stop. *"Where's the Boar?"* He cast the question to the ancestors as he crept forward on silent feet, skirting around one of the broken buildings, a few of the volunteers going with him.

"He is destroying so many."

The cry of rage from the ancestors was strong enough to send Michel-Leon reeling back. He cursed under his breath and blocked them away. If they weren't able to help, he wasn't going to leave himself vulnerable to them. He scanned the ruins again. Something was keeping Vautrin away from the death of his soulless creations. He must consider it more important.

Screams alerted Michel-Leon, different from the screams of battle. These were higher, shriller and tinged with fear.

Michel-Leon headed in that direction. The shrieks came from the building near the strange edifice. The burned-out shell had been reinforced, and more of those twisted humans stood guard outside. Michel-Leon considered the odds and gestured to his companions. He couldn't waste any time.

The fight was short and brutal and as soon as the creatures were dead, Michel-Leon forced open the door. They had hollowed the building and erected a guarded penned enclosure on one side and an opening to the edifice dominating on the other side. Vautrin stood at a table, his face drawn into a demonic mask as he concentrated. Red light pulsed between his fingers, dragged upward from the bodies surrounding him. When it became a fiery corona, he hurled it toward the edifice, which appeared to absorb the offering.

"Bring me more," he shouted. "We're almost there. And start loading the eggs. Go! Go! I will show him how it's done."

Michel-Leon lifted his pistol, but he sensed the ancestors' presence right before his finger froze on the trigger. "Vautrin. It's over. Help me destroy the nest."

Vautrin snarled at him as more of his creatures entered from the enclosure, dragging a group of people with them. They were weeping, their mouths open, pits of horror, their clothes tattered, their eyes hopeless shells. They saw the bodies on the floor and cried out in renewed fear, desperate to get away. A scraping noise caught his attention, and Michel-Leon spied Raul hiding under one of the long worktables, trying to make himself as small as possible. Vautrin had twisted his grandson's face into a similar mask, and Michel-Leon's heart ached for him.

"Bring them here," Vautrin ordered his creatures. "Protect me from the intruders." He turned away as if Michel-Leon didn't even exist, muttering again under his breath.

The screaming started again as light tugged under the skin of Vautrin's new victims. Michel-Leon dropped his sword and pistol and dove at Vautrin, ramming into him through his worktable. He may not be able to kill Vautrin, but he could sure as hell knock him out.

"Leave me be!" Vautrin howled and clawed at Michel-Leon with stiffened fingers. "I'm so close."

"You are not killing more in the process," Michel-Leon snarled back. He landed a punch on Vautrin's jaw that hit solidly, but Vautrin didn't notice in his maddened state. "You're not just killing their bodies, damn you, you're destroying their souls."

Vautrin threw Michel-Leon off and rolled to his feet in a low crouch. "What are a few compared to the thousands I'll save?"

"You think they'll thank you?" Michel-Leon circled him, his hands outstretched. "When they're burying their loved ones, do you believe they'll praise you for it? Laud you instead of the chevaliers? *Non*, they'll only see what they've lost. Your name will become a curse."

"*Non*," Vautrin hissed. He grabbed for the tools at his worktable and threw a hammer at Michel-Leon. He ducked out of the way, and Vautrin put the table between them. "I will be their savior. Get the eggs! Load them on the ship."

The soulless men abandoned dragging their quarry forward. The men and women bolted for escape, but bound as they were together, their efforts were hampered. Some of Michel-Leon's companions worked to untie them, and the others hurried to the enclosure. Michel-Leon observed the soulless men disappear into a darkened doorway that led down. That had to be the entrance to the catacombs. The nest couldn't be far.

Michel-Leon circled around as Vautrin began chanting again, and the screams of his victims renewed. He picked up the hammer, hefting it in his hand. He'd knock him out and decide what to do with him later.

"Let me," Constantin said softly as he appeared by Michel-Leon's side. "He needs to understand what he is doing."

He appeared pale and drawn, his mouth pinched at the corners, and his eyes were impossibly old. Michel-Leon had an inkling of what he intended. "Be careful." He stepped away, trusting Constantin to tackle this monster in a way Michel-Leon was denied, and kept his eyes on Vautrin. He didn't trust him to react in any rational way.

"I will," Constantin replied.

Chapter Thirty-Three

CONSTANTIN FIXED HIS gaze on Vautrin as he gathered more energy from his stumbling victims. "Stop this," he thundered in a voice impossible to ignore.

Vautrin threw Constantin a sneer and chanted faster. Several of the people collapsed as the red lights under their skin swirled faster. Constantin retched as what they felt shrouded him, and he lurched toward Vautrin. He grabbed the Boar, caging his head in his hands. "You will understand," he rasped.

With grim resolve, Constantin forced a link between them. He let Vautrin sense what he sensed, the agony of his victims, the terror and fury of the trapped souls, and the terrible emptiness of the soulless men. Vautrin's eyes widened in a silent scream, and he fell to his knees.

"What have I done?" He clutched at his hair, staring with wide, horrified eyes at his victims. For a moment, sanity reflected in his eyes. Then he saw a youth cowering in hiding and screamed. "*Non…non*! I will destroy them."

He lurched to his feet and ran, stumbling toward the entrance to the tunnels beneath.

Michel-Leon walked over to Constantin and laid his hand on his shoulder. Constantin felt bolstered by the quiet support. "You didn't kill him."

Constantin shook his head. "He had to know what he'd done." Gesturing helplessly to the wounded people sinking to the ground, he continued, "Vautrin had to understand the consequences and live with it."

They hurt so badly, worse than Gabrielle's pain, and again amplified by the fact there were so many. Constantin felt his knees give out, and he hit the ground hard as he fought to keep all those screaming souls from overwhelming him. With it came the hunger to feed again. The dark side of him that had fed off Nightingale whispered seductively. All those souls already trapped, stolen from their bodies. With that power, he could do so much. He could destroy the nest with his mind alone.

"Feed. Feed. Feed."

Constantin shook his head violently, fighting off that voice as well.

Michel-Leon knelt in front of him, his handsome face concerned as he talked earnestly to him with words Constantin didn't understand past the trauma enveloping him. Michel-Leon believed in him even when Constantin hadn't believed in himself. He had to show them both the faith wasn't misplaced. Constantin had to do it for Gabrielle and all the children victimized by magicmen. He would not become one of them.

He turned away from Michel-Leon and reached his hand out toward the wounded souls. Vautrin hadn't had a chance to transfer the stolen bits of them to the ship yet. He gathered them to him as the hunger snapped with vicious teeth. He poured the energy back into the people, healing the ragged edges of their spiritual wounds as he went, and the hunger disappeared under the gentle warmth of healing.

Constantin sagged back on his heels as the warmth vanished. He felt scooped out and cleansed but exhausted from his efforts. Michel-Leon eased him down until he was sitting on the floor. "What did you do?" he asked as the people next to them cried with tears of joy and disbelief as they struggled to their feet.

"I healed them." Constantin turned his troubled gaze on the ship. It was a thing of beauty, meticulously made and dark with stolen power.

"You are an amazing man." Michel-Leon clambered to his feet and glanced toward the dark hole of the ship. "What about Raul? Vautrin's grandson. He's hiding around here."

Constantin couldn't be sure if he'd been among the number of souls he'd healed. "I'll check on him," he promised as Régine called their names from outside.

"I'll get her and the soldiers," Lyon said with a grim glare around the ramshackle building Vautrin used for the headquarters. "Then we'll end this."

"I need to deal with Vautrin and destroy the nest. Lyon should stay with you. I don't think you'd be able to handle yourself in a fight," Michel-Leon said as he helped Constantin to his feet and waited until he'd steadied his legs.

Constantin tore his grim gaze away from the ship long enough to give Michel-Leon a reassuring smile. He caught Michel-Leon's arm and gave it a squeeze, trying to convey the depth of his emotions. "Be careful. Come back to me." He thrust his chin out toward the ship. "I have to deal with that. Make sure the souls get released. The longer they are trapped there, the more they are warped."

Michel-Leon squeezed his arm back. "You be careful too."

Régine came in on Lyon's heels and eyed them both. "There are no more soulless men swarming around outside." Her fingers flexed on her bloodied sword. "Where's Vautrin and the nest? Are we ready to end this?"

"I'm staying here," Constantin replied to her. "There's still work to be done. You two better come back soon."

Régine touched his cheek, her eyes brilliant. "I'll see you soon, brother."

Michel-Leon gave him a tight smile and nodded at Lyon. "I'm leaving some soldiers and volunteers with you. Do what you can to get answers out of our victims and guard him."

Constantin watched them go, carrying fresh-lit torches. He longed to go with him, to be by Michel-Leon's side when he faced the creature that had been one of the root causes of the downfall of the chevaliers. But they needed him here more.

He turned toward the ship and glanced down at a small cry under the table. A boy, no older than Constantin was when he'd faced the streets, tried to scurry away, whimpering in fear. Vautrin had twisted the boy's face into the strange shape of the soulless, but he didn't appear inhuman. Tears leaked from his oddly shaped eyes as Constantin crouched down. This must be Raul.

"*S'il vous plaît,* don't hurt me." His words came out garbled from the misshapen mouth, but they were clearly words.

"He's the old man's grandson," a prisoner cried out. "Seize him. Make him pay."

Constantin put himself between them and their prey. "Go home, all of you. Free the other prisoners, and go home. The chevalier and soldiers will deal with him."

It took some more convincing, but the remaining soldiers got involved and urged them on. Constantin looked down at the boy, who eyed him in terror. He had found a small opening between stacked materials and wedged himself in there. Constantin reached out with his senses. The child's soul was intact, and he suspected the changes to his face could be reversed, given time.

"I won't hurt you. I won't turn you over to them," Constantin soothed. "The chevalier will have questions for you, but don't be afraid of him. He's good. He's been worried about you."

Tears ran runnels down the boy's dirty cheeks. "*Grandpère* is sick."

"I know," Constantin replied heavily. "I need to undo some of his damage. Can I trust you not to run, or do I need to make sure my friends guard you?"

"I won't run," the boy whispered.

"What's your name? I'm Constantin." As much as Constantin could tell, the boy had been altered through the sacrifice of Vautrin's own personal energy, one not tainted by blood magic. He must've been one of the first. Maybe even as an attempt to protect him from the mists, but he wouldn't be able to test for sure until after he'd dealt with the ship. The call was too strong.

"Raul."

Constantin nodded and turned back to the ship with half-closed eyes. Through his senses, he could see the souls struggling to escape, pushing against a barrier that made it appear as if the metal rippled. The screaming impression of faces bulging out only to be sucked back in, eddied throughout the structure. Constantin reached out his hands to feel for any weaknesses in the barrier. He drilled a mental hole into a softer spot and called for the newest prisoners, the ones they'd been too late to save. They slipped out and vanished as they were put to rest.

He widened the hole and stretched out more. The deeper he went in, the harder they fought back, converging on him instead of on the escape route — the souls who wanted to break free and wreak vengeance on everyone still living, the ones who tried to twist him in return, believing he was Vautrin.

Sweat popped out on Constantin's brow as he struggled to funnel them on. Several broke free and surrounded him, dark wraiths with distorted faces. *"Use us,"* they hissed, their words sinking into Constantin's brain like parasites. *"Use us. Use our power. Make him pay. Make him understand."*

Constantin rocked his head violently, trying to stave off the insidious whispers that hit at his darkest desires. Vautrin did deserve to pay. Realizing what he'd done and escaping into insanity once again was not enough to atone for his crimes. The hunger awoke, yearning to take what they so freely offered, to use the energy of their souls to hurt Vautrin.

This was different. This wasn't like Nightingale. These souls were sacrificing themselves for a greater cause. With their energy, he'd never have to hide in the shadows. People would hide from him.

The thought jerked him out of the temptation of the dark souls. Sickened by his reaction, Constantin came back to his body to find Lyon right beside him, his hand on Constantin's arm. That was not the life he wanted at all. He couldn't take care of Gabrielle if he was that kind of a man.

"I will be fine." He drew himself up and faced his tormentors, who still circled around him. "Go, leave this plane."

They hissed again and rushed at him. Constantin threw up his hands in an instinctive shield. More and more dark souls broke through the crack and surrounded him. The whispers ate into his brain. They swiped at him with mental claws, opening real gashes that bled. The world around him fell away again as he fought back.

Instinctively, he struck back, but it made the hunger worse, the temptation to take what they offered. Sensing his weakness, they pressed closer, sinking into him, whispering promises that called to the darkest parts of his soul. Constantin curled into a ball, covering his head with his arms, and they attacked again. Most of the barrage he deflected with a shield, but every one that got through weakened him further.

Constantin struggled to hold on to his sanity and sense of self. He brought to mind the best memories of Michel-Leon, Régine, and Gabrielle. The warmth in Michel-Leon's eyes when he told Constantin he loved him. Why hadn't Constantin said the same in return? He had to survive. He had to tell Michel-Leon. The wonder and gratitude in Gabrielle's expression after he had healed her soul of the damage the magicman had wrecked. The affection in Régine's gaze when she had called him her brother.

Michel-Leon's voice came back to him. *"We will find a way. You won't be doomed. You can fight this. You can find a way. The fey kissed are meant to be soul healers. So do that. Heal, don't destroy."*

Constantin lifted his head and fixed his gaze on his closest tormentors. They drew back and hissed, sensing his resolve. He pulled himself to his feet, swaying as he recalled what he did with Gabrielle. Throwing out his hands, he caught the closest and most twisted in a blanket of light enveloping the corrupted souls with his own energy. The souls called to him, filling him with the overwhelming need to heal and pushing back the hunger. The call became everything, blotting out the pain of his wounds. He filled them with the light, and the twisted, stunted remnants grew strong and whole again.

They passed on, leaving a sense of gratitude, and Constantin moved on to the next victims. He was aware on one level of a trembling exhaustion, but the need to heal pushed him further as the link between his mind and his body became tenuous.

Then the last soul was gone, and Constantin snapped back to his body and fell to the ground, gasping for air. The foreman crouched beside him, slapping at his cheeks. "Constantin! Constantin! Snap out of it." Lyon leaned over him, his expression concerned as Constantin focused his gaze on him. "I thought we lost you."

Constantin drew in a shuddering breath and filled air-starved lungs. Chaotic activity surrounded them. "What happened?"

"I'm not sure. You went into a trance." Lyon gave him a troubled look. "Something we couldn't see was hurting you, but we couldn't get to you. There was a barrier around you."

"Some of us saw things." One of the crew handed Constantin a flask, and he gulped the fiery brew thankfully. Another dabbed at his wounds with a damp handkerchief. The gashes stung, but he didn't think the wounds were too bad. "Spooks. Then whatever was being built over there crumbled."

Constantin nodded and handed back the flask before struggling to his feet with their help. "There were many spirits haunting here, courtesy of Vautrin. They have passed on." Constantin looked around the ruined work yard. The wondrous ship had sustained damage, but perhaps he could fix it. It would be a marvel to fly to the stars.

"Did we rescue anyone?" Constantin asked as he pawed through the pile of sketches and intriguing diagrams. Some showed the ship, others unique inventions. He'd take them all and study them when things calmed.

"*Oui*, monsieur," Lyon reported. "There were near a hundred people locked up in pens in the ruins. More that escaped when their captors deserted them."

"Good." Constantin crouched and discovered Raul still hidden among the materials, curled into a ball as small as he could make himself. Michel-Leon would want to talk with him. "Come on out. It's safe. There are no more monsters here to scare you."

Raul eyed him for a long moment with wary eyes. "The voices say I can trust you," he finally whispered. "Am I crazy like *grandpère*?"

"*Non*." Constantin shook his head and held out his hand. "You are a chevalier, like my friend. The voices are your gift if you use them correctly. Michel-Leon will help you."

Raul grimaced. "*Grandpère* says the chevaliers are all bad. But I met one once. He seemed nice." A tic in his cheek spasmed. "*Grandpère* is bad."

"But not you." Constantin gave him a reassuring smile. "Come, I'll take you to the chevalier."

After another long moment, Raul crawled out. He was filthy and undernourished, but Michel-Leon would be elated to see him alive. Constantin laid a hand on Raul's shoulder and then looked around for his lover. "Where is Michel-Leon? Have he and Régine returned?"

Chapter Thirty-Four

MICHEL-LEON TOOK the lead and headed down the winding staircase that plunged into the heart of Paris. The heart of hell. It opened into the first of the narrow, dark tunnels of the old quarry system. There was a hushed quality despite the crackle of the torches and the stamp of the soldiers' feet behind him as they followed. From somewhere deep within the tunnels came muffled screams of pain and fear.

That's all the trail he needed. They reached a junction where the corridors branched in several directions. Michel-Leon consulted his map and compass. He sensed a faint whisper of a song but wasn't sure if it was memory or reality.

"*Mon Dieu*, what is that?" a soldier whispered and Michel-Leon jerked his head up, searching the shadows. At first he didn't see anything. Then the shadows undulated near the top of one corridor.

Michel-Leon crept closer, motioning for more light as he pulled out his sword. For a moment he saw it, the impression of a limb or snake, something long and eel-like stretched along the ceiling. Then it blended in again perfectly with the surrounding rock. He listened down the corridor. The screams sounded louder in that direction. He checked the other corridors as the soldiers fidgeted with nerves.

"We'll take the first one," Michel-Leon announced and led the way without a backward glance. There was a soft moan of fear behind him, but the soldiers fell in line. Michel-Leon kept an eye on the surrounding walls and ceiling. On occasion, he'd see a flicker of movement overhead that told him whatever they'd seen was still with them, but there was no sign of the nest.

Partway down the tunnel, the mists began, lying low and wispy on the ground. The sight confirmed they were going in the right direction but made it harder to see. Again he heard the song, louder now and still so faint. Old and rich, the melody lacked the power it once had, though it still tugged at his heartstrings.

"Put on your filtering masks, in case. We'll need them anyway, with the amount of smoke we will produce in these tunnels." Michel-Leon fitted his over his face, and then as they went deeper, the mist thickened until they were feeling their way down the corridors. The tunnels spilled into the catacombs, and grinning skulls layered in rows stared out at him through empty sockets. "Is that thing still over us?" a soldier asked in a low voice.

"I would hazard *oui*." Régine glanced up and then at Michel-Leon for confirmation. He nodded, resisting the urge to hunch as the ceiling lowered. "Let's not agitate it at this point."

The screams died to whimpers of animalistic agony. Tension thrummed in the air as a steady, slow thumping started up, like the heartbeat of a dying god.

"Stay back," Michel-Leon ordered. "The mists haven't affected us, but I'm not sure what we will find. I'll move forward ten feet. The next crypt should be near. When I give the order, move to me and I'll inch forward again."

"I'll take the rear and make sure that creature above us doesn't try anything once we pass a certain point," Régine said, and Michel-Leon smiled, though he knew she couldn't see it. He knew how much she wanted to be first, but she was right. That was a weak point, and he trusted her to stay steady.

All his instincts screamed the danger wasn't past, even though the ancestors were silent. They observed, nevertheless, and their presence screamed caution. He moved forward the ten paces. The tunnel abruptly ended, and Michel-Leon froze in the entranceway. He could make out the cries of pain. Most of them seemed to be concentrated in this area, and shapes shifted in the swirling mists, but they were too nebulous to define. He waved his torch over the area, feeling the damp on his skin that made his flesh crawl as black threads reached out to surround him.

No one coming down had ever stood a chance. Not if they hadn't been inoculated or, in the case of Vautrin's creatures, forcibly mutated. The nest reacted to the presence of food and used the mists to lure them closer. It was still a hypothesis, but it stood to reason that if the swarm fed off the population after hatching, it would crave the same sustenance while incubating.

Michel-Leon called the others forward. In the gloom and mists, with the masks distorting their faces, they were a chilling sight. He called for more torches and set them up in close intervals, hoping it would make the damp recede some. The light reflected off the mists and illuminated the ceiling, where the shadows shifted and wriggled. The beating drum and song were directly over them.

"Help me," an agonized reedy voice croaked from somewhere in the crypt.

"What is that?" a soldier asked sharply, and Michel-Leon threw up an arm to keep him from moving closer.

"The Boar is dying. Dying badly in pain and despair at what he's done.

We understand now."

Michel-Leon threw up a mental wall before the ancestors could share the details with him. He'd take the time to understand later. He did not need to be incapacitated now. "It's Vautrin. He's dying. Stay put. The mists are clearing up some, and I don't want any of us to make a misstep."

"The pain in his voice," Régine said with a wealth of sympathy. "Is there anything we can do to help him?"

Michel-Leon swung his torch back and forth as he inched forward. He made out the bodies of Vautrin's creatures first, some struggling on the rocks in which they lay, others inert and appearing to sink into the stone. It took several moments before his brain registered what his eyes were seeing. It wasn't a pile of rocks at all. It was the start of the nest.

"Be careful, but come forward. Don't touch anything that looks like a rock. It's an egg." Michel-Leon stepped forward again and the closest victim rolled his eyes around, his gaze filled with terror and pain. The harder he struggled, the quicker he sank into the eggs until his body disappeared and his face remained. He cried out one last time before he vanished completely.

Someone behind Michel-Leon retched.

"We need to put them out of their misery," someone else whispered. "Here, help me pull him free," the soldier ordered, his voice gaining strength.

"Don't touch them!"

The force of the command pushed through Michel-Leon's shield and blossomed with a headache that radiated pain out from his temples. "Don't!" Michel-Leon snarled harshly. "Give me a moment. Let me clear some of this mist out and see if I can get us better light. The torches aren't dissipating the mists."

He'd prepared the spells, as much as he hated using them,

because they often attracted other things. Who knew what else might lurk down here in the catacombs? But it was a risk he needed to take at this point before they blundered into a trap.

He muttered under his breath, steeling himself for the strain it would put on him to hold the spell in place. Light splashed across the roof of the cave, spilling out in undulating, colorful waves and with it came a dry heat that pressed down on them. The ceiling appeared to flinch, and the thudding picked up in speed. "Stay steady," the commandant ordered as the soldiers cast anxious glances upward.

The mists retreated, curling around their feet in a thick soup. The horror before them was revealed, and Régine gasped. Michel-Leon forced himself to examine it dispassionately. The eggs looked like natural rock striated in yellows, creams, and grays to blend in with the limestone and grinning skulls. They were vaguely ovoid, and the mists seeped out from them, growing thicker on the ground but unable to engulf the group.

He may not have much of a use for magic usually, but he praised it now. The nest had many defensive mechanisms. They were designed to survive. Vautrin moaned again, and pity twisted Michel-Leon's heart.

"Will I be safe if I use my sword?"

The ancestors were quick to reply. *"We think so. Don't touch him with your bare skin."*

"I believe they came down here to do their master's bidding to pick up the eggs and carry them to the ship. They were immune to the mists, but whatever immunity they had wasn't enough when they handled the eggs," Michel-Leon said to the waiting soldiers, and they stirred uneasily.

"The mists lure their victims to the nest and once they contact them, they are absorbed and consumed." Régine shuddered, her eyes dark with horror. "We have to do something."

He pulled out his sword. "If anything happens to me, burn the nest and get out."

"Wouldn't it be better to use our pistols?" Régine asked with a restraining hand on his arm.

"*Non*. Something may splash and we don't know the effect it will have if it touches skin." And Michel-Leon couldn't imagine the din that it would create in these close tunnels. Once one started shooting, others would follow. That could also attract trouble.

"We should try to help them now!" A soldier pushed past Michel-Leon and dodged his grab. He approached the eggs cautiously and halted beside one of the mutated men. Its leg stuck out, still wiggling and jerking. The soldier grabbed ahold of it in both hands, braced himself and pulled.

Michel-Leon held his breath as it began to slide free with a squelch.

"It's working!" the soldier cried. "Help me."

A darkness rose, an oppressive feeling more of the mind than reality. On the edges of his consciousness, Michel-Leon thought he sensed a roaring of wings and a vast chittering cry as the song increased in magnitude. But before he could examine the sensation, the solider screamed. He dropped the leg, holding his hands to his ears, his eyes mad as he screamed again.

"Michie." Régine's hand tightened on his arm, and she yanked him back into the dubious safety of the corridor as the ceiling undulated again. Black and silver limbs uncoiled down and grabbed ahold of the screaming man. Before Michel-Leon or anyone else could react, they flung the soldier onto the nest. A convulsion went through the eggs, and the ones in contact with the man appeared to soften as he sank in. The screams began again, this time filled with agony, and the rest of the soldiers fired up at the creature over them. The caverns echoed with the roar of gunfire. More limbs came down, and Régine shouted for a retreat as she dragged Michel-Leon deeper into the corridor.

"The mother guards and feeds her young," Michel-Leon said softly, struggling to keep himself in the present as the ancestors converged on him.

"She is old and tired, weak from starvation. All the food went to the eggs."

The ancestors babbled at each other as they experienced Vautrin's dying agony and compared it to experiences in the past. It was a sound theory that made sense, but Michel-Leon didn't have time for theories and suppositions. He struggled against the voices as Régine shouted his name, and he dimly felt the sting of her slap. Not now. He could not let them overpower him. With a wrench, Michel-Leon staved off the voices.

"Be silent!" he ordered savagely, and to his surprise, they obeyed.

Régine's tight expression eased as Michel-Leon focused on her. "If you ever have the leisure, consider lecturing your ancestors about their horrible sense of timing."

Michel-Leon grimaced and raised his hands into claws. The necessity pained him, but they could not deal with the nest without first dealing with the mother. He muttered words under his breath and felt the drain on his energy, and electricity sparked between his fingers. Then lightning lashed out, stabbing deep into the wounded creature clinging to the ceiling. It shuddered once, hard enough to shake the ground, then fell.

He glanced around at the remaining soldiers. The corridors were eerily silent; the heartbeat gone. The commandant gave him a grim look, blood running down his face from a slash. "The monster is dead. It's over."

"*Non*, it's half over," Michel-Leon corrected. He approached the nest, his fingers tightening on the hilt of his sword. Régine fell into step beside him. The carcass of the creature half buried the nest and the eggs quivered as they accepted the new offering.

"She's beautiful," Régine said softly. The camouflage ended with its death, revealing the creature in its entirety. Natural black armor encased most of it, though the undersides gleamed like moonlight underneath. A bulbous head had sunken in on itself and sprouted near a dozen limbs that tapered down to points. Lacy wings covered it like a shroud.

Michel-Leon agreed and wished he had an opportunity to study her more, but the fresh food was having an alarming effect on the nest. The nest shivered with a low hum as it pulled pieces off the huge carcass that disappeared into the eggs.

One of the soldiers was still alive, his nails dragging along the ground as he struggled to pull himself free from the devouring nest. The light was fading from his eyes and Michel-Leon pulled out his sword. It was too late for him. They only thing he could do was provide mercy.

"Wait, allow me." Régine laid her hand on Michel-Leon's wrist. Her expression filled with grim resolve as she witnessed the soldier being consumed. "We cannot risk you. If it doesn't work, burn it down before it gets me."

"With the mother dead, it should be safe." Knowing she wouldn't back down, Michel-Leon passed over his sword. "I warded the blade, for what it may be worth."

Régine nodded. The blade flashed in the undulating light, and the soldier's screams were silenced. This time, the eggs closest to them rocked. Michel-Leon yanked Régine back in case another attack was imminent.

"They appeared withered," Michel-Leon said, crouching down for a better look. "If you observe closely, the ones that have the bodies attached are sleeker. I suspect Vautrin might have inadvertently been starving them when he diverted the nest's victims for his own purposes. I suppose my inoculations added to the process." Michel-Leon said as he examined each body for signs of life, but most were already gone. "Which would explain why the mists were so erratic. Their life cycle had been interrupted."

"They are starting to crack," Régine said urgently. She pointed to minute striations appearing across the shells as Michel-Leon paused in front of Vautrin.

The tortured eyes opened. He was still alive, barely. "Raul?" Vautrin asked with a gasp.

"He's with my men. We'll keep him safe," Michel-Leon promised.

"*Non!*" Vautrin cried out weakly as Michel-Leon raised his sword. "Let it be through the fire."

Michel-Leon nodded and raised his hands again. "Step back into the corridor, all of you. I'm not sure what will happen, but there are a lot of eggs. This will take some doing."

He waited until the soldiers stepped back, though Régine stubbornly remained by his side. "Someone needs to guard your back," she said in an undertone. "You're going to be vulnerable while you're working the magic."

"I have learned not to argue with you."

Régine gave him a tight smile. Michel-Leon locked eyes with Vautrin as he muttered the words to alter the spell. The light on the ceiling pulsed, then lanced down, striking through Vautrin and into the nest.

Vautrin's scream cut off mercifully quick as fire burst through the eggs, incinerating the closest and racing back through the rest of the nest. A roar of wings filled Michel-Leon's mind, followed by a vast chittering. The song this time was young and filled with an unrelenting hunger. The sound overwhelmed him, knocking him down to his knees. In the distance, humans shouted with terror, and he struggled to get to his feet again, to see, but wings and tentacles and teeth blotted out the world.

Michel-Leon drew his pistol and sword, striking out against the horde, but it was impossible to get a bead on any of the monsters attacking him.

"It's in your mind! It's not real!"

The voices of his ancestors shouted through the din, barely heard. *"Don't lose the fire. Don't falter."*

Michel-Leon struggled to hold his concentration. A terrible fear pressed down on him, and he sank to his knees under the weight of it. In the background, the soldiers screamed. Régine's breath came in sobbing pants. The ancestors reacted to the psychic attack with a roar of their own that partially shielded him and gave him a moment to think.

He narrowed his eyes and forced himself back to his feet. The catacombs were a nightmare of grinning skulls and smoke as the eggs turned to ash. He pushed forward down the corridor, dragging the light and fire with him through a pure effort of will as he continued to burn them out. Smoke filled the long dark hallways and the screams from his past echoed with the renewed screams of his family in his head.

Fear flashed through him and then eased back as the spiritual wounds Constantin healed didn't have the power they once did. Michel-Leon blocked away his family and concentrated on the fire. He had to get through this. He had to see it to the end. When he emerged, he was going to kiss Constantin senseless.

Chapter Thirty-Five

SMOKE BILLOWED FROM the catacombs and rose in a black, noxious column to the sky. Constantin tried to contain his fear while he examined the soldiers after they'd stumbled outside. The smoke had to be a sign the plan was working.

"Where's Michel-Leon? Is he behind you?" Constantin asked as he offered water to the commandant.

The commandant shook his head, gulping down the water until he coughed. He wiped a hand over his face, smearing blood and soot. "Don't know. Those things hatched and attacked. We lost him in there."

Constantin reached for the man's mask, hanging from his fingertips. His chest tightened with worry. That didn't make any sense. If the swarm had hatched, they would be in the middle of hell and trying to find what shelter they could. Not one monster had come out with the smoke. He'd have to see for himself. Michel-Leon and Régine had not emerged with the others.

"Constantin!"

Constantin looked up at the urgency in Régine's voice. She surfaced from the catacombs, as covered in soot and fluids as the rest. There were some scratches on her, but it appeared as if she had done more damage than taken. She tore off her mask. "Michel-Leon went deeper in, and I've lost him. I need your help. You can track him."

Constantin leaped to his feet and grabbed one of his constructs. "Is the plan working?"

"I want to say *oui*, but I don't know to what extent." She dragged her hair back from her face and slipped the mask back on. "Vautrin's dead, as are his assistants. The nest can protect itself, which I'm sure Michel-Leon will find interesting later, but I find quite terrifying. There's so much to tell you, but there is no time. He's in the heart of the fire."

"Hold it." Constantin grabbed her arm before she could dive back in. He concentrated on Michel-Leon and sent a construct skittering in. "It will make sure we find him and don't get lost returning."

"The smoke is still thick," Régine said, leading the way with a lantern as he donned the mask he took. "So, I'm assuming he's still burning. There's so many of them." In terse sentences, she relayed the rest as they found the trail.

"He'll be fine," Constantin assured her and prayed he was right. "If anyone is used to mental noise barraging him, it's our chevalier."

They found the first room with the seared ashes, bones, and shell fragments. Several soldiers were down, hacked to death with their own weapons. "We went mad. All of us," Régine whispered with a shudder. "They made it appear as if the swarm were attacking."

"A potent defense mechanism." Constantin paused to get his bearings from the construct leading them deeper inside. "The trail of ash leads in the same direction as the construct. Michel-Leon went that way."

Régine nodded and plunged ahead. The catacombs were a maze

of twisting tunnels, often with uneven pathways. In some places, the ceiling was low enough that they had to crouch. Others held pools of water that he supposed the nest found convenient. It was eerily silent, so when they emerged into another crypt, a weak chittering immediately attracted his attention. He crouched low, where the smoke was thinner to get a better look around the chamber.

Shadows skittered in the corner, accompanied by a faint flutter of wings in his mind and the soft threads of a haunting song. Régine hissed and drew her pistol. "Get out of my mind," she snapped.

"Hold the shot." Constantin drew his own weapon and inched closer. "A few may have hatched. It's not surprising Michel-Leon would miss some, given the number we are dealing with. We'll have to be careful and make sure we leave none behind us. Bring the light closer."

Régine approached, and the light fell across a small cluster of eggs that were singed, but otherwise intact. The top had broken off one and a form had slithered out to rest in a puddled heap. Long, transparent, webbed wings gleamed wetly in the smoky light, swaying back and forth to dry. Constantin had the impression of a squat, fat body with writhing appendages.

"Michel-Leon would give his right arm to study one of these," Constantin said as he slipped off his pack. "We could learn so much, maybe even discover a way to prevent them from nesting."

"Constantin, I don't think this is one of your more intelligent ideas," Régine warned as Constantin took off his coat to use as a makeshift net.

"It can't fly yet," Constantin observed. "Its wings are still wet."

Those wings froze with an awful stillness, and Constantin was assailed with a powerful sense of hunger before the creature leaped at him, teeth gleaming from an open maw, tentacles reaching out. A gun blasted and it fell to the floor with a screech. With its death, the hunger vanished.

"Merci." Constantin's heart pounded as he approached and nudged the corpse with his toe. "Fast buggers." He eyed the remaining two unhatched, unburned eggs. "You said the eggs had defense mechanisms. What do we need to do to get rid of these?"

"Don't handle them. Don't let any part of them contact you." She lit a torch from the lantern and handed it to him. "Your reach is longer than mine. Be careful. If anything happens to you, Michel-Leon will never speak to me again."

"I feel that goes both ways." Constantin kept his distance, stretched out, and set the two remaining eggs on fire with his torch. Again, he sensed the chittering wings, the hunger and fear, but they quickly vanished as the blaze tore through the shells. They were easier to burn out than he expected. The susceptibility to fire might be one reason the mother nested in caves near water. "I think what makes the psychic attack so powerful is the numbers. As individual eggs, they are weaker."

"I don't care to analyze it." Régine shouldered her bag again. "I want them gone."

Carefully, Constantin wrapped the creature Régine killed in his coat and stowed it in the pack. There was too much to learn about it to leave it behind. He couldn't risk fire destroying it. It may make the task of fighting the swarm easier for future generations.

As they followed the trail, the smoke grew denser, and Constantin was grateful for the improved masks. Piles of ash lay everywhere, the scale of it sobering. If this had hatched, Paris would've been doomed. A ping from his construct alerted him. "Michel-Leon?" he called and urged Régine forward. "He's right around the bend."

Constantin spied him first, slumped against the wall, his hands limp at his sides. *"Mon Dieu,"* he breathed and rushed to kneel by Michel-Leon. He checked his fluttering pulse. The sound of his breath coming through the mask was slow and even.

He was alive, but unconscious. Constantin glanced over his shoulder to where Régine prowled the crypt. "Any eggs left we need to worry about?"

"Appears like he did a pretty thorough job," Régine said in an awed voice. "He had to have pushed himself to the limit. We'll need to come back after the smoke clears and comb through every corridor and crypt to be sure we have them all. However, they are easier to deal with in smaller groupings. I can guide the soldiers through while you both recover."

Constantin wanted to argue, but he didn't have the energy. The mental battle he'd gone through had sapped him. He'd been feeding off the need to find Michel-Leon, and now that he had, he had enough left in him to get them out. Régine knew what she was doing. She reminded them of that often enough.

He helped Michel-Leon up and threw him over his shoulder with a grunt. The construct whirred toward him, and Constantin sent it a mental image of Lyon. "Get us out of here."

"We should be getting mobbed by spirits after the amount of magic Michel-Leon expended." Régine followed behind him, lighting the way with her lantern. Smoke hung heavy along the ceiling, moving with little eddies as they passed through. "They're attracted to magic."

"They're grateful," Michel-Leon said with a groan and stirred. "Sweet Saint Jeanne, Constantin, set me down. I can walk out of here on my own two feet."

Constantin eased him down and took off their masks now that the smoke had dissipated some along the floor. He needed to be sure Michel-Leon was all right. He stared at Michel-Leon's pale face in the flickering light. He appeared exhausted, but lucid, as he slumped against the wall for support. "Damned if you didn't do what you set out to do, despite all the odds. Your ancestors would be proud."

"We did it." Michel-Leon looked between Régine and Constantin.

"It took all of us. Is Raul safe?"

"He is. He's with the soldiers. I told him you'd want to talk to him." Constantin pulled Michel-Leon in a rough hug. "You did it, you glorious bastard. I should've said this before. *Je t'aime.*"

"*Je t'aime aussi.*" Michel-Leon hugged him back with a weak chuckle. "Hold on, I promised myself this."

To Constantin's surprise, Michel-Leon dragged down his head and kissed him thoroughly, leaving him speechless. When Michel-Leon let him go, he flushed to see Régine watching him with an amused grin. "Look, get moving, you two. You can get emotional later. Both of you are on your last legs, and I'm not carrying either of you."

Michel-Leon pulled Régine in for a hug as well. She squeezed them both back and pulled away. "March." They turned obediently to follow the construct out, discussing their encounters.

"You faced your deepest fear, your darkest temptation," Michel-Leon murmured with a sideways glance at Constantin. "I knew you had it within you."

Constantin considered that and recognized there was a newfound peace within himself. He didn't fear what he was anymore. "I think we'll be fine," he replied.

Epilogue

"I DON'T KNOW how you can concentrate with that cacophony outside."

Michel-Leon glanced up at Constantin's voice, awareness flooding back to him and with it the noise of construction under his window. He'd left it open to let in the warm early summer breeze laden with the scent of green and growing things. Constantin stood in the doorway with a workman's smock covering his clothes to protect them from the dust that covered everything. "I'm used to constant noise. It's soothing. Quiet is unnerving."

"Have you finished yet? I thought you might walk with me to check out the progress we've made." Constantin was no longer the man who hid behind rags and dirt, moving on from one city to the next, leaving behind only impressions. He'd laid foundations here in Sampigny as solid as the new foundations of the home they were building over the ashes of Michel-Leon's ancestral home.

It was at times like this, in the quiet moments, Michel-Leon marveled at the turn his life had taken and how happy he was with those changes. He could remember many times being content, but Constantin and their love for each other had shown him a whole new world. The fact he could do the same for his lover was intensely gratifying.

Michel-Leon scanned over the notes he'd made about the woodwose they'd encountered a few weeks ago and shut his journal. His progress on updating the records was proceeding smoothly because of Raul. The young man was a prodigy of organization and found a like mind with Janvier.

Between the three of them, the chevaliers of the future would have detailed records to work with when battling monsters and investigating phenomena. Constantin was contributing as well with his intricate diagrams and pictures when needed. Régine preferred to stick to the practical training, which left Michel-Leon free to work on his records and experiments.

"I believe I have worked enough for the day." Michel-Leon rose to place the journal in its assigned spot on the shelves lining his new study. He did not want to see Raul's look of reproach if it was in the wrong position. He had taken on one too many mannerisms from Michel-Leon's valet. "Has Janvier returned to the inn?"

Once his old friend had assured himself Constantin and Michel-Leon would take care of each other, he'd accepted his pension. It didn't stop him from checking on them and Régine every few weeks. But after he'd satisfied himself all was still well, he'd return to his books and fire and great-grandchildren.

"He has, with considerable irritation over my hovering. It hasn't escaped his notice that either you, I, or Régine accompany him each time." Constantin stole a kiss, his brown eyes warm with affection. "Lyon has made considerable progress. The quarters for the new chevaliers are almost finished. They should be ready for occupation within a fortnight."

"We have never used a school. It should be an apprenticeship with the ancestors overseeing."

The grumble from his father was so predictable Michel-Leon smiled. The other ancestors were silent about the school. Saint Jeanne approved and that was all they needed. Michel-Leon had not forgotten his promise to her to build a better world. After they'd returned to the inn a few years ago, they set about doing that.

"Well, let us see what you've wrought. After they complete the barracks, we should focus on the workshops and library next." They left their suite of rooms and headed outside. It did wonders for his heart to see his ancestral home renewed. He had delayed it too long.

This section had been completed first, with rooms for themselves, Régine, Raul, and Gabrielle. They made a strange family, but a family nonetheless. Which reminded Michel-Leon how quiet it had been for the last hour. "Where are Raul and Gabrielle?"

Constantin grimaced. "Gabrielle snuck out of her studies again, and Raul followed. I caught them because once they thought they were safe, they started squabbling. I passed them off to Régine, and she chased them around with a weapons lesson, which pleased her to no end. Once I deemed they had enough, I sent them to Lyon for chores. Tomorrow, they should be too tired to sneak off."

Michel-Leon laughed as they stepped out into the sunlight. The courtyard teemed with activity. Régine's red hair gleamed as she leaned against the inner wall and studied her afternoon students' sparring. She lifted her hand in a wave, and Michel-Leon returned the gesture. The barracks roof was completed and the stone walls would last for generations. Lyon emerged from the doorway, two figures in his wake who broke away as soon as they spied Michel-Leon and Constantin.

Gabrielle, as usual, was in front, clad in the trousers she had taken to wearing in imitation of Régine. Once Gabrielle had reunited with Constantin, and he reassured her she always had a home with him, her confidence and daring blossomed. Raul had been slower to trust. Though Constantin had healed most of the damage wrought by Vautrin, his mouth still carried a small, permanent slant that appeared as if he had a secret smile. Michel-Leon thought the expression suited him.

"Constantin! Monsieur Lyon let us install some windows! I used the hammer." She glanced at Michel-Leon through her lashes. "I mostly completed my studies first."

"Weren't you supposed to see me afterward for more lessons?" Michel-Leon asked in a grave voice to tease her, and her eyes widened innocently.

"Régine says exercising our bodies is as important as exercising our minds," Gabrielle swiftly countered, and Constantin affectionately tugged on her braid.

"I think half your sentences start with 'Régine says,' *ma petite chouette*."

"We knew you were close to finishing your report," Raul came to Gabrielle's defense. Despite their initial rocky start and many arguments, the two had become family in their own way. "We didn't want to disturb you. Did you finish?"

"I did and returned the book to its proper place." Michel-Leon laid his hand on Raul's shoulder. For a long time, that had been the sole expression of affection he'd allowed. He had grown again, and soon Michel-Leon would be looking up at him instead of right in his eyes. He had become a young man and was more than ready to take on the mantle of chevalier. It wouldn't be too more many years before Gabrielle would be fighting to go out at his side.

"Why don't you two show us our new barracks?" Michel-Leon suggested. "We can go back to the lessons tomorrow."

"They won't be able to keep their eyes open over their books," Constantin said with a laugh as they raced off again. Each one eager to be the first to show them the new developments. "Well, Gabrielle, at least. Raul appears more interested in that aspect of his training."

"It doesn't hurt to take a step away and run out to play in the sun from time to time," Michel-Leon said, and Constantin cut him a laughing glance.

"I wish Janvier and Régine were around to hear that one."

"Especially since Raul has been hinting more and more about his willingness to take on easier assignments. We ought to consider bringing him along on occasion," Michel-Leon suggested.

"We can discuss that later." Constantin cast a glance around at all the activity and then directed a look at Michel-Leon filled with heat. "After Gabrielle and Raul give us our tour, what do you say to running away for the afternoon to play in the sun?"

Michel-Leon smiled shyly at him. "I think I could be persuaded." He touched his hand to Constantin in unspoken anticipation of that moment. "Let us take a look around, and then it will be solely you and I for a time."

Constantin's answering smile warmed all the places in Michel-Leon's once lonely soul.

"My lord, my lord!"

Michel-Leon spun about at the call and saw a messenger riding in from the direction of the inn. There was urgency in his voice, but not fear. That was a good sign, though it might mean their afternoon was interrupted.

"What news do you bring?" he asked as the man slowed his horse to a walk.

"News from Alsace, my lord. The goblins have returned, and the villagers are asking for you to come parlay."

Michel-Leon glanced at Constantin, his eyes wide with surprise, and then glanced toward where Raul and Gabrielle had disappeared before throwing back his head and laughing.

"What is it?" Constantin asked, his gaze mystified.

"A nuisance, no more. The goblins found their loophole." Michel-Leon turned his attention to the messenger. "Let them know we will be on our way within a couple of days and remind them not to antagonize the little beasts. It will make the situation worse."

"It appears Raul will have his chance," Michel-Leon murmured as the messenger rode off. He smiled at Constantin, a smile filled with promise. "We can tell him later, after our time in the sun."

"I am looking forward to it, my love."

Acknowledgements

There are so many people who made this book possible. It took me a long time to work through how to make all the elements mesh. First off, Keir, for your input. Janvier wouldn't be who he is without you and thank you for listening to me try to work out the lifecycle of the swarm. Thank you for giving me my love/hate relationship with horror. I know how happy you would be that it's finally finished.

For all the awesome people on the Writer's Block Discord channel, you have been a rock. Most especially Wobs and Graves. For Ella and Maridyan, who also beta read it, I appreciate you and all your input.

About the Author

Marguerite Labbe loves to spin tales that cross genre lines, where stubborn men build lifelong ties of loyalty, friendship, and family no matter the odds thrown against them, and where love is found in unexpected places.

When she's not working hard on writing new stories, she spends her time reading novels of all genres, enjoying role-playing and tabletop games with her friends, and taking long walks with her dog.

Email
margueritelabbe@gmail.com

Facebook
Marguerite Labbe

X
@MargueriteLabbe

Website
www.margueritelabbe.com

Connect with NineStar Press

Website: NineStarPress.com

Facebook: NineStarPress

X: @NineStarPress

Instagram: NineStarPress

BlueSky: NineStarPress

Threads: @NineStarPress

www.ingramcontent.com/pod-product-compliance
Lightning Source LLC
Chambersburg PA
CBHW060305100726
47907CB00002B/288